ENDOWED WITH DEATH

ENDOWED WITH DEATH

A KENZIE KIRSCH MEDICAL THRILLER
BOOK EIGHT

P.D. WORKMAN

PD WORKMAN

ISBN: 9781774686041 (KDP Paperback)
ISBN: 9781774686058 (KDP Hardcover)
ISBN: 9781774686072 (Large Print)
ISBN: 9781774686096 (Lulu Paperback)
ISBN: 9781774686041 (ePub)
ISBN: 9781774686089 (Accessible Audio)

ALSO BY P.D. WORKMAN

FIND MORE BOOKS AT PDWORKMAN.COM

MYSTERY/SUSPENSE:

Kenzie Kirsch Medical Thrillers

Unlawful Harvest

Doctored Death

Dosed to Death

Gentle Angel

Rushin' Death

Posed for Death

Death of a Corpse

Endowed with Death

Shattered to Death (Coming Soon)

Captured in Death (Coming Soon)

Zachary Goldman Mysteries

Private Investigator

She Wore Mourning

His Hands Were Quiet

She Was Dying Anyway

He Was Walking Alone

They Thought He was Safe

He Was Not There

Her Work Was Everything

She Told a Lie

He Never Forgot

She Was At Risk

He Drowned in Memory

Their Walls Were Empty

They Came for Him

They Sought Vengeance

She Was Their Target

His Fear Was Real

Parks Pat Mysteries

Police Procedural Set in Canada

Out with the Sunset

Long Climb to the Top

Dark Water Under the Bridge

Immersed in the View

Skimming Over the Lake

Hazard of the Hills

Knows the Hills

Spanning the Creek

Sanctuary in the Stream

Echos of the Engine (Coming Soon)

Bench with a View (Coming Soon)

Beneath the Icy Depths (Coming Soon)

High-Tech Crime Solvers Series

Virtually Harmless

AND MORE AT PDWORKMAN.COM

For all the little ones
Those who grew up...
...and those who didn't

1

Kenzie's ringer sounded. That wouldn't have been unusual except that she had it turned to silent mode during their visit with Lorne Peterson and his partner Patrick Parker. The ring wasn't just her generic ringtone, but the "urgent" trill that meant it was a work call, and it was programmed to bypass silent mode so that she couldn't miss it.

Zachary's head went up and he looked at her, dark eyes surprised. "What's that?"

He knew very well that it was her ringtone for the Medical Examiner's Office.

"Sorry," Kenzie apologized, standing up from the breakfast table. "I need to take this."

"You're not supposed to be on call today," Zachary objected as she hurried away from the table.

"I know that," Kenzie snapped. Which meant that something serious was going on. A mass casualty event? What would justify Dr. Wiltshire's calling her when she was supposed to be off all weekend for their visit to the Petersons?

She retreated to the guest room she and Zachary were sleeping in, pulling out her phone and swiping the answer slider so that it wouldn't go to voicemail before she had a chance to pick it up in private. She closed the door and raised the phone to her ear.

"Kenzie here."

"Kenzie, I'm sorry to call you on your weekend off," Dr. Wiltshire apologized, his voice sounding stressed. "Believe me, I didn't forget you were supposed to have the day off today."

"What's happened?"

"The perfect storm. We have an autopsy that needs to be done right away. Urgent political pressure. Which is fine; normally, that would not be a problem and I would just take care of it."

"Right."

He was a well-trained, experienced medical examiner, the man who was teaching Kenzie everything she needed to know. There was no one better qualified to do the autopsy.

Especially one that apparently had political repercussions.

"The thing is... I broke my hand."

"What?" Kenzie heard her own voice go up several notes higher than usual. "How did you do that?"

"A stupid accident. That is not important right now. What is important is that this autopsy cannot be put off, and I'm sidelined. I haven't had a chance to line up someone who can do overflow work for us while my hand is healing, and they want it done now."

"Yes. I understand. I'm sorry about your hand. I guess... I'll say my goodbyes here and get packed and come back. I'll be a couple of hours." Kenzie ran one hand through her long, spiraling curls.

"I apologize. It shouldn't have happened. You need your down-time. But..."

"It is what it is," Kenzie agreed, shrugging. He couldn't control the fact that he was getting pressure from above to do the important autopsy immediately. And he certainly had not planned to break his hand.

How bad was the break? He could be out of commission for anything from a few weeks to months of healing and physio. Or if he were unable to regain full use of his hand... Her stomach plummeted at the thought of his having to leave the medical examiner's office.

"I appreciate it, Kenzie. I'll be here to provide any assistance or advice. I just can't do the manual work."

"Okay. I'll see you in a few hours, then."

Kenzie terminated the call and looked around the room. They hadn't brought much with them. They had only stayed over one night so Zachary would have time to visit his sister Joss as well as the Petersons. Lorne was an old foster father of Zachary's, the only parent he had stayed in touch with over the years, bonded by a love of photography and Lorne's dedication to a lost and broken boy he thought he could do something for.

Rather than immediately telling Zachary about having to return to Roxboro and pulling him away from the discussion with his chosen family, Kenzie started packing. Pajamas, Zachary's meds, and charging cables went into the suitcase. The door opened and Zachary peeked in.

"You're off the phone?"

"Yeah."

Zachary looked at her for a moment, then down at the suitcase. The smile disappeared from his face, replaced with an expression of concern.

"What happened?"

"They need me to come back to do an autopsy. Something urgent. Dr. Wiltshire broke his hand."

"Oh, no!" He sounded immediately concerned for Dr. Wiltshire, which made Kenzie feel guilty because she had expected him to be upset about cutting their visit short and had been prepared to defend herself, pointing out that she had no control over the circumstances. "Is he going to be okay?"

"It sounded like it. He said he'll be waiting for me at the office, so he must not be at the hospital." The morgue was in the basement of the police department building, not at the hospital. "I'll find out when I get there. I didn't ask for details."

Zachary looked around the room. "Do you need help with anything else?"

"I've got this. Check the bathroom to make sure neither of us left anything in there. And... I'll make apologies to Lorne and Pat."

"It's fine. They understand that sometimes things come up. You can't exactly control when people die."

Kenzie appreciated the support. He was being understanding and supportive, but she was angry. It was the first time in a year that she had specifically booked off a full weekend for some downtime with Zachary and his family. She couldn't blame Dr. Wiltshire for the circumstances, but she was ticked off and wanted someone to take it out on. She closed the suitcase, which was soft-sided and did not respond with a satisfying bang.

"Let's just get ready."

Zachary left the bedroom ahead of her and walked down the hall to check the bathroom while she walked the suitcase to the door.

"I'm so sorry," she apologized to the two men. "I'm not supposed to be on call. Nothing was supposed to happen to interrupt me this weekend. But…"

"Things happen," Lorne said understandingly.

Pat nodded his agreement. "I'll put the coffee in travel cups for you. And I could make some breakfast sandwiches while you guys get ready…"

Kenzie looked toward the table, where they had just started to eat the delicious breakfast spread Pat had prepared. She hated having to leave so abruptly. Having Pat make it into sandwiches for them would take a few minutes and be extra work on his part. Still, the alternative was leaving all of the food and not being able to appreciate his efforts. Her mother's voice in her head told her it was rude not to eat it after he had gone to so much work.

"Uh… sure. That would be lovely."

Pat brightened at her words, obviously having anticipated that she would say no. "Great! It will take no time at all. Just give me a couple of minutes while you put your bags in the car and say goodbye."

Kenzie smiled and nodded. Pat picked up the eggs, ham, and other ingredients to make into breakfast sandwiches and retreated to the kitchen.

"Thank you," Lorne said with a smile, laugh lines fanning out around his eyes and mouth. "You made his day."

"Happy to help. And it saves us having to stop somewhere on the way for gas station snacks or fast food. My body and my taste buds will thank me for it."

Kenzie gave the older man a quick hug as Zachary returned from the bathroom, holding up his empty hands to show that there wasn't anything else to go in the suitcase. Kenzie took the luggage out to the car, leaving him to say his goodbyes.

"Did he say who died?" Zachary asked, as he smoothly maneuvered the car through multiple lanes of traffic, the speedometer climbing.

"He knows it will take a couple of hours," Kenzie told him. "Slow down."

Zachary looked at the speedometer and touched the brakes to slow the car down just slightly.

"He didn't say who it was," Kenzie said. "And I didn't stay on the phone to ask. The sooner I get there, the sooner I'll know everything and be able to get started on it. He said it was political, so I assume..." Kenzie shrugged as she thought about it. "Probably some old guy. Dropped dead in his club or mistress's bedroom and they want to stay ahead of the gossip and headlines."

Zachary grinned. "But you're not cynical or anything."

"I know too much about how politics works from Dad's work. Dr. Wiltshire didn't give me any details, but just the fact that he said it is political makes me assume it's not someone who just died in their sleep last night."

"No, you're probably right about that," Zachary admitted. He made a quick lane switch that made Kenzie's heart race. But no one honked and, so far, she had never seen him pulled over by the cops for speeding. If he were, they would probably let him off with a warning if Kenzie apologized and pled that she was trying to get back to Roxboro quickly to get to a law enforcement matter. And maybe it would teach Zachary to take things a little more slowly.

But probably not.

They got into a clear lane, and he leaned back, relaxing, getting into the groove of a highway drive, which always seemed to calm his ADHD brain.

It didn't take the full two hours to get to the medical examiner's office, and Dr. Wiltshire didn't mention anything about the time when he met with Kenzie.

"Again, I'm sorry for doing this to you," he apologized, "Thank you for making the time. I know this is not how you expected to spend your Sunday. Can I get you something? You probably need lunch."

"No, I ate on the way. I'm good for a while. So, what have we got?"

The first shock was that it was not an old man. Dr. Wiltshire led Kenzie to her usual autopsy table and pulled back the sheet from a very small figure. A boy, a toddler of two-and-a-half or three, by Kenzie's guess. Slight build. Blond hair and a round face.

Kenzie shook her head. "I thought you said this was political."

Dr. Wiltshire sighed. "Michael Wade, son of Crispin 'Cash' Wade. Friend of the governor, currently a congressman, moves in all the right social circles."

Kenzie took this in. She shook her head, thinking about it. "So he and the governor are putting pressure on the medical examiner's office to have the autopsy done instantly, so there are no questions raised in the newspapers or social media."

Wiltshire nodded. "People like this don't want there to be any lingering questions about a death in the family. They want a statement as to the cause of death. A tragic accident, unavoidable, all that kind of thing. We'll oblige them the best we can. It looks like a simple open-and-shut case, but you can never predict complicating factors."

"No," Kenzie agreed. She looked at the body on the table.

It was, at first glance, unremarkable. The child looked as if he had been healthy in life. The cavitation in the front of his skull indicated he had met with a pretty strong force. A car accident or fall from a significant height, most likely. She shuddered, glad that she did not have any children of her own. She couldn't imagine trying to deal with the sudden and tragic death of a child she had thought healthy and happy. It had been hard enough when they had lost Amanda, Kenzie's sister, as a young adult, after a long and protracted battle with kidney disease. At least they had known what was coming and knew that she was no longer suffering.

"What's the story?" Kenzie asked. She picked up the file on the counter, which should have the basic scene details, but she wanted to hear everything Dr. Wiltshire thought might be important from the start.

"Fall from a third-floor window. Apparently, the boy's caregiver was not with him, didn't realize he had gotten into a room he wasn't supposed to be in. There was a balcony. He went climbing like kids do and went over the rail." Wiltshire's voice was flat and clinical, removing himself from the situation. There was no point in their getting wrapped up in the emotions of a tragic case. They carried a lot of burdens and couldn't spend a lot of time and energy grieving over the loss of a person they hadn't even known. Enough of the tragedy of a case would seep in through the cracks in the walls they built around themselves without their opening the door.

Kenzie nodded and followed his lead, not letting herself think about the family's loss and the tragedy of a young life cut short. She was lucky to live in modern times when the death of a child was a rare event rather than something that every family went through multiple times. In days gone by, it had not been unusual to lose several children in infancy or early childhood. They were privileged. There were places in the world where that was still true.

She dressed, scrubbed, and tapped the button on the floor to make her initial recording. She introduced the case with the patient name, date, and details of the death they had been given. It was clear that George had already examined the body for any forensic evidence and washed it in preparation for Kenzie's arrival. Kenzie hadn't seen him in the outer suite when she had come in. He had probably been called in especially for this case, as she had, and had gone home when he was finished preparing the body for her.

Kenzie proceeded with a gross examination of the body, carefully noting any defects, bruises, cuts, or anything else that might be important later. No birthmarks. A variety of bruises, as was the case for most toddlers. Kenzie studied them closely, and moved the body from front to back and then front again.

"Something of note?" Dr. Wiltshire asked.

"No. I don't know. There are bruises on his arms, upper and lower, and on both his back and front."

"Recent? From today?"

He could see the coloring as well as Kenzie could, and had drilled her in the past about the colors the bruises went through from the time they were inflicted until a week or two later. Everyone healed at different rates, of course, but the order of the colors was always the same, and the timeline could be estimated.

"No, nothing that is obviously today. But they wouldn't be, would they? How long before the accident did he get out of bed?"

"Not long. It wasn't clear from the report from the police at the scene whether he had been up interacting with a caregiver before the incident, or went straight from bed to the balcony before they knew he was up."

There would be a number of people to interview, Kenzie suspected, and anyone who was closely connected to the boy might be too distressed to give a clear statement in the first few hours of the investigation.

"The bruises are a variety of ages," Kenzie observed. "I know that kids get into trouble, some of them more than others. And some kids bruise quite easily. But… it seems like a lot."

"Make sure they are all documented. You may want to try an alternative light source as well. You may be able to see other bruising under ALS."

Kenzie nodded. It was tedious to measure, take pictures of, and describe each bruise. And the ones on the shins, knees, and elbows seemed to be the typical accidental injuries of a child just learning to get around in the world. But the documentation needed to be done before moving on to other things.

"What position was the body in when the police got there?" Kenzie asked, as she examined the signs of livor mortis, the settling of blood in the body after death.

"The child was on his back but had obviously been moved. The damage to the skull is in the front. That has to be the position he landed in."

"Did the parents say they had moved the body?"

"They probably don't know. It's instinctive to turn the person over, look them in the face."

Kenzie nodded. She recorded her thoughts and questions and proceeded. When she had finished with the gross examination, she moved on to the eyes, ears, and mouth. Unsurprisingly, all three showed traumatic changes. That would happen when plunging face-first into the pavement, even falling from just a few feet up. Kenzie took pictures and set aside one eyeball for microscopic examination.

She looked at the mouth, frowning. Dr. Wiltshire looked up at the screen as she took a few pictures and moved the camera in for a closer, enlarged view.

"Observations?" Dr. Wiltshire asked.

"No broken teeth. The blow was closer to the top of the head than the front of the face. But there is significant bruising and tearing of the frenula."

"There is," Dr. Wiltshire agreed.

Kenzie met his eyes, then returned to the autopsy. She examined the mouth injuries closely and considered the color of the bruising. Not bright red. Not sustained in the fall.

3

Kenzie would need to do a microscopic examination of the eyes to gather all the information she could. There was blood visible on gross examination, but she would need more magnification to make a full evaluation.

"X-rays?" Kenzie asked.

Dr. Wiltshire nodded. She didn't really need to ask; she knew what needed to be done. "What will you x-ray?" he prompted.

"Head, of course, we will need to see how extensive the skull fracture is. Neck and shoulders." She paused. "Ribs, front and back. From there... we'll see."

He nodded his agreement.

Kenzie proceeded as planned. Dr. Wiltshire took a break while she did the films, so he didn't have to worry about a lead shield. Kenzie could see him through the window to the observation room, swigging some pills down with a bottle of water. She eyed his splinted hand while waiting for the machine to perform each of the x-rays she needed. It appeared to be a temporary splint, not a full cast. Hopefully, that meant it was only a minor injury, a hairline fracture or two that would heal quickly and without further intervention. She hadn't been able to see how much swelling and bruising there was because of the way that it was wrapped, so she couldn't guess at the extent of his injuries.

When Dr. Wiltshire came back in, she queued up the x-rays and they reviewed each one. The most important ones in determining cause of death were, of course, the skull x-rays. The massive fracturing from the fall was certainly extensive enough to have caused the child's swift demise. But it didn't sit right with Kenzie. It didn't match up with some of the other observations that she had made.

The neck and shoulders were also consistent with a fall from a height, with the heaviest part of the child, the head, hitting the ground first.

Kenzie put up the rib x-rays without a word, and she and Dr. Wiltshire studied them.

"What do you see?" Dr. Wiltshire invited.

Kenzie sighed and shook her head. She used the mouse pointer to indicate the callus formations on the posterior of several ribs, bright white on the x-ray. "String of beads," she said. "That's how my professor described it in med school."

"Which indicates?"

"The child has been squeezed or shaken hard enough to fracture ribs. In the absence of any brittle bone or connective tissue disorder... abuse."

"Resulting in death?"

"No. The calluses are healing fractures. Meaning it happened at least a few weeks before death."

Dr. Wiltshire nodded. "Follow-up questions for the investigators?"

Kenzie considered, then recorded several questions for the police to follow up on. Whether the custody of the child had changed recently. Whether there were any previous investigations into abuse. How many doctor and emergency room visits he'd had, and for what. Whether he had any diagnosed disorders.

"And we'll need to take bone samples to review for disease," Kenzie said, anticipating his next question. "See whether there is another explanation for multiple rib fractures."

At least there wasn't any danger of a child being inappropriately apprehended by DCF for abuse when there was actually an underlying disorder, traumatizing the child and putting unnecessary stress on the family.

But they would need to be mindful of the political consequences of any questions or reports that included allegations of abuse. Cash Wade was not a man to be trifled with. A number of ruined careers lay in his wake.

Eventually, they reached the point at which dissection was necessary. Kenzie wished that it could have been avoided. If there had been no findings in the gross examination and x-rays, and everything was consistent with a fall, Kenzie could have chosen to dispense with a full autopsy, ruling it an accidental death and avoiding any further indignity to the body.

But that was not the case.

Kenzie was bothered by the head x-rays and her observations of the tissue around the fractured skull, so she started there instead of with the Y-incision. Dr. Wiltshire made no comment or correction.

Kenzie made her cuts and peeled back the skin and tissue covering the skull to examine it, then removed pieces of the shattered skull to examine the bone and the bleeding within the subdural layer.

Except there was no bleeding.

She took a series of pictures of the membranes around the brain. The shards of the skull created by the explosive impact had cut into the membranes, blood vessels, and brain tissue. Yet there was little blood.

Kenzie pressed her lips together tightly.

"There was no bleeding from the fall. The victim was dead *before* he fell from that balcony."

Dr. Wiltshire shook his head, but it was in regret, not disagreement. "I concur."

The revelation that Michael Wade had not been killed in the fall from the window was only the first part of the answer. There was still more work to be done. And much of the evidence might have been compromised by the fall.

Any bone breaks could be the result of the fall or might have been inflicted earlier. The damage to the frenulum, Kenzie had already noted, could not have been perimortem. Neither were the previously broken ribs. Though looking at the x-rays under magnification, Kenzie could identify recent hairline fractures. Not starting to heal yet. Possibly caused by the fall or possibly broken within the previous few days.

Before proceeding with the dissection of the torso, Kenzie took a closer look at the bruising inside Michael's mouth and also dissected one eyeball under magnification. She was straightening up and arching her sore back when she saw that a couple of police detectives were in the observation room. A male cop she recognized as Detective Tuttle, and a woman she didn't know. Dr. Wiltshire had undoubtedly called them when Kenzie had discovered the boy was already dead before he fell. Kenzie instructed the computer to turn on the speaker in the observation room.

"Did Dr. Wiltshire fill you in on everything?"

Tuttle stepped forward, closer to the mic in the observation room. He pressed the click-to-talk button and addressed her.

"He told us there was no bleeding from the skull fracture, so Michael was dead before he fell."

Kenzie nodded. She waited for anything more, but that was all the detective had to offer. Dr. Wiltshire had only given them the minimum they needed to know to get them there and give them a heads-up that it was now a homicide investigation. Michael hadn't climbed over the railing. Whoever had dropped him off the balcony had intended to cover up the actual cause of death, and that suggested homicide, not accident or natural causes.

"We have made a few other findings that you need to know about for your investigation."

"Go ahead."

Kenzie showed them the pictures of the torn and bruised frenulum. "This is Michael's frenulum. It is that little string of tissues that holds your lip to your upper gums. As you can see from the dark bruising, this happened several days ago, not today."

"What causes that kind of injury?"

"This is sometimes referred to as a bottle jamming injury. It can be caused by a bottle, pacifier, spoon, or other object being forced into the child's mouth. Usually by a frustrated caregiver trying to force feed or quiet them. It can also be caused by a hit or slap directly to the mouth."

"Not an accidental injury, then."

"It would be very rare for it to be an accidental injury. It is almost always indicative of abuse."

"But you don't know by whom."

"Obviously, I can't tell that from the bruise."

Kenzie showed them the x-rays, indicating the damage that was definitely caused by the fall, the healed or healing fractures that were not caused by the fall, and recent breaks that could not be determined to be one or the other.

"Have there been any previous investigations into abuse?" she asked.

"Not that we are aware of. We will look into it."

"Is that everything you have so far?" the female detective asked.

"Not yet. I've just been investigating the ocular injuries," Kenzie gestured to the organ she had been dissecting.

"Eye injuries?" the woman inquired.

"Right." Kenzie pulled up the photos she had taken so far and indicated areas of damage. "There are a number of retinal hemorrhages. Areas where the tiny blood vessels of the retina have bled. Experience tells us that this is usually caused by traumatic head injury."

Dr. Wiltshire had returned to autopsy, but did not interrupt, letting Kenzie deal with the presentation and answering any questions.

"Like the one sustained by the victim?"

"Not from the fall from the balcony. If the head injury did not bleed after the fall, then neither did the eyes. These injuries were sustained before death. They appear to be recent. It's possible that the drop from the balcony was meant to obscure another head injury. And if that was the intent... then so far, they have succeeded. I'll be doing a more thorough examination of the skull and brain to see what preexisting injuries I can identify. As well as the hemorrhages, you can also see some retinal tearing."

"That's quite serious," Tuttle suggested.

"Yes, retinal tearing can lead to blindness. The tears in this case are quite small. Still, retinal tearing in children is almost always associated with trauma, unlike in adults where it can be spontaneous, part of the natural aging of the eye."

"Caused by being hit in the head?"

"Hit in the head or shaken violently. It could be the result of injury sustained in sports or roughhousing, but in most cases…"

"It is indicative of child abuse," the female detective finished.

Kenzie nodded. She looked the woman over. "I don't think we have met before, Detective…?"

"Oh, sorry. Detective Baker."

"Baker. Yes, retinal hemorrhages and tearing are common signs of Shaken Baby Syndrome. But they can occur in older children, too, not just infants. It is easier to cause damage shaking an infant, because their heads are so heavy and they have little control or stabilization until they get a bit older."

"So did these happen when he was a baby or more recently?"

"The hemorrhages are recent. The tears do not show any sign of healing or scarring, so I assume they were both caused recently."

"And is that all you've got?" Baker inquired.

"Do you need more than that to begin your investigation?"

"No, no. I just don't want to race out of here if you still have more to tell us." Baker gave her a little smile to show that no offense had been intended.

"Okay. Yeah, that's all I've got for you so far. But as you can see, I'm not done with this autopsy. I imagine Michael still has a few more things to tell us. But it will probably be along the same lines… signs of recent child abuse as well as older, healed injuries. You can see from the bruising…" Kenzie brought up a few representative pictures, "that these injuries are different ages. This is not just one incident of a parent losing their temper."

Baker and Tuttle both nodded.

"We'll look into it further," Tuttle confirmed. He looked hesitant. "You have heard, I assume, that this is the child of…"

"Cash Wade," Kenzie filled in. "Yes, so I heard. But he is not immune from investigation. If he or his wife had something to do with this…"

"We'll find out. I just mean… you will need to be careful of what you say. Keep this very quiet, don't let anything leak out. If there are accusations or innuendo made in the media before the facts are established…"

"It won't leak from here."

"Good." Tuttle nodded. "I don't mean to make any accusations. Just to make sure you're aware of how sensitive the situation is and how easily it could get out."

"I'm sure that Mr. Wade's PR people will be feeding the story to the press with their own spin," Dr. Wiltshire said. "But that won't stop people from speculating. There will be accusations of abuse made without anything coming from this office. And unfortunately, we will not be in a position to refute anything that is said. All we will be able to say for the time being is that it is under investigation."

Tuttle looked like he would argue, but he just nodded again, keeping his lips pressed tightly together.

"Keep us informed as to what is happening in the investigation," Wiltshire requested. "Any circumstances we need to be aware of to interpret our findings. And if you have any questions regarding scenarios or the specific injuries we have found…"

"We'll keep in touch," Baker agreed.

She and Tuttle left the observation room, expressions grim.

4

It was past their usual dinnertime when Kenzie arrived home. She was tired from the physical work and emotional toll of the autopsy, glad to be home where she could rest and regenerate.

She had called Zachary to let him know she was on her way home, so she was a little disappointed to see that he hadn't started dinner preparations by the time she arrived. It must have shown on her face.

"I have a plan," Zachary assured her quickly. "But I didn't want to start too early. I figured you would want a shower and change before you eat. You usually do."

It was true. After a particularly grueling autopsy, she always felt sweaty and disgusting and wanted a nice hot shower to scald it all away.

"If you need something right away, I can bring you a drink," he offered.

Since she shouldn't drink alcohol on an empty stomach, that would be a fruit juice or soft drink. She could have a glass of wine later with dinner.

"Yeah, that all sounds good. Why don't you bring me a grapefruit juice?"

Zachary's relief at her reaction was obvious. "Will do!" he agreed.

Kenzie retired to the bedroom to drop off her purse and other items. She started the shower warming and began to undress. Zachary brought her a glass of grapefruit juice.

"Your drink, Miss."

"Perfect." Kenzie had a long sip, then set it on the dresser as she finished undressing.

"I don't know how you can drink the stuff," Zachary said, shaking his head. "I mean... I can force myself to, but I don't enjoy it."

"Well, considering your usual diet... I wouldn't expect you to."

While his palate was expanding, he still returned to childhood favorites when he was tired, stressed, or wanted to celebrate. Chicken and stars soup, macaroni and cheese, pizza, burgers. His love affair with garlic bread provided endless amusement.

Zachary watched Kenzie divest of her clothes appreciatively. But he didn't try to start anything. He knew by now that she needed the shower more than anything else and wouldn't want him to touch her.

"You'd better start on that dinner now."

"Yes, ma'am."

"A minute ago, it was Miss."

"Well..." he looked flummoxed for a minute. "It's ma'am when you're giving orders."

That made sense. He had probably been well-trained by foster mothers and social workers to show respect and "yes, ma'am" for all he was worth when he was told to do something.

"See you in a few minutes. I'll try not to be too long."

He probably had a good idea that it would be at least half an hour before she was out of the shower, which was why he hadn't started dinner before she arrived home. A nice long, hot shower was just what Kenzie needed.

When she dressed and returned to the kitchen, Kenzie found that Zachary had been hard at work. With his ADHD and PTSD-related executive dysfunction, coordinating the different parts of preparing a meal was challenging. She was lucky if he could get breakfast on the table without forgetting anything, or one main dish for supper.

But he had managed to get plates, cups, and cutlery on the table, a jug of water, a wine glass in case Kenzie also wanted a real drink, a salad with a choice of bottled dressings, and a couple of microwaved dinners from the freezer.

"Good job," Kenzie approved. "This looks great."

He draped a dishtowel over his shoulder like Pat Parker often did when working his culinary magic in the kitchen. "Did I forget anything? Anything else you want me to get?"

Kenzie took a careful look and shook her head. "No, I think you got it covered."

"And we can have ice cream for dessert."

"Ice cream sounds good."

Kenzie sat down and started to dish up. Zachary waited a moment to see if she would discover something she was missing and, when she did not, sat down across the table from her.

"So, how was the autopsy? Took longer than you expected?"

Kenzie rolled her shoulders. Everything had loosened up in the shower, and she felt much more relaxed. "It's not done yet," she told him. "Sometimes it takes a few days to get everything done."

"Because you're waiting on tests?"

"No, because we're taking extra care to be thorough. We can't take the chance of a case like this going sideways. Everything has to line up and be presented perfectly."

"A case like this? Because it is political?"

"It isn't political... but there is political pressure."

Zachary took a bite of his microwave dinner and chewed slowly. "How is that?"

"Because it is not a public figure who died, but someone in his family."

"So he will bring his position to bear, even though it isn't actually anything politically motivated?"

Kenzie nodded at the assessment. Zachary didn't ask who the deceased was or who he was related to. He knew that information would be confidential. When Kenzie discussed her cases with him, she never named names.

"Was it like... a kid with a drug overdose? Or a spouse?"

He would find out sooner or later. And Kenzie knew that he was careful not to repeat anything they discussed about the medical examiner's office.

"No. It is a child. A young child."

"Tragic. Lots of public sympathy," Zachary suggested.

"Yes. But there are going to be some problems with them portraying themselves as grieving parents. At least once our findings are published."

"They aren't the parents?" She could see that Zachary's mind immediately went to foster care or adoption, an affair, or a second marriage.

"I haven't checked into any of that. But… they lied about what happened. And the victim shows signs of abuse."

"Oh, boy. Well, that's going to be a problem."

"It's a very delicate situation."

"Yes, it is."

Zachary's eyes went hazy. He was no longer looking at Kenzie or imagining what kinds of problems they would encounter in the media. Instead, Kenzie was pretty sure he was back in his own childhood; abused in his own family, placed into foster care, and exposed to more abuse from caregivers, other foster children, institutional care, and probably a lot of other situations he had never told Kenzie about, and maybe never would.

Kenzie put her hand over his on the table. He flinched, but then kept his hand in place and gradually refocused on her.

"It's okay," Kenzie assured him. "Just stay with me."

5

"I'm okay," Zachary told her immediately, shaking his head as if to shake off the memories. "Sorry, I just spaced out for a minute there."

"It's okay to talk about it. I can see how this might disturb you."

"It's fine," Zachary said. "We both know that I have a past." He shrugged. "We don't need to go over all of that again. Tell me more about the case. What did you find in the autopsy?" He took a bite of his dinner, though he didn't look like he was enjoying it.

Kenzie outlined her findings so far, watching him carefully to see if anything would push him over the edge. She didn't need to go into anything in detail if it appeared to bother him. She could stop at any time and they could change the subject. He could tell her about what he had been working on that day, if he had any interesting cases in his PI business.

"So those things are pretty conclusive?" Zachary asked. "They aren't things that you would see on a child who was just hyperactive or clumsy?"

"Some of them, on their own. Bruises of different ages on shins, knees, and elbows, but not the stomach and back or around the arms. He could conceivably fall and hit his mouth against a piece of furniture. Toddlers do things like that. The ribs..." She shook her head. "Unless he has brittle bones, somebody squeezed him very hard."

"Not just the paramedics trying to resuscitate him, because they were healing."

"They didn't happen during CPR or the fall," Kenzie confirmed. "They happened some weeks ago."

"And everything else is different ages, so it's ongoing, not just one incident."

Kenzie nodded her agreement. "I'm not sure what we're going to find is the cause of death, but they tried to cover it up so, chances are, it wasn't just Sudden Cardiac Death or choking on a candy or toy. Whoever threw him over that balcony is involved in the abuse and complicit in his death."

Zachary continued to eat, chewing slowly. "What if it was natural, and they were only afraid that it was caused by something they had done to him?"

"I supposed that's a possibility. Or that they were afraid we would see evidence of the abuse that had occurred before his death and would jump to the conclusion that was what he died of. But I think either way, it suggests a guilty mind."

"Definitely trying to cover something up. Why else throw him off of a balcony?"

They both ate in silence for a few minutes. It was Zachary who spoke next, voicing what they had both been contemplating.

"There are other possible reasons. Rage, loss of control over something that the child did. Hate for him. Punishing the spouse by causing indignity to the child's body."

"Those... seem like a stretch. I hope."

"Yeah. I don't know why it feels better that it was just a logical decision to cover up a possible homicide. Like it's worse if it was an emotional reaction."

"I think... it's the depth of that emotion that is chilling. Having that much anger or hate for either the child or the spouse... that he would be willing to go to those lengths after his child—or a child in his household—had died..."

Zachary nodded. "That's a lot of anger."

Kenzie pondered it. "Right now, I'm going to proceed on the assumption that it was to obscure the evidence. Which means that I'll be looking very hard at the body to catch every clue."

"Yeah. It doesn't really make any difference to your autopsy what the motive was. You're dealing with the body on the table. It might matter to the cops investigating the case, but they'll develop their own theories and explore all possible avenues."

"We'll exchange information; each investigation will inform the other."

Zachary scraped up the last of his frozen dinner. Kenzie noted that he hadn't helped himself to any salad. But at least he was eating. She was watching his mental state and weight carefully as the days shortened. She knew his thoughts would be returning to Christmas, and his annual depression reasserting itself. It wasn't a big deal that he didn't eat the salad. He was still eating, and his weight was at a healthy level, his cheeks filled in rather than hollowed out. His dark eyes were bright and interested, despite the potentially traumatic subject matter.

"You never think about things like that happening in wealthy, upper-class families." Zachary pushed his empty dinner tray away from him an inch. "At least, I don't. I always associate abuse with the lower classes. The stress of too many mouths to feed and not enough money. People brought up in the cycle of poverty and abuse. Fostering kids just for supplemental income. Drinking and arguing getting out of control."

Kenzie smiled. "Rich people still have stresses too. They still drink and get into arguments. There are a lot of egos, power plays, high expectations."

"Huh. Yeah." He raised his eyes to hers. "But you never...?"

"No. My mom and dad never hit me or abused me in other ways. There were plenty of arguments when Dad was at home, but they didn't get out of control and never led to violence, as far as I know. They got along pretty well, as long as they weren't together for too long." Kenzie ended on an ironic note. She'd never really thought about the dynamic between her parents very deeply. It was just the environment she had grown up in and it seemed perfectly normal.

"So maybe your dad's work taking him away from home was a good thing."

"Yeah. It probably was. Most of the time when he was home, he was very loving and generous. I didn't hear many arguments between them. They were generally behind closed doors, voices lowered. When they were on display, they spoke to each other civilly, even lovey-dovey. I told you I didn't even know when they got divorced."

Zachary chuckled. "That's so crazy. I can't imagine."

"I was on my own by that time, halfway around the world, and they didn't want to bother me with it. I didn't notice any difference when I saw them. They were still fine with each other when I saw them together. I think their relationship now is probably better than it ever was when I was growing up and they were still married. Dad still has a space to park his car in the garage, a study in the house to work in when he is in town. I haven't asked about sleeping arrangements." Kenzie's cheeks got hot. She did not need to know whether her divorced parents slept together when Walter was in town. Or if they were sleeping with anyone else when they were apart. They were both healthy adults. She assumed they had interests other than lobbying and fundraising.

Zachary laughed at Kenzie's discomfort. "What was the point in getting divorced, then?"

She shrugged. "I suspect Mom wanted independence. Being able to manage her own affairs without worrying about the money she made going to Dad, or vice versa."

"But she runs his family foundation."

"Well... yes. But she always has. Since before I was born."

"You don't think that's strange?"

"Of course I do. But if it works for them, who am I to say anything about it?"

He shook his head in amazement. "What about your friends when you were growing up? In school or whatever. You must have seen signs of abuse in other families?"

6

_____

enzie had to think about that one. Her first instinct was no, none of her friends had been dealing with abuse at home, against themselves or others in the home. If they had been, she would have noticed it. She would have reported it to her parents, a school counselor, or teacher. Of course.

But she knew the statistics. Upper class or not, the stats said that a number of the kids she had been going to school with were experiencing domestic violence. But she had always figured that if parents of that class didn't want to take care of kids, they had the money to hire someone to do it for them. There was no need to deal with the frustrations of child-rearing if they weren't cut out for it.

"I guess there had to be, but I don't remember seeing any red flags for abuse. I never thought that someone might be getting hurt..."

Zachary nodded. "Kids get pretty good at hiding it, avoiding questions and reports. Reassuring anyone who suspects that something might be going on."

"Still... you would think that I would have noticed something. Been uncomfortable. Seen bruises or other signs."

"Most abusers won't hit you in the face where bruises would be visible. Slaps, maybe, as long as you don't bruise too easily. But anything that might cause bruises or scars… under your clothes. Or learn how to hurt without leaving a mark."

Kenzie's heart ached when she thought of the experiences Zachary had been through. His childhood experience had been the complete opposite of her own. She'd always had food on the table, parents who were kind and generous and usually patient with her. And Amanda, her baby sister. Even though Amanda's kidney disease had put a lot of extra stress on the family, they had pulled together rather than being pushed apart, as many families in the same situation were.

Her mind shifted to the boy on her autopsy table. No bruises on his face. The torn frenulum was hidden from view, but clearly indicated violence, something being shoved into his mouth to keep him quiet. The damage she observed in the ocular exam and the burst eardrums suggested shaking and blows to the head. Broken ribs showed that he had been squeezed, someone crushing the breath out of him, probably to stop him from crying. Multiple restraint bruises and blows to the stomach and back. That poor boy had been through so much. And what Zachary had said was true; someone had gone to lengths to hide the violence, both before and after the boy's death.

"That's so awful," she told Zachary. "I can understand a parent who gets frustrated and loses it once. But not… systemic, ongoing abuse. Being careful enough to hide it means that they are making a choice. Instead of choosing not to take out their anger or frustration on the kid, they're choosing to hide it. To… get whatever satisfaction they get from letting go and keep anyone from finding out."

"Or pleasure," Zachary said.

"Hmm?"

"It doesn't always have anything to do with anger or frustration or being drunk. Sometimes it's just because they like to cause pain."

Kenzie nodded, swallowing. Was that true of someone in Michael Wade's orbit? They just liked to hurt little kids?

"There are tricks for hiding it," Zachary went on, continuing his previous line of thought. "So that friends at school or teachers don't notice it. Hiding bruises with long sleeves and pants, even when it's hot out. Makeup to cover it, though that's not as easy for a boy.

Avoiding gym or any kind of sports or activity where you have to change."

Kenzie cast her mind back to school. There had been kids who wore jackets or long sleeves all year. Vermont might not get hot like the desert states, but it was warm enough that such things were uncomfortable. She had always rolled her eyes at kids, usually the less-popular students, who felt the need to hide under voluminous hoodies and layers of clothing and wouldn't look her in the eye.

"Oh, man. I was so blind."

Zachary nodded. "But even if you had known to look for those things... they aren't proof, are they? Even a teacher who is looking for them can't force a kid wearing long sleeves to roll them up to make sure he isn't covered with bruises, cuts, or cigarette burns. They can't call DCF and start an investigation just because the kid doesn't participate in gym. And the kids who are drowning... sleeping in class, drinking, repeat runaways... they're just seen as bad kids. Best to get them out of school so that they're not a negative influence on the others."

"Even now, when we're supposed to know better?"

He shrugged. "From what I've seen... yes. There may be some enlightened educators who can reach these kids, but most of them get jaded pretty fast when faced with the 'bad attitudes' of kids who don't trust anyone and lash out at those who try to help them."

"I guess. We figure that if they need help, they should be asking for it. They should be grateful and take the first hand that's extended to them."

"Yeah." Zachary toyed with his fork. "But a kid caught in the system or with a bad family... he knows he can't trust anyone, and that if he tries to get help, it's just going to backfire and generate more abuse."

Not that there was anything a toddler *could* do. By the time a child was old enough to find some trusted adult outside the family, it was too late. He'd already been trained to be quiet and not to trust anyone.

"Time for the ice cream," Kenzie declared.

Zachary looked relieved. He stood up and went to the freezer to get it out.

7

Kenzie went through her usual routine of processing all the emails, voicemails, and deliveries that had come in while she was gone. One day, maybe she would have a morgue of her own and be able to employ somebody to do those things for her but, for now, she *was* the person employed to do them. She had to keep everything in the office running smoothly. She was not expected to do more than assist with postmortems, not to do everything herself. But Dr. Wiltshire had left her a brief note indicating that she was to call him if she had any questions that needed to be answered and, in the meantime, to continue with her usual work and finish the autopsy of the Wade boy. Kenzie frowned, looking down at the messily scrawled note. It wasn't Dr. Wiltshire's usual precise script. But he had a broken hand, so he was either writing with the broken one, or with his non-dominant hand, neither of which was likely to produce neat penmanship.

She had performed autopsies, or portions of them, without Dr. Wiltshire supervising her. Still, he didn't like her to do too much without his watching over things. He was responsible for any of the work she did, so he wanted to ensure it was done right.

It seemed odd that he would want her to proceed without him on a case that was so potentially explosive as the dissection of Cash Wade's son.

Kenzie continued with her administrative work, then finally called Dr. Wiltshire.

It took a few rings for him to answer and, when he did, Kenzie could hear a lot of background noise. Like he was in a garage or a department store.

"I guess you got caught up on another case?" Kenzie guessed. That would make sense, at least. He had a competing call that he had been required to attend.

"No. I have to see the surgeon about my hand," he dismissed. "What's up, Kenzie?"

"I just wasn't sure about proceeding on the Wade case. I can do it, of course, but... I thought you would want to be back here for it."

"I don't know when I will be in the office, so you'd better take care of it. I'm sorry."

"Oh, okay. Sure, of course. You can review my photos and notes before signing off on anything. I won't release the body until you've had the chance to look everything over carefully."

"Are you concerned that you got something wrong? Do you have a question that needs clarification?"

"No. I just thought you would still want to have a hand in." Kenzie winced at her own inadvertent pun. "I haven't even gotten back to it yet."

"Well, I'm available if there is something that concerns you. Something that you have questions on or want me to double check."

"Thanks. I had some questions about the original scene survey...?"

"Well... how detailed are these questions? The fact is it appeared to be an accident scene and we didn't do an extensive scene review."

"Things like how far the other rooms were from the balcony that he 'fell' from. Where is his bedroom? Whose room was it? What rooms are close? If he was dead before he went off the balcony, which we know to be the case, then there could be blood evidence or other trace that needs to be collected."

"I didn't go into the house. In fact… I wasn't present in person at the scene."

"Oh." Kenzie knew that he had to sign off before the body was removed. He hadn't sent Kenzie because she'd been out of town. Any of the death investigators could do it, of course, but Dr. Wiltshire was usually pretty particular about what he allowed.

"I had Ralph attend, and he took the footage and broadcast it to me on my iPad so that I could see what he did firsthand. The ME is allowed to attend virtually. I can't always get to every site in a timely manner in person."

"Right, of course, and this one looked like it was a pretty clear-cut accident."

"Exactly. We don't go into every death investigation expecting to find out that it was homicide. There are plenty that are attributable to natural causes, accidents, and suicide. And you can rule out suicide with a child so young."

"Right, of course. If he climbed or jumped, it wasn't because he intended to kill himself. Except he didn't climb or jump. And now we're looking at…"

She didn't use the word "murder." It could still be something else. Murder was a legal definition rather than a medical one. He could rule homicide, but it would be up to the police investigation to determine whether it was murder, manslaughter, or something else. Motive wasn't something that could usually be determined through an autopsy.

Dr. Wiltshire sighed heavily. Kenzie could hear pages going out over the hospital PA system. "You'd better go back there," he decided. "You'll need to find out the answers to your questions and take any samples or trace you identify."

Kenzie hadn't been expecting to visit the scene of Michael Wade's death when she had left home that morning. She had hoped to finish the autopsy with Dr. Wiltshire and had not prepared herself for investigating the scene of the death on her own. She asked for the police to assign someone to accompany her. There was no way she would just show up at the scene and expect to be let in, and she also did not want to walk into a homicide scene without some kind of protection. Of course the killer of a child would not necessarily pose any threat to Kenzie, but she wasn't going to walk into it blindfolded. And she also didn't need any accusations that she had planted evidence. She needed someone else there to confirm her story.

She expected to be assigned a young officer, someone they could spare to hang around with her for a while without being needed anywhere else. But it was Detective Tuttle who showed up and told her he would be going over with her.

"Are you sure?" Kenzie asked uncertainly. "I could be a while out there. You probably have better things to do. You don't want to send someone junior?"

"I'd like to be there, see what you see, bounce ideas back and forth. The scene survey is a pretty important piece of the puzzle."

"Well, yes, it is," Kenzie agreed. That was why she had called Dr. Wiltshire about it when she hadn't been able to find what she wanted on the file. That was why she was going out there. Essential evidence had been missed when they had first arrived at the scene. Would it have been sanitized in the twenty-four hours since then? They couldn't take the risk of it getting any more degraded. Or lost. Or cleaned. "Okay. I just wanted to make sure that it wasn't a waste of your time."

"I can't imagine it would ever be a waste of my time to attend a scene with you, doctor."

Kenzie eyed him, trying to decide whether he was teasing, flirting, or just clumsy in his attempt at a compliment. He gave her a small smile and she still wasn't sure.

She grabbed her death kit and double-checked to ensure it contained everything she expected to need. If it turned out that a more extensive scene investigation was required, she would need to get techs out there with her.

8

Kenzie had grown up with the rich and powerful of Vermont. Her parents were not as ostentatious as many of the others she knew. They were more low-key, willing to work behind the scenes and not get a lot of recognition for the charitable donations and other work that they did. Walter Kirsch and Lisa Cole Kirsch were recognized as part of the ruling elite in Vermont politics, even if they did not hold governmental positions. There was power, and then there was power.

And there was rich, and then rich. Kenzie had grown up in luxury, given everything she needed, always with her own room and plenty of space to roam. She had nice clothes, good food and, when she was young, lots of playdates and parties. Her parents had been wise enough not to give her everything she wanted. She still had to do chores. So she had not been completely spoiled, but she certainly had not understood how the outside world worked back then. One of her responsibilities had been helping out with Amanda. The playdates and parties had ended when Amanda had been diagnosed with kidney disease. They had spent a lot of time in the hospital and taking care of her at home. The family's focus had turned intensely inward, and they had shut off the chatter of the world outside of their little circle. Until Kenzie had turned eighteen and donated her kidney to

Amanda and, for a while, Amanda had been better. Kenzie had entered college life, had traveled, and had explored the big wide world outside of her family and Vermont to find her place.

The Wades, though, apparently had no clue what it meant to be understated or do their good works behind the scenes rather than in the spotlight. Their mansion put the Kirsch home to shame, and Kenzie knew that the Kirsch home was needlessly extravagant, especially with only her mother living there now. The Wade home was built like a Roman temple, with white marble and columns, a big white, shining block in the midst of the changing leaves of the grounds. There were fountains and greens and gardens, a gazebo that probably seated fifty, and no fewer than three swimming pools. It must take an army of staff to keep it looking so fresh and beautiful, like a painting of a house, with not a blade of grass out of place. Kenzie let out a whistle.

"I know, right?" Tuttle asked, shaking his head. "Can you believe that people actually live like this? And then have the gall to complain about how their lives aren't perfect?"

"Well… no one's life is perfect."

"But you can apparently get darn close."

Kenzie looked at the house and nodded. But within those perfect walls, a child had suffered over weeks or months and had died. The pure white stone hid the dark secrets within. It had not been a happy home for Michael Wade. Who knew what other suffering those beautiful halls hid.

"It would be nice if living in a home like this could actually make you happy," she told Tuttle.

He shrugged and drove down the long driveway that led to a circle in front of the house, then turned out of the ring to park in a small lot to the left of the house, out of sight. He had apparently been shown his place previously. Police were like staff. Helpful to have around when you needed them, but meant to be invisible when they were not.

She followed Tuttle to the door—the big front door, not a servants' entrance. He rang the doorbell. It was not long before the door was answered. Despite it being such a big house, someone kept close to the front door to ensure that visitors did not have to wait long. The person who answered the door appeared to be a house-keeper or personal assistant. A woman in a plain, understated skirt and blouse rather than the liveried butler Kenzie had anticipated. The woman's eyes flicked over them.

"Yes, how may I help you?"

"Detective Tuttle, ma'am. And this is Dr. Kirsch from the medical examiner's office."

"Yes?" She eyed Kenzie with disapproval.

"We have some things that we need to follow up on with regard to the young boy's death, ma'am. Some evidence that we need to gather that was not dealt with yesterday."

"They said yesterday that the scene was released. We could go back to normal. That woman and... was it you?"

"Yes, it was me. But some new facts have come to light that require our further investigation. I'm sorry to be a bother, but if we could come in and complete our business, we'll be as quiet as we can and get back out of your way again."

She pressed her lips together in disapproval. "Come in while I look into this."

She ushered them into a sitting room to wait, disappeared for some time, and eventually returned. She spoke to Kenzie rather than Tuttle. "I am Hilda Mathers. I am in charge of the household. If things are not kept running smoothly, that falls on me. Do you understand?"

"Yes," Kenzie agreed. If they were to mess something up or draw the ire of the lady and man of the house, it was Hilda who would take the blame. It was in her best interest to keep trouble out, not to grant Kenzie whatever she said she needed. "Like the detective said, we'll be as quick and quiet as possible. We don't want to interrupt the whole household. If we could see the child's room and the room he acciden-tally fell from, that may be all I need. If there is something else, we'll talk about it then."

"No one needed to see them yesterday. Just where the boy fell." Hilda gave a little shudder. "That poor boy. And his poor mother. So very tragic."

"It is," Kenzie agreed. "And we don't want to make it any worse for anyone by drawing this out longer than needed. They'll want us to finish the examination and the autopsy as quickly as possible, so they can lay him to rest."

"Yes, that's right."

"If you can help us to get this taken care of, I'm sure they'll be very appreciative."

"It's very unusual. We are not used to a *police presence* in the household."

"And you're not used to the tragic death of the young master, either. This whole thing is very usual."

"Yes," Hilda admitted. She took a deep breath and let it out slowly, then seemed to make her decision. "All right. I will take you there, but you cannot wander the house or disturb the servants. It's very important."

"We'll talk to you before we do anything else."

Hilda didn't appear to like that, but maybe she sensed that it was the best offer she was going to get. She nodded stiffly. "Follow me."

Kenzie and Tuttle followed. Hilda led them through back hallways used by the servants rather than the more public spaces where they might run into members of the household. They climbed a couple of flights of stairs to get to the third floor, which, according to the information Kenzie had been given, was the floor Michael had fallen—or been dropped—from. Hilda opened double white-paneled doors that slid into wall pockets, and gestured to the room.

"This is—was—Michael's room. The nursery."

"Thank you. We'll start here. And the room he crawled out the window from...?"

"Do you want me to show you now? Or when you are finished with this room?"

"Uh... now, if you don't mind. Then we don't have to bother you again until we are done."

"This way."

It wasn't simply across the hall or next door to the nursery. It was down two hallways, on a different side of the house. Hilda pointed inside the room, across to the balcony outside the sliding glass doors.

She didn't look in the direction her finger was pointing, but looked studiously away from it. "There. That is where it happened."

Kenzie gave the room a cursory glance and nodded. "Okay. We'll start with the nursery and then in here. And we can reach you...?"

"On any of the house phones." Hilda indicated an ivory and gold antique-style telephone on one of the side tables. "Just dial one."

"We will."

She and Tuttle returned to the nursery and the housekeeper went her own way after one more disapproving look.

Kenzie and Tuttle shut the sliding doors so that no one walking by could see what was going on, and looked around the room.

"Anything in particular you are looking for?" Tuttle asked, donning gloves.

"Mainly anything that would indicate where or how he was hurt before being thrown off the balcony. He was killed somewhere in this house, presumably on this floor, in this room or the one with the balcony."

Tuttle nodded and began a slow walk around the room, looking at the neatly made bed, a rocking chair beside it, and the various toys and furniture around the room. The heavy drapes were closed and the room was dim. Kenzie switched on her ALS and shone it around the room, sweeping it quickly at first to see if any large areas had been soaked or spattered with bodily fluids, and then moving it more slowly in small arcs, especially around the rocking chair and the pillow of his bed. Tuttle looked at the taut sheets as Kenzie shone her light on them, looking for any spots that showed up under the light.

"The sheets have been changed," Tuttle said. "No way they looked that crisp after the kid slept on them, even after just one night."

Kenzie nodded her agreement. "I think you're right. We'll have to follow up with Hilda on where the other sheets went. This is why it is a problem to return to the crime scene after they have had time to clean things up."

"I know, but it didn't look like a homicide," Tuttle told her, irritation clear.

"Sorry, it wasn't meant as an accusation. It's just... an observation. We only have the evidence we have. That's not your fault."

He looked at her for a moment, then nodded. Kenzie ran the light over the sheets and pillow once more. "With a toddler, I'd expect spots of saliva and urine, at least. These sheets are practically new out of the package. Take the pillowcase off."

Tuttle obeyed and held the pillowcase out toward her. Kenzie shook her head. "I want to see if anything soaked into the pillow."

They examined the pillow. Several splotches showed up under the ALS. Kenzie nodded, satisfied. "They didn't change the pillow, just the pillowcase. Let's take that with us."

"It isn't blood."

"No," Kenzie agreed. "Probably saliva. But we may be able to tell if it was held over his face."

"Ah." Tuttle nodded and put the pillow into an evidence bag.

The room included a small fridge and space suitable for preparing a bottle or snack. There was also an en suite bathroom with a bathtub. Of course. Why would they take the boy halfway across the house for a bath? Kenzie shone her light around and didn't find anything too alarming. "Let's take samples from the trap. Both the sink and the tub." The garbage had been emptied and sat with a fresh white bag in it. The under-sink storage area—appropriately secured with child safety latches—included bleach and other run-of-the-mill cleaners. Dangerous when swallowed, but nothing unusual or alarming. The medicine cabinet over the sink contained cartoon bandages, several ointments and sprays, lotion, a children's melt-in-the-mouth painkiller, and, of course, a child's toothbrush and toothpaste.

"Let's document all of this. Take a few photos."

"Any reason to take the toothbrush?"

"Uh… yes, let's. If there is a significant amount of blood…"

He collected it in an evidence bag, handling it carefully to avoid damaging any fingerprints. "Could the mouth injury be caused by a toothbrush?"

"Yes, especially if he was resisting, trying to keep his mouth closed when… whoever was trying to brush his teeth tried to force it in."

Tuttle nodded his agreement.

"Anything else? In here or the nursery?"

"I'm not seeing any blood spatter using the ALS. Or any areas that have been bleached. I mean..." Kenzie shone it around the toilet's base, "you can see that bleach has been used here, but that's perfectly normal for a bathroom. Especially a little boy just learning to use the big potty."

"And then we're on to the other room."

Kenzie nodded. She was reluctant to move on to the room with the balcony, but she obviously had to.

9

"Were you in here at all yesterday?" Kenzie asked, looking around the room.

"Briefly," Tuttle confirmed. "We were told that he had wandered in and climbed over the balcony rail, so we took a quick look around to ensure that everything matched their story." He shrugged. "There wasn't anything to refute it. Nothing that we found, anyway."

"What was it like?" Kenzie asked. "How did the household feel? Were there people in here?"

He considered her questions. "It was late morning. Everybody was a bit frantic, as you can well imagine. Wanting to do something when... it was too late to do anything. The glass doors were thrown all the way open..." He thought about it. "I don't think a child would open it all the way. More likely he just squeezed between them, and whoever came in here to see what had happened pushed them open the rest of the way. Went to the balcony, looked down..." Tuttle shook his head. "We didn't measure trajectories or anything. He fell close to the house, as would be expected in a fall. It is a long distance. A child falling onto concrete from up here, on his head... No one thought he had a chance."

"Did anyone attempt CPR?"

"I don't think so. None of the emergency responders. If one of the staff did, they neglected to mention it. It was clear from the condition of the body that there was no point. It was obvious he was too badly injured. The deformation in the skull..." He shrugged expressively.

Kenzie nodded. From the sparse notes on the file, it didn't sound like anyone had attempted any lifesaving measures, but it was essential to establish all of the facts as early as possible.

Kenzie shone her light on the handles of the balcony doors and along the carpet in front of them. No signs of blood there.

"We need fingerprints taken here," she indicated the handles, "and out there on the railing."

"Yes, ma'am," Tuttle agreed. "And we'll need elimination prints from anyone who might have touched them."

Of course they were always phrased as elimination prints, even when their purpose was to identify possible suspects. Everyone who had touched the door handles around the time of the boy's fall was a suspect.

"No one actually saw him fall, obviously," Kenzie suggested.

"No. No one claimed to."

If someone had, he would be lying, since things had not happened that way. If someone claimed to have seen him fall, then either he was the person who had dropped the body off the balcony, or they knew who did.

"Is there normally anyone back here that time of day?" Kenzie gazed through the doors at the big blue pool.

"I don't know how much they use the pools and how much they just lounge beside them," Tuttle said. "It didn't look like anyone had been in it. No water on the deck that I noticed. There are some lounge chairs with fresh towels beside them. It was late morning, so it's possible that someone had been in earlier, or that someone would be out getting a bit of sun. But no one said that they had been outside. We'll have to follow up on that a little more carefully."

"It's a bit chilly to be swimming."

"The pool is heated."

Of course it was. Kenzie could imagine jumping into the warm water on a brisk fall day. It would be perfect. Until she had to get out, of course, into the cool air again.

Had the killer considered putting Michael's body into the pool? But doing so would not hide the broken skull. They would still have to be able to explain that, and there was no way the boy could have hit the side of the pool with enough force while swimming or playing in the pool to do the damage he had sustained.

Kenzie left the window to look around the rest of the room. It was the sitting room of a suite, but did not appear to be in active use. Guest quarters, Kenzie guessed. Not in constant use. Would the door usually be left open so a child could wander in? Could Michael manage doorknobs? Did he wander a lot?

"Who was supposed to be caring for him?" she asked. "He must have been under someone's supervision."

"According to the statements we got yesterday, he was supposed to be sleeping in his room. No one was sitting watching him sleep."

"Late morning? Almost noon? Why was he still in bed? I don't know of any kids that sleep that late."

"Maybe he had gone down for a nap. Or maybe he was up late the night before."

"Maybe a nap," Kenzie conceded. He could have been up and around in the early morning, then worn himself out and been put down for a sleep. Toddlers that age still napped, didn't they? Amanda had napped even older than that, when she was five or six. In the afternoon, not the morning. But Amanda had been sick. Her energy had been low because of her kidney disease.

Kenzie shone her light all along the walls and carpets, looking for any sign of blood or anything else suspicious. But the room appeared to be spotless under the ALS as well. There were no toys that might indicate the boy had wandered in there on his own or often played there. If he had interrupted someone in the room and been killed there, then they had cleaned it up or covered it up well.

Thinking about the possibility of evidence being covered up, Kenzie checked the walls behind the paintings and the carpeting under a fancy silk rug, but they all appeared to be clean as well. She shook her head at Tuttle. "I don't think he was killed in here. There's no sign of it. We'll need to check the other rooms on the floor."

He grunted. "Why don't you go back to the nursery and call Hilda about seeing the rest while I take care of the fingerprints and check the balcony. You might find out who is available for further interviews as well. See if their statements today match their statements of yesterday. Ask any of the questions that have been prompted by your autopsy." He paused. "But don't ask any questions until I'm with you. Just see who is available."

Kenzie nodded her agreement. It would be essential for her to have a witness, and she was not a trained police interrogator. Tuttle would get her back on track if she messed something up.

She stopped at the windows again, looking out at the balcony. She wouldn't touch the doors to open them up until the fingerprint evidence had been gathered. But then she should make a careful examination of the balcony and see if there was any blood out there.

"If you want to leave the ALS here, I'll check after I print," Tuttle told her, guessing her line of thought.

"Okay, yeah. The floor of the balcony and the railing especially. Whoever threw him over the edge might have rested the body on the top rail before pushing it off. Bodies aren't as easy to move as you see on TV."

"No," he agreed. "Though a child that age does not weigh very much."

"Still awkward. Would either of the parents have been able to lift him over the railing?"

"Either one, I would think. Mrs. Wade is tall and doesn't look like a weakling. Cash is…" Tuttle shrugged. "I don't think any man would have a problem lifting that little boy over the railing. And Cash is built like a bull."

Kenzie nodded. "Okay. I'll go back to the nursery and let you do your thing here."

She left the ALS with him and went back to the nursery to have one more look at it and call Hilda for permission to search the rest of the rooms on the floor.

10

ilda returned to the nursery at Kenzie's call, and considered her with a pinched expression.

"You said you would only be a few minutes. That you just needed to look at this room and the one with the balcony."

"We would like to look at the rest of the rooms on this floor. We need to gather evidence."

"You can't have the run of the entire house."

"This floor—"

"And when you are finished snooping through this floor, you will want to look at the other floors. This is a private home. Citizens have the right to privacy. You don't need anything in any of the other rooms. Mr. and Mrs. Wade's rooms. The child wandered into a room where he was not allowed and climbed over the rail. That is what happened. You can't make it into something else. You don't need access to any other rooms. Leave this family to their mourning."

Kenzie hadn't even heard any voices on the floor while she and Tuttle had been there. Either the Wades were somewhere else, or the soundproofing in the house was very good.

"If you don't give permission for us to see those rooms, then we will need to get a warrant," Kenzie advised. "Because we do need to see them. Getting a warrant will cause extra publicity in this case. There will be rumors. Is that what you want?"

There would soon be rumors and more people involved anyway, but Kenzie knew that Hilda did not want any of those things to happen and would do what she could to avoid them.

"I can't," Hilda said stoically, shaking her head. "I'm not allowed to give you permission to search any of the rest of the house."

"Then you'd better call them and explain the situation."

Hilda stared at Kenzie stubbornly but, eventually, she caved. "I will talk to them again. But you will not get permission."

Kenzie nodded her understanding.

"Where is the other one? The detective? He'd better not be snooping anywhere else."

"He's in the other room, gathering some evidence. He won't go anywhere else."

"He'd better not," Hilda affirmed. "Or there will be trouble. Mr. Wade knows the governor. The attorney general. The police commissioner. If either of you steps out of line…"

"Haven't we followed your instructions while we have been here?"

She glared at Kenzie for a moment, then nodded. "Good. See that you do. You stay here until I get back to you."

"I will."

With one more glare, Hilda left the room, her hand immediately going to her pocket to retrieve a cell phone. But she didn't use it while within Kenzie's sight and hearing.

While Hilda was gone, another woman appeared in the doorway of the nursery. She peered inside, a frown on her face, and saw Kenzie.

"Oh, there is someone in here. Who are you?"

"I'm Dr. Kirsch. With the medical examiner's office. We're just following up on…" Of course, anyone in the household knew what she was following up on. Kenzie made a little motion to indicate the nursery and what had happened the day before.

The diminutive woman's eyes welled with tears. She shook her head. "My poor little Michael. I just can't believe it. How could such a thing happen?"

"Come in," Kenzie motioned for her to enter, indicating the rocking chair beside the bed. Kenzie perched on the edge of the bed while the woman sat down. "Are you the..." Tuttle had said that the boy's mother was tall so, clearly, it wasn't this woman. And she was too old to be Michael's mother. Maybe a grandmother?

"I help take care of Michael. Or... I did."

"Oh, I'm sorry. This must be particularly hard on you, then."

She sniffled and dabbed at her nose with a tissue. "Yes. I just can't get over it. That poor little boy. He was the light of my life." She wiped her leaking eyes with her palm. "You might think I'm being dramatic saying that, since he wasn't my own child, but it's true. He was the bright spot in my life. A child brings so much joy and *life* into your life."

Kenzie nodded. She tried not to think about Amanda and how Kenzie had been a second mother to her and had helped raise her. When she had died... it had left a great hole in Kenzie's heart. She had never considered having a child of her own after that heartbreak. She didn't know how she could handle it if something were to happen to a biological child. She didn't know how she would be able to go on.

"I know what you mean," she said softly. "I'm so sorry for your loss."

The nanny nodded her head and sniffled some more. "My name is Sylvia Arnold." She held out a wet hand momentarily and then withdrew it, changing her mind. "I'm sorry; I should have introduced myself."

"That's okay. Can you tell me what you saw yesterday? What you observed personally?"

Sylvia looked uncertain. She shook her head. "It was such a shock. I came here to check on him." She looked around the room as if she might find something of importance or comfort. "He wasn't here. Usually, he stays here to play. But he wasn't. So I looked for him. When I realized what had happened, saw him out there by the pool..." Her eyes swam with tears and she shook her head in disbelief. "I couldn't make myself believe it. How could such a thing happen? That baby. That poor boy."

"What happened? Do you know?"

"He had climbed out over the balcony railing and fell... I couldn't believe it. I still can't. What would possess him to do that?"

"Was he... an active child? Did he take a lot of risks or not seem to understand when something was dangerous?"

"What child understands all of the dangers, even when they are told? It's built into their nature. They need to experiment, push outside the boundaries, explore the world around them. That's what children do."

"It is," Kenzie agreed. "They have to separate from their parents at some point and find things out on their own. But he was still pretty young. Kids that age are not usually so daring."

She blubbered, wiping her nose and eyes. "You must think I'm so silly, he wasn't even my child, but I can't help it. I've been taking care of him since he was a baby. He was so special to me."

"Was someone supposed to be with him? What was he supposed to be doing?"

"I couldn't be with him. I had been given other tasks to do. They said... that he would be fine. He would be with one of the other staff members or his parents. They could all look after him. Everybody chipped in now and then. I couldn't be with him twenty-four hours a day. I still needed to sleep, have days off, run errands..."

"Of course you did. I'm not saying that you did anything wrong in letting someone take care of him. I'm just curious about what the arrangements were."

"I was to be helping out in the kitchen for a few hours. I thought everything would be fine."

"I heard he was sleeping, and this happened when he got out of bed without anyone realizing it."

"Sleeping?" Sylvia repeated, looking puzzled.

"Yes, I was told that he was asleep. That he had gotten out of his bed and gone into the other room and climbed out before anyone realized that he was up."

Sylvia nodded slowly. "He might have been down for a nap,

maybe. He was up early in the morning. Maybe he was tired or was not feeling well."

"How was he the last time that you saw him?"

"He was fine. He seemed…"

"Happy?" Kenzie suggested, when Sylvia couldn't seem to come up with the right word to finish her sentence.

"Yes. Well… not, maybe not happy. He was a little stormy. He was like that sometimes. But I knew how to handle him. He just needed some attention. Maybe he was cutting a tooth."

"Right. So he was grumpy? Upset?"

"His cheeks were red… I would probably have given him a pain reliever, in case it was his teeth. That usually helped."

Kenzie wondered how often painkillers were required for injuries rather than teeth. Of course being hurt would make a child grumpy and harder to deal with. And from what she had seen, Michael was probably hurt a good amount of the time.

"Was he a moody child? What was he like?"

"He was colicky when he was young," Sylvia admitted. "He cried a lot and was hard to settle. His mother was at her wit's end. I would rock him." Sylvia rocked the chair. "Hold him for hours until he settled, and we both fell asleep here."

"Did they ever take him to a doctor to see if it was something physical? Something they could do something about? Maybe reflux medication or a different diet?"

She shrugged and shook her head. "It was just colic. You can't do anything about colic. Just wait for them to outgrow it."

Kenzie nodded slowly. Had Michael been colicky? Or had the abuse started way back then, and he was crying in pain? Or maybe both—he'd been colicky, which had precipitated the abuse.

"Did someone change the sheets on the bed yesterday?" Kenzie asked.

Sylvia shook her head. "Wednesday is the day the bedding is changed."

"Maybe he wet the bed? And it needed to be changed earlier?"

"He was dry when I got him out of bed."

"But then he apparently went back to bed. Maybe he had an accident during or after his nap. Maybe that's what woke him up."

Sylvia shrugged. "If he did, no one said anything to me about it. That wasn't normal for him. He was dry during the day. Sometimes, he still had accidents at night, but not during the day. He was very good."

"So you don't know who would have changed the sheets or why."

"No. What makes you think they were changed?"

"I could see that they were fresh, unused sheets. Still starched and ironed. They hadn't been slept in."

"I don't know. I don't think that could be true." She didn't offer any further explanation as to why someone might have seen fit to change the sheets on the bed after the child had died. They wouldn't be expecting anyone else to sleep in the bed anytime soon.

"Michael is the only child in the house, right?"

"Yes. Well, usually, he is the only child here. Sometimes a visitor... but no, he was the Wades' only child." She dabbed at her running nose. "His poor mother. What she must be going through right now."

Kenzie sighed. "I can only imagine. I remember how it was when my sister died. And she wasn't that young. She was sick for a long time, so we knew it was possible, but when it did happen, it was so sudden..."

"Really?" Sylvia leaned forward slightly, getting closer to Kenzie. "That must have been very hard for you."

Kenzie nodded. She rolled her eyes upward, trying to keep them from filling with tears. Bringing up her own loss during the discussion would not be helpful. Not to her, anyway. She needed to keep her emotions under control and not think about Amanda and that loss of years ago. She could separate from it. Compartmentalize it until she was somewhere safe to think about it again. Not in the middle of an investigation.

"So, if you were Michael's nanny, what are your plans now? Will you keep working here, doing something else? Maybe until there is another baby?"

"Oh, I don't think I could." Sylvia shook her head sadly. "I could not stay here and take another baby. I would be too afraid... that it would happen all over again."

Which was far more likely if she were talking about the abuse, rather than Michael going off the balcony. She couldn't bear to see another child abused. It would be too hard for her to handle.

"Was Michael happy here? Were they a happy family?"

"Of course, of course," Sylvia assured Kenzie without enthusiasm. "This was his home. Of course he was happy here. What child wouldn't be? He had toys, lots of room to run around, the pool. The staff was very good to him and Deanne would make cookies for him, even though Mrs. Wade said he didn't need them." She smiled conspiratorially at this memory. "Michael loved chocolate chip cookies."

"And I'll bet that Deanne made really good ones."

"Oh, yes. They are to d—they are so delicious. Just the right amount of sweetness, crispy on the outside and chewy inside." She gave the tips of her fingers a chef's kiss. "Perfect."

Kenzie leaned forward slightly to ask her question, hoping that she would not scare Sylvia away, but pull her in, where she felt safe to share confidences, as she just had.

11

"Did Michael fall down a lot?"

Sylvia looked at her, frowning. "Fall down? No. This fall... it was just... no one could have foreseen that such a thing could happen. There was a railing. He would have had to climb over it."

"No, I mean just when he was walking or playing. He had a lot of bruises."

"A lot of bruises?" Her expression went stone-faced. Blank. "No, no, he didn't fall down a lot."

"Where did the bruises come from, then?"

"He did not have a lot of bruises."

"I'm the one performing the autopsy, Sylvia. I know exactly how many bruises he had, where they were on his body, and the approximate date he received them. Think about that."

Sylvia sat there frozen, thinking about what Kenzie had told her. The color slowly drained from her face, but she still tried to tell Kenzie that she was wrong.

"Those must have been from the fall. It was so awful. He must have been black and blue from falling that far."

"No, they weren't from the fall. He didn't bleed after the fall because he was dead. When the blood isn't circulating through your body anymore, you don't bleed or bruise. And I told you that I could tell how old the bruises were. They weren't all received yesterday. They spread out over weeks."

"Well... he must have gotten them playing, I don't know. Some people bruise more easily than others."

"If you were the one who was taking care of Michael, then you must have seen that. How many bruises he had. You didn't bathe him?"

Sylvia looked torn between not making herself look any more guilty and lying and making herself look uncaring. She kept shaking her head. "Yes. Yes, of course I bathe him every night before bed. I did."

"Then you saw the bruises."

"Yes," Sylvia admitted reluctantly. "I told you they must be from playing."

"How would he get a bruise in the middle of his back while playing?"

"If he... fell backward out in the garden. Or walked into something backward. Children can be so silly, running backward and inventing all kinds of games."

"He had a lot of friends to play with, did he?"

"Well, no. There were not a lot of children visiting the Wades. He mostly played by himself or with one of the adult members of staff."

"And you think one of them hurt him like that?"

"No, no, I didn't say that!" She quickly tried to cover the suggestion. "He could have hurt himself playing alone."

"How did he get the bruises on his stomach?"

"He must have run into something."

"So he got a lot of bruises playing. Did you ever take him to the doctor to find out why he hurt himself so much? If there was something wrong with him? A brain tumor or blood disease?"

"No. That would be up to his parents, not to me."

"And when did they last take him to the doctor?"

"I don't know. Usually, they would have a doctor come here to check on him. But only if there was something that needed treatment. If it was just a bruise…" She shrugged helplessly with one shoulder. "Who would take a child to the doctor for that?"

"When was the last time he saw a doctor, do you remember? And if I could get the name of his pediatrician, that would be helpful. So I could follow up with him on Michael's medical history."

"I don't know. I can't give that to you. His mother would know."

"Was she ever concerned about the bruises?" When Sylvia opened her mouth to answer, Kenzie pressed on. "Or did she tell you to ignore them?"

Sylvia closed her mouth. She looked at Kenzie. "I think… I should not answer any more of your questions."

Tuttle appeared in the doorway of the nursery and looked in at them, one eyebrow raised in question at Kenzie.

It wasn't until then that she realized she had done exactly what she had promised not to do. She had interviewed the nanny by herself, without anyone recording or being able to verify what she had said. The nanny could claim that anything Kenzie reported was made up.

Not that she had provided any real information. There were hints that she was aware of the abuse and certainly someone that close to the child should have been aware and had a pretty good idea who was doing it.

"This is Detective Tuttle," Kenzie told Sylvia. She motioned for Tuttle to come closer. "And this is Sylvia, Michael's nanny. Sylvia, why don't you tell the detective about Michael and how you think he got those bruises?"

Sylvia was clearly terrified about talking to the detective. It was one thing to talk one-on-one to a sympathetic woman doctor. It was quite another to have to answer the questions of a burly police detective.

"I told you I don't know anything about it," she protested. "I don't know how Michael got any bruises. He was a child. He had accidents."

"That was a lot of accidents. Do you think he had a brain tumor or something that made him keep falling down or walking into things?"

"No. I don't know. He's just a little boy. I don't think there was anything wrong with him. He just got bruises."

"You realize," Tuttle said in a slow, thoughtful voice, "that whoever was hurting him could turn around and say it was you."

"I would never do anything to hurt him!"

"You're the one that was with him the most, aren't you, the one who was charged with his care? So if he was getting bruises while he was under your care, that must mean that you are the one who was hurting him."

"No! He didn't get hurt while I was taking care of him. I took good care of him."

"So he didn't fall down and walk into things when you were taking care of him?" Kenzie asked.

Sylvia considered the question, her eyes darting from one to the other. "No. No, he didn't get hurt when he was with me. Only when he was with... someone else."

"Who else?" Tuttle asked.

"I don't know. I couldn't tell you what happens when I am not here. Other people look after him. He doesn't tell me how he got hurt."

A toddler didn't tell her how he got hurt? Whoever was abusing him must have scared him pretty good. That was a hard lesson for someone so young to have learned already.

"You must have a pretty good idea," Tuttle pressed. "His mother? His father? Someone else on the staff?"

"What is going on here?" a loud voice demanded. "What do you think you're doing?"

12

They all looked up to see who it was. Kenzie knew without turning to look at the doorway who would be standing there. The belligerent, authoritative voice could only belong to one person. The master of the house. Crispin Wade. Always referred to as Cash.

He was a heavyset man, his body appearing to be solid muscle rather than fat. He was formidable. He seemed to fill the doorway. Sylvia was gasping, hand to her mouth, trying to stop her tears, sit up straight, and do whatever else she was supposed to do when the master entered the room. Stand and salute? Cash certainly seemed to have the presence to order everyone around, with the clear expectation of being obeyed.

"Ah, Mr. Wade." Tuttle didn't turn a hair. He had his own presence. He stood with his thumbs hooked in his pant pockets, making himself appear bigger and wider than he was. Not the same class as Cash, maybe, but enough to command respect. "Detective Tuttle. I believe we met yesterday."

"Yes," Cash agreed. "So what are you doing back here today? I thought you got everything you needed yesterday."

"Well, things are not as they appeared. Which means that we

needed to come back today to collect more evidence. I appreciate your cooperation."

"That cooperation is over. You do not have permission to interview my staff. You've seen what you need to, and I would ask you to leave. You will not be welcomed back into this house again. Keep that in mind before you bother coming out here again. Stay on your own side of town."

Those were fighting words. Kenzie looked at Tuttle, concerned about how he would react to Cash's superiority. There was a red flush at Tuttle's throat, but he kept his expression neutral and didn't move a muscle to show any threat to Mr. Wade.

"We were hoping for your permission to search the other rooms on this floor."

"No."

"If you don't grant it, we will be back with a warrant. In fact, I won't actually leave. I'll sit in my car and wait for it to be delivered, and then I will search the other rooms."

"You can't do that."

"I can't leave the scene without ensuring I've obtained all the evidence. There is no other option."

"Get out of here. I know the governor!"

"Yes, sir. You're not the only one. But you don't think he's going to help to obstruct a police investigation, do you? What kind of a political leader would he be if he didn't look out for the most vulnerable in his state?"

"He will not allow you to make a spectacle of this household. We are personal friends."

"I'll have to get a warrant before a judge," Tuttle said meditatively. "And if it takes more than one judge to get a positive answer, I will shop it around until every judge in the county has seen it and either denied or granted me the right to search the rest of the rooms in your house. That will probably make a pretty good stir at the courthouse. People will start to ask questions. Will want to know what or where the warrant was for. It might be confidential, but word still gets around."

"You can't do that."

Tuttle shrugged. "We'll see."

"What are you looking for?"

"Evidence in the death of your son."

"You already did that yesterday. The boy fell from the balcony to the concrete below. It was a tragic accident. You have investigated. You have gathered evidence. And now it is time to close your investigation."

"We know what happened."

Tuttle said it quietly, but everyone in the room froze. Everyone in the adjoining rooms where servants worked and talked froze and listened.

"We just need to find out where," Tuttle said.

"You know where. We know what happened. Why are you stretching this out? We are mourning the loss of our son. This game you are playing is going to backfire in your face."

"Maybe," Tuttle agreed.

"I'm asking you to leave my house now. My property. Go back where you belong."

Tuttle nodded his agreement. He looked at Kenzie to make sure she was with him. They gathered their various evidence bags and were escorted out of the house.

Tuttle and Kenzie sat in the car and Tuttle proceeded to make several phone calls to try to get the warrant that they needed. Kenzie didn't want to be accused of hovering or eavesdropping, so she did her best to ignore him and look at her phone, checking her email and what else she could do remotely. She had not planned to be sitting in the car for hours.

But as it turned out, they would not be sitting there for hours. Tuttle got a call from his sergeant calling him back to the police station.

"Sir," Tuttle protested. "We need to search those other rooms. If we don't do it today, evidence could be destroyed. Some cleanup was already done since we were here yesterday. And I don't think that coming back a third time would get us in any more hot water than going back in today."

Kenzie could have told him there was no point in arguing with his boss about it. The decision had been made, and with Cash Wade's full weight behind it, there would be no talking his way into a warrant. The governor would make his calls. The attorney general. Maybe even the police commissioner. And they would all ensure that no warrant was granted or even applied for. If Tuttle didn't want to end up riding a desk for the rest of his career, he had better know when to back off.

He listened to what his sergeant had to say, his skin taking on a grayish tone. He said a few "yes sirs" and then terminated the call. He looked at Kenzie and shook his head.

"We're not getting it today."

"We're not getting it at all," Kenzie said.

"Maybe not." He pressed his lips together and cleared his throat, uncomfortable. "I hate politics."

"I know."

"I want to get this guy dead to rights. This guy probably beat his kid to death, and he's going to stand in front of me and threaten my case and get away with it? With everyone throwing their support behind him? How can we call it a justice system if it only applies to those who don't have any power? If there are two different sets of rules?"

"It's not justice," Kenzie agreed. "But maybe we'll be able to get him another way."

"You have a way?"

"I don't know yet. We have more evidence to process." She indicated the bags in the back seat, "and I need to finish the autopsy. I don't know what I will find yet. But I can tell you, I won't be finding that he climbed over the balcony rail and fell to his death in a tragic accident."

Tuttle licked his lips and nodded. "Yeah. When that is made public, the family will have to answer for it. One way or another."

"I just hope they don't try putting it on the nanny or some other innocent servant."

"You think the nanny is innocent?"

"I can tell you she is a lot more broken up about Michael's death than his father is. I haven't seen the mother, so I can't speak to what is going on with her, but Sylvia is about as grief-stricken as a person can be over an unexpected death."

"You think she'll talk?"

"I hope so."

"Okay. I guess it's time to get back to the office."

Kenzie nodded and sighed as they turned around and left the big white building behind them. She was glad that she hadn't grown up in a place like that. It might have damaged her irreparably. She had a pretty good idea that if she had grown up like that, her parents would have seen to it that she could not follow her passion to go into something like the medical examiner's office. She would have been given a choice between charities, maybe. The choice as to what highbrow politician she wanted to intern with. But she would not have been allowed to follow her heart.

13

Despite the fact that Kenzie had been thinking about Lisa and about her own growing-up years, and despite Cash blustering that he knew everyone of any importance and would be able to apply whatever political pressure was necessary to get his own way, Kenzie had not been expecting the call.

She was at the morgue long enough to get all the evidence and samples properly cataloged for processing. She was thinking about whether to take lunch before she restarted the autopsy, when her phone rang.

Kenzie pulled it out tiredly and looked at the face to see who was trying to reach her now. She swiped the call.

"Oh, hi, Mom."

"MacKenzie. How are you doing, dear?"

"I'm okay. Pretty busy at the office," Kenzie offered, hoping this would encourage Lisa to get to the point, since Kenzie had work to do. "Dr. Wiltshire is off, so I'm trying to hold down the fort."

"Well, you have certainly made yourself useful there. He puts a lot of trust in you."

"Yes, he does," Kenzie agreed, allowing herself a smile. She was proud of how she and Dr. Wiltshire worked together and how much trust he put in her. It was rewarding to see how much she had grown and learned since she had first started there, when it was purely an administrative position. She had hoped that it would grow into something where she could put her medical skills to use and get experience in the field so that she could qualify one day for real medical examiner work. Dr. Wiltshire had quickly advanced her so that she was doing more than she had ever hoped to in her job. One day maybe she would have her own morgue to run. "So I can't take too long to chat. How is everything?"

"Things are well. I am working on a fundraising drive for the Kidney Foundation, of course, and we are looking forward to Christmas to decide which campaigns to participate in or donate to. There are always so many worthy causes, but we can only help so many. And we're hoping to include some mental health advocacy or research causes this winter. How is Zachary?"

"He's good so far. I'm braced for his depressive cycle, but so far so good."

"Maybe it won't happen this year."

Kenzie shook her head. "Maybe."

"And your father is well. Have you talked to him lately?"

"Yes. Well, it's probably been longer than it should be. I'll make sure to give him a call." Kenzie paused, waiting to see if that was why her mother was calling. Just to tell her to talk to her father? Did that mean that something was going on with him, or just that Lisa wanted to ensure they continued to have a good relationship?

"I'm sure he'd be happy to hear from you. The two of you should go out for dinner the next time he is in town. Or the three of you—take Zachary with you. No need to leave him at home by himself."

Except it would probably be doing Zachary a favor to keep him away from Walter, who wasn't his favorite person. They both tried to be positive about him and not discuss his negative qualities and their negative experiences with him. If Kenzie were going to keep up a good relationship with him, she had to let go of past hurts and misconduct. Walter was a good man who cared about his family. That was what she needed to focus on. It wasn't easy for either of them, and Kenzie knew that Zachary had a particularly difficult time forgiving Walter's offenses against Kenzie.

"Was there anything you needed, Mom? Papers to be signed or something…"

"I just thought it had been a while since we talked last, and I would try to get ahold of you. I'm sorry if I've caught you at a bad time."

"I do have a lot of work to do here."

"I understand you are working on that terribly tragic death in Congressman Wade's family. I can't tell you how shocked and saddened we were to hear what had happened to him."

Kenzie stiffened, her muscles tensing before she even had a chance to process what Lisa had said.

"I can't talk to you about active cases," Kenzie told her woodenly.

"No, of course not. I understand completely. But it has been all over the news. We were so sorry to hear of his loss. You remember how it was when we lost Amanda… nothing can prepare you for that. And they didn't have the warning that we did or the happy years that we had with Amanda. His son was so young. An unbelievable tragedy."

"Yes, it was," Kenzie agreed. "But you don't know the details, so I don't think you should talk about it as if you do."

"The poor family just wants to move on. To be able to put it behind them and grieve in private. It is so difficult when you are a public figure and everyone wants to know every detail of your life. They want to see how upset you are, to see and hear and intrude on all those private times. It is a very difficult situation."

"Yes, I'm sure it is," Kenzie agreed. She had not been the one in the spotlight when Amanda had died. She was just the sister, not the father or mother. She was a side story, and not a very interesting one. They wanted to see her mother cry. Lisa stood strong in front of the cameras and continued to pound the drum, raising money for the research that could have saved Amanda. Every question was pointed back toward the need for more research, for a cure.

Cash Wade, on the other hand, was not interested in fundraising, talking about domestic abuse, or naming something on his son's behalf. He was only interested in silencing everyone and putting it behind him so that he and his wife and their entourage could continue to enjoy the good life that he had established for himself.

"You'll be careful, won't you, dear?" Lisa prodded.

"Careful of what?"

"You know how things can get blown out of proportion. I just mean that something insignificant should not be turned into a circus. Into something that it is not. You know that the Wades are a fine, upstanding Vermont family. They have been in the state for almost as long as the Coles and Kirsches have."

Almost, Kenzie noted. Almost as long. So the Wades were "new money" Vermonters. Not part of the old guard. The congressman wanted to make himself a part of the old fabric, to hobnob with the old Vermonters and be seen as one of them. But he was still a bit too much *new money* to do so.

"You know that I don't make any determinations in the work that I do based on someone's position in the government or in Vermont society," Kenzie said sternly. "I am looking for the truth. Not a sound bite."

"Oh, I would never imply that you are just seeking publicity. But things can be taken the wrong way, and you don't want anything you say to be taken the wrong way. People like Cash Wade—" Kenzie noted that it was Cash now rather than Congressman, "—are very good at spinning things the way they want to. And very sensitive to anything that might be... exactly what they want to hear."

"The Medical Examiner's Office will publish its findings, whether Cash Wade likes it or not."

"I thought you would be a lot more sympathetic to an old friend than—"

"It doesn't matter who he is friends with," Kenzie insisted. "We will publish the truth. And right now, that is *not* something that Congressman Wade will want to read."

There was a small intake of breath. A little gasp that Kenzie would be so bold and would insinuate that Wade might have been in the wrong about something.

"What do you mean?"

"I've already disproved the story Cash Wade and his wife would like us to believe. So I wouldn't believe anything he and his cronies might whisper in your ear. Take everything they say with a grain of salt. Maybe a full teaspoon of salt. Because he is a liar. And we will not be supporting his lies in our final report."

"MacKenzie," Lisa reproved. "You can't go around saying things like that."

"I wouldn't say it to anyone else but you. We won't put it exactly that way in the report. But you should know the kind of person you are dealing with. Cash Wade is a bully and a liar, and if you think that anything he is saying about the loss of his son is true... you'd better wait until you see our press release."

"What are you saying?"

"I can't say more than that. I can't give you any specifics. But you should know that he is lying. His son did not climb over a balcony rail and fall to his death."

Lisa was silent. Kenzie could hear her breathing on the other end, still there but unsure what to say.

"You understand?" Kenzie asked.

"Yes, of course. You are very clear. And very sure of yourself."

"There is no doubt."

"And you won't have any mercy for an old friend?"

"No, Mom. I can't. I have to stay impartial. No matter what happens, I can't let family or friends affect the way I investigate and report on this child's death. I won't write anything that is not the absolute truth."

"And you can't... I don't know... excuse yourself from this case."

"No, I can't. We don't have a big office. It is Dr. Wiltshire and I and some other staff members that help with gathering evidence or dealing with transportation. And Dr. Wiltshire is out of commission with a broken hand, which will take weeks or months to heal enough for him to use again. So it's up to me to keep things moving and finish the autopsy on Michael Wade."

"I see. And there is no way to... soften your findings. To make it less... inflammatory."

"I haven't released anything yet. I don't see how you could ask me to be less of anything. We haven't said anything to the public. If anyone says that we have, they are lying. We will release our findings when the investigation is complete."

"Of course," Lisa agreed. "Well, good luck with that. I hope everything goes well and smoothly, and that you do not attract too much… negative attention. Let me know if you need anything."

"I will."

"I mean it, MacKenzie. Anything. Just call me. Understand?"

"Okay, Mom. Thanks. Take care of yourself and give Lola a kiss for me."

"I will, dear."

Lisa terminated the call.

Kenzie suspected Lisa would not actually give the dog a kiss on her behalf.

14

Kenzie moved Michael Wade's body back to autopsy and made sure that all of her equipment was ready before starting. She tapped the button on the floor and dictated the date and time and her own name. She paused for a moment, used to adding that Dr. Wiltshire was present as well, even if he wasn't attending to the same dissection as she was. He was usually in the room to discuss the case with and to take a second look at any findings.

It felt very strange to be starting without him.

But Kenzie eventually began, performing the Y-incision and exposing the viscera. She made initial observations, taking pictures of any areas of bleeding or bruising, trying to identify each individual injury on this boy who had been a punching bag for some adult in the home for the past weeks or months. Perhaps for all of his short life. It made her furious, but she had to keep her focus and remain objective and dispassionate. Even though she knew what had happened to him and who was likely responsible, she had to pretend she didn't. Imagine this was a new case that had just come across her table and she knew nothing about his history or what had happened to him. It was a puzzle to solve, that was all. She would find all the pieces and put them back together in a way that made sense.

She would expose the truth, just as she had exposed the internal organs for examination.

Kenzie removed each organ, making observations, weighing and measuring them, and probing them for any damage or unusual pathology. There were lacerations in the liver, and scarring where previous lacerations had healed on their own. The damage to his body went much deeper than the bruises on the surface.

After cracking the ribs, she was able to remove the lungs. She weighed them, looking at the number on the scale and frowning before making note of the numbers. She dissected them and made several slides to be examined later. She took samples of the fluids and made extensive notes.

She called Dr. Wiltshire, hoping to be able to discuss her findings with him. There was no answer. Had he been at the hospital all day waiting for a consult on his hand? She would have thought that his position would afford him some special treatment in getting a scheduled appointment at the head of the line rather than having to wait all day like a walk-in.

Kenzie continued with the postmortem, deciding it would be advisable to dissect the throat as well, looking for any internal bruising or damage that was not visible from the outside. She would need to be able to answer all questions about how Michael had died.

It was a long day. Kenzie never did manage to get ahold of Dr. Wiltshire. Hopefully, that was just because he was in the hospital and had his phone turned off while he had his consult. Maybe they would decide it didn't need surgery and would cast it right away. She hoped for the best possible outcome for him.

Zachary was at his computer when she got home, lost in some case. He looked up briefly when she walked in the door and said something unintelligible, then was once more immersed in whatever was on his screen.

Kenzie removed her shoes and outer clothing, and took her purse to her bedroom where she put it down. No comment from Zachary.

"What case are you working on?" she asked as she went to the fridge and poured herself a glass of water. There was no response. She might as well have been talking to the wall. "I'm going to have a shower. Then we'll pull something together for supper. Unless you want to order in."

Again, her comment was met with silence. Kenzie shook her head and retreated to her bedroom, where she stripped down and hopped into the warm shower. She let the hot water work on her sore muscles. Anyone who thought it wasn't hard work to move bodies around and spend half the day bent over an autopsy table, cutting through bone and tough sinews should try it for a day. It was no walk in the park.

And that was aside from the mental and emotional strain. Even though she had done her best to keep from getting invested in the case, not to worry about how things would turn out or who was responsible for the abuses she uncovered, she couldn't completely dissociate herself from the experience. She knew she had been working on a toddler. She knew those things should never happen to anyone, let alone an innocent child.

The shower felt good. Cheap therapy. Wash away all of the sweat and grit and bad feelings, and luxuriate in fresh, warm water, steam cleansing her pores and her lungs, and breathing in the aromatherapy of her shampoo, conditioner, and body wash. It was like a whole spa treatment, right in her own house.

She put on flannel jammies, even though it wasn't really late enough to be wearing jammies, and walked back out to the kitchen.

Zachary looked up from his computer, paying more attention to her this time. "Oh, you're home," he said, looking at her and then down at his computer, frowning. "I didn't—did I see you come in?"

"Well, you gave a lousy rendition of 'Hello, how was your day,'" Kenzie advised. "It seems like you were a little focused on your work."

He looked at his computer screen again. "I had no idea it was so late. Sorry, you've had a long day."

"It was," Kenzie admitted. "I hope they're not all like that for the next few weeks."

He stood up from the couch and stretched. Kenzie wondered how many hours he had been sitting there, lost in his investigation before she had gotten home. He needed to move more than he did. But the same was probably true of her.

"Why would they all be like this?" Zachary asked. He gave her a hug and a quick kiss. His body was warm and musky and she held on to him for a couple of seconds longer than he held her.

"Because Dr. Wiltshire is out of commission with a broken hand."

"Oh! Did I know that? I don't think you told me. Unless it was a whole conversation we had while I was working on this file..." He motioned to the computer, grimacing.

"I know better than to keep talking to you when you're hyperfocused. I told you about Dr. Wiltshire yesterday. That's why we had to come back."

"Oh yeah. Sorry. How badly is it broken?"

"Well, any break is bad for someone who works with their hands like we do."

Zachary nodded and looked down at his own hands. She wondered how many times he had broken a finger or another small bone in his hand due to abuse or fighting. He avoided fighting; he wasn't someone who immediately resorted to violence when faced with a threat. But it had only been a couple of months since he had broken knuckles fighting for his life and the lives of Bridget's twin girls before the police had been able to get there to effect a rescue and arrest the culprits.

"I don't know how badly it was broken," Kenzie said. "He didn't talk to me about it. I don't even know how he got it. But I hope he heals fast and I don't have to do all the work without him for the next few weeks."

"You'll need to get someone in there to help. A sub."

"Yeah." Kenzie wasn't sure how many people were available to do that kind of thing. Any medical doctor could do a postmortem, but she wasn't about to turn the lab over to anyone who didn't have extensive knowledge about forensic pathology and the standard procedures to follow. But maybe the hospital could loan them someone a couple of days a week. "That would be good."

Zachary looked at the fridge. Even without his opening the door, Kenzie could tell that he wasn't interested in anything he might find there today. Even if Kenzie were cooking, which she wouldn't be, he wasn't going to be tempted by anything remotely healthy. Whatever case he was working on stressed him enough that he was looking for comfort food. Junk, deep fried, dripping with cheese.

"You want to order pizza?" Kenzie suggested, before he could think of something even more unhealthy to eat.

He let out his breath and nodded. "That would be good."

At least they'd had salad the night before. Or Kenzie had, anyway. Kenzie sat down at the table. It felt good just to sit and relax for a few minutes. Zachary got one of the pizza flyers out of the drawer and made a call to order their dinner.

"We should have Tyrrell over one day," Zachary suggested. "Him and Robbie both."

Kenzie couldn't even begin to think of entertaining. Not after the day she'd had.

"Not today," Zachary clarified. "I just think that we should do it sometime. When you're not stressed out."

"I'm not stressed out, just tired."

Zachary eyed her. Kenzie thought about the autopsy and the call from Lisa and threats from Cash Wade.

"Well, maybe I am," she admitted. "There is a lot going on with this case."

"Is it the same one? The little boy?"

"Yes."

"I saw a story in the news today about a boy who died in an accident. In a fall."

"Probably the same one."

Zachary gave a low whistle. "There is going to be a big stink if you don't find the way they want you to."

"I know that already. And I know that I'm not going to say what they are hoping I will."

"And you don't have Dr. Wiltshire to fall back on."

Kenzie nodded. "Bingo."

"But he'll still look at what you've done. Approve it. Say that he agrees with your findings."

"Yeah. I would hope so. But it's going to be brutal, even with him backing me."

"What's he like? Did you meet him?"

"The father?" Kenzie asked. "He's... loud. Forceful. Not the kind of person you want to cross. He's already making all kinds of threats about the kinds of trouble he is going to cause, all of the people who he can talk to about getting me... I don't know, thrown off the case... forced to say what he wants me to say. I don't know exactly what he hopes to accomplish by calling anyone political to try to stop me. It isn't like I'm going to run for office."

"Who's he going to call?"

"He's already been making calls. Got Detective Tuttle blocked in requesting a warrant to search the rest of the house. And Lisa called this afternoon." Kenzie wrinkled her nose to express her displeasure at this development. "To tell me that I need to be careful not to rock the boat, and won't I make an exception for an old friend?"

"Cash Wade is an old friend of hers?"

"I guess. I didn't know there was any connection between them, but she says that his family has been in Vermont almost as long as hers."

"Which means...?" Zachary knew better than to speculate on the political world the Kirsches were a part of.

"Which means he is a new money Vermonter. Not as high on the social scale, but still significant. And maybe if he has *enough* money, he can buy the rest of what he needs."

"They always can."

"No, not always," Kenzie disagreed. "You need a combination of blood, breeding, money, and influence. All the money in the world won't buy you the rest."

15

"I can't believe that they were able to hide the abuse," Kenzie mused. "The people in the household must have known. Anyone that they did things with socially must have known. I know you told me about them making sure they didn't bruise his face and keeping him in long sleeves and pants when necessary, but they couldn't hide it from the nanny who bathed him. What about the children he played with? Swimming? They have three pools!"

Zachary shrugged. "He wouldn't necessarily have had suspicious injuries all the time. If he did, they could say he was sick and couldn't go swimming or have any playdates. They could tell people that he was sickly or had an immune disorder and couldn't go out to visit. They have a social life. They can go wherever they want to without him. And at home, it's just the staff. Just the nanny and anyone else who took care of him, if there was anyone. It could even be the nanny. People *do* hide it, Kenzie. No one wants to believe their friends are abusive. They'll look the other way and believe whatever excuses they are given."

"He must have been in terrible pain much of the time. And it doesn't seem like he saw any medical professionals. Maybe a doctor who came to see him at the mansion if he was sick, but they couldn't call him if the boy was bleeding internally or had any suspicious bruises."

"The rich pay them off. The poor... wait and see if the child survives. If not... dump or bury the body somewhere and never tell anyone what happened."

He stared off into space, and Kenzie didn't want to know what he was remembering. Whether he was thinking of something that had happened in his own family, or a foster family, or to someone like Ben Burton, who had hired him to find out what had happened in his past and discovered a tragedy he had kept locked away for far too many years.

"We should probably change the subject," Kenzie suggested.

Zachary nodded.

The pizza arrived, and they decided to be decadent and watch in front of the TV instead of visiting at the table. Dr. B, who led their couple's therapy, suggested they turn off all screens for supper and focus on each other. But they had already done that, discussing the difficulties Kenzie was having with her job, and they needed to just relax and not think about it anymore.

At bedtime, they exchanged massages, working on the knots in each other's muscles to help them relax for sleep. But Kenzie knew that Zachary was doing a much better job on her than she had done on him. Her massage of his muscles had been too short, and she had not really put the attention into it that she should. She hit the spots that she knew usually got sore when he was sitting on the couch hunched over his computer, but she had not really explored any other areas. She was so tired that giving him a massage made her *more* sore and took energy she didn't have. He could tell that she was tiring and had insisted it was her turn for a massage when really, she'd barely touched him.

Zachary, on the other hand, worked his way over Kenzie's back, neck, and limbs slowly, kneading at the sore and knotted muscles, rubbing fragrant lotion into her skin, and generally making her feel relaxed and safe and ready for sleep. She kept dozing off while he worked on her. Eventually, he put the bottle of lotion to the side, pulled the blankets over her, and lay beside her running his fingers through her curly hair and rubbing her scalp as she drifted off the final time.

Kenzie awoke a couple of hours later to an animal-like cry from Zachary, followed by staccato, broken sleep-babble as he tried to reason with his demons. Kenzie fought her way through the sheets to put her arm around him.

"Zachary. Zach. It's okay. Wake up." She stroked his short, stubbly hair and neck, waiting for him to surface. "You're just dreaming, Zachary. Wake up. You're okay." She knew better than to grab his arm or shake him. Nothing that might make him fight back, thinking she was the enemy.

"*No!*" His body convulsed as if he'd been hit or had flinched to brace for a blow. Then softer, "No."

She thought that the second "no" was a conscious echo. Repeating himself and trying to orient himself to his surroundings and figure out what was happening.

"It was just a dream," Kenzie told him again. "You're safe. You're with me."

She knew she should say "Kenzie" instead of "me," because how was he supposed to know which "me" she was? Waking up out of a dream, he might think her to be Bridget, or his mother, or some other woman from the past. But calling herself by name felt awkward and a little silly.

"Kenz?"

"Yeah. You're okay. Do you want to tell me about it?"

He cleared his throat and moved around restlessly, looking around the room, re-establishing himself in space. This was where he belonged now, but he hadn't lived with her for long enough to automatically know where he was when he woke up. She knew he still thought he was in other places first. An old apartment, a place he had lived in with Bridget, maybe Bonnie Brown, an institution he had spent time in as a child.

"No, just a dream," he murmured.

"Yeah. Was it something from the past?"

"No."

She knew it wasn't the fire. She could usually tell when it was the fire. He was far more frantic, shouting to his family, curling up in a ball with his arms over his face, trying to hide from it, just as he had done as a ten-year-old.

"No," Zachary repeated. "Your case. I think it was just because of your case."

Michael Wade. It wasn't a shock that he would dream of the abused child. He had spent much of his childhood being abused and trying to protect the other children from abuse. If he had been in the same home as Michael, he would have tried to protect him. Hide him, step in front of the blows, distract the abuser with something else. A punishable offense that could not be ignored.

"I'm sorry."

"S'okay." Zachary felt for Kenzie and pulled her gently closer, tucking her against his body, his warm breath on her hair, arms around her protectively. "Not your fault." She snuggled into him, enjoying the closeness even though she had been jerked out of a sound sleep by his nightmare.

"You're one of the good guys," Zachary went on, his voice a low murmur, barely more than a whisper. "You'll protect him. Find out who did this and put him behind bars."

"I can't arrest anyone. But I'll give the police everything I can, and they'll get him. They'll take care of it. They won't let a child beater go free just because of his money."

Zachary gave a grunt of disapproval at the mention of the abuser going free. Kenzie stroked his jawline and neck, and rubbed the back of his head with its short stubble. He purred at that. Kenzie hoped that if she could keep it up long enough, he would drop back off and get a nice long night's sleep. She knew from experience that it was unlikely, but she could try.

"When will it happen?" Zachary asked. "When will you release your report and they will be able to arrest him?"

"I'm still waiting for some test results back. Going to go over some slides and samples tomorrow. Not a lot. Some tests can take months to get back, but I can release my initial findings before that.

I'd really like to go over everything with Dr. Wiltshire first. And... I need to read over the parent and witness statements. I should have done that today, but I didn't have time to finish everything. I want to do this right. To make sure that all of my conclusions are rock-solid and no one can fight it."

"Yeah." Zachary stretched and relaxed, kissing the top of Kenzie's hair. "But be careful. You know guys like this. You don't want him gunning for you."

"I don't know how I'm going to stop him from being upset with me. He isn't going to like what I have to say. Hopefully, they'll be able to arrest him quickly. I'll coordinate with the police... make sure their investigation has run parallel to mine and come to the same conclusions. They know Michael was being abused. They don't doubt that."

"That's good." Zachary rubbed Kenzie's back.

She closed her eyes briefly, luxuriating under his touch and, without meaning to, drifted off to sleep again.

16

When Kenzie awoke in the morning, she was alone in the bed. Zachary always got up before she did, so that was not unusual. She hoped that he had been able to get back to sleep after the nightmare and hadn't been up since then.

She pulled on her housecoat and wandered into the living room, unsure whether she would find him asleep on the couch or hard at work. He was at his computer, tapping away. But not so lost in his work that he didn't notice her approach.

"Morning," he greeted. He squinted at her for a moment. "Have a nice sleep?"

"Yeah, it was good. How are you doing? Did you get back to sleep?"

He shrugged. "No. Couldn't settle back down again."

Which meant he had probably only gotten a couple of hours of sleep.

"You might want to take a sleep aid tonight, then," she said neutrally. If she told him he had to or really pushed for it, he would resist. It was better if he felt like he could make that decision for himself and her suggestion was only a thought to consider. He was the one who knew his brain, his meds, and his sleep requirements. As much as Kenzie wanted to insist, to dictate how he handled it and force him to take the meds she felt he needed, she couldn't do that. She needed to let him make his own choices.

And he'd been doing well at it. He was in a good place. So far.

One short night's sleep like that might throw him off the rails in December, when his traumatized brain was trying to figure out how he could survive the Christmas season, but now he was still in a good place, and he would handle it just fine. As long as she didn't keep bringing up child abuse cases that kept him awake at night.

She had seen terrible things before. She didn't need to take them home to Zachary.

"You want coffee?" Zachary asked.

"No, not yet. I'll get myself together first. Just wanted to say good morning."

Zachary nodded, smiled, and looked back down at his computer.

There were an unusually high number of messages on the office's voicemail system with queries or instructions about the Wade case. Lots of reporters and curious members of the public were hoping to learn more about the case. A few calls from government officials who "had an interest" in the case and wanted to know how things were going. A polite call from a funeral home saying that they had been authorized by the family to pick up Michael's remains and would she please call as soon as they were ready for transport.

There were no threats. No angry tirades from Cash Wade himself detailing what he would do to her if the autopsy results were not satisfactory. Apparently, that kind of thing was reserved for the confines of his home, when there was no one but his own staff to overhear. People he knew he could control.

Dr. Wiltshire had left a couple of messages with things that he hoped she would have time to follow up on, but which Kenzie highly doubted she would be able to get to. Where was he? She had assumed that he would still come in to deal with the desk work, at least, and to go over everything with her before she released her findings in the Wade case.

After taking care of the administrative functions that could not be avoided, Kenzie had Julie take over the reception desk and phones, and shut herself in the boardroom away from the constant ringing to review the statements on the Michael Wade case.

Cash Wade's statement was brief, and pretty much what she expected after speaking to the detectives and the nanny. He was in a different part of the mansion from Michael and, as far as he knew, Michael was sleeping in the nursery. The first that he knew something was wrong was the shrieking of the nanny. It was clear that it was more than just an argument with someone on the staff, but that something was really wrong.

He had hurried toward the sound, but then been distracted by the sound of staff members rushing downstairs and outside to the pool area. He had looked out a window and seen them gathering around something on the poolside deck. The screaming nanny forgotten, he followed to see what was going on. And that was when he had seen his son lying on the ground, unresponsive. Looking straight up, he could see the balcony overhead and knew that was where he had fallen from. He concluded that the nanny had not been watching the boy closely enough.

Which was a bit odd, because if he blamed the nanny, why was she still at the mansion? Why hadn't she been terminated on the spot? Even if he didn't blame her for his son's fall and death, it would still have made sense to let her go after his demise, since there were no other children for her to take care of.

But Kenzie had been under the impression that Sylvia also had other household duties. She had not introduced herself as the nanny, so maybe that was something she had only taken on as they had needed her to.

Still, Cash had not yelled at her for talking to Kenzie or being in the nursery. He had not made any bitter accusations about how his son would still be alive if she had only done her job. But maybe that was just Hollywood stuff. In real life, people didn't behave like they did in the movies. The scenes written for the silver screen were just that—scenes invented out of someone's imagination for the best dramatic effect. In real life, maybe someone like Cash kept his mouth shut and let the housekeeper or his lawyer deal with Sylvia's employment. Maybe he didn't even think about what her part in his son's death had been while he was trying to get the prying detective and assistant medical examiner out of his home.

Or he was waiting until they were out of the way to lay into her.

Or he didn't blame her at all.

Because he knew that she had not been the cause of Michael's death.

Maybe.

Kenzie went on to the mother's statement. Terri-Lyn Wade.

She also claimed to have been elsewhere in the building. Unlike Cash, who claimed he had been conducting business, she said she had been eating a late breakfast after her Pilates workout, which was her usual routine. Kenzie didn't judge her for starting her day so late. Before Kenzie had gone back to medical school, she'd followed a similar schedule, going to events in the evening, with plenty of socialization going on into the early morning hours, eventually crashing at home and sleeping until mid-morning or later. She didn't have a Pilates class, but she frequently didn't have her breakfast until many people were contemplating lunch.

Terri-Lyn had also been startled by Sylvia's screams. She had been on the main floor in the breakfast room, with windows at the front of the house rather than the back, so it wasn't until people started shouting and running toward the pool that she knew something had happened outside. She initially thought that the staff would take care of whatever had caused the disruption, but eventually decided that she'd better see what was causing all of the commotion.

A couple of staff members had blocked her way, not letting her go right up to her son, telling her she didn't want to see him like that and that there was nothing she could do. Cash would not allow her to get close, no matter how she begged. She didn't see his face before they zipped him into a body bag and took him from the house, and could only imagine the extent of damage that had been done by the fall.

Rather than blaming the nanny, she blamed herself for not going to check on Michael after her Pilates session and for the fact that he had been able to get through the sliding doors to the balcony. Rather than abdicating responsibility as Cash had, she blamed herself for things she probably had no control over. Whoever had used the balcony last and had not fastened the doors securely. Maybe a faulty door lock. The fact that Michael had been sleeping alone and she hadn't known that he had gotten out of bed on his own.

All of the things that she should have done or foreseen because she was the mother.

Even if there was no way she could have controlled ninety percent of them.

Her son was dead, and she blamed herself for it.

Kenzie smoothed the report pages as though they were crumpled or wrinkled, but they were not. She pictured the two parents. Cash she had met, so it was easy to put those words in his cultured, angry voice. Terri-Lyn was more difficult because Kenzie had never met her. Was she a small, mousy woman who always let Cash push her around? A strong independent woman who did her own thing and was only married to Cash for convenience and money? Something in between? Kenzie had met all types in the upper echelons of the Vermont social structure.

Tuttle had said that she was tall and well-built. She had been doing Pilates so, in theory, she should have strong core strength. Not a little old lady. Not a shrinking violet, Kenzie suspected. Someone who could stand up to Cash when he got carried away with his orders and tried to control her life as well as the rest of the mansion.

Someone who felt a huge well of guilt for not having been there when her son went over the edge of the balcony. A mother who had wanted to protect and care for her son, but had not been able to.

Sylvia had implied that neither parent had the patience to deal with Michael when he had been a colicky baby and she had stepped in to hold him until he had cried himself to sleep. Maybe Terri-Lyn was not someone with much instinct for child rearing or who hadn't had the time to properly establish a bond with him. It could be challenging to bond with a child with colic or medical issues that kept them in constant pain or discomfort. They weren't the cute, cuddly bundles people expected, the baby you could hold or rock for hours just staring into his eyes. A baby who screamed, cried, and pushed or kicked against his caregiver was not easy to love.

Maybe Terri-Lyn recognized that she didn't have the proper mother-child bond with Michael, and that was what she felt the most guilty over.

That and the fact that she or her husband had been beating on him, eventually causing his death.

Maybe she felt guilty about that.

17

It was the nanny's screaming that had alerted everyone that something had happened, so she was clearly the one who had discovered his body after it had been dropped from the balcony. Kenzie moved on to her statement, which was quite a bit longer than either parent's.

Sylvia said she had been working in the kitchen, the same thing she had told Kenzie. She had taken a break and gone to look in on Michael to make sure that everything was okay. She didn't say who was supposed to be watching him during that time, if anyone. She had gone to the nursery and, not finding him there, had begun to conduct a room-by-room search.

She didn't say if she had called for anyone else to help her, or that she had alerted either parent to the fact that he was out of his room and she didn't know where he was. So maybe it was a fairly regular thing. Although Sylvia had told Kenzie that he would usually stay in his room to play.

She had reached a room with the door standing open and had entered to see if that was where Michael had gone. Looking around, she did not find him, but she felt a breeze and realized the balcony doors were open. She went to secure them, but it occurred to her that they were open wide enough to admit a child and checked to make sure that Michael was not on the balcony.

And that was when she had looked over the edge and seen Michael on the white concrete pool deck below her, splayed out and unmoving.

Her narrative ended abruptly. Kenzie imagined the screams that had drawn everyone in the household to the back of the house where Michael's body lay. Sylvia probably had little recollection of what had happened after she saw Michael there. Neither parent had said that she made it down to the main level or ran out to Michael's body. Perhaps she had collapsed, or someone had gone to her and comforted her, keeping her away from the body, just like they had prevented his mother from rushing out to see him like that.

More details had been added later. Bits and pieces of information that Kenzie imagined the detectives had managed to coax out of Sylvia and had her add to her statement.

"I did not see him climb over the rail. I did not see him fall."

"I heard a noise. That was why I went to find him."

What kind of a noise? Kenzie could imagine Tuttle prompting her. *Did you hear Michael playing? Crying?*

"Not Michael. Just a noise that made me think I should check on him and make sure he was okay."

Kenzie pondered this. What had Sylvia heard? She seemed to have refused to give the detectives any description of what kind of a noise it was. Footsteps? Voices? Toys being thrown? Something falling? Just "a noise."

Something that made her think she had better check on her young ward.

She said it was not a noise Michael had made, so maybe it was the parents. Maybe one of them had said something within her hearing that made her worry for Michael's safety. The boy had not just wandered out of the nursery and climbed over the balcony rail. He had been killed by someone before he had been dropped from the balcony. And that someone might have said something in Sylvia's hearing that tipped her off to the fact that Michael had been hurt again.

She was used to his getting hurt. She knew he would need painkillers. That she would need to rock and soothe him and try to keep him still so that the injury could start to heal on its own. She must know how badly he had been beaten in the past. She wasn't stupid.

So she had gone looking for him, only to find that she was too late and they had already killed him and disposed of his body in a way intended to obscure what had been done.

Kenzie heard a door open and looked up. It had not been the door of the conference room she was hiding out in, but one of the other doors in the suite. She waited for a moment, head cocked, trying to identify any other familiar signs to figure out whether it was George returning with a transport or Julie getting a cup of coffee from the kitchen.

But it didn't sound like it. She stood up from the table and left the boardroom to see who it was.

Dr. Wiltshire's door opened down the hall. Kenzie waited to see if he was going to the kitchen for a coffee and, when he didn't, she went to get him one anyway. Even though it was an inconvenience for him to be injured and to put everything on her, that wasn't exactly his fault, and she wanted him to be in a good mood.

She prepared his coffee and then went down the hall to his office. She entered through Dr. Wiltshire's open door, tapping on the door as she went by.

"I heard you come in."

He looked up quickly, startled even though she had knocked and been careful not to sneak up on him.

"Oh, Kenzie!"

She tilted her head and laughed. "I *do* work here."

She stepped forward and put the cup of coffee on his desk, switching at the last moment to putting it on her right, his left, so he could use his other hand. She looked at his right hand, still in a splint.

"What's the word? No cast needed?"

He sighed. "The splint is temporary. It needs extensive surgery and hardware if I am going to regain full function. They are trying to get a specialist lined up to do it. I'm not sure how long I will have to wait. Hopefully, just a day or two. And then the recovery period after that and physical therapy..." He shook his head, frustrated. "I would like to tell you that I'll be back on the circuit again in a month. But it could be as many as six. Assuming I get full function back again. Fine motor... it's vital for our work. I can't just be hacking and slashing. Even if I leave the sewing up to someone else, there is still so much more that I need full motor function for."

"Yeah," Kenzie agreed. With less dexterity, it would be difficult for Dr. Wiltshire to continue in his position. "You must have really done a number on it. What exactly did you do?"

"I'm embarrassed even to say. Suffice it to say that I do not have a future in the PGA. Or any other sport, for that matter. You would think I would have learned as a young man that sports are not my thing. But with what I do here, the coordination required, thoughtful planning, reflexes... I assumed that my work proved I had all of those things." He picked up his coffee with his left hand and sipped it carefully. "Sadly, there is still something vital that I lack."

Kenzie frowned at this response, which was really not an answer to her question at all. Dr. Wiltshire was avoiding answering. He had said it was embarrassing, and she supposed that was why. He didn't want to have to admit whatever had happened. Kenzie had experienced enough of those moments herself to be sympathetic. Stubbing her toe on something she knew was there. Possibly even the heel of her other foot. Tripping over a crack in the sidewalk or nothing at all. Walking into a closed door in the dark, thinking it was open. There was a long list of stupid accidents in her past too. Everybody had them, so why was Dr. Wiltshire so hesitant to admit his?

She'd heard him joke about playing golf before. Mostly about how his wife wanted him out of the house or wanted him to have a hobby before he retired so that he wouldn't think he could stay home all day with her. He had never actually claimed to be good at it.

But what could he have done to break his hand so badly while playing golf? Swung into a tree? Fallen down a slope and tried to catch himself? An accident with an electric cart?

"No need to look so serious," Dr. Wiltshire assured her. "At least your position here is assured, as there is no one else to take over the work at the moment."

"Will you be looking for someone to do some part-time work? When things pile up and two people are needed to handle the workload?"

It was a quiet time of year, but when December hit...

"I will see who I can find. I was already talking to the head of pathology at the hospital in Burlington, seeing who he could suggest."

"Good. Not that I want someone else to take over, but I don't want to be here twenty-four hours a day. I'll end up a zombie, and not the good kind."

He chuckled. "Fair enough. So, how are things coming on our big case?"

18

"**A**re you talking about Michael Wade?"

"Who else?"

"I just wanted to make sure. Because he's a small case and a big case."

Dr. Wiltshire stared at her, and Kenzie wondered whether her comment had been difficult to follow.

"A small boy," she explained. "But a big political situation."

"Right, of course," Wiltshire agreed. He took his glasses off and wiped them as if dust had prevented him from seeing her point. "Small but big. So what have we got?"

Kenzie pulled up a chair and settled in to discuss it more fully. "There are a number of things that I wanted to talk to you about."

"This may be a case where it is in our best interests to... leave things a bit vague."

Kenzie felt like she was the one staring at him now, in disbelief at what he was suggesting. "Leave them a bit vague? It's our job to provide as much clarity as possible. For the sake of the public and to give the police the best possible chance to catch the culprits in a case like this."

"I'm sure that there are some things that are... ambiguous. And perhaps it's best if they are just left that way. Digging down too far, we run the risk of accusing or even just implicating the wrong person. And that would be doing the family a huge disservice."

"Someone in that household was abusing him."

"So it would appear. But again… perhaps it was someone outside the home. Or someone who was only an occasional guest. And throwing shade on the family brings with it the danger of lawsuits. Defamation of character. False accusations."

Kenzie shook her head.

"There are… discrepancies in this case," Dr. Wiltshire tried approaching it from another direction. "Inconsistencies between what the witnesses report and what the body is telling us. We could simply state that there was disagreement between those things and the justice system would have to investigate and take it to its conclusion."

"But we know that the body is right. Not the witness statements. Someone could swear that they saw him walking around outside today, and it wouldn't make any difference because we know he wasn't. He's on a table in the cold room. That's the truth. And we need to be clear as to what the truth is. That is not in doubt. There's no *interpreting* the truth."

"I think it can be managed. If you'll bring me your first draft, I can go over it, or we could go over it together, and discuss the best way to word those *truths*."

"I really don't think…"

"You and I both know that things are not cut and dried. There is often more than one cause of death or mitigating factor. We interpret what we find based on the clues at the scene and what the police find and communicate to us. Technologies change. We decide what tests are required or are not required. Our budget constraints require that we be conservative in how much time and money we spend on each case, pinching pennies like a grandma on a pension."

All of that was true, but Kenzie still didn't like what Dr. Wiltshire was suggesting that she do. Or what she thought he was asking her to do.

If Cash Wade was guilty of killing his heir, Kenzie wouldn't bury that fact.

. . .

She didn't have a lot of success going over her findings with Dr. Wiltshire. He was distracted and complained about being unable to focus due to the painkillers he was on for his hand.

He agreed with each point she brought up, but then tried to spin it so that it was irrelevant or ambiguous in meaning. She had to assume that he either knew the Wade family or was receiving significant pressure from the people that Cash Wade had promised he would call. He had the influence he claimed to; Kenzie would give him that. Old money or new, the man had clout. He had clawed his way into Vermont society and had it by the throat.

Dr. Wiltshire left after just a couple of hours, signing off on whatever reports he could and apologizing that he didn't have the energy or focus to spend any longer with her.

"We'll go over this later," he promised. "Maybe put it to the side as 'undetermined' for now, and we'll revisit it when I feel better."

Kenzie just smiled at him. She didn't disagree with him aloud, but there was no way she was going to set the case aside or waffle on the cause of death. She had been raised by a couple of people who were adamant about standing by what they believed, and she wasn't going to cave to any pressure to do otherwise. She would uncover the truth and do whatever she could to ensure the culprit was caught and punished.

Since Dr. Wiltshire was gone and the phones and reception desk were already being covered, Kenzie decided that a field trip was in order. It was time she visited some of Vermont's hospitals.

The Roxboro hospital was small, but Kenzie knew from experience that it was staffed by competent and talented staff and that their emergency room was second to none of the city hospitals. When the wait time was long in Burlington or Montpelier, people would drive to Roxboro, knowing that they would get in and dealt with faster there, even considering the driving time.

A couple of people she had gone to medical school with had been posted to the hospital, so Kenzie made a couple of phone calls just to say hello and see if they were still there. And to casually mention that she would be by to pursue an inquiry.

When she spoke to the nurse at the triage desk in the emergency room, she smiled and nodded. "Dr. Pulman said that you might be stopping by and that I should help you out however I could."

"Well, that was very sweet of him," Kenzie said with a smile. "If there is someone I could talk to, I don't want to take you away from your duties here…"

Nurse Harris leaned over to look around Kenzie, emphasizing the fact that there was no one standing in line behind Kenzie and very few people sitting in the waiting room for their names to be called.

"I think you are safe."

Kenzie chuckled. "Okay. I don't want to cause problems. Dr. Pulman seems like a nice guy, but you never know what kind of a boss someone is…"

"He's not my boss," Nurse Harris said comfortably, "And my boss will not get after me for helping out the medical examiner's office when I am not inconveniencing any patients."

Kenzie nodded. She turned her phone around, showing it to Nurse Harris.

"Now, I know you get tons of people through here, so this is a long shot, but I wonder if you recognize this boy as having been a patient here before."

Nurse Harris looked at the picture for a moment, then nodded. "Yes. I recognize him."

19

K enzie leaned in, surprised. "You know him? You're sure?"
She nodded again. "I've got a pretty good memory for
faces. I know I've seen him here before." The corners of
her mouth turned down. "What... what did he die from?"

Kenzie had done her best to make the picture look as if the boy
were just sleeping, even going so far as to add a pink filter to brighten
up his gray skin, but it was still obvious, to a nurse at least, that the
boy was dead.

"I haven't released my findings yet. Would you pull up his records
for me, please? His name is Michael Wade."

"Sure, of course." She turned to her computer and tapped in the
name. She shook her head, frown lines appearing between her brows.
"Hmm. W-A-D-E?"

"Yes."

"I do not see that name here anywhere. Is it possible that he was
admitted under another name? Mother's name, stepfather's? A lot of
kids have several different last names these days. It can be a bear to try
to untangle them all."

"No." Kenzie hadn't seen Terri-Lyn Wade's maiden name
mentioned anywhere. She was always Mrs. Wade or Terri-Lyn Wade.

She couldn't imagine why Michael would be going by any other name.

"Well…" the nurse shook her head. "Do you think you could find out? I can't really pull up his file without a name."

"You would check ID, wouldn't you?"

"Yes, we check." Nurse Harris looked squinted her eyes up at the ceiling while she thought. "Oh… I wish I could remember more about the circumstances he was brought in under. He was brought in by his mother, or maybe his grandmother. He had fallen…" She pursed her lips and shook her head. "Or something had fallen on him. I think that was it. She was very upset. The mother. Said that she had only turned her back on him for a minute and then he had pulled something over on himself. You know how kids do. Climbing a tall piece of furniture or something."

Kenzie nodded. She tried to think of a way to find Michael's records if she was not registered under the right name.

"So he received treatment. Do you remember what day it was? How long ago?"

"No. A few months ago. I can't be much more specific than that."

"And he was brought in by his mother?"

"Umm…" the nurse stared off into space, thinking about it. "An older woman, so maybe stepmother or grandmother. It's so hard to know these days when you have women getting pregnant into their fifties or adopting or becoming parents to their partner's children. You just never know."

"Can you remember what she looked like? A tall, well-built woman?" Kenzie regretted that she had not seen Terri-Lyn Wade face-to-face, nor even looked up her picture online to see what she looked like. She could find a picture on her phone to show Nurse Harris. Kenzie hit the home button on her phone to search for it.

"No," the nurse said. "No, a little woman."

Kenzie stopped what she was doing and looked at her. "A little woman?"

"Well, you know, not *little*, little. Not like a dwarf. But quite short and small-boned."

"Dark hair?"

"Yes."

"And what did he call her? Did he call her Mom?"

"The little fellow wasn't calling anyone anything. He was quite badly hurt." The nurse nodded toward Kenzie's phone. "Not *that* badly, but it was pretty serious. We had to get him into surgery immediately."

Kenzie almost let herself tear up, thinking about what someone had done to that little boy. Pulled the furniture over on top of himself? She highly doubted that. It did happen, of course. Children died of crush injuries or head injuries from such accidents with regularity, despite the advice to parents to tether furniture to walls to prevent it. They didn't bother, or didn't know their kids were that mobile yet. Or thought that their children were too smart or mature to do something stupid like scaling a bookshelf to reach what they wanted.

But the injuries she had seen on Michael suggested ongoing abuse. Not just a single accident. Or one several months ago and one the previous Sunday.

"Funny about your question about checking ID, though," the nurse said thoughtfully. "She didn't have his birth certificate with her. We checked hers, of course, and set up his chart based on that."

"Arnold?" Kenzie suggested. "Could it have been set up under Michael Arnold?"

Nurse Harris typed the new name into her system and brightened. "Bingo. So he did go by her name."

"No." Kenzie shook her head. "She wasn't his mother. That was his nanny. Sylvia Arnold."

The nurse skimmed over the information on her screen, nodding in agreement. "Yes. That's the name of the woman who brought him in. The woman who said she was his mother." Harris paused, reading more that Kenzie could not see. "She said that she had no insurance. So we didn't need to collect that information. He had to be treated or he would probably not have made it. It was lucky she got him here when she did. She should have called an ambulance."

They probably wouldn't let her. They probably wouldn't let her call any authorities to the house. No paramedics, no police, no one who might have recognized the abuse and connected it to the Wade family. They didn't want anyone like that at the mansion. So Sylvia had done the only other thing she could, taking him away from there to a place where he was safe and could be treated for his injuries. Had his parents known about it? Had they allowed it? Or had she done it without their permission, knowing that Michael would die unless she did?

They hadn't fired her, so maybe they knew and approved of what she had done. Or maybe they didn't even know. She might have done it covertly, and if she was his primary caregiver, his absence from the home had gone unnoticed.

"Can you print that off for me? And anything else you have on file?"

"Of course." Nurse Harris started the print job and then paged through it on her screen. "It did look like what she had said. Something heavy fell on him. He had deep bruises, broken ribs, liver lac, fluid in his lungs. It was very serious."

"Could it have been caused by a person squeezing or crushing him?"

Harris looked at her for a moment, mouth open. "Well... I wouldn't have thought of that scenario. You would have to ask one of the doctors who dealt with his case, and he may not be able to remember enough after this long. We see a lot of cases."

"But you remembered him. Maybe he would too."

Harris nodded, but didn't look hopeful. "Michael was not a big child," she said, considering. "I don't think it would take a lot of force to do that kind of damage. But you should talk to someone in DCF with experience. *They* would have a better handle on that."

"I will look at some case studies as well," Kenzie told her. She was still waiting to hear from the police on whether there had been any DCF reports made concerning Michael Wade. She didn't want to be the one to call them. Not after Dr. Wiltshire had made such a big deal about avoiding any accusations of defamation. "Was he treated here for anything else? Or was that the only time he was brought in?"

"It wasn't the only time. That's probably why his face was familiar to me. Always brought in by Sylvia Arnold, no insurance, no birth certificate. It's not unusual for undocumenteds. But Arnold doesn't sound like an immigrant name." Harris rolled her eyes. "Not that you can tell by someone's name. But I mean, so many of them are Hispanic or else names you can barely pronounce. Arnold is so... American. And she didn't look foreign."

"No. She doesn't," Kenzie agreed. "I think she just didn't want him to be identified by his real name. That was why she could never bring a birth certificate or any insurance. She might not have been able to get him treated if she admitted she wasn't his mother."

"We would still have had to treat him. But it would have presented some additional problems. Thinking it was just an insurance problem, we didn't dig deeper than that. Was she... you don't think *she* was abusive, do you? I don't see how such a small woman could have caused those injuries."

"No, I don't think she was the one. She is the only one who seemed to care about him enough to get treatment."

And yet, it nagged at Kenzie. Sylvia had been the one to take Michael to the hospital to make sure that he didn't die, but she didn't care enough to stop the abuse. She hadn't taken the steps necessary to have him removed from the home. Once he was at the hospital, she could have told them that Michael was being abused by his parents or someone else in the household. She could have had him removed.

But she hadn't.

20

Kenzie went home early. She could continue working from her home office, making phone calls to the other hospitals in neighboring towns with the names Michael Wade and Michael Arnold to see if he had been treated in any other hospitals.

He had.

Sylvia kept taking him to hospitals with stories of accidents to have him treated, but she hadn't turned him over to DCF. It didn't appear that she had made any effort to stop the abuse. She just kept bringing Michael to hospitals, injured, worried about whether he would survive. She knew the bruises were not caused by clumsiness, falling down, or bumping into things, even if that was what someone had told her. She had recognized that Michael's injuries were serious.

"Kenz?"

Kenzie rubbed her eyes and sat back in her chair. She faced Zachary, but didn't look at him, her palms still resting over her eyes.

"Yeah. What time is it?"

"I thought you might want something to eat. I know you're working, but..."

"But I need to take care of myself," she finished for him. She removed her hands from her gritty eyes, recognizing that her body was telling her she'd been at it for too long. Zachary was absolutely right to interrupt her. She looked at the system time on her computer. It was nearly nine o'clock.

She swore. "I had no idea it was that late. You should have said something earlier! You must be starving. Or did you already eat?"

Usually, Zachary was the one who got so lost in his work that he didn't know what time it was or that mealtimes had passed him by. She'd better not be picking up that habit. But she knew how hard it was to decide whether to break his concentration and bring him back to reality. She didn't like to stop him when he was immersed in something important.

"Do you want me to heat up some pasta for you?" Zachary suggested, without answering the question. "Or one of those rice bowls?"

"No. I can do that. I really do need to get off the computer. I can work on this tomorrow."

"I can heat something up. Really. I'll even take the plastic off when I'm supposed to. Put a warm cloth on your eyes or something for a few minutes while I do it."

Kenzie chuckled at him mothering her, just like she chided him when he was not taking care of himself properly. "Okay, I will. Work is put away. I'll eat whatever you heat up. And I'll take a few minutes to relax while you do it."

"Good." He nodded briskly. "I'll be five minutes."

What had he been doing all night? Had he been working on his own projects and also lost track of time, or had he been monitoring her, trying to decide when the best time was to interrupt her? Weighing just how important the work she was doing was against her need to relax and regenerate at the end of the day?

They sat at the table together twenty minutes later, eating and visiting, Kenzie still trying to put the concerns of the day aside so that she could relax properly. She told Zachary about Sylvia Arnold taking Michael to different hospitals, passing him off as her own son.

"I really can't understand her. If she cared at all about Michael—and she clearly did, or why would she be taking him to the hospital for treatment, probably behind her employer's back—if she cared about him, why didn't she report them to the authorities? They could have given him a safe home. Gotten him out of the place where he was being harmed."

Zachary nodded. "But the system itself has a lot of flaws. A much higher percentage of children die in foster care than with their own families."

"You can't tell me that she knew that. The perception of the foster care system, for those who are outside of it, is that it will provide children with a safe environment. Get them out of a dangerous one to where they can be safe. And for most kids, that's exactly what it does. I know that isn't your experience, but many kids only have one foster home, and they grow up there, safe and loved, until they are ready to be on their own."

"Or sent back to their biological families."

"Yes, I know that reunification is a big goal. But only when they believe it is safe. Only when the parents have gone through counseling and retraining and all of that stuff and are ready to take the child back again."

"I saw a lot of kids who bounced back and forth between foster care and their bio families. Social services... wasn't the best at determining that a parent was... reformed."

Kenzie thumped her fork down on the table with a bang that made Zachary jump. "I'm not talking about your experience. I'm saying that in *this* case, Michael at least would have had a chance of surviving if he had been removed and put in foster care. But no one did that. No one was willing to admit to the abuse they saw going on in that household every day and do something to protect Michael. No one did! They just let him die!"

Zachary stared down at his dinner, nodding. His face was blank, devoid of any emotion. She knew that her sharpness hurt him, but she wanted him to be as outraged about it as she was. She wanted him to see her perspective and to quit telling her it was an imperfect system. She already knew it was an imperfect system. But without it, Michael Wade had not stood a chance.

That little boy, hardly more than a baby, had not stood a chance because no one in the household was willing to step up, tell the truth, and get him out of there. They were all too worried about losing their jobs and any references from the Wade family. Maybe they were worried about the political fallout. Of being shunned and unable to get another job because of their political power.

But a child had died!

They should have stepped up. Everyone who knew about or suspected the abuse should have made a report and stayed on top of it until Michael was taken out of that home where he was tortured and killed.

Zachary's Adam's apple bobbed up and down as he swallowed. He moved mechanically, probably not tasting what he was eating.

He had hated foster care. He had been abused and institutionalized and had seen terrible things happen to other children. But he had survived. He had grown up and aged out of the system. And so had all of his siblings. It was true that they all had their difficulties and emotional problems. Some of that could be blamed on the system, and a lot of it came from the family they were taken away from. She couldn't allocate how much trauma had been caused by the foster system. And neither could Zachary.

"How was Dr. Wiltshire?" Zachary asked eventually, after a long silence that neither of them wanted to aggravate the other by breaking. "Did he make it in today? How did you say he hurt his hand?"

"He was in for a couple of hours. But... it was frustrating. He's on painkillers for his hand and I don't think he is thinking very clearly. He signed the paperwork he needed to and went home again."

"I hope he's not driving if he's in that bad of shape."

"I'm pretty sure he used a service. I didn't actually escort him out to the parking garage."

Zachary flinched. Kenzie felt bad for her mood and wished she could get past it. Zachary didn't deserve to be snapped at and to have to endure her grumping around all evening. But a lot had happened and Kenzie didn't know how to deal with it.

"He was telling me to be vague in the postmortem report," she explained, trying to give Zachary some basis for her irritation on the subject of Dr. Wiltshire, who he had thought would be a safe topic.

"He is worried about political backlash and the Wades coming back at us with a lawsuit. He wants the manner of death to be left open. Requiring further police investigation. Let them take the flak for it."

Zachary looked at Kenzie, brows up in surprise. "Can you even do that?"

"Of course I *can*. Technically. Sometimes it is impossible to tell what killed someone, and you are left with saying that it is natural causes, even though you are pretty sure there was something hinky going on. If you think it might have been homicide, but don't have any proof, or only have a few clues that all point in different directions—maybe natural, or maybe an accident, or maybe homicide—then you can go back with 'undetermined.' But that is not the case here. I know that it was homicide. I can't say I don't know."

Zachary nodded slowly. "You can see his point, though. Maybe if you initially say it is undetermined and just let the police continue to investigate until they have overwhelming evidence that it was the father, then you avoid any accusations by the family that it was politically motivated or that you are incompetent or trying to slander him."

"But that isn't right."

"I know. I think he is just trying to make it easier on you."

"He's trying to make it easier on himself. He is the one who has to take responsibility for what I put in my report."

Zachary looked surprised at this. "Is he? Not you?"

"He's the medical examiner. I'm just an assistant. Anything that comes out of the Medical Examiner's Office is his responsibility."

"Of course. That makes sense. I had just never thought of it before. I thought that if you were doing the autopsies, then any complaints would come back to you."

"Sort of. But ultimately, to him."

Zachary scraped his dish for the last of the pasta sauce. "I know it wouldn't be right for you to say it was undetermined when you know it was homicide."

"But you still think I should."

"No." Frown lines appeared between Zachary's eyes as he looked at her. "Of course not. I would expect you to do what you knew was right."

Sometimes, the simplest things could just melt Kenzie's heart.

Lisa had warned her to be careful what she put in her report and how she handled the case. Dr. Wiltshire had suggested that she fudge her report. Both claimed to care for her well-being and wanted what was best for her. She had expected Zachary to fall in line behind them, agreeing that even though it didn't feel like the right thing to do, sometimes she might have to bow to the rich and powerful to succeed in life. Sometimes real life forced you to outgrow those ideals, and you just had to be grown up about it and let it go.

"Thanks," Kenzie told him sincerely. "It's really nice to hear you say that."

"I would never tell you to hide the truth."

They were truly matched on that one thing, if nothing else. They were worlds apart in other areas. But Zachary Goldman was also a truth-seeker and truth-teller. He might intentionally obscure the truth to protect someone else, as he had when he had rescued Madison and Luke, leading the criminal enterprise they escaped to believe they were both dead. He might hide his feelings and lie even to himself about what he was feeling. But put him on a case where the truth was inconvenient, dangerous, or political suicide, he would still pursue it to the ends of the earth.

Just as Kenzie would any of the cases on her table.

21

K enzie had hoped that she would be able to sleep soundly after her long day. Her body and her mind were both tired, and she wanted nothing more than to just fall into bed and drift off into dreamland. Or, not to dreamland, but to nothingness. Not having to think about her work, feelings, or the tragedy of Michael Wade's death, but just to sleep.

And that hadn't happened. She had slept, but fitfully, with periods of restlessness in between, flipping back and forth as she tried to find a comfortable position and force herself to go back to sleep. The day's events and how she would write everything in her report kept pushing its way into her conscious mind. Her brain wouldn't let her push it off until the next day. She repeated phrases and tried to figure out the most clear, concise language to use to convey her findings and point the finger at Michael's father and the rest of the household.

There was plenty of guilt to go around.

She shouldn't have to feel guilty too. She wasn't the one who had been in the house, seen what was happening, and refused to do anything about it. By the time she was on the scene, Michael was dead; all she could do was try to see that justice was served on his behalf. That was her job. To speak for the dead.

"Kenzie."

Zachary's warm hand was on her shoulder, resting very lightly. Soft but solid, something anchoring her to the physical world.

"What?" She turned and looked at her phone to see if it was ringing, but there was no call and no alarm. "What's wrong?"

"You were dreaming. Sorry. I didn't know whether to wake you."

Having contemplated the same dilemma herself many times, she didn't blame him for waking her up. "Was I? Was I making noises?"

"Yeah. I was afraid... I didn't know if it was because of..."

It hadn't been a dream about the kidnapping. At least, Kenzie didn't think so. She couldn't remember much about it, but a few images still floated in her mind's eye.

"I think it was just the case. I can't let it go tonight."

"Do you want to read? Get up for a while and put something on TV?"

These activities sometimes helped her relax and get back to sleep on a bad night, but Kenzie was too tired to consider them tonight. "No. I really need to just sleep. I *was* asleep..."

And then he had woken her up. She didn't mean to accuse him or suggest that he had done something wrong, but it felt like she had barely dropped off. How was she supposed to get a good night's sleep when he woke her up at every disturbance?

"Sorry. You sounded upset. I didn't want you to be caught in that dream."

"I know." Kenzie snuggled up against his warm body, head on his chest, trying to reset. "It's okay. I just... I'm so tired."

"What can I do?" His arms encircled her and he rubbed her back in gentle circles. He kissed the top of her head.

Kenzie murmured something that wasn't really an answer, but told him to just keep doing what he was doing.

And he did.

Morning came too soon. Kenzie didn't wake up feeling relaxed and well-rested. All the burdens she had tried to put aside as she slept came rushing back to her. And now she couldn't keep pushing it off; she had to deal with it. She had to deal with the calls from the press and the various governmental offices who had absolutely nothing to do with the medical examiner's office but thought that they would give their input into her process and what she should be doing. She had to figure out how to write each finding in her postmortem report so that it was clear and unequivocal, and the police would have to act on it. Whether she or the office suffered a backlash from it or not, she didn't care. It had to be done anyway. Michael deserved the truth.

She put her coffee cup down on the table more forcefully than she had intended, and Zachary jumped and whipped his head around to look at her.

"Sorry," Kenzie told him without meeting his eyes. "Just slipped."

He shrugged and looked away from her again. "No problem."

They each asked the other how they had slept the night before, each of them knowing that the answer was that they'd slept like crap. But they made encouraging noises and said that they would sleep better tonight. Kenzie rubbed the middle of her forehead, knowing everything would not be resolved in a day. She would probably be sleeping restlessly for weeks, trying to get the report worded just right, and then dealing with the blowback, and whatever was in the papers, and having to deal with Dr. Wiltshire and his ire. He would probably be grumpy, strung out on painkillers, irritated she hadn't listened to him and followed his advice, angry that he couldn't work and had to wait and rehab his hand, worried that he would never regain the full use of his hand.

What had he done to it, anyway? Was there any soft tissue damage? Muscles? Nerves? If it was a crush injury, there could be all kinds of damage done to the connective structures. Damage that would prevent him from being able to use it properly even after the bones were healed nice and straight and strong.

"This afternoon?" Zachary was asking.

Kenzie let her fingers fall away from her face and looked at him. "Sorry, what did you say?"

"I just..." He looked awkward. "I just wanted to make sure that you remembered it's couple's therapy today. I know you've got a lot going on. Did you want to reschedule it? If you are too busy, I could just do a personal session today."

Couple's therapy. It was on Kenzie's calendar. She knew it was their week to attend Dr. Boyle's office together. Dr. Wiltshire knew that she took every second Wednesday afternoon off, and that was fine when he was around, but she hadn't thought about how her schedule might be affected while he was away from the office.

"Uh, yeah. That shouldn't be a problem. Julie will know that this is our week. I'll just double-check that she's okay with it. Dr. Wiltshire isn't there so, if something comes up… well, I'll let you know."

She had missed couple's therapy once, and that oversight had permanently affected his outlook, worried every time that Wednesday afternoon came around she was going to forget about it. It was such a small thing to have made such a significant impact, and she couldn't help but resent how he held that one mistake against her, even if he said he did not.

Did she and Dr. B hold it against Zachary that he had missed his own therapy appointments not just once, but multiple times? Sometimes because something was really wrong, and sometimes because it had just slipped his mind. And, of course, she always believed it was because something was seriously wrong, especially since her abduction, brief though it had been. The world no longer felt like a safe place and she worried that he had been abducted. A situation that was not improved by the fact that he *had* been abducted not so long ago to stop him from making trouble for a pharmaceutical research company that had been related to his case.

"Sounds good," Zachary said, his voice airy and casual. But she knew by his eyes that he was still worried. He wouldn't say anything else about it but, for the rest of the morning, until she left for work, he would be watching her and silently worrying that she would forget again.

They had talked it over, both during therapy and on their own, and had agreed that forgetting once did not mean that she had abandoned him or that he was less important to her than her work. No more than it meant that she was not important to him when he was distracted or followed a compulsion that took him somewhere other than where he was supposed to be.

They had talked it to death, and now it was all resolved. Except that he still watched her the same way and waited for her to do it again.

"You don't think Dr. Wiltshire will be in today?" Zachary asked.

"I don't know. I'm not counting on it. He was hoping to get into surgery in the next day or two if a specialist could fit him in, so I might have a message on my office voicemail telling me that he got in today and will be incommunicado for a day or two as he recovers. And that means I have to keep everything else moving forward. I still plan to be there, but I can't promise that something won't come up. I'll let you know if it does, and you can go ahead and have an individual session with Dr. B, and we'll do couple's next week."

He nodded. "Next week, things won't be as crazy."

Kenzie wasn't making any promises. Who knew where the case would go in the next week and what kind of craziness *might* jump out at her. "Could be a natural disaster," she pointed out.

"Could be a zombie apocalypse," Zachary deadpanned in the same tone of voice.

"Could be a train derailment."

"Could be the rapture," he suggested.

Kenzie shook her head and had a sip of her coffee. It was strong. She wondered if she or Zachary had switched it over to a stronger brew without realizing it. Or maybe he had done it intentionally, knowing that Kenzie hadn't slept well and figuring she would need a stronger kick to keep her going through the morning. "Hoo. That's strong. Wasn't expecting that."

"Is it okay?" he asked. "Do you want me to get you another cup? Less strong? Or stronger?" He smiled wickedly at the suggestion.

Kenzie made a face and shook her head. "No. This is just right."

"You want some sugar?"

"No." Kenzie took another sip of the potent brew and smiled to show she was fine with it.

The toaster popped and Zachary supplied her with toast and marmalade. And after a moment of staring at her blankly, a knife and tub of butter.

"Thank you."

Kenzie asked him about his day and the cases he was working on, the largest of which was an insurance fraud investigation. He was involving his sister Heather in the surveillance, which they were both enjoying immensely. When they had first met Heather, Kenzie hadn't had any idea how much like Zachary she was. She hid the trauma better and, being a woman, tended to do better at the social stuff than Zachary did. But they were both intensely interested in investigative work and solving puzzles, in bringing injustices to light, and had a mischievous sense of humor. Heather didn't have the same learning disabilities as Zachary and enjoyed organizing things in a way that was optimal for his ADHD brain, having raised two ADHD children of her own. They both had different strengths, but were interested in the same kinds of things.

Zachary cleared the table as Kenzie made the final preparations to go to work. Zachary kissed her goodbye before she exited to the garage.

"See you at couple's therapy this afternoon," he told her with a slightly strained smile.

Kenzie gritted her teeth. "I'll be there," she promised again. "Or I'll let you know."

enzie told Zachary that she was running late, but would be there. She needed to focus on finishing her report and couldn't keep texting him a countdown every two minutes.

She was only ten minutes late, and he had probably only been talking with Dr. Boyle for five minutes. And most of that would be introductory small talk. Dr. B checking in on how his life was going and if there were any new issues to be addressed in his personal sessions.

Their eyes turned to Kenzie as she hurried in the door, apologizing and out of breath. She didn't like to be out of breath or to have to apologize for her behavior. But she knew an apology was in order, even though she had been doing her best to arrive on time and the delays had not been her fault.

"I'm here, okay?" she snapped at Zachary when he turned accusatory eyes toward her. "I told you I would be. I didn't forget, and I'm here. It just took a few extra minutes."

Zachary didn't say anything at first. His eyes flicked toward Dr. B and then back to Kenzie. "Sure," he agreed. "No problem."

Kenzie sat down, blowing out her breath. "I'm sorry. I'm cranky and it's not your fault at all."

"You're under a lot of pressure right now," he said neutrally.

"Why don't you tell us what's going on right now that is stressing you out? Get it off your chest," Dr. Boyle suggested.

"Zachary already knows."

Dr. B just raised an eyebrow and waited.

"Okay. I'm getting a lot of political pressure on a case right now. From my mother, my boss, and various other political bigwigs who have nothing whatsoever to do with it. And my boss broke his hand, which means I need to do all the physical work. And he isn't even showing up for the paperwork and to discuss cases. I *need* him to be there, but he's been…"

She shook her head, knowing that Dr. Wiltshire was doing the best that he could and she would just have to be patient and understanding about the whole thing.

"He has to take care of personal stuff, and I guess I resent it that he's allowed to have a personal life and to deal with things like breaking his hand. It's silly, because of course he has to be allowed to have time off for illness and injuries."

Dr. Boyle smiled and nodded. "We understand that kind of thing intellectually, but our feelings are playing a whole different tennis game."

"Yeah. My emotions are all over the place. It isn't fair to anyone else that I'm feeling and behaving this way. But… I don't know how to change it."

"Why don't we break some of these feelings down a little. Your boss not being there feels like… what?"

Kenzie stared out the window behind Dr. B, trying to figure out what she felt and put it into words. "Like he's abandoned me, honestly. I know he didn't choose to hurt himself, but suddenly he's unavailable to me."

"Can you think of other times you have felt this way?"

"I'm not usually such a walking ball of prickly feelings. I'm a mess. I've always managed my feelings pretty well, so I don't know why I am so out of control this time."

"Have you always had to 'manage' your feelings?"

"I guess so. Everybody does, don't they?"

"What happens if you don't manage them? What if you just feel what you feel?"

"Well, you can *feel* whatever you like, but you can't walk around like a little storm cloud making everyone else miserable."

"Who do you think you heard that message from?"

Kenzie considered it. "I guess... from my mother. Maybe both of my parents. We've always been a little repressed," Kenzie joked, and gave a laugh. "My mother has always told me the *proper* way to behave in any social situation."

"But that isn't always a way that affirms your feelings."

"No. But you can separate your feelings about something from how you behave. People do it all the time. That's just... being civilized. Showing consideration for other people in society."

"So when you feel abandoned, how should you behave?"

Put that way, it sounded ridiculous to Kenzie. "I don't know how you should behave... I guess you just put the feelings aside while you're with other people and... serve and support them. My dad was away for a lot of my childhood and, when he came home, it was for my mom or because Amanda was sick and needed him. It wasn't for me."

"So you felt abandoned by him. Felt like you didn't matter. Your feelings didn't matter."

"I guess. And really... they didn't. As parents and as a family, we had to do what we had to do, no matter how any of us felt about it. None of us wanted Amanda to be sick, but that's what we got. And you just play the hand you're dealt."

"But you're still allowed to have feelings."

"As long as they don't get in the way."

Dr. B nodded. "And your boss being hurt and not coming into the office and dealing with his work feels like when your father was away, and only came back to deal with family problems. He wasn't there for emotional support when you needed it."

"But I'm not looking for emotional support from Dr. Wiltshire. He's not my father, and he isn't a father figure in my life." Kenzie paused, considering that. "At least, I don't think he is."

Dr. Boyle smiled. "Our feelings like to play tricks on us sometimes. You may never have intended to see him as a father figure, but he still is. Or he may not be, and you're just feeling extra pressure with your boss being gone that you want him to come back and take care of."

"Yeah. That's how I would describe it. I don't expect him to swoop in and 'there, there' me. I don't need any strokes or special praise. I just want him to do his job. So that I don't have to."

"When was the last time you talked to your father?"

Kenzie frowned. "Didn't we just establish that this wasn't about my father?"

"No. We're just discussing feelings. And they can change, or conflict, or hide other feelings. We want to look at the whole picture. Not just your work life and Dr. Wiltshire, but also your home life and your nuclear family growing up. These things all affect each other and, if things are off balance in one, they can cause problems in the other."

"I suppose." Kenzie looked over at Zachary. He knew quite a bit about her relationship with her father and how difficult it was, but he didn't volunteer anything or speak on her behalf. "It's... been a couple of weeks since I talked to Walter, I guess."

"And did he call you or did you call him?"

"He called me."

"When was the last time you called him?"

"I don't know. Maybe to wish him a happy birthday or something."

"You don't normally call him?"

"No, I don't. He's a busy guy. He isn't often free when I try to reach him, so I just let him call me when it works for him. Maybe that's being lazy, but it saves me a lot of aggravation."

"I would like to give you an assignment. I want you to call him during the upcoming week. Not for anything special. It's not an event. Just call him to chat for a few minutes. Would you accept that challenge?"

Kenzie squirmed. Usually, Dr. Boyle's suggestions were things for her and Zachary to do together. It was couple's therapy, after all. It was supposed to be about her relationship with Zachary, with Dr. B mediating, helping each to see the other's perspective. They were getting better at communication, learning how to talk to each other in language that was clear and didn't leave them with so many misunderstandings. They both came from such different backgrounds that it had taken time to build a solid foundation.

Kenzie really wasn't there for advice on her dad.

"I'll think about it. Maybe."

Dr. B nodded. "Don't make a big thing out of it, because it isn't. It's just one tiny thing that will take five minutes of your time and minimal effort. It's not a mountain to climb."

"Okay."

They were all silent for a few minutes. Kenzie shifted uncomfortably. She looked at Zachary, waiting to see if he had something to say, either about her being late and stressed out, or something about her relationship with her parents. He said nothing.

23

"How have things been going between the two of you?" Dr. B asked after a few minutes. "With things being so stressful at work, have you found that overflowing into your home life? How are the two of you managing?"

Kenzie didn't look at Zachary before answering this question. She stared out the window, taking a few deep breaths and trying to relax.

"I know that I have been more emotional. Less patient than I usually am. I've probably bitten Zachary's head off a few more times than I would have normally. But I also think... despite that, we're still communicating pretty well. We haven't gotten into any big arguments. I know that sometimes... I say things that hurt, and I regret that." She ventured a look at Zachary. "But Zachary's been very patient with me through it all. He hasn't lashed back at me. And he sure could have."

"That's good. Do you wish that you had more engagement from him? Are there things you want to discuss that you think he is avoiding? When you are impatient, is there a particular behavior you are looking for? Are you snapping about the same things?"

"No, I don't think so. I think it's just because I'm stressed. I get impatient because... he takes longer to do certain tasks than I would.

Or he makes assumptions about how I want something done or about what I need, and it's wrong."

"Like?"

"When I'm just venting, and he wants to jump in and fix things or tell me what I'm doing wrong."

"That's a pretty common complaint between couples."

"I know. It's nothing. It doesn't mean there's anything wrong with our relationship. It's just normal couple's stuff. But *he* thinks I'm halfway to breaking up."

"No," Zachary protested, finally sitting up and taking part in the conversation, "I'm just trying to help out. To be a supportive spouse. And she's fine. She thinks she snaps all the time, but she doesn't. Not like…"

"Not like Bridget," Kenzie finished. "Well, I'm glad I don't sound like a screaming lunatic whenever he does something I don't like. But I wish that wasn't the standard. Zachary acts like I'm a saint, and I'm not."

"When does he act like you're a saint? When he's talking to friends?"

"No, it's not like that. Not to show me off. Just when it's the two of us, and he acts like I could do no wrong, which is clearly not true. I know I get impatient and hurt his feelings, but he won't admit it."

Dr. B looked at him. "How about it, Zachary? Is Kenzie perfect?"

He looked trapped. He looked at Kenzie and then at the therapist, his face getting pink. "There's no right answer to that question."

"It isn't a trick. No one is perfect. So is Kenzie perfect?"

"No." It seemed to pain Zachary to say so. He grimaced and shook his head. "She's great. She's a supportive partner. We do things together. She is interested in my work and I'm interested in hers. We have a good time together. We're communicating well…"

"But she's not perfect."

Zachary ran his fingers through his short hair and scrubbed at the back of his head, wincing.

He didn't answer.

"You see?" Kenzie said, and shrugged. "And, of course it is an impossible standard. He makes me feel like I can't do anything wrong

116

or I will disappoint him. I won't be the perfect Kenzie anymore. I'll be… tarnished. Disappointing."

Zachary's brow furrowed. "No."

"You felt like you needed to be the perfect daughter growing up, didn't you?" Dr. B's eyes were alight with interest. "It's often true of the firstborn. You felt like there were a lot of expectations, and you had to meet them all."

"Sure. I guess. I tried to do what my parents wanted me to. Tried to listen when they told me my responsibilities or the right way to do something. And I did my best."

"But you weren't perfect."

"No." A shrug. Of course not.

"And when you made a mistake, they corrected you. They didn't tell you it was okay to fail. They asked you to do better. To live up to their standards, even if they weren't realistic."

"That's what parents do. They teach their kids the right way to do things."

"Yes. And they need to correct them when what they do is dangerous to themselves or others. But when they tried their best and failed, that's okay."

"I suppose."

Kenzie thought about little Michael. Had he been punished when he hadn't been able to do what his parents told him to? A toddler could not be expected to follow every instruction given to him. Probably not even half of them. They needed to try, and try, and try again to build their skills. They needed to be allowed to fail again, and again, and again.

But Michael had been punished harshly. Maybe for things he had done wrong, and maybe just for existing. For being there when his parents didn't want him around. For making a mess, as kids do. For making noise. For following them around. For wanting one more drink of water before bed.

"Kenzie?" Dr. Boyle asked quietly.

Kenzie wiped at the tears that suddenly wet her cheeks. "I don't know what this is all about," she said, embarrassed. "It isn't about this conversation," she gestured between herself and Dr. B. "It's... the case I'm working on. The abuse case."

Dr. B nodded sympathetically. "It's a terrible thing."

"I just can't understand it. I know that people get frustrated or angry when children can't or don't do what they're supposed to do. But... kids aren't just short adults. They have to learn and to try and make mistakes and try again. It isn't fair to expect them to be perfect."

"No, it isn't."

"Michael— this boy was just little. Barely two years old. And they just... how could they do that?"

Dr. Boyle didn't try to explain it. And that really wasn't what Kenzie was looking for. Dr. B probably dealt with parents who were in counseling. Children who had been damaged by abuse, as Zachary had. Families who were in conflict, maybe hurting each other. She saw it from both sides and knew what could happen when things got out of control.

"I'm sorry, Kenzie," the therapist said gently. "I truly am."

24

"I know this has been hard, Kenzie," Dr. Boyle said. She glanced toward the clock. "Our session is drawing to an end. You have an assignment, should you choose to accept it." She gave Kenzie a teasing smile. "Have you considered medication? If this case is triggering memories of your abduction or putting a lot of extra strain on you, you might want to consider it."

"No," Kenzie dismissed the possibility immediately. "I don't need medication." She was a doctor. If she needed medication, she would have sought it. But extra work was not something that could be medicated away.

"I have offered it before. It can be helpful in dealing with your traumatic memories. And it doesn't have to be permanent. Many people take an aid for a few months and then are able to continue without it. It isn't a lifetime commitment."

Zachary flashed a look at Kenzie. She was always getting after him to take his medications, even when he didn't think he needed them.

But she wasn't being hypocritical about it. Zachary needed medication to function every day, to sleep at night, and to help him with his compulsive behaviors. It wasn't the same as Kenzie dealing with a little extra stress.

"I don't need anything right now," Kenzie asserted.

"Okay. That's fine. The offer is open if you change your mind or find that things are getting worse and you get to the point where you need something. Don't feel embarrassed because you said no and then find that you do need something after all. You are a doctor, so you know it isn't a sign of weakness to need some pharmaceutical support if things get too bad. It doesn't make you any less perfect." She winked at Kenzie. "You don't have to give up the rest of your superpowers."

Kenzie laughed along with her. Not because it was that funny, but because she felt obligated. It was hard to admit that she wasn't perfect and that she was constantly chasing that perfection, even though she knew it was unachievable. She was a grown adult, and it was hard to admit that she still wanted or needed her parents' approval. She should have been long past that stage by now.

Dr. B met her eyes again, firm, holding the connection for a second longer than was comfortable. Kenzie tried to act as though she was much more "together" than she really was, keeping her eyes steady and not immediately looking away. Dr. B gave a nod and then turned to Zachary.

"I hope you don't feel neglected today. You are part of this dynamic too. Kenzie's stress and her feelings and what she is going through all affect your relationship and how you feel about yourself."

"I'm here to support Kenzie. What she's going through is important to me."

Kenzie felt like it was a little too pat. A careful, perfect, supportive answer, bare of any emotional baggage. Not the way he really felt. Like Kenzie's, his emotions could be a hot mess. Just because he appeared calm and collected, that didn't mean he was.

"Zachary," Dr. B's voice was reproving. "Are you 'fine'?"

Kenzie had to chuckle at that. One of the rules was that when one of them asked the other how they were, "fine" was not an acceptable answer. Or anything else that might be swapped in its place. No socially acceptable brush-off. Dr. B apparently didn't think he was being truthful about his emotions either.

Zachary opened his mouth to object, squirming in his seat. He looked at each of them, looking for the right response.

He might not have been the perfection-seeking child that Kenzie had. In fact, he'd been a hyperactive, impulsive, anxious child who was always screwing up and who his mother deemed incorrigible. She abandoned him because she didn't want to have to handle him and his siblings anymore. But he was still always seeking the approval of those close to him. Foster parents, his ex-wife Bridget, Kenzie, and his therapists. He was frantically trying to read them and figure out the right thing to say.

Because even though the poor guy had picked just the right thing to say, it had not rung true to either of them and they knew he was just trying to display the expected behavior.

"We talked about me too," he said. "I don't feel left out. I *do* want to help Kenzie."

"I believe that. But I think there's something else going on that you're not talking about. Now, we have about five minutes left. I can give you another five minutes over that if you need it. So… let's talk about what's bothering you."

Kenzie looked at him again. She hadn't realized that there was something else going on beneath the surface. He had fooled her.

"I'm not… there isn't really anything that I need to talk about. It can wait until next week."

"Yes, we can talk about it in your next session. And if you start today, even with just five minutes, you will have something to think of between now and then and maybe some strategies to try so that you can be that much further ahead when we meet again."

He stared at the carpet, fingers rubbing the arms of his chair anxiously. "I don't think it's anything. It's just that Kenzie's case… stirs some things up. Stuff starts rattling around in my brain." He shrugged. "Not really anything new. There's always something bouncing around in there."

"It's okay to say that this case is triggering for you, even though it has nothing to do with you."

"I'm not… hijacking Kenzie's issues."

"You're not," Kenzie and Dr. Boyle both said at the same time.

"It's just… like I said, stirring things up."

"Memories?"

"Not... clear ones. Mostly just feelings. I can't attach them to anything. And I know it is Kenzie's case, not mine. And not anything to do with my life."

He sounded frustrated. Kenzie could relate. She didn't want to be feeling what she was, either. She didn't want to be subject to emotions beyond her control. Illogical, inconvenient feelings.

"Okay. That's understandable. And you're doing a good job of trying not to butt in while Kenzie was discussing her feelings. But now the floor is open and you can talk about yours too."

Zachary shrugged, staring down. Kenzie could see the sweat on his face. While he appeared to be calm, the emotions were clearly having an effect on him. Dr. B had worked with him long enough to notice the tells. Kenzie had been oblivious to them, dealing with her own issues.

"Not really much to say. Anxious. Jumpy. Feeling like... I need to watch everyone. I might be in danger."

"Those are probably all pretty familiar feelings, considering your history."

"Yeah."

"You were able to identify that it was Kenzie's case that triggered them?"

Zachary considered. "I guess so. They started when she was talking about it."

"And they aren't attached to any particular memory? Something about a young child? You or one of your siblings, or one of the other children that you lived with?"

"There have been a lot," Zachary said helplessly. "Sometimes you see them hit. Sometimes... you just know that they were. Something telegraphs it, even if you can't put your finger on it. I don't remember any of the kids in the homes I was in dying, but I knew that could happen. I guess maybe as foster kids, we had talked about it; we knew of other cases where kids *had* died."

"And you were a witness to at least one death in institutional care as well."

"At Bonnie Brown. Yeah. But that wasn't the same. I mean... it was, because they hit her when she bit one of the guards... but she died later, not because of that."

"You don't know that," Kenzie interposed.

He looked at her. He had told her about Annie before. Reluctantly. She was one of the ghosts in his past. An autistic girl who had died in the children's center Zachary had sometimes been housed at. In the room next to his.

"You don't know that wasn't why she died," Kenzie pointed out. "She could have had internal bleeding or other injuries."

"They told her parents that she'd just died in her sleep. I knew that... they left her in handcuffs all night, so she asphyxiated."

"That's what you assume, and you might be right. But they might not have told the parents the truth, or all of it. Things were a lot less regulated then. They might have told her parents that she died in her sleep when they knew very well that it was because of internal injuries."

Zachary looked sick at the thought. Kenzie realized belatedly that she should have just kept this to herself. He had probably thought of Annie's death as peaceful, fading away in her sleep because she wasn't getting the oxygen she needed while restrained. He hadn't thought of her as being in pain and bleeding out in the cell beside his. He put his face in his hands. Kenzie bit her lip and looked at Dr. B. She hoped her apology was clear. She hadn't meant to make Zachary's pain worse.

"It was a long time ago," Dr. Boyle told Zachary. "And it's best to know the full truth, or as much of it as possible, even if it is upsetting."

"Uh-huh."

"But it wasn't Annie that you were thinking about specifically."

"No, just... all of them. All the kids that I knew, or didn't know."

"And yourself. You were not killed, but you were physically abused. You have those memories, even if no specific ones are coming to your mind. Your physical abuse probably goes back just as far as that of the child Kenzie is dealing with."

Zachary wiped away sweat or tears without pulling his hands all the way away from his face. "We always tried to protect the little ones. At home… in all the homes I was in. We always tried to keep them from getting their hands on the youngest children."

"But you weren't always able to. And early in your life, that child was you."

"Michael didn't have anyone to protect him." Zachary sniffled. Kenzie's eyes were burning again.

"No," Dr. B agreed, looking at Kenzie to see if she had anything to contribute. "He was the only child?"

Kenzie nodded. "Yes. And I hope they never have any others."

"They won't stop," Zachary said with assurance, probably thinking of his own parents rather than Cash and Terri-Lyn Wade. He didn't know them or what their plans were as far as more children were concerned. But he knew that Zachary's father had gone on to have several more children after Zachary and his full siblings had been taken into care. More victims of abuse. Who knew how many families and children the guy had around the state or surrounding area.

"Okay." Dr. B was using her "closing" voice now. Wrap up, summarize, and send them on their way until the next session. "We can discuss this more at your next session if you like. I think it's good if you each know what the other is going through right now. Do you agree?"

They looked at each other and nodded. Kenzie wasn't sure how she would handle Zachary's emotions on top of her own and everything else that was going on. Was she supposed to walk on eggshells around him? Not mention anything else about her case and investigation? That was what held the two of them together, their mutual interest in investigation and digging up the truth. If she couldn't talk to him openly because it was triggering his anxiety, what were they going to talk about?

Dr. B gave them both understanding smiles and sent them on their way. For the next week, they would have to map their way through the minefield themselves.

25

They had their usual ice cream after the session, a tasty tradition Kenzie had instituted to help Zachary feel good about their therapy sessions. A sweet association that would tell his brain to look forward to the sessions instead of dreading them.

But it turned out that it was just as important a tradition for Kenzie herself. And after today's session, she needed it more than ever before. They didn't discuss anything heavy over ice cream. They rarely did. But it was an essential part of reconnecting after the intense "inner work" that was part of their session.

Then Kenzie had more work to do. She couldn't afford to take off the entire afternoon and evening like she did when Dr. Wiltshire was in the office. She was too anxious about staying on top of everything while he was recovering.

She called Julie for messages and found that Dr. Wiltshire had not left any for her, though there was a slew of other messages. They would be in Kenzie's email when she logged in.

Kenzie had been putting off calling the Wades. After meeting Cash, she wasn't too eager to talk to his wife, but she would probably be much easier to deal with. Hopefully. A grieving mother might be impossible to get any information from. Still, at least she wouldn't be screaming at Kenzie like Cash. And if she did, what was easier than disconnecting the call? There was no danger of retaliation. Or physical retaliation, anyway. If she got another slew of phone calls from friends of the Wade family in high political positions, she would deal with that.

So, shut away in her home office, with the door shut so Zachary knew not to interrupt her, she called the number on the mother's witness statement. It rang a few times and she figured it would go to voicemail, then it was picked up.

There was a click and breathing, but no words.

"Hello?" Kenzie tried. "I'm looking for Terri-Lyn Wade."

More breathing and a sniffle. "Yes?"

"Is this Mrs. Wade?"

"Yeah. Who is this?"

Kenzie cleared her throat. "This is Dr. Kenzie Kirsch from the Medical Examiner's Office. I was hoping that you could answer some questions about your son."

"What?" There was a squeak of outrage in Mrs. Wade's voice. "You have no right to call me!"

"It's part of my job, actually. There are a number of unanswered questions, so I would like to get some details from you about your witness statement."

"No. No, I don't want to talk about it. This is cruel. You can't just call and interrogate me about my son's death like I'm a criminal."

A little unfair, since Kenzie had not asked a single question yet, let alone accused her of any wrongdoing.

"I don't think you're a criminal, ma'am. I'm sure you want this dealt with as quickly as possible, so I'm doing what I can to keep things moving forward."

"Well, I don't have any intention of answering any questions. You and the rest of the ghoulish doctors at the medical examiner's office can just leave me alone."

Kenzie frowned. She wasn't aware of anyone else from the office having called Terri-Lyn, so she wasn't sure why she would react to Kenzie's call this way.

"I just have a few questions."

"I'm not answering them."

"It would only take a few minutes, and I promise to be sensitive to your—"

"Cash said not to talk to anyone. He said that if anyone called me, I should ask for my lawyer. So that's what I'm doing. Lawyer, lawyer, lawyer. You can't ask me any other questions."

That wasn't quite how it worked, but Kenzie wasn't going to argue the finer points of the law with the woman over the phone.

"All right, Mrs. Wade. I'm sorry to have bothered you."

A few notes in Kenzie's ear notified her that the call had ended, so she didn't make a fool of herself talking to dead air. Kenzie was pretty sure that Terri-Lyn Wade had slammed the phone down.

She sat just looking at the phone for a few minutes.

There was no way she would call Cash to ask him about his statement. She had hoped that the questions she had about Terri-Lyn's statement would cover them both. But she didn't want him screaming at her.

While she was sitting there staring at her phone, she decided she might as well follow through on her assignment from Dr. Boyle and call her father. Dr. B had warned her not to make a big deal out of it and build it up to make it bigger and more onerous and difficult than it was; just make a casual call.

If Walter were busy, he wouldn't answer, and he would follow up with her another time. If he were free to take a call, then she was sure he would pick it up. He was a family man. He enjoyed his work, his calling as a lobbyist, but at the core of everything was his commitment to his family and making the world a better place for them. She tapped over to her favorites list and found his name. Another tap and the call was going through.

He was much quicker to answer than Terri-Lyn had been, which was satisfying. Kenzie would like to think that he was eager to talk to her.

"MacKenzie?"

"Hi, Dad."

"How are you? Is everything okay?"

Kenzie smiled and quirked her head. It was a telling question. She didn't call him often enough for him to consider it a normal occurrence, and he was worried that something was wrong.

"Yes, I just thought I'd touch base and see how you were."

"Ahh." He sounded like he was stretching out and settling in for a long conversation. "I'm delighted to hear from you. Things going okay with you and Zachary?"

"There are always bumps, but yes, we're doing just fine. Had the afternoon off to spend some time together." He didn't need to know that it was for therapy. It was technically true. And it was more important to their relationship than an afternoon museum date or going out for drinks.

"Excellent. Glad to hear that you're taking time together. You're like me; it is very easy for me to get caught up in my work and lose all track of how much time I'm actually spending at work instead of at home. One of the dangers of loving your work is that you're happy to spend too many hours doing it."

Kenzie agreed with his assessment of himself. She wasn't so sure it described her. She made sure that she spent time with Zachary. But it was true that she spent longer at the office than she was strictly required to. She worked longer hours than an office worker. But less than she had as a medical student.

"I suppose I might do that sometimes," she said tentatively.

He chuckled. "It's hard to admit. You're not supposed to prefer your work to the rest of your life. But who wants to spend time making dinner and cleaning the bathroom when you could be doing something more interesting, like pushing a bill through the legislature —or stopping one in its tracks."

"Or investigating an interesting medical puzzle," Kenzie contributed.

"Better than TV," Walter told her.

Kenzie laughed. It was. She often found herself getting bored with what was on TV. That didn't happen in the middle of an autopsy.

"Your mother told me about this case with the congressman's son. What a tragic loss."

"Yeah. It's a very sad case."

"Too bad you don't get to choose which cases you are involved with."

"Just pick the cheerful ones?" Kenzie suggested.

Walter's low, rumbling chuckle cheered her. "Okay, I suppose you probably don't have many of those," he admitted. "Though there are a few politicians I wouldn't be sad to see on your slab." He laughed again, at himself this time. "What a terribly inappropriate thing for me to say. A person can't go around making jokes like that. What if something actually did happen to one of my political opponents?"

"Would you be sad?"

"I would not," he asserted.

"Were you at Mom's?" Kenzie asked, circling back to his reference to Lisa.

"Yes. Spent a few days in Burlington for a conference recently. Had a very nice time visiting with her."

"You two have a good relationship."

"Best thing we ever did was get divorced. Though I wouldn't recommend it to anyone else," he warned seriously. "Things are okay with you and Zachary?"

"Yes."

"You haven't made the same mistakes that we did. We were too quick to rush into marriage, seal the deal because that was the expected thing. I don't think either of us was cut out for it. I don't regret that we got married. I wouldn't have had you and Amanda in my life if I hadn't, and I can't imagine my life without you."

Kenzie thought about the possibility of children in her and Zachary's life. She knew he would like children, but she had never been too keen on the idea herself. She had helped to raise Amanda. And then had lost her. She wasn't eager to do either one again. Zachary could enjoy his nieces and nephews and spend time with them. He could interact with them when he felt good, but they were not devastated when he had to be hospitalized or was not in good shape to see them.

"I'm glad that you made that mistake," Kenzie offered.

"Me too. But I'm glad that we straightened things out and dissolved the…" He hesitated, looking for the words that gave a sense of what he intended. "The onerous legal relationship and responsibilities dictated by the government. We are free now to have whatever relationship we want without it affecting our financial commitments or legacies."

Kenzie wondered if it also left them both free to pursue other relationships. She wasn't aware of any other serious relationships either of them had pursued. Neither of them had introduced her to any boyfriends or girlfriends. She was sure they must both have someone to take with them to charity and political events from time to time. But they were no longer limited by social convention to choose each other.

26

Kenzie found herself feeling more at ease at the office the next day. She was not surprised that Dr. Wiltshire wasn't there and was no longer expecting to hear from him each day. If he got back to her, he did; if he didn't, she would just deal with it. He was the one who would have to take responsibility for anything not done; that wouldn't fall to Kenzie. She felt reassured after talking to her dad, some of those feelings of anxiety and abandonment trickling away. Or maybe it was just because she had talked about them to Dr. B. Either way, she was glad to feel lighter and a bit more like herself.

She had a backlog of filing and other computer work after having Julie cover the desk for the last day and a half, so she spent extra time getting that done before it could become unmanageable.

The phone rang and she picked it up without more than a glance at the caller ID.

"Medical Examiner's Office."

"Is this… Dr. Kirsch?"

"Yes, how can I help you?"

"I want to talk to you."

Kenzie looked impatiently at the display on the phone. She saw WADE in front of the string of numerals and focused on the woman's voice. One of the other staff members in the Wade home? Someone who had finally decided to step forward?

"Uh, yes, of course," she agreed calmly. "Can I get your name?"

"This is Terri-Lyn."

Not a staff member, but Mrs. Wade herself. Kenzie tried to keep her breathing smooth and not give away the change in her attention level.

"Thank you for calling me back, Mrs. Wade. I'm glad to hear from you."

"It's Terri-Lyn."

"Okay, Terri-Lyn."

There was a pause. "Do you know who I am?"

"Yes. Terri-Lyn. Michael Wade's mother. We spoke briefly yesterday."

Another moment of silence. There must be a problem with the phone connection, with each of their voices being delayed a second or so, leaving too-long pauses when no one was talking.

"Yeah. You said you had some questions about my statement."

"Yes. If you just wait for a moment, I need to refer to my notes." Kenzie didn't want to miss any of the important notes she had written down. "Okay. You indicated that you were having breakfast when the... incident was discovered."

"Yes."

"And that you thought Michael was still sleeping at the time."

"Yes."

"But he had been up for some time."

Another pause as Kenzie's comment was relayed over the ether to Mrs. Wade. Then perhaps another second or two while Terri-Lyn considered how to respond to the comment. The seconds ticked by, making Kenzie wonder whether she had lost the connection at first.

"No. He was still in bed. He just got up and... went to the window without anyone knowing he'd gotten out of bed. If any of us had known that he was out of bed, we would have been able to stop him..."

"When had he eaten last?"

"Uh... the night before. Suppertime, I would guess."

"His stomach contents were partially digested. So if he had last eaten the night before, he died an hour or two after supper. If he died in the morning, when he was found below the balcony, he'd been up for a couple of hours and had already eaten breakfast."

"No, that can't be right."

"Those are the facts, Mrs. Wade. Either he died the night before, or he had been up for several hours before he died in the morning."

Kenzie already knew which it was. The death investigators who had retrieved the body had done their job competently and recorded the body temperature. It was still warm when they arrived. Not a child who had died the night before and then the body thrown off the balcony in the morning to disguise time of death.

He might have been killed an hour or more earlier than the family had reported, but not ten or more hours before.

"I… I don't understand it. I thought he was still in bed. Sylvia must have gotten him up. But why would she leave him alone?"

"You can understand why I have questions."

"Yes… I understand. It is confusing. I guess things get confused when something like this happens. There are always pieces that don't quite fit, aren't there?"

It was true. All of the clues didn't always point in the same direction in real life like they did in a movie, and there were often things left unexplained after an arrest and conviction. The human body was not always as predictable as she would have liked to believe.

But it was strange to hear someone outside of the medical profession or law enforcement express this thought. Most people who picked up all of their forensic knowledge from TV had expectations that far exceeded what could actually be done in real life. Or what was done when budget, time, and other resources were at a premium. There were not DNA or fingerprints at every scene. Or there was too much. Not every body that came through the medical examiner's office was dissected. People went unidentified and cases went unsolved. In many cases, the cause of death could not be determined from the body itself, and they needed more information from the police as to what had happened at the scene to make a determination.

"No, everything does not always fit," she agreed. "But in this case... I think the answer is quite simple. You and your husband would prefer to place yourselves as far from the scene as possible. You don't want to put yourselves in close proximity to him or to admit that he was up and active, and didn't just wander off for an instant and get himself into mischief."

"Whatever happened had nothing to do with me," Terri-Lyn objected. Effectively demonstrating Kenzie's point. "It must have been Cash. I wasn't around. I had been attending to other things all morning. I had my Pilates class and... other things."

"If you don't give me and the police the truth about what really happened, you just end up making yourself look bad."

There were prolonged sniffles on the other end of the line. Terri-Lyn's voice was breaking when she spoke again. Or she did a really good imitation of the grieving mother, now that she had been trapped. "I don't know what happened, MacKenzie, but it wasn't anything to do with me. I didn't hurt my son. I could never do that. You have to believe me."

"Someone *was* hurting him. There are a lot of unexplained injuries."

"I don't know what you're talking about. If there are other injuries... he must have hit something on the way down. He must not have fallen straight down from the balcony, but maybe... off to the side and he hit a tree or part of the house that stuck out..."

"I wish you would reconsider your answers. You must know that I can tell the difference between injuries obtained yesterday, or last week, or last month. And they don't look the same as injuries obtained at the time of death or shortly before."

A longer silence from Mrs. Wade. She continued to sniffle and breathe raggedly, at least keeping up appearances while she thought through the possibilities.

"I'm not even supposed to be talking to you," she said in a near whisper. "He told me not to, but I thought *you* would understand. That you would help me."

"I am trying to help you. My first responsibility is to the truth and finding out what happened to Michael. And I'm sure that's what you want to know too. It's a terrible thing to be left wondering for years afterward exactly what killed him." Kenzie thought about Zachary and the girl that had died at Bonnie Brown. Even now, decades later, he was still broken up over the thought that she had died of her injuries that night instead of just peacefully drifting off in her sleep. How would Mrs. Wade feel if Kenzie never identified the cause of death or fudged her report to hide it? Like Annie's parents and Zachary, she would wonder for years, and it would tear her up inside. "I know you want to find out the truth too," she told Terri-Lyn.

"It's Cash. I'll need to... I'll have to find a way to see you. He could overhear anything that I say at the house."

"We can work something out. If you come down to the medical examiner's office, we have a comfortable boardroom where we can sit down and discuss it."

"No. I can't come all the way there. It will need to be somewhere else. Somewhere he wouldn't know what I was doing. We could meet halfway, couldn't we? Get together for lunch so that he thinks it is just a friendly chat, not anything to do with Michael."

Kenzie doubted that she needed to pull a bunch of cloak-and-dagger tricks to avoid being seen by Cash Wade. Wouldn't he be off working? She was pretty sure that congressmen couldn't just lie around all day, but had to attend meetings in person. A lot of events, both political and charitable. Appearances that were just for visibility as well as those that were required to get things done.

"Yes, I guess we could meet for lunch," Kenzie agreed. "Today? Tomorrow?"

"I need to check my calendar..."

Kenzie shook her head, irritated. Terri-Lyn had known who she was calling and why, and Kenzie was sure she at least knew whether she was having lunch with anyone today or not, even if she didn't know her schedule for the rest of the week without looking.

"Do you think... a late lunch today?" Mrs. Wade suggested, pretending that she was looking at her busy schedule. She couldn't be expected to be anywhere but at home just days after her son had died. She could have canceled anything she wanted to.

"When and where?" Kenzie prompted sharply.

"Today at one-thirty... two o'clock...? I'll send you the address."

Two o'clock certainly was a late lunch. Kenzie wouldn't be able to wait that long without something to eat. She would have to grab something from the vending machine to hold her over for a few hours until she could get to the restaurant Terri-Lyn had picked out.

"All right," she agreed. "Send the address to my cell phone." Kenzie dictated the digits slowly to give Mrs. Wade time to write them down or enter them into her phone.

"Thank you," Terri-Lyn said distantly, and then the call was terminated. Kenzie looked at her desk phone in irritation. The woman could have at least had the courtesy to say goodbye, or to wait until Kenzie confirmed she had received the address.

She hung up the receiver and slid out her cell phone to look at it. No text. She laid it on her desk and worked on other things while she waited for the phone to light up with the arrival of the text. Mrs. Wade couldn't very well expect her to show up at a restaurant she never named or sent the address for.

The termination of the call had been very abrupt. Maybe Mr. Wade had walked in at that moment, and she'd had to end it before he could figure out what she was up to. And then she hadn't been able to send the address right away as she had planned.

A few hours passed, and Kenzie started to wonder whether something had happened to Mrs. Wade. If there was physical abuse going on in that household, then Michael might not have been the sole target. Cash might have no qualms about beating on his wife, especially if he guessed what she was up to.

That was when she really started to worry. Should she call the police and report it to them? She could fill Tuttle in and see if he wanted to go over to the Wade mansion to check on her.

She didn't really have any evidence that Mrs. Wade was in any danger, but she had to wonder. If Cash Wade had killed Michael, he wouldn't just sit around waiting for someone to find out about it. If he felt like his secret was threatened, he would take action.

27

It was a quarter to two when a text finally came through to Kenzie's phone with an address. Unknown caller. Kenzie navigated to the number to assign it Terri-Lyn Wade's name and found it to be a long stream of letters and numbers, clearly sent through some kind of anonymizer service. So Terri-Lyn did not want Kenzie to know her private cell phone number. She hadn't just blocked the number, maybe anticipating that, as someone involved in law enforcement, Kenzie might be able to see even a blocked number.

It was a relief to get the address and to know that Terri-Lyn was okay, whatever games she was playing. Domestic violence situations were fraught; it was difficult to know when things might explode. And things had definitely exploded at the Wade residence once already. Kenzie didn't want to be responsible for another because she had reached out to Terri-Lyn Wade as a witness and her husband found out about it.

Sending her the address so late meant that there was no way Kenzie would be able to get there by two. She had to wrap things up at her desk, make sure the phones were either covered or forwarded, hike to the underground parking to get her car, and then drive most of the way across town to reach the restaurant.

And Terri-Lyn hadn't even said what the name of the restaurant was, so Kenzie couldn't fix exactly where it was in her mind. She would have to use her GPS and look at the numbers on the buildings or signs.

Knowing that she would already be late and that it was Terri-Lyn's own fault for taking so long to get her the address, Kenzie didn't rush. What difference did it make if she were ten minutes late or half an hour late? Terri-Lyn would probably be late herself, knowing that social strata. She expected Kenzie to get there in a rush and then would blow in herself half an hour or an hour later, innocently surprised that her guest was angry and frustrated because of the wait.

The restaurant was not a restaurant, as it turned out. It was a private club. There wasn't even a name on the outside of the building. One of those places that the elite would refer to as "the club" and expect everyone to know what they were talking about. Or at least, expecting their peers to understand what they were talking about. And if they didn't, they were not social equals.

Kenzie walked into the reception area. Thick, plush carpets, dim lighting, and lots of black marble and brass accents. An older woman at the reception desk raised the glasses on a chain around her neck to her eyes to scrutinize Kenzie closely, emphasizing the fact that Kenzie had never been there and was not a member.

"Good afternoon. How can we help you today?" she asked politely.

"Dr. Kenzie Kirsch," Kenzie said firmly. She paused, waiting for the receptionist to think of the name and all the associations with the Kirsch and Cole Kirsch connections. "I'm here for a meeting with Terri-Lyn Wade?"

Maybe there wasn't even going to be a lunch. Since it was so late, Kenzie wouldn't be surprised if the lunch she had been invited to ended up being nothing more than coffee. A social necessity.

"Ah, you are Mrs. Wade's guest. We are delighted to have you, Dr. Kirsch. Mrs. Wade has booked the Wade family boardroom. Third floor, to your left when you get off the elevator." She nodded to the ancient-looking lift in the corner. Kenzie supposed people were supposed be impressed with its provenance, but instead she wondered how long it had been since it had been serviced and inspected. She looked at the grand staircase instead. A little more work to get to the third floor, but at least she knew she would make it to the top. She would leave the lift to the lifetime members, those with rooms named after their families and who were not physically able to make it up the stairs anymore.

"To the left of the stairs," the receptionist said, following Kenzie's gaze.

"Thank you."

"Have a lovely day, Miss—Dr. Kirsch."

Kenzie gave a curt nod and headed up the stairs. There was a big, wide staircase to the second floor, then it split into right and left arms heading up to the third floor. Kenzie took the left arm, through a reverse, and then turned left at the top of the stairs, hoping she was facing the correct direction.

The second door down from the stairs was dark wood with a brass plaque that read "Wade Boardroom." Kenzie sighed that she had made it to the right place.

Terri-Lyn had not, Kenzie suspected, chosen the boardroom that bore her husband's name in their private club simply because she wanted to have a private conversation with Kenzie away from any eavesdroppers, including her husband. She had wanted to signal to Kenzie just who she was, how rich and influential in their small Vermont community. Terri-Lyn Wade was no one to be trifled with. She and her husband's family were semi-royalty.

Kenzie wasn't sure of the etiquette when arriving at a private boardroom such as this, but Lisa had trained her to be polite and confident when dealing with the elite. She was one of them. Her parents' names had an immediate effect on any of Vermont's old money families. And if the new money had not heard of them, they had clearly not been moving in the right circles. Kenzie knocked on the door, a polite three raps, and then turned the handle and pushed it open.

She wasn't sure what to expect. Terri-Lyn and her husband as a surprise? Terri-Lyn and her lawyer? A boardroom table surrounded by Terri-Lyn, Wade, and a coterie of lawyers? What was the proper collective noun for lawyers? A bevy? A murmur?

But there was just one person seated at the table, head bent over a notebook so that her shining platinum and silver locks formed a curtain that prevented Kenzie from seeing her face for a second or two. Then the woman looked up.

Kenzie stared in shock, instantly recognizing her.

Kenzie did not know her as Terri-Lyn Wade, but Terri-Lyn Ellis, a girl she had known in school.

"Terri-Lyn?" she asked in disbelief.

The stranger with a familiar face stood up. She looked older than Kenzie. She was too young for the gray that streaked her hair. Most people Kenzie knew would have gone to great lengths to conceal such signs of aging, resorting to dyes and treatments to maintain their youthful appearance. But not Terri-Lyn; she carried her gray locks with an effortless grace, as if it were a deliberate fashion statement crafted by a skilled stylist. Kenzie had seen models with hair dyed gray. Twenty-somethings like silver foxes.

Terri-Lyn's face was also more wrinkled than Kenzie would have expected, more like Lisa's face than Kenzie's, even though they were the same age. It looked like she'd lived a very hard life, aging her prematurely.

"I thought it was you," Terri-Lyn said, taking Kenzie's hand in her slim one and pressing it slightly. "When I heard your name, I had to look you up, see if it really was you." She raised an eyebrow and shook her head. "How in heaven's name did you become a medical examiner?"

Kenzie laughed. Terri-Lyn made it sound like she had just stumbled into it, waking up one day after a night of drinking to find herself in the position by serendipity. "A lot of years of school and hard work," she said.

"But... why? Why would you become such a thing?"

"I enjoy it. It's very fulfilling."

Terri-Lyn continued to shake her head. She leaned toward Kenzie, put her hands on her shoulders, and bussed her cheeks with air kisses. Fake hugs and kisses.

"Sit down, please." Terri-Lyn resumed her seat and gestured to the room, palms up. "Well, what do you think? The Wade Boardroom."

"It's really something. Your husband must have made a pretty hefty donation to get his name on a door."

Terri-Lyn looked disappointed. Maybe Kenzie was supposed to refer to it as Terri-Lyn's name, not Cash's. Maybe the money had come from Terri-Lyn's family coffers.

As Kenzie remembered it, Terri-Lyn's family had old money, and plenty of it. She hadn't kept track of the Ellises over the years, but she had a vague notion that Terri-Lyn's father had passed away. Maybe her mother had too. Maybe she now controlled that wealth. But then, why not have the room named after her family? Or maybe Kenzie was supposed to assume that the room had been named after the Wade family based on influence alone, not any kind of monetary donation. But in Kenzie's experience, things like that didn't just happen without a large amount of money passing hands.

"Yes," Terri-Lyn agreed, her mouth downturned.

Kenzie pulled out a chair and sat down. There was coffee service on a sideboard, and various platters with tiny sandwiches and wraps, decoratively arranged fruits and vegetables, and a large bowl of salad accompanied by various salad dressing cruets. But apparently, they weren't eating yet.

"I didn't *think* you knew who I was," Terri-Lyn said. "When I called you on the phone, I said I was Terri-Lyn, but you just kept saying Mrs. Wade, and I didn't know if it was because you weren't allowed to call me Terri-Lyn, or someone was in the room with you, or… you just didn't know who I was."

"You could have said Terri-Lyn Ellis," Kenzie pointed out.

"Yeah… it's funny how I never use my maiden name anymore, even in circumstances like that."

Kenzie didn't think it was funny. It was downright weird. Why wouldn't Terri-Lyn introduce herself to an old friend by the name she had been using back then?

"Wow. I had no idea," she told Terri-Lyn. "I really didn't. I just thought you were doing that thing, asking someone to call you by your first name 'cause you're not comfortable with them using your last name. Or because you want to disarm them. I thought it was just 'call me Terri-Lyn.'"

"Right. I'm sorry for the confusion."

Kenzie stared at her old friend, trying to figure out where to begin. They clearly had a lot of ground to cover. "So… how are you doing? I had no idea that you had married Cash Wade."

"It was a thing," Terri-Lyn said vaguely. "I talked to your mother at the time. I think you were traveling. France or something."

Kenzie strained her memory. Had Lisa ever relayed that information? Had there been an invitation? Was it just assumed that Kenzie would not be able to be there, so her mother had answered on her behalf?

Lisa's more recent call came back to Kenzie now. *You won't have any mercy for an old friend?* Kenzie had thought that her mother had been talking about Cash, about how his family and the Coles had been friends, or the Wades and the Kirsches. She hadn't had a clue that Lisa had been talking about someone that *Kenzie* was friends with.

All the hours that Kenzie had spent on the Michael Wade case so far, and she'd had no idea that Michael's mother was her old school friend. She'd had no idea at all about her personal connection with the case.

28

Kenzie felt sick.

How could Terri-Lyn be involved in this? How could she know what her husband did and not do something to protect that little boy?

The Terri-Lyn she had known had been an idealist, interested in protesting against injustices, attending rallies, and helping to spearhead fundraisers for street kids and other similar causes. She hadn't exactly been radical, but she had been persuasive, talking people into helping out a cause that they probably wouldn't have looked at otherwise. Lisa had taught her step by step how to run a campaign and to ask people for money. Her own parents had not been interested in such things. They would open their wallets when necessary, making a splash in the news, but it had been Lisa who had taken Terri-Lyn under her wing and shown her what to do.

"I don't even remember hearing about you getting married," Kenzie confessed. "That was before Amanda died. And... a lot of the stuff around then is kind of wiped out by what happened afterward. I wasn't really myself... Then I decided to..."

"Change your whole life direction and become a medical examiner," Terri-Lyn finished.

"Well... that's not exactly how it happened. But I knew I wanted to go into medicine. I didn't know what I was going to do with it yet. I was interested in forensics. I had done a lot of the work on figuring out what Amanda had, even though it was too late..." Kenzie's throat constricted, hot and painful. She cleared her throat as if she just had a tickle, and paused for a moment to make sure she was okay before she resumed. "I was always interested in biology in school, and we were so involved in Amanda's treatment... I was often the liaison between Mom and the doctors. After she died, I was ready for a change in my life. Something with meaning."

Kenzie wondered if she had put her foot in her mouth by saying that. She didn't mean to imply that Terri-Lyn's life had no meaning. She was sure it did. Terri-Lyn had been involved in causes, and Kenzie was sure that hadn't stopped just because she got married.

"I mean... I felt like I didn't have any direction. I was just messing around before that. Sowing my wild oats, I guess. Travel, parties, going to the events Mom wanted me to attend."

Terri-Lyn nodded. "I remember how focused you were on your sister before we graduated. Everybody else is talking about prom dresses and limos and after parties, and you're like, 'the day I turn eighteen, I'm donating my kidney to Amanda,' because your parents vetoed it while you were still a minor."

It was the truth. Kenzie remembered that there had been graduation ceremonies and parties, and she knew she had been at her grad dance. Had probably even gone to it with one of the jocks, but it was all a blur. That hadn't been what was important to her. What had been important was saving Amanda's life. Finally escaping the chains that Walter and Lisa had put on her so that she could do the one thing that mattered.

"I don't know how my parents managed to hold out on my giving my kidney to Amanda. If it was me, I don't think I could have stopped the one thing I knew could cure my daughter. We all loved Amanda so much. How could they say no to that and make me wait for years before I could do it?"

"They just thought that was the right thing to do," Terri-Lyn said, her voice a little wistful. "One thing you could always count on was for your parents to do the right thing."

"Or what they thought was right," Kenzie corrected.

Terri-Lyn shrugged. "What's the difference?"

"Because they were wrong. I should have given my kidney to Amanda before that. We could have saved several years of extra pain and illness if I'd been allowed to give it to her when I wanted to. How can that be the right choice?"

"Because they didn't just have one daughter, they had two. They needed to protect you just as much as they needed to care for Amanda." Terri-Lyn looked stern. "Your parents adore you too, MacKenzie. You always act like Amanda was the only one who ever mattered, but they love you too."

"I know that. But it never... impacted on any decisions that I made."

Was that an awful thing to say? She hadn't depended on her parents' love. She hadn't considered it when she had decided to travel or go into medical school or any of the other things that she had decided to do in her life. She hadn't thought that those decisions had any impact on her parents. Of course they did; but Kenzie was supposed to separate from them and make independent decisions about the direction of her life, not just make the safe, prescribed decisions that her mother would have picked out for her.

Kenzie shook off the reminiscences. Enough of the stroll down memory lane. She didn't like where she knew it would lead. She gestured to the food on the sideboard.

"Can we eat now? I'm starving."

"Yeah, sure, of course," Terri-Lyn agreed. "Help yourself. That's why it's there."

"You're going to have some too, aren't you?"

"I don't have much of an appetite lately..." Terri-Lyn sighed and looked at what had been arranged. "Yes, of course I'll have something."

They both stood up and went over to the buffet. Kenzie selected a number of the small sandwiches and other items on offer. She could just imagine what Zachary would have said about those sandwiches if he'd been there. Or what he would think because, of course, he wouldn't speak his mind in front of Terri-Lyn.

"So tell me about your life," Kenzie said. "Since you seem to be familiar with mine, but I lost track of what you were doing. You got married when I was in France."

"Yes."

"That was a few years ago now." Before Amanda's death. Before medical school. How long? Ten years? "But you didn't have children right away."

"No, we wanted Cash to get established first. It's a lot of work, a political career like he has. Well, your dad would know about that. He's the 'kingmaker' type. He works behind the scenes, but he knows what goes into it. I didn't think we needed the extra stress children would bring."

They finished serving themselves and returned to the table to eat. Kenzie hadn't asked anything else, but Terri-Lyn continued describing what had happened to her over the years.

"The first few years, things were pretty good. We were kind of wild and free, Cash was climbing the ladder quickly and there were a lot of fun events and appearances. I felt like I'd escaped my family and could finally be happy."

Kenzie frowned at that and ate her first tiny sandwich. She tried to remember what Terri-Lyn's family situation had been. Terri-Lyn had come to Kenzie's house a number of times, but Kenzie had only gone to Terri-Lyn's house once. Maybe twice. It had not been the type of place Kenzie wanted to spend a lot of time.

Terri-Lyn's family home had been nice enough as far as architecture went. Everything looked fine on the outside. It was a little smaller than the Kirsch home, but that was not unexpected or a problem. A lot of the kids lived in more modest homes than Kenzie did. She'd never said anything about them or said anything to indicate that she looked down at them.

But inside, it had been a different story. Not the decor which, like the outside of the house, was perfectly fine. But her parents had made Kenzie very uncomfortable. Even at the school and around other parents, they had never talked to one another in a civil tone. They would snipe and be sarcastic. On a good day. On a bad day, they would scream across the house at each other, yelling and throwing things.

Terri-Lyn was mortified by this behavior, of course. This was probably one reason that Kenzie didn't go over there more than she had. That and the fact that she was afraid of them. She had never seen anyone have a knock-down blowout fight and was terrified that they would kill each other in front of her.

They hadn't hit each other while she had been in the same room, although Kenzie suspected that they had in the next room, out of her sight. And once, she had seen Terri-Lyn's father slap her across the face.

And it had been over nothing. Terri-Lyn and Kenzie had been doing their homework on the dining room table. A group project, maybe. Any parent should have been delighted to see their child working diligently away. Terri-Lyn had been a mediocre student. She struggled in some areas, which affected her average, even though she was very good in a couple of subjects.

They had been making a poster together, carefully lettering each information panel.

"Terri-Lyn. Your mother needs the table for supper," her father had announced. "Put your stuff away."

"It's homework," Terri-Lyn protested. "If we put it all away, then we have to start out all over again. Can't we just eat in the kitchen tonight?"

"No. I'm not eating in the kitchen like a servant. Get your stuff moved out of the way."

Kenzie looked sideways at Terri-Lyn's father and started to put the felt markers and other supplies away.

"Dad!" Terri-Lyn protested, drawing it out. "That's not fair. I need to do my schoolwork."

"You can get it out again after supper. Better yet, do it in your bedroom so you aren't underfoot. I don't know why you set up here to start with."

"Mom said that—"

Mr. Ellis backhanded her across the face. Kenzie was so surprised and frightened she nearly wet her pants. She grabbed the papers and supplies she could and bolted out of the room.

Maybe Mr. Ellis had forgotten that she was there. Maybe he just hadn't cared, thinking that she wouldn't tell any tales or that he would be able to counter them if she did. Kenzie ran up the stairs to Terri-Lyn's room and shut the door.

After doing so, she realized she was trapped and should have run out the front door and gone home. If he came after her now, there was nowhere to go but out the window. She was examining the latch and the screen when the door behind her opened quietly, and Terri-Lyn entered. She was sniffling, but tried to pretend that nothing had happened out of the ordinary. Kenzie was on high alert, waiting for Mr. Ellis to come barreling after Terri-Lyn to hit her again, or to yell at the two of them. She'd seen plenty of after-school specials on TV, she knew how abusers would threaten their victims and everybody else not to talk *or else*.

But he didn't come. Only Terri-Lyn did. Her cheek was a hot red where she had been struck, but she didn't talk about that. She just brought up the rest of their schoolwork and put it in her room. "We'll finish up here after dinner," she informed Kenzie. "It's better. We can turn on our music and everything. It will be fun."

Kenzie nodded, looking around. She looked at her friend, waiting for the explanation, the excuses, the "This has never happened before." But it clearly had happened before. Terri-Lyn took it in stride and just tried to pretend that it was nothing. Everyone's parents embarrassed them sometimes. Terri-Lyn's father had just embarrassed her. Life went on.

Kenzie couldn't remember much more about that day. She had apparently gone back downstairs to the dining room to eat dinner with Terri-Lyn and her two parents who couldn't speak to each other civilly. She had made it through the meal and then returned to the bedroom to get their homework finished.

And they had never spoken about it.

29

Kenzie had told Zachary that she couldn't remember worrying about anyone at school being abused at home. Had she blocked out everything she had known about Terri-Lyn? Had she buried that memory of Terri-Lyn being hit by her father and just written it off as "one of those things"? Parental discipline. Like a spanking, except that Terri-Lyn had been older, so it had been across her face instead of her backside. Parents had the right to discipline their children.

She was sure there had been other signs that Terri-Lyn did not come from a happy home. She was always at Kenzie's house, talking to Lisa, but Kenzie hadn't really thought anything of it. Most of Kenzie's friends thought that her mom was cool. Lisa was pleasant and didn't treat them like little kids, but like grown adults who could reason and make decisions by themselves.

There had probably been other signs. Maybe bruises covered up with makeup so that Kenzie wasn't really sure they were there. Just a shadow she had seen for an instant, and then hadn't been sure there had really been anything there. A trick of the lighting. Terri-Lyn's attitude toward her parents had always been negative. It wasn't that she rolled her eyes, shook her head over their behavior to her friends, and whined about the things that all kids did—bedtimes or curfews that were too early. Family vacations. Strict standards of dress, makeup, or dating. Terri-Lyn's complaints had been more general. Harsher.

I hate them.

I would be happier if they were both just dead.

I would be happier living on the streets than with them.

Kenzie would exchange looks with the other girls and shrug. How did you argue with something like that? They could compete about whose parents were the strictest, but Terri-Lyn didn't participate. What would she say? "My dad beats the hell out of me"?

This all flashed through Kenzie's memory in an instant. Cash had taken Terri-Lyn away from all of that. She must have seen him as her savior. Someone had finally come along who said she didn't have to stay with them anymore, didn't have to put up with any more abuse. She had been happy with her new life.

"But things didn't last?" Kenzie guessed. "I guess sooner or later, you had to settle down to domestic life."

"I hate that word. Domestic. Who was domesticated? Me? Him? Why do people have to be domestic? Why can't they just do what makes them happy? Why do we always have to do things to please others?"

"Well…" Kenzie was uncomfortable with the suggestion. "We want people to see us a certain way. It doesn't mean we have to make everybody happy, but we have to choose… what kind of a person we want to be. I decided I didn't want to be a socialite like my mom. That never interested me. I wasn't interested in politics like my dad, either. I wanted something else. It took me a while to figure out what that was."

"Be glad you found it," Terri-Lyn said, toying with her food. She didn't look at all interested in actually eating anything. "I wish… I'd been able to pick the kind of life I wanted."

Kenzie studied her. "What kind of life would you have chosen?"

"I'd love to be… just a normal family. Like mom, dad, and kids, working at… a bank or an office. Normal hours, normal house. Kids come home from school and… I don't know. Everybody is happy and normal. Like at your house when we were growing up. Don't you want that? Kids, and parents who are home and do things with them..."

"Do you think that my dad worked normal hours?" Kenzie asked with a laugh, "That he was home all the time with us girls? He was away all the time. He'd come back for dinner and then he'd be off again for days. It seemed like weeks sometimes."

"Well, that would have been okay too."

"If you didn't have to see Cash for a few weeks?"

Terri-Lyn nodded and shrugged. "I wouldn't mind a break from him now and then. It's hard being his wife. I thought it would be so great. I thought we would be *that* couple, like your parents." She sighed. "Not like mine."

"Does he hit you?" Kenzie asked directly. Maybe she should have been more direct with Terri-Lyn when they were younger. Talked about the domestic violence rather than pretending that it wasn't happening. Maybe if she'd had some support, Terri-Lyn would have been able to avoid getting into the same kind of relationship again. Maybe she could have broken the cycle. How different would Terri-Lyn's life have been if Kenzie had reported what she had seen to a teacher all those years ago?

"Cash is fine most of the time," Terri-Lyn said. "Just sometimes, when he has too much to drink and too much pressure from his job... he needs a release valve. And if I'm all stressed too instead of helping him to unwind..."

"It isn't your fault if he hits you."

"Isn't it? You think you would let anyone say anything to you and it would never get you upset enough to hit someone? A man like Cash doesn't need a wife who always challenges what he says and second-guesses him. He needs someone who is supportive and looking for ways to help him and give him what he needs. Not harping on him like some shrew."

"He shouldn't hit you. Whether he is irritated or stressed or drinking or what. He doesn't have any right to hit you."

"I'm glad your life is perfect, MacKenzie. Not all of us can say the same."

"I'm not saying that my life is perfect. I have a lot of challenges and stresses of my own. But I don't take them out on my partner, and he doesn't take his out on me."

"Yet. How long have you two been together? It's still the honeymoon."

"A couple of years."

Terri-Lyn shrugged. "Like I said. Honeymoon. You haven't really been tested yet. Just wait and see. It doesn't stay like that."

Kenzie shook her head, thinking about her ups and downs with Zachary. Mental health issues, his depression, and his obsession with his ex-wife. Dangerous cases, beatings, and assaults that brought old, buried memories to the surface. Therapy sessions and wondering if he was dead. Being abducted herself and thinking she might never see him again.

They hadn't been tested? Most couples did not have to go through all of that.

"He was always better when I was pregnant," Terri-Lyn said. "I thought he would settle down if I could give him a son. Become more of a family man. Doting."

"Domesticated," Kenzie suggested.

Terri-Lyn laughed shortly. "Yeah."

"You were pregnant more than once?" Kenzie was pretty sure that Michael had been an only child.

"Yes. I had a couple of miscarriages. And then... a couple of terminations too. I didn't want to have a girl."

Kenzie felt the frown lines crease her forehead. "Why not? I thought you would like to have a little girl."

"Boys are better," Terri-Lyn said decisively. "That was what Cash wanted. A little boy to take after him. That he could do things with. What can you do with a girl? Girls are... too distracting. I would always have to watch her, make sure she stayed out of his way."

So Terri-Lyn had terminated any pregnancies that were not boys and then given Cash Wade the son he wanted. Or the son that Terri-Lyn believed he wanted.

"But things didn't turn out the way you had imagined?" Kenzie guessed.

Terri-Lyn looked at her, her eyes looking hollowed out and far away. "Things never turn out the way I imagine. It's like a curse. I'm just not supposed to be happy, I guess. Just enough to give me these brief glimpses… these ideas that I could be happy if I made all the right choices. But it doesn't matter how hard I try. Things never turn out the right way."

"Being pregnant didn't stop Cash from hitting you. And having a baby did not make him settle down and take responsibility for his actions."

"He's good to me," Terri-Lyn insisted, as if Kenzie had been the one to make the accusations and she had to defend her husband. "He's given me everything. Literally everything. I can have anything I want. Cars and pools and that house. It's like living in a dream. Only I always thought that when I had all of those things, the hitting would stop. I didn't think that things happened like that to people who were really wealthy and powerful. They didn't happen to *your* parents."

"No," Kenzie agreed. She hesitated about what to say. Terri-Lyn made it sound like abuse was just something that happened to people. That it could strike out of nowhere. Like it was a virus that some couples caught. "My parents *chose* not to behave that way. It had nothing to do with how much money or influence they had."

"It did," Terri-Lyn would not be deterred. "My dad said that if he had all of the opportunities that your dad did, he wouldn't have been that way. It was because of all of the stress he was under that he was the way he was."

"You don't think that my dad was under any stress? With a daughter who was dying of kidney disease?"

"She wasn't dying. She was on dialysis," Terri-Lyn said scornfully. "And then she got your kidney, so she was cured. That's not such a big deal."

Kenzie was flabbergasted. She stared at Terri-Lyn, trying to understand her viewpoint. Everything that Terri-Lyn's dad had said and done had twisted things up in her mind. He thought that if he had all of the advantages, he would be a different person. He told himself—and her—that he would have been able to control himself, or would never have gotten angry enough to hit his wife and children.

"Amanda *was* dying," she told Terri-Lyn. Terri-Lyn should have known that. She had been one of Kenzie's best friends. Before... whatever it was that had split them up. "A person can't live on dialysis forever. Sooner or later, the body gives up. It starts to fall apart. And even after she had my kidney... she was freer. She could get out to do the things that she had dreamed of. But she still had to take anti-rejection meds, go in for scans to ensure everything was functioning, and follow a careful diet and all of the other things that they told her would help her live longer. Transplanted organs still fail. They don't last forever. The kidney she had from me only lasted for a few years, and then she had to have another transplant. And that was what killed her."

"But she had good years in there. I'm just saying that your dad wasn't worrying about her all of the time. He could just go on with his life, do what he wanted, and not worry about his family. It wasn't like that with my dad. He didn't have any choice in his life. He had a good job, but it was never good enough. He had money, but it was never enough. There were always still more bills to be paid, and every time he thought he was catching up, one of us would buy something stupid. He wasn't made of money."

Kenzie could hear Mr. Ellis saying all of those things. Maybe she had heard him say them in real life, and maybe she could just imagine it from the complaints she had heard from him. But Terri-Lyn had bought into it and taken those same attitudes with her into her life with Cash. A man that she thought would have it all so he would never put his hands on her. Or had she always known that sooner or later, he would?

30

"We need to talk about Michael and what happened to him," Kenzie told Terri-Lyn.

A trip down memory lane was fine when you met an old friend under different circumstances. But she was there because of Michael, Terri-Lyn's son, who had died after months of physical abuse. It wasn't exactly a high school reunion.

"It was an accident," Terri-Lyn said. "A tragic accident. I don't know what he was doing climbing around like that. He wasn't usually that daring. But we tried to keep him safe. Childproofing. That room should have been locked. One of the staff must have left it open after cleaning it. No one could know that Michael would wake up and go exploring like that, would climb over the edge..." She trailed off, dabbing at her eyes.

Kenzie fixed Terri-Lyn with a firm stare. It felt familiar, Terri-Lyn telling stories or going off on a tangent and Kenzie having to be the one to demand the truth.

"Terri-Lyn. That's not what happened. I already told you that I know that isn't what happened. Michael was not killed in that fall."

"He was. There are a ton of witnesses. Everybody in the house can tell you that's what happened."

"As far as I know, only one person actually saw him fall. If there were others, they have not come forward. Everybody is just going with the story that they didn't know what had happened or that there was anything wrong until Sylvia screamed. And she screamed when she saw him on the ground. She didn't see him go over the edge."

Terri-Lyn's eyes welled with tears. "Don't be like that, MacKenzie. Please. I know you're probably still mad at me, but don't mess up this case because of something that happened years ago."

Kenzie shook her head and tried to read Terri-Lyn's expression. "What are you talking about? I am telling you what I know about your son's death. It doesn't have anything to do with... anything else."

"I always figured you knew. You just shut me and everyone else out and pretended you didn't care anymore. But that was high school, MacKenzie. Can't you let it go now?"

"Let what go?" Kenzie was baffled. She had no idea what Terri-Lyn was going on about. It was true that she had become more withdrawn during high school. She and her parents had been so focused on Amanda and keeping her happy and well until Kenzie was old enough to donate her kidney that Kenzie had neglected her friendships. But what did that have to do with anything?

"You know," Terri-Lyn prompted. "With Frankie Carter."

A flood of memories was attached to that name.

Kenzie had always thought it strange how people could forget about traumatic things and bury them so deeply that they didn't even remember what had happened. She knew that it was true, it happened, but she was always a little bit suspicious. Did they *really* forget completely? Maybe they just avoided thinking about it. She could begin to understand it with someone like Zachary, who had gone through such terrible things in his past. One trauma wiped out another. Children's brains were more malleable, and they simply couldn't live with all the memories and still function.

But she *had* forgotten about Frankie Carter. She hadn't thought about him in years. If Terri-Lyn thought she was making decisions based on what had happened with Frankie, she was sadly mistaken. The boy had not even crossed Kenzie's mind in over a decade.

"Frankie Carter. What does he have to do with anything?"

Terri-Lyn looked down, avoiding Kenzie's eyes. "You can't hold that against me after so long. I'm sorry for what happened, but it was just... a prank. Kids do things like that to each other. I guess I was a little jealous of you. You always seemed to have everything that I wanted. But I just... it was stupid what I did."

"What *you* did."

"Yes."

Kenzie had never known who was behind the "prank." She had thought that maybe it had been one of Frankie Carter's friends. Or one of the mean girls who didn't like Kenzie and her friends. She hesitated to call herself and her small circle of friends a clique, but that was probably how other people had seen them. They were always together, and Kenzie had to admit that it had been a closed society, excluding others she probably would have been compatible with. But they had drawn together and kept others out. Other girls who wanted into the circle of friends, who wanted to be noticed, who had felt slighted by one of them; any of them might have decided to turn the tables and pull a prank on Kenzie to put her in her place.

It had been Terri-Lyn? Terri-Lyn, one of *her* girls, one of her best friends? One of the girls who was supposed to have her back? Kenzie had always defended the other girls in their group. They had been a sisterhood when Kenzie hadn't actually been with her sister.

Kenzie swallowed, her throat tight. "That was you?"

"I'm sorry, MacKenzie. I really am. I didn't mean you to get hurt, just... I don't know. I wanted to see you fail at something. It was mean and I was a terrible friend. But please don't hold that against me. After all these years... you can let it go, can't you?"

"Terri-Lyn." Kenzie looked her directly in the eye. "I haven't even thought about that in years. It doesn't have anything to do with Michael's death."

"No, but you wouldn't be acting like this if... if we were still friends. You wouldn't be trying to put this on me, to say that it was my fault when it was just a horrible accident."

"I didn't even know until I walked into this room that *you* were Terri-Lyn Wade. I thought I was dealing with a stranger. I would approach this the same way even if you were someone I had never met before."

"But you do know me," Terri-Lyn grabbed Kenzie's hand and squeezed it, trying to convey the desperation behind her words. "You do know me, and you can't do this to me. You know that I wouldn't do anything to hurt anyone. You *know* me, and you know that I didn't have anything to do with Michael's death."

"I can't treat you any differently than any other witness."

For now, she would keep referring to Terri-Lyn as a witness rather than a suspect.

"I know that you can't in front of anyone else," Terri-Lyn said, holding on to Kenzie's hand tightly. "That's why we're meeting here, where no one else can hear what we have to say. A room I know isn't monitored or recorded by anyone."

Kenzie tried to pull gently out of Terri-Lyn's grasp, but the woman held on, not releasing her. "Kenzie, this is *me.* I know that in front of everyone else, you have to act like you believe the worst of me, and not even act like you know me. But we were kids together. You know I would not hurt my son."

Kenzie stopped arguing that she wouldn't treat Terri-Lyn any differently from anyone else. Terri-Lyn clearly wanted preferential treatment. As Lisa had suggested—for Kenzie to show mercy to an old friend. Had Terri-Lyn called Lisa? Had she planted that idea and been the cause of the phone call? She and Lisa had always been close.

"You know what happened to Michael," she told Terri-Lyn

"No, I don't know. Michael was just fine. He was sleeping. There was nothing wrong with him."

Had she looked in on her son and seen him lying on his bed, already dead? Is that why she was so convinced that he had been sound asleep? Had the killer left him there for a time, while figuring out how he would deal with the inconvenient body?

"You know that your husband abused him," Kenzie asserted. So far, Terri-Lyn hadn't actually admitted to that, though she had implied it.

"No," Terri-Lyn's mouth was a thin line as she pressed her lips together. "Cash might have been too rough with him sometimes… when he'd been drinking or was stressed out. Maybe he grabbed him or shook him when he was upset, but that's all. He wouldn't have done anything to hurt Michael on purpose."

"Your nanny knew. She took him to the hospital. If she knew that your son was that badly hurt, why didn't you? You were his mother!"

"Sylvia?" Terri-Lyn shook her head angrily. "She's always been jealous of me. She wanted Cash for herself. Didn't want another woman in his life. She's been a problem since the day we married."

Kenzie tried to understand why the older woman would be jealous of Terri-Lyn. She had a crush on the much younger man? She was old enough to be his mother. Kenzie had a flash of inspiration.

"Was Sylvia Cash's nanny?"

"Yes." Terri-Lyn nodded impatiently. "And she didn't want anyone else giving him any attention. She didn't want him to love anyone else. She's the one who told me to give him a son." Terri-Lyn's voice rose. "She said that he would settle down and be happy... that he would have a purpose, and he needed that..." She blinked, eyes shiny, but no tears fell. "But I think she just said that because *she* wanted a baby. *She* wanted Cash's son."

31

"Sylvia told you to give Cash a son?" Kenzie repeated, completely flummoxed at this revelation. "How did that even come up?"

"I was lonely. I was upset because... things weren't going well with Cash. We were having problems. And Sylvia was a shoulder to cry on. Someone who knew him and I could talk to her about him... she wouldn't be shocked by anything, because she knew him better than I did. She said that his father had been like that... wild... spending too many nights away from home... being... angry. I didn't know what else to do. It was something I *could* do, instead of just sitting around feeling sorry for myself and watching him drift further and further away."

"And she told you that having a baby would solve the problem."

"Yes. She said it had worked with Cash's father. He started coming home more, wanted to be around his family, settled down... I *wanted* that. She said it would work, and I thought she was thinking of me and how to make things better for me and Cash. But that wasn't it at all."

Kenzie shook her head.

"When Michael was born, she took over. He was so fussy and I was tired and didn't feel well. It was too hard for me to look after him all the time, and Sylvia swooped in and took over. She didn't even ask. She just said that was what she was doing. And I wasn't exactly eager to stop her. Having a baby is really hard."

Kenzie made sympathetic noises, encouraging Terri-Lyn to go on and tell her about what had happened.

"I had postpartum. That's what the doctor said. I couldn't do anything. I tried. But I didn't have any energy, and I was so… I just couldn't make myself move. I wanted to stay in bed. Just lie there and pretend that nothing had happened. That I didn't have a baby to take care of, or a family, or a household, or a husband."

"It was that bad?"

"Yeah. The doctor prescribed some stuff that eventually helped. I think. Things got better, anyway. I'm still not a hundred percent. I'm not back to the way I was before he was born. I'm working on my body, you know, doing the Pilates and everything to get it back into shape. But how do you shape up your… brain? It's not a muscle. You can't just exercise it and have it snap back to where it was before."

"Are you still seeing your doctor?"

"No. Just to get the prescription renewed. Why bother? He can't really do anything."

"You might try some therapy. It could help."

Terri-Lyn shrugged. "I've been through crap before. I guess I'll get through it again. But all this stuff…" She made a gesture that encompassed the room, but she wasn't talking about anything in the room. "You can't think I had anything to do with Michael's death. It was just an accident. Like I said from the start. Like everyone said from the start. I don't understand why you're making a big thing out of it. Michael just climbed over the balcony railing."

"You know that he didn't."

Terri-Lyn's mouth was a stubborn line. She let go of Kenzie's hand.

"So we're not friends anymore. You can't do anything to help me."

"Not the way you are talking about. I can't say that you and your family had nothing to do with it. If you want to help clear yourself and them, I need the facts. Not made-up stories. And if I show you any kind of bias, then everything will blow up. People will think I was bought off, pressured by the government, or persuaded by an old friend to look the other way. I can't do any of those things. I have to just do my job."

"Then why did you even come here?"

"Because that was the only way you would talk to me."

Terri-Lyn looked angry about this at first, but then she gave a little smile. "That is what I did, isn't it?"

"Yeah. And then you haven't answered any more of my questions. I'm no further ahead than I was."

"Well, I can tell you," Terri-Lyn leaned forward. "That neither of us had anything to do with it. So if you if you think that Michael was being abused and was killed by someone before he fell from that balcony... you should be looking in another direction. Maybe check out the person who was actually supposed to be taking care of him."

"Sylvia said that she had something else that she was working on, away from the nursery. That she wasn't with Michael twenty-four hours a day."

"Then where was she? And why wasn't she there when he fell?"

Both good questions.

"And Sylvia has been taking care of Michael since he was born?"

"Any time he wasn't with me. He had colic when he was little, and I couldn't handle it. All of that constant crying, for hours. I don't know how anyone can live through that. I seriously don't."

"I've heard it's pretty tough," Kenzie agreed. "And how often did Cash interact with Michael?" When she thought about Sylvia and Michael, Kenzie couldn't picture the nanny hitting him. And Michael *had* been hit. Those bruises had not been sustained in falls or walking into things. No connective tissue disorder or brain tumor had shown up in the autopsy to explain his sustaining such bruises through his own play.

"Cash didn't spend much time with him. He was too busy. Too important. When he saw Michael, he didn't want to play with him or do anything with him. He wanted to show him off or to pick him up for a minute and then put him down and not deal with him again two minutes later."

"He didn't have a lot of patience for Michael?"

"Who could? You don't have any kids, do you?"

Kenzie shook her head. "No."

"Well, they take a lot of work, and they're messy, and they don't care how you feel. They're selfish, greedy little energy hogs. And if you want one to be quiet, do you think they'll stay that way?" She shook her head. "Not on your life."

"Neither of you had much patience for him."

Terri-Lyn rolled her eyes. "No. The person who spent time with him was *Sylvia*," she insisted.

Kenzie hated to think that the little woman who had so clearly adored Michael could have been the one who hurt him. Still, she couldn't deny the possibility and keep looking in the opposite direction. Sylvia was the one who was Michael's primary caregiver. She was the one who had taken him to the emergency room, aware of his injuries and taking it upon herself to see that he was treated, possibly without his parents even knowing about it.

"All right," she conceded. "I'll look into it. Thank you for that information. And I *am* sorry, Terri-Lyn. I would never want to accuse you of anything, but I can't protect you either. I will do my best to figure out exactly what happened to Michael and see that justice is done."

32

K enzie knew before even getting home that supper was going to be a bust. She would have to eat late, if she had anything at all. She hadn't exactly stuffed herself with the tiny sandwiches, fruit, and salad, but she wasn't feeling at all hungry.

"I'll just make myself a sandwich and we'll visit," Zachary promised. "You don't have to eat if you're not hungry."

That made Kenzie feel a bit guilty for all of the times she had forced him to eat when his medication had taken away his appetite and he was so nauseated. But she had done that for his benefit. He needed to eat in order to stay healthy, and he wouldn't eat unless she pushed him.

But luckily, he was off of those meds now and finding it much easier to eat and keep up his weight.

Kenzie didn't need to worry about losing weight because she didn't eat one evening.

She told Zachary about discovering that a witness she had contacted—she didn't give him any information on which case it was or that Terri-Lyn was possibly a suspect—was an old friend of hers from school. Zachary shook his head at the coincidence.

"That's why women should never change their names when they get married," he said. "It's impossible to keep track of people."

Kenzie snorted. "This from the private eye."

"Do you know how hard it can be to track down a woman who has changed her name with each of four marriages?" He rolled his eyes. "It's crazy. Why do they do that?"

"I don't know," Kenzie confessed. "I think that in a lot of cases, women like to take on a new identity. To start fresh. To be associated with their husband more closely. And that's not even talking about tradition and the taboo about single mothers and babies born out of wedlock. There is a lot of social tradition to deal with if you don't change your name."

"There are countries where the kids take both parents' names automatically. Or take the mother's."

"Or the parent's first name," Kenzie filled in. "Anderson. Jackson. Peterson. Can you imagine trying to track people down in those countries?"

"There must be tricks, but I wouldn't want to be doing it."

"Yeah. It would be pretty crazy. My mom has friends who do genealogy and say it is almost impossible in those countries."

"So you guys just lost touch over the years? Going in different directions?"

"Well, it was more than just that. I mean, part of it was my being involved with Amanda's care so much. I might not have had a long time with her, and I was waiting for when I could donate my kidney to her. It was really important to me to be with her. And other kids didn't understand that. Terri-Lyn says she wasn't dying, she was just on dialysis, and then she was cured with the transplant, but that doesn't even begin to describe the kind of life we were leading, watching her fail from day to day, hoping that she wouldn't get a virus or pneumonia that might end her life. Trying to be happy around her and act like it was all okay. It was really hard."

He nodded. "I can imagine."

"And then... I mean, it was high school and kids do crazy stuff. Stupid stuff. Some of the things that those girls did..."

Zachary raised his brows. "What? You didn't want to be involved in what they were up to?"

"No. It was... I didn't even know that it was Terri-Lyn at the time, but there was this boy I had a crush on. Frankie Carter. He was on the football team. Big jock. Big everything, he was really popular in school, had all of the girls swooning over him. I was no different than anyone else."

"I don't know about that."

"No, I wasn't anything special. And then… I started getting notes from this boy. Left in my locker, or people who approached me and said they were supposed to give them to me, or whatever. There was all of this cloak and dagger, very romantic; I'm sure my marks were trash at the time because my head was in the clouds, daydreaming about him. And writing in my notebooks; you know how girls do. *MacKenzie Carter. Mrs. MacKenzie Carter. Mrs. Carter. Frankie and MacKenzie. MacKenzie loves Frankie.* All of the lovesick teen girl stuff."

"Aww," he crooned, as if it were cute.

"And the notes were very exciting. Poems, little vignettes of how he had seen me the day before, doing something totally mundane, and had been dreaming about me since. And… spicier stuff. Suggestions. Talking about getting together. Talking about how… excited he was to meet me."

"But he wasn't the one writing the notes," Zachary guessed.

"No. I should have known, but I didn't see it. I was completely blind. Why would a jock like that be interested in me? And if he was, why wouldn't he just walk up and talk to me? He wasn't shy. I saw him talking to plenty of other girls. Being bold and stupid other times. He wasn't the kind of guy who walked around hiding behind a fringe of hair and blushing anytime a girl spoke to him. He was more than capable of walking up to any girl in the school and asking her out."

"But he didn't. And…"

"And so I started flirting with him more and more obviously, thinking that he was into it and he was the one writing me all of these notes. And saying things to him, little secrets that had been in the notes. Until one day…"

Zachary grimaced, anticipating it.

"I asked him if we could get together sometime. You know,

privately. Since he'd been sending these notes saying that he wanted to..."

"And he had no clue."

"Nope. He had no idea who I even was. I thought he was joking at first when he asked who I was. Because we'd been connecting, in my mind. We had this emotional relationship already. And when he asked who I was, and said that he wasn't interested and would appreciate it if I would give him some space and stop acting so creepy around him..." Kenzie closed her eyes and shook her head, her cheeks warming up as she remembered the humiliation. "And, of course, it wasn't just the two of us alone when this finally blew up. It was in the cafeteria with half the student population watching. Or that's what it felt like, anyway."

"And it was your best friend who set this all up? This woman who is a witness in your case?"

Kenzie nodded. "What a mess. I never knew it was her. But maybe, on some level, I knew she had enjoyed it and liked seeing me put in my place. She didn't gloat, exactly, but maybe I sensed that she was a lot happier about it than she should have been."

"That's terrible." Zachary's voice was pained. He rubbed his forehead. "I know how cruel teenagers can be, sometimes without actually meaning to be. But that was carefully planned out and executed. She knew exactly what she was doing."

"Yeah. And maybe we drifted apart because she felt guilty about it."

"Or because she was jealous, the emotion that started it all in the first place," Zachary suggested. "Maybe she couldn't be around you, seeing all your successes."

"My successes?"

"Happy family. Good marks. Whatever else she was jealous about."

"Yeah, I guess so. I never knew there was all of this negativity going around. I just... I needed to be with my family and school was secondary to everything else. I didn't really care about it anymore."

"But to Terri-Lyn, the school community was still the most

important thing in her life, and maybe seeing that it was not all-important to you anymore pushed her away."

"Anyway… by the time we graduated, I was already gone, emotionally. I remember a bit of the graduation stuff. Walking across the stage, the dance. I think I went to an after-party. But it wasn't a big deal to me."

She had left it all behind her with the rest of her childhood. Until suddenly, Terri-Lyn reappeared in Kenzie's life, the grieving mother of a homicide victim. If she really was grieving. It was hard to know exactly what Terri-Lyn's feelings toward Michael were. He was her child, and she had cared for him to some degree, but it was hard to tell how deep her feelings about him were. Some people felt things deeply, but showed little on the surface. Other parents made a huge fuss and pretended feelings of loss that they did not feel. It was diffi-cult to tell from the outside.

They talked about other things, and Kenzie made sure they covered several other topics before returning to the Michael Wade case, so that Zachary wouldn't immediately know that was the case that her friend was involved in.

"What do you think about the possibility that the child might have been abused by the nanny?" Kenzie asked. "It's a twisted sort of relationship. She was nanny for the boy's father, talked the mother into getting pregnant, then kind of hijacked the kid's care while the mother was battling postpartum depression. The baby has colic, and the mother can't handle his care, but the nanny is already living in the house, so she jumps in and does what she does best. Taking care of babies."

Zachary shrugged. "Anyone can be an abuser. You can't tell just by looking at them. It isn't always a father or stepfather. There could be any relationship. Anyone close enough to hurt him or manipulate him."

"But she is devoted to him. She is the one who took him for medical treatment when no one else in the household did. And she's this little, tiny old lady. I really can't see her in the role of an abuser."

"Huh." Zachary gave a short laugh. "You don't have to be big and strong to abuse someone. She was still a lot bigger and stronger than a small child. And some of the women that I knew in care... Mrs. Phipps at Reachout..." He gave a shudder.

Kenzie had heard mention of the woman before. Usually in reference to her ability to beat and bully the teens in the group home she worked at.

"Just a little tiny woman," Zachary said. "Under five feet. And she was crip—handicapped. She had this leg that dragged, and she needed a cane to get around. I don't know what was wrong with it. Maybe a stroke, or maybe she was born that way. She could handle that cane like a ninja. You would think you were out of reach, and *whack* she'd bring it down across your knuckles. Or in the knee. Or jabbed straight in the spine. A few seconds, and she could have you curled up on the floor, which was right where she wanted you. Right where she could whale on you. A few whacks with that cane would have the strongest boy in the house begging for mercy."

"I can't imagine."

"She was wicked. It wasn't just to keep us in line. She enjoyed hurting and humiliating us."

"That must have been awful. I'm so sorry you had to deal with that."

He made a motion as if pushing it into the past. "Long time ago now. I've recovered. I'm just saying... she was maybe the smallest caregiver I ever had, and physically handicapped, but she was *vicious*. Terrifying."

Kenzie thought about this. Was that what Sylvia was like? A grieving, heartbroken caregiver to the rest of the world, but perhaps also the person who had caused Michael's visits to the hospital and his eventual death? It was still hard to believe, even with Zachary's story. She pictured his Mrs. Phipps as a wizened old witch with a hard face, her weapon of choice always close at hand. Not at all like the devoted nanny she saw in Sylvia Arnold.

33

It seemed like Kenzie was getting more and more behind at the medical examiner's office. She hoped that Dr. Wiltshire would stop in to sign the paperwork on his desk and maybe take a few things off her hands. In the meantime... she could only do what she could. Julie had spent a lot of time on reception lately, so she was off working one of her other jobs, leaving Kenzie to either man the phones and reception desk or to direct calls to the voicemail system and deal with other duties.

She decided she'd better stay at her desk and get some of the paperwork done. It was too easy to become buried in just a few days by the amount of paper that the medical examiner's office produced. She focused on clearing the voicemails, phone message slips, and emails that had accumulated to make sure that nothing got overlooked.

Detective Baker had left a couple of messages, so Kenzie called her back to see what she needed. She didn't want to be responsible for holding up the Wade investigation.

"Hello? Oh, Dr. Kirsch. How are things? I understand Dr. Wiltshire has left you in the lurch."

"Well, sort of. I'm doing what I can. What can I help you with?"

"You've had a couple of discussions with the folks at the Wade household."

"Yes. Mostly the nanny and Terri-Lyn. Mrs. Wade."

"Anything interesting?"

"I wouldn't know where to start… if you want to stop by here, we can go over it. I need to write down what I can, but I'm not sure what is relevant to the autopsy report and what you need to know. A lot of it doesn't directly impact the autopsy report, but you might want to explore further…"

"Okay. I'll take you up on that. And the other thing is, you might be interested to know that there *was* a DCF visit. Two of them, in fact."

Kenzie sucked in her breath. "I thought they came up clean."

"Well, they did initially. But it seems that some of the documentation got… misfiled."

"Intentionally?"

"Maybe?" Kenzie could picture Baker's shrug. "I wouldn't say that it was not a possibility. But of course, I don't have any proof that it was buried or interfered with."

"Just the name on the file should be enough proof of that," Kenzie said in disgust. "You wouldn't believe the amount of pressure I am getting to obfuscate in my report."

"Oh, wouldn't I?" Baker returned dryly.

Kenzie laughed. If there were anyone who was probably under more pressure than she was with regard to the investigation into Michael Wade's death, it would be the detectives.

"Maybe you would," she agreed. "What do you think? About your investigation so far, I mean. Was the additional evidence that Tuttle and I supplied of any help?"

"Most of it is still being processed. It is an interesting case. No lack of possible suspects. But unfortunately, the kind who can ruin your career if you point a finger in the wrong direction. Not that I'm in the habit of carelessly pointing out potential killers."

"Yeah. Can you shoot me a copy of the DCF reports?"

"Already on their way. If they aren't in your inbox yet, they should be soon. And I will try to get down to talk to you today or tomorrow to find out what you discovered in your conversations. Any high points?"

"Well… you should probably know that, unbeknownst to me, I actually know Mrs. Wade from way back. I didn't know that until yesterday, because I've only heard her called by her married name. So… it won't affect my autopsy report, but you should be aware of the possible accusations of bias. Obviously, we haven't kept in touch, so I don't think I can be accused of being a close friend. I haven't seen her in years and years."

"Understood," Baker agreed crisply. "In a place like Vermont, you can't really expect not to run into people you know from time to time. I know I have as well."

"Okay, good. I wanted to make sure that you knew right away."

"I'll make a note on file, including the date you disclosed it to me."

"Aside from that… well, pretty much what you would expect. Everybody denying that they know anything about what happened to Michael and pointing their fingers at each other."

"Trouble in paradise?"

"Mrs. Wade made it clear that all has not been well between her and her husband. But even more finger-pointing toward the nanny. I don't think there was any love lost between the two of them."

"Why didn't she fire her, then?"

"She was Mr. Wade's nanny."

"Oh. Ohhh…" Baker drew the syllable out thoughtfully. "Well, that *is* interesting, isn't it?"

"I doubt if Mrs. Wade would have been allowed to fire her. And I don't think she was prepared to. From what she said, she's not up to raising a young child on her own. She would have had to find someone else before firing Sylvia Arnold."

"Anything to it, do you think?"

"Maybe…" Kenzie didn't want to commit to anything. "I find it hard to picture her as an abuser or murderer, but my partner reminds me that it doesn't really matter what she looks like. Outer appearances can be deceiving."

"That they can," Baker agreed.

"Sylvia Arnold was the one who took Michael to the hospital when he was injured. She can't deny knowing about the abuse, even though she tried."

"Maybe it's time for us to have another chat with her."

Kenzie nodded her agreement, even though Baker couldn't see her. "Yeah, you might want to. I hate to think of her doing something to that little boy. She seemed so broken up about it. But we've all seen mothers weep over their kidnapped or murdered children, only to find a few weeks later that they were the perpetrators. Looking sympathetic doesn't mean anything."

"Some of the most horrific killers have been sweet-faced. Okay, I'll leave you to your work. Will stop by later."

Kenzie hung up the phone and went immediately to her inbox to scan for the DCF reports. They had just arrived. She printed copies and filed the electronic copies immediately, then started to skim-read as the reports came off the printer.

DCF had twice been called out to the Wade mansion. Considering the amount of influence Cash Wade wielded, it had taken some guts for someone within the household to make a report. Even though the details of such reports were supposed to be kept from the accused abusers, this kind of information often leaked out. So a reporter could never be sure that her identity would remain unknown. As such, Kenzie thought that she must have recognized that the abuse had become extreme, or she wouldn't have dared make the report.

34

The first call that had been investigated by DCF had been a report of suspected abuse. The subject child had significant bruises, cried a lot, and was often sick in bed. The case worker, a Moriah Wright, had apparently not been expecting the Wade mansion when she responded to the report. There were a lot of details in the report describing the property, both exterior and interior. This had clearly been a novelty for someone who was used to investigating homes with six children sleeping in a single-room apartment or a house on its way to being condemned for health code violations. She was used to reporting any red flags in the child's environment in detail, so she followed a similar process for the Wade mansion, listing everything she thought argued against a child being neglected or abused there. Poverty was a red flag for neglect and abuse. Extreme wealth was not.

She detailed meeting with each of the women who took care of Michael, Terri-Lyn Wade and Sylvia Arnold. She conducted the interviews separately. She was also introduced briefly to Michael. Wright reported that Michael appeared to be healthy and well-nourished. He was clean, dressed in clean, well-maintained clothes. His hair was combed. His face washed. No sores or rashes that would suggest he wasn't getting the vitamins he needed. She didn't report any bruises.

When she asked for the opportunity to examine Michael more closely by having him raise his shirt and pant legs, the request was denied. Not much the social worker could do about it. Without concrete evidence to back the abuse allegation, she could not take him into custody and take him to a doctor herself.

The child's father was not available. He was out of town on business. The case worker reported that he was a congressman, though Kenzie wasn't sure what relevance that had. She supposed that if he were a construction worker or unemployed barfly, those would have been red flags. The case worker wanted to cover all of the bases so that she couldn't be accused of being biased or so blinded by the family's wealth that she hadn't done a thorough investigation.

Both of the women had denied there was any possibility of Cash Wade being abusive. Both described him as a loving, caring family man.

Wright had been shown to the nursery and reported on everything being clean and neat, with no apparent hazards to such a small child. She was told that he was supervised at all times and, during the interviews, he had been taken to the kitchen, where he was given a chocolate chip cookie and looked after by one of the kitchen staff until they were finished.

She reported that each of the women was cooperative and concerned about the allegations that had been made, but denied that there was any possible truth to the reports. Both women were well-dressed and well-groomed, presenting themselves well. They were calm and did not show any sign of deception or contradict themselves or each other. Both suggested that perhaps the report had been made by a former employee who wanted to get back at his ex-employers for perceived wrongs. Sometimes people did things like that, making false reports as a method of retaliation. Wright, of course, knew this to be true. She did not confirm or deny the identity or position of the person who had made the complaint.

The allegation was cataloged as "unsubstantiated" with no recommended follow-up.

. . .

The second report that sent a social worker to the Wade mansion suggested that Michael was abused and the victim of medical neglect. There was no indication whether the report had come from inside the mansion or was made by a former employee. Still, Kenzie assumed from the contents that it must have been made by someone on staff. How else would they have known to call when they did?

Upon arrival, the case worker, this time Delia Rose, found Michael Wade sick in bed.

He was pale and lethargic. Kenzie's stomach tightened as she read these details. She wrote down the date of the report to check later whether it matched up with any of the emergency room visits. Rose did not see any injuries on Michael's face that suggested abuse. Like Wright, her request to examine Michael more closely was denied. She was not allowed to pull down the blanket, pull up his shirt, and see whether there were blackening bruises or signs of internal bleeding. She was told he had the flu and would probably bounce back in a day or two.

There were bottles of water and a pediatric electrolyte solution on the bedside table, as well as saltine crackers and a bowl with remnants of what appeared to be porridge or pablum. They suggested that he was being properly taken care of during his illness. There were no medications in evidence. Kenzie didn't suppose that a social worker would look kindly on medicine left within reach of a child, no matter how sick he was. A bottle of syrupy children's Tylenol could be swallowed in a few seconds, leading to great harm.

When she touched him, Rose found Michael to be warm, but not burning up. If he had a fever, it was low grade, nothing to be concerned about. He didn't engage with her or answer questions, but he was only a toddler, and he was sick. Not someone that Rose expected to get more than a word or two out of.

Sylvia Arnold sat in the rocking chair beside the bed, where it was evident she had been spending a good deal of time. A wastepaper basket filled with crumpled balls of tissue and food wrappers suggested that she was spending all of her time there. The mother, Terri-Lyn Wade, had made a brief appearance, checking in on her son and talking to Sylvia and Rose for just a few minutes.

She indicated that Sylvia was watching over Michael most of the time, with Terri-Lyn or someone on the house staff taking over when Sylvia needed a break. Terri-Lyn said Sylvia had some medical or first aid training and was the best one for the job, but didn't go into detail. Sylvia didn't offer any credentials, just saying vaguely that she had experience with sick kids.

Rose suggested that the boy be taken to the doctor if he hadn't already seen one. Terri-Lyn indicated that a family doctor would make a house call if his condition worsened or was prolonged. If they had any concerns, outside medical treatment would be sought. No expense would be spared.

Rose obviously knew they had the money to follow through on these promises and would not hesitate to take him to the hospital due to lack of funds or insurance. There was no reason to suspect that they would avoid treatment. At the time, the best place for the boy was in bed in his own home. If things got worse, the hospital was not far away.

Rose recorded the second report as being unsubstantiated and, as with Wright, did not recommend any follow-up action.

35

The case workers seemed to have been diligent, recording the details of their visits and everything that they had observed while there. Kenzie had read a number of DCF reports, and nothing seemed amiss. She couldn't see any gaps that the case workers should have filled.

The only troubling factor was that they had not been allowed to examine Michael for injuries. As Zachary had told Kenzie, serial abusers frequently learned to avoid facial injuries or scarring on the arms or other places they might be seen. Michael's worst injuries had been focused on his torso, both belly and back, which the social workers would have been able to see if they'd been allowed to look. But the legislation said that bruises alone did not constitute evidence of serious bodily injury. There had not been any indications of abuse or risk factors noted in the SDM Risk Assessments the social workers had performed. So they hadn't insisted that Michael be examined by a medical professional.

Kenzie was not looking forward to the next step, but she knew she had to do it anyway. She dialed the number for DCF and asked for Moriah Wright. She introduced herself, planning to ease gently into the conversation. But Moriah's voice immediately choked up and the sniffles started.

"I saw the notice on that poor boy," she cried. "We get a notification when one of the kids we have visited... when something happens like that. I feel so awful. I don't know what to say. I've talked to my supervisor and gone over the investigation. She says I did everything right and couldn't be blamed for what happened. But... I'm not trying to get out of being blamed. I want... I want to know what I should have seen. What I could have done differently. Everything I saw said that he was being supervised appropriately. My boss says it's just one of those things. People can't be expected to watch their kids twenty-four hours a day, and sometimes these things just happen when they think that they're asleep or their backs are turned for a few minutes..."

"I'm afraid I have more bad news for you," Kenzie cautioned. She hated to push this sensitive woman further into despair. She would need to toughen up if she were going to pursue a career in social work. "The evidence shows that Michael Wade did not die in the fall from the balcony."

"Oh, dear... how long was he lying there before...?"

"No, he was dead before he fell from the balcony."

"How could he be...?" Wright's voice was mystified.

"Someone threw him off of the balcony after they killed him. To obscure the cause of death."

There was a sharp intake of breath from the social worker. Shocked out of her tears, for the moment at least. "He was killed? What happened to him?"

"I haven't issued my final autopsy report yet. But there were signs that he had been severely physically abused over the last few months. Bruises in various stages, broken bones, scarring. Investigation into emergency room admissions shows that he has been treated a number of times over the past year for potentially life-threatening injuries."

"No... I did a medical records search. We look for that kind of thing."

"He was admitted under the nanny's name. Michael Arnold rather than Michael Wade."

"Without a birth certificate or social?"

"It was an emergency situation. They checked the nanny's identification and used the name she gave them. There was no insurance claim, so they never took the further steps to verify it."

"How did you figure it out? You can't search under every potential name someone might have used."

"One of the ER nurses recognized him and described Sylvia Arnold as the mother. We tracked it back from there, and found the pattern."

Wright sniffled again. "What did I miss? How could I have known that he really was being abused? Everything seemed fine. There were *no* risk factors. No sign that he'd been injured."

"You never interviewed the father?"

"He wasn't there. They said he was often on the road with his work. He obviously wasn't one of the primary caregivers."

"But you have to check everyone in the home."

There was no answer for a moment. "Do you know how many people are in that home?" Wright asked. "There was more of a chance that the cook or chauffeur or a maid was hurting Michael. They were there every day, the father wasn't. I interviewed the people who had the most contact with him. The mother and the nanny."

"Did you know that the mom had postpartum?"

"No. No one ever mentioned that." Kenzie could tell from Wright's voice that she knew postpartum depression was a red flag for an overwhelmed caregiver. It didn't make them an abuser, but it did increase the risk.

"And that she was abused?"

"No. How did you know that? She told you?"

"I… am familiar with her from a number of years ago. Know a bit of her history."

"I didn't have any idea. She didn't disclose that in our interview."

Kenzie didn't imagine she did. And there had probably never been an investigation into abuse in Terri-Lyn's family of origin. Even if there were, the records would have been destroyed long ago.

"They didn't want you to examine him more closely because he was covered with bruises. You would have known immediately that he was being abused."

"I couldn't insist. There was nothing else to indicate that he was being abused. No evidence that the caller who reported them was telling the truth. Both caregivers seemed caring and engaged. The child was taken care of. I watched him with them... he seemed more partial toward the nanny, but that would be expected, if she is the one taking care of him most of the time. I didn't see any behavior that suggested he might be hurt."

"And I assume he wasn't verbal?"

"No. Pointing. Whispering a word in his nanny's ear. Nothing more than that. He didn't want to talk to me, or engage with me. Shy. He just wanted to go play so, when the cook came around and offered him a cookie to keep him out of the way during the interviews, he was happy to go."

"I'm sorry to be the bearer of such bad news," Kenzie told her. "And I agree with your supervisor. I don't think you did anything wrong. If you had insisted on a physical examination, the abuse would have been discovered. But bruises themselves are not conclusive. And if there hadn't been obvious bruises, DCF could have been sued, and Cash Wade is a very powerful man."

"Thanks. I do appreciate that."

"I wondered if there was anything that didn't make it into your report? That you thought about later, or noticed at the time but didn't think was important enough to be included in your report, or maybe something that you wished could have been investigated further, but wasn't."

"Well, I wished that I could have examined him more closely for bruises, obviously. But more to clear the Wades than to accuse them. Everything I saw seemed perfectly fine. I was sure there was nothing to worry about." She sniffled, and Kenzie heard an echo in her head. *Nothing to worry about.*

"Okay. If you think of anything after we hang up, please call me. I'd like to know before I issue my final report."

"Sure. I will."

"Ms. Wright..." Kenzie tried to capture Wright's attention again before she could hang up.

"Yes?"

"If you had to guess, which of them do you think was hurting him?"

Wright sighed. She hummed while she considered the question. "I don't really think I should say."

"I won't put it down anywhere. I'm just curious as to your impressions."

"Well... I would say the mother. She didn't seem as involved in his care. But then... it's usually the person who has the most contact with him, isn't it? And that would make it the nanny."

36

Kenzie expected the conversation with the second social worker, Delia Rose, to go much the same way. It took a few transfers to get to the woman's voicemail, so she left a message, not leaving very much information. She didn't want the worker to avoid her because she was calling from the medical examiner's office and thought she was about to get her hands slapped. Or to go into a tailspin like Wright because she thought she should have done something more to save Michael Wade. Both of them had been put in a difficult situation, unable to establish any pattern or evidence of abuse before the boy had been killed. It was a difficult situation for anyone, regardless of how experienced they were.

She heard a familiar footstep in the hall and looked up to see Dr. Wiltshire approaching. He gave her a wry smile as he walked up to the desk.

"The dead rise again," he said, with an embarrassed chuckle. Kenzie guessed he was feeling bad about leaving her in the lurch and not getting back to her on exactly what was going on and what his plans were.

"Well, I certainly hope not," Kenzie told him. "That could make our business quite challenging."

He laughed more openly at that. "If you could accompany me to my office, I'm still not very good at dressing and undressing with this contraption."

His arm and most of his hand were covered by an overcoat, so Kenzie couldn't see what kind of cast he had on now. She stood and followed him to the kitchen, where he set down his peace offering of a dozen donuts, and then to his office. She helped to pull his jacket off so that it didn't get caught on the external hardware. Dr. Wiltshire's hand and arm were enclosed in a high-tech-looking external fixation cage and cast combination. What little she could see of his fingers was black and blue. It looked like he'd been trampled by a horse.

"Ouch," Kenzie said expressively. "Exactly how did you do this?"

He looked at her, expression pinched. "I don't think full disclosure is required at this point."

Kenzie raised her brows. Whatever he had done to it, he had done a magnificent job.

"They think you'll be able to regain full functionality?"

The repairs had obviously been done by a skilled orthopedic surgeon. It wasn't just a slap-dash cast put on by an intern still getting his hours in.

"He is hopeful," Dr. Wiltshire said, looking critically at the fixation device as if it were the first time he was seeing it. "Luckily, there were no torn tendons or ligaments. Didn't seem to be any nerve damage." He grimaced. "All of the nerves seem to be functioning fully, from what I can tell." He rolled his eyes expressively.

"Is it in a lot of pain?"

"Not as much now as in the beginning. With all the bones held in place and the swelling going down, it is definitely improving. But it isn't a walk in the park."

"I guess not." Kenzie hung Dr. Wiltshire's jacket up on his coat rack. "So, are you just in for a few minutes to sign off on work?"

She wanted to set her expectations correctly and not expect him to be back full time if he were only going to be there for an hour and then take off again. It would also help her prioritize his tasks, ensuring they hit the most urgent and important cases first.

"I'm not sure yet how long I'll last. Between the pain of the injury and the wooziness caused by the painkillers, it has been hard to find just the right balance. I'll stick around for as long as possible, but if I'm seeing double from the painkillers, then I'm not much help to anyone around here."

"Okay. Understood. If you want to start on this pile here," Kenzie pointed to it. "That will cover off the most vital stuff."

He looked at the pile but didn't pick up a file. "We need to talk about the Wade case."

Kenzie nodded. "I am getting close to being able to issue my postmortem report. But I'll definitely want you to look at it to ensure I haven't missed any key points or said anything that could be construed as... controversial."

He leaned back in his chair and rubbed the point on the bridge of his nose where his glasses sat. "The more convoluted and ambiguous, the better, on that file."

"I'm not going to bury the truth."

He sighed. "Of course not. I know that."

She sat down in the chair across from him. "So, what did you want to talk about?"

"Somebody is leaking."

In the morgue, that statement could have several very different meanings. Kenzie shook her head. She knew she had not said anything that had reached the news circuit. She had been very careful. Reporters had been calling her nonstop, but she had remained firm. She had been careful not to say anything of substance to anyone outside the medical examiner's office. One never knew what ears might be pricked nearby.

"I've been very careful. What has been released?"

"Starting a couple of hours ago, there have been several stories posted about Cash Wade's son being killed in an accident."

Kenzie nodded. Not surprising. A lot of people knew that. It had been bound to hit the press sooner or later. The Wade family had been lucky to keep it out of the media for the first few days.

"The publicity seems to go in two different directions. First, about whether there was any foul play. If the congressman himself was involved in the death or was there at the time."

Kenzie nodded. "Something I wouldn't mind knowing for sure myself. But I don't think anyone in that household will tell us. Maybe I'll be surprised and he will confess or Terri-Lyn will come forward to say what really happened. Or maybe we'll be able to get someone else for it. But right now, Cash is still a pretty good candidate."

"The other direction the publicity is taking is to question the competency of the medical examiner's office. Why do we still have the body? Why hasn't it been released along with the autopsy report? Is there some conspiracy? Some cover-up?" He shrugged. "You know how it is."

Kenzie nodded. "They're always impatient. But sometimes, it takes time. Especially when I am working on my own."

He grimaced. "Yes, I'm sorry about that. I have not been available. But you've done well to hold down the fort and I appreciate that. How close are you to being able to issue your report?"

"I just found out that there were DCF reports. So I'm dealing with that right now. I've talked to one of the social workers, and I'm waiting for a callback from one. I'd like to find out what impressions she had, if anything, about what was going on in that house."

"Of course. Such background is always helpful."

"And I had a long talk with the mother."

"Glad to hear it. She was rather evasive last I heard. How did that go?"

"Well, it turns out I know her from way back when I was in school."

"Medical school?"

"High school."

"Oh." He pursed his lips. "Well, that *was* a while ago now."

"I'm not quite as old as *that*," Kenzie laughed, "but... yes, it was a long time ago. Longer than I would like to admit. We were close friends once, but we drifted apart. I haven't even thought of her for years, let alone seen her. I didn't even know she was married. Or that she had married Cash Wade."

"I see. That doesn't sound like a problem for us. And did she give you any details of what happened that day?"

"I got some things to look into, but she didn't confess. It would be really nice to have a confession, you know."

He chuckled. "It would make things much easier. Well, you leave that to the police detectives. There is only so much investigating that you can do from your end. Leave the police work to them."

"I know. I will. And I've liaised with them and let them know everything I found. I'll give them a copy of the report before I release it. Make sure there's nothing else to be considered from their end."

He nodded his approval. "It sounds like you have everything under control. I assume any results I need to review are in this pile?" He indicated the high-priority pile that Kenzie had pointed him at.

"Yes. If you work on that one, it would really help me out."

"Leave me to it. I'll get done what I can."

"Let me get you a coffee. That should keep you focused," Kenzie offered.

"That would be brilliant. And there might be some donuts in the kitchen…?"

"I noticed that," Kenzie said dryly. "I'll bring you one."

37

Walking back toward her desk, Kenzie heard her phone ringing. It sounded somehow more urgent than usual. Talking to Dr. Wiltshire about the stories circulating in the news, she felt a stronger push to close the Wade case quickly. But at the same time, she couldn't do that before she was finished gathering the evidence, assembling it, and considering it carefully. She needed to know what had happened. Not just a guess, but certainty about the cause and manner of death, even if she couldn't point her finger at who the police should arrest.

She dashed the last few steps, though she slowed enough that her shoes would not skid on the tiled floor. She didn't want to go crashing into the desk because she couldn't stop. She grabbed the phone before it could go to voicemail.

"Medical Examiner's Office."

"Medical Examiner's Office?" a woman's voice repeated flatly. "I don't know if I have the right number. Someone asked me to call back? Do you have a Dr. Kirsch?"

"Speaking. Sorry about that. I was running for the phone." Kenzie puffed a little bit. "Whew. Who am I talking to?"

"Delia Rose. DCF. I gather if I'm talking to you, it is not good news."

"Unfortunately, no. Do you remember a child you investigated a report on named Michael Wade?"

"Yes. I remember him. Sick in bed. Had the flu. But that was weeks ago. He didn't die from that."

"No. And I suspect it wasn't the flu that caused him to be in bed when you went to see him."

"What do you think it was?"

"I think he had been beaten. He had a number of old injuries. There was a hospital visit around the time that you made the report. Lacerated liver. They said that he climbed a bookshelf and pulled it over on top of himself."

"A bookshelf. I don't remember seeing any freestanding bookshelves at that house. Everything was built in. Or antique. No bookshelves that I remember."

"Yeah, we don't think that's what really happened."

"No, I doubt it."

Neither of them said anything for a minute. Kenzie cleared her throat.

"So what do you want from me?" the social worker asked eventually. She was tough, ready to move on. Nothing like the tenderhearted Moriah Wright who had cried and blamed herself for Michael's death.

"I was just hoping for your impressions of the home. Things that might not have made it into the report. You have to put anything concrete in there, but your own feelings and instincts, even though they may be just as important, do not necessarily make it to paper."

"I figured there was something there." Kenzie pictured Rose as a square-jawed bulldog of a woman. Fierce. Someone who had seen the worst of humanity and was still sticking it out. "It was the second report, and you don't usually get two reports on a family unless something is going on. That doesn't mean you can prove it. And people do make reports just to be vindictive. But two calls on the same child within a few months of each other... and it wasn't someone who had any skin in the game. Not someone who wanted custody or was interested in one of the parties involved. Sometimes if a woman doesn't want her love interest's kid around, she'll make a little call to DCF to stir things up and make people suspicious..."

"But you didn't see that in this case."

"The reports came from two different parties. I figured there was probably a reason for that. Wouldn't you?"

Kenzie nodded, the phone to her ear. "Yes, I would be suspicious."

"The nanny was the primary caregiver. Mother not so interested. Father was not present when I visited, and I was told he was not there very often. I made a couple of phone calls to him. He answered me, but kept canceling appointments for me to go see him. Something important came up that he had to handle. Big corporate. Politics. He was oh-so-important. Like trying to nail down Jell-o."

Kenzie laughed at the expression. That described a lot of the lawyer and political types that she had dealt with in the past. They were slippery, that was for sure.

"But eventually, you managed to meet with him?"

"Eventually, I gave up. He wasn't at home. I talked to him several times. No red flags that I could find and another report had not been made since we had visited. Eventually... I just issued my report."

"And you didn't see anything in particular that worried you?"

"No. Nothing that I could put in a report. Father was absent, but responsive. If he wasn't there, he couldn't be hurting the kid. He was sick in bed, but appeared to be properly taken care of. All of the expected precautions were in place. He was well-nourished. Had someone beside the bed watching him, which honestly, most kids do not have when they are sick, even at that age. Parents will put them down in the crib and check back every so often to make sure they are still breathing and haven't developed a fever or a rash. Sleep is the best thing, and most parents do not have the resources to hover over the kid for a day or two without a break."

"Did you check out the bathroom attached to the nursery?"

"Nope. What was in the bathroom?"

"A lot of painkillers."

"Well, that's not that unusual. Kids get into things. Fall and hurt themselves. Teething and need something for their gums. Sore and irritable after vaccinations. The doctor suggests a certain painkiller, so the caregiver buys a bottle on the way home. They don't bother to check what they already have at home or ask the doctor if they can give him something else."

"Yeah. It's certainly not a smoking gun. But the child had multiple emergency room visits and the postmortem x-rays show a lot of previously broken bones."

"We didn't find any record of hospital visits. There was a family doctor, but he didn't see the boy very often. He hadn't had any occasion to notice anything suspicious."

"The nanny took him, admitted him under her name."

Rose made a disgusted noise. "So now you know there was abuse. No one covers up an emergency room visit unless there is something to hide. A pattern of injuries."

"Yeah."

"The nanny knew that he was being hurt. Did Mom?"

"I assume she did. Michael's injuries were quite severe, both when he had to go to the emergency room and at his death. I don't see how any parent could not be aware."

"She could be the abuser."

"Yes. That's one possibility."

"You favor someone else?"

"Not favor… but there are other possibilities. The father. The nanny."

"Was the father home at the time of his death? It didn't seem like he was around very often."

"Yes, he was. And I think… at least some of those trips away from home were fictional. I think he was home most of the time. At least during the evenings. I don't think he was really traveling or putting out fires or whatever he told you."

"Abusers lie," Rose admitted philosophically. "You can't expect people to tell you the truth. He's an accomplished liar if that was all made up."

"Politicians," Kenzie said with a shrug.

"Yeah. Professional liars."

38

It wasn't until evening that Kenzie had time to read what was in the news about the tragic death of Cash Wade's son. She figured by the time she finally got to it, things would be fairly well-developed. News traveled fast. Especially bad news. Speculation ran rampant and the juicier, the better.

She hoped that it wouldn't be too bad. But if Dr. Wiltshire had already seen it and was worried about it, then it wasn't just a whisper. As soon as she typed the name Cash Wade, the window filled with news stories, social network discussions, and every other form of news she could think of. The story had been picked up by print papers, radio, and TV.

"What's up?" Zachary asked, when he saw Kenzie leaning forward to sort through the headlines to figure out where to start.

"Cash Wade. He is all over the internet."

"Oh? What's going on?" Zachary typed it in on his own computer, and whistled, shaking his head. "Is Cash Wade a suspect in the death of his son? What is the ME covering up? Where was Cash when his son died? Tragic accident or foreseeable tragedy?"

"Yeah," Kenzie agreed. "Wow, this is really exploding."

"The conspiracy theories are taking off," Zachary observed, scrolling down farther and looking quickly through headlines. He might have difficulty digesting long-form articles—his learning disabilities caused him significant problems—but scanning through headlines and boxes filled with videos and conversation threads was right up his alley. He was a big-picture guy and would be quick to pick up on any patterns or anomalies. "Is it a government cover-up? Is Michael Wade really dead? Insider reports that his body never arrived at the ME's office."

"Really?" Kenzie laughed in disbelief. "I think they'd better find a better insider."

"Apparently, Dr. Wiltshire's broken arm is probably the result of him not complying with the orders to hush the whole thing up. Either that, or he fought off ninjas armed with nunchucks who broke in to steal the body."

"Broken hand," Kenzie corrected, chuckling. "He won't tell me how he broke it. I would think that if it was ninjas, he would have told me about it!"

"He's keeping things from you. It's a big conspiracy. They beat him into submission."

"Well, that's one secret he's kept very well."

Zachary was quiet for a few minutes as they paged through the different reports and clicked from one article to another.

"Not good for Cash," he murmured after a while. "Financial trouble. Infidelity. Rumors of government corruption."

"No wonder things were stressful at home. How long has this been going on?"

Zachary shrugged with one shoulder, looking at her for an instant and then back at his screen. "There's no telling if any of it is actually true. It could have been going on for months or years, or be a complete falsehood."

"True," Kenzie agreed. There were bound to be all kinds of rumors once people started to ask questions about whether Cash had been involved in his son's death. There would be all kinds of speculation that was utterly untrue from people who didn't even know him or his family. "Do you think you can sort out which rumors have some basis in fact?"

Zachary grinned. He was always happy to put his expertise to use in one of her cases. Just like he was happy to call on her when there was some insight she could provide for one of his. Their mutual interest in solving puzzles had been one of the things that had pulled them together. Zachary wasn't one to shy away from the more graphic medical information that Kenzie could provide, and Kenzie had come to admire Zachary's investigative ability when it came to internet searches, background checks, finding patterns, and seeing the things that no one else did. His obsessive nature was a benefit in the investigative field.

"Sure," he agreed, "I can dig into this. But your police investigators will already be on top of it."

"I'm sure they will. But they're not you. And they won't share any information with me that they don't think directly relates to Michael's death."

Zachary nodded, his eyes intent on his screen as he rapidly typed in searches, popping open a new tab with each one. She probably shouldn't have given him an assignment in the evening. There would be no more conversation as he dove deep into the research project, and it might keep him awake far into the night. She should have waited until morning to ask.

39

Kenzie's phone rang and, knowing that Zachary's attention would be otherwise occupied for the rest of the evening, Kenzie looked at the screen to see who was calling. Walter. She sighed. Did she really want to talk to him again so soon? But she tried to take Dr. B's advice to heart and not make talking to him a big deal. She could have a short conversation without it taking too much energy, keep it light, and feel good about having regular contact with him. The less of an "event" it was, the better. She pasted a smile on her face and swiped to answer.

"Hi, Dad."

"MacKenzie. Glad to catch you, honey. I just wanted to check in and see how you were doing." His question trailed off on a tentative note.

"Fine, Dad. What's up?"

"I just know there has been a bunch of publicity around this case of yours. I imagine you're getting a lot of phone calls. And then the way it's blowing up on social media, you might be upset..."

Because they were accusing her of incompetence or being involved in a conspiracy or cover-up. That made sense. She could see how he would be worried about her.

"Oh, no. I'm fine. I don't invest too much energy into what the internet trolls are saying. You know how they say you can't please everyone all the time?"

"Sure."

"There are some people you can't please any of the time. They'll always find something wrong with what you are doing. And these trolls don't know anything about me. They're just making stuff up for their own entertainment. Who cares what they have to say?"

"Ah. Well, that's a healthy attitude to have. Good for you. Young people today can get so invested in their online image."

Kenzie was amused that he thought of her as a young person. But of course, in his mind, she was still a kid. His kid. She would never catch up to him and be a peer. She would always be less experienced and need to be protected and sheltered.

"I'm not one to worry about my online image," Kenzie assured him. "I stay in touch with close friends, but I don't live online."

"Well, I hope you'll have this case cleared up soon. It must be stressful for you."

"It shouldn't be too much longer. I have written most of what I need to. There are just a few missing pieces I would like to fill in. If we can."

She might never know the exact circumstances of Michael's death. As far as she knew, the police were still being blocked from getting a warrant to search the rest of the Wade household, even just the floor Michael had apparently been dropped from. That meant they might never have the full crime scene details that would help inform Kenzie's report. More unknowns than she would like.

But if the police could not get into the house again, or even if they could get into the house but everything had been sanitized, they could not identify exactly where Michael had been killed or gather any more forensic evidence. Kenzie would have to be satisfied with what she had.

"I assume there is a reason you haven't issued it yet?" Walter prodded. "I take it that means that it wasn't just a child falling from a balcony, as has been reported."

"You know I can't share any of that with you."

"Oh, no, of course not," he agreed heartily. "I wouldn't expect you to share any details with me. From your report not being issued, and the chatter online and offline, I'm deducing there is more to it than that. Maybe someone in the household is lying. Maybe someone was complicit in his death. Just negligence, or more...?"

"Mmm." Kenzie didn't give him any indication of whether he was on the right track or not. It wasn't any of his business. He could speculate all he wanted to, but she wouldn't give him the information he wanted. If the congressman, governor, or one of Walter's other cronies had asked him to do damage assessment or control, they would have to be disappointed.

"Your mother reminded me that Cash is married to Terri-Lyn, that girl you used to go to school with. Michael was her son."

"Yes. That was a bit of a shock. I guess Mom knew right away, but I didn't even remember hearing anything about the wedding. I was out of the country. And Terri-Lyn and I had drifted apart."

She had never told either of her parents about the prank, and hadn't known it was Terri-Lyn. As far as they knew, Terri-Lyn's and Kenzie's estrangement was solely due to the fact that they no longer ran in the same circles. They had gone to school together and, when school had ended, they didn't have the same opportunities to see each other.

"I think we went to the wedding," Walter said vaguely. "Your mother and I."

"Did you? Well, that was nice of you. Was there anything else, Dad? Things are going okay with you?"

"Oh, yes. Certainly. Couldn't be better. Just thinking... I'm sure you want to get this case off your desk as soon as possible. Maybe it would be best to leave some questions unanswered. But that's just me worrying about my girl. You know how parents are."

"Sure. I've got to go. I think Zachary is calling me, so—"

"How *is* Zachary? I know it's getting later in the year, the days are getting shorter and that affects him."

"It isn't so much the shorter days as just Christmas itself. So far, he's doing great." She glanced over at Zachary, expecting that he would still be deep in his data, completely unaware of her conversation beside him. But he was watching her curiously.

"Are the two of you considering children? It's a big step, I know, but you're not getting any younger."

Kenzie opened her mouth, and no words came out. She was shocked that he had asked. Lisa sometimes hinted about grandchildren, but Walter usually stayed out of her private life.

"Uh…"

"I'm sorry, MacKenzie. I know that's taboo. I shouldn't be asking. It's totally up to you. I have just been thinking, with this case, about your friend Terri-Lyn having a child. I don't know whether it is something you are considering."

"I don't know, Dad. Not now."

"Okay." His voice took on a lighter note. "None of my business. I won't ask again."

He was a good man, and he cared about her, her relationship with Zachary, and her plans for the future. Even if it was irritating to have him poking his nose into her business and checking up on the Wade case, she knew he had her best interests at heart.

"Love you, Dad. Take care."

"You too, sweetie."

He hung up. Kenzie lowered her phone to her lap. Zachary was still watching her out of the corner of his eye.

"What's Walter up to?"

"I'm not sure whether it is personal interest or doing damage control for Congressman Wade. Or both mixed together. You know how he is. When he gets his teeth into something, he doesn't let it go."

"He was asking about me?" Zachary asked.

"Uh… yeah. He often does. Wants to make sure that everything is good between us. He wants me to be happy, and part of that is…"

"Me being happy," he finished. "Keeping you happy."

She shrugged. "They know about your depression. You've been open about that."

He nodded. As hard as it was to let people know how much he

struggled, he was trying to push back against the stigma of mental illness by talking about it. Bringing it out into the light rather than making it a shameful secret.

"Yeah," he agreed quickly. "I just... it's a little disconcerting to hear people talking about me."

"I thought you were still focused on that," she nodded at his computer. "I should have put it on speaker and let the two of you talk to each other directly. I don't mean to treat you like... an object, like you're not even in the room."

"No, it's okay. Being open is being open. I wouldn't care if you were talking about me... getting a sunburn or not liking brussels sprouts. Why should talking about my depression be any different?"

"But I wouldn't talk about other medical issues with him. So there is a difference."

Zachary nodded, scratching his jaw thoughtfully. He looked back at his computer. "Something to think about. Maybe talk to Dr. B about what she thinks."

"If I've crossed a boundary line, it's okay to tell me. Then I know better for next time."

"I don't think so. Discomfort doesn't necessarily mean that you did anything wrong. It might just be something I need to get used to. Maybe because deep down I still feel like I have to cover it up. I don't know."

"Well... I'll try to be more sensitive about it. Let me know how you feel... when you figure it out."

He chuckled at himself, cheeks pink. "Yeah. One day I'll have this all sorted out."

"You *are* feeling pretty good right now, aren't you?" Kenzie asked. "I mean... maybe you're uncomfortable because I think you're fine when you're not. Or because I told someone that you were, and I was wrong."

"No. I'm pretty good right now," he echoed her words. "Watchful... because I don't know when it will hit. But still in a good place for now."

"Good. You can tell me if you're worried about it. Or if things start to... get dark."

"I will."

Kenzie swallowed, a hot lump in her throat. There was nothing like thinking of Zachary's pain to get her choked up. Each year, she hoped he would be able to manage the Christmas season better. With the last med change, maybe this would be the year.

40

Kenzie wanted to have another chat with the nanny. She knew a lot more now than she had the last time they had talked, and she wanted to confront Sylvia with some of the facts and hoped that she would break down and give Kenzie the scoop on what was going on in the household. If she were the one who had been abusing Michael, maybe she would confess. That was a long shot, but she still felt like she would get more information from Sylvia now that she had completed the autopsy and talked to Terri-Lyn.

She looked up Sylvia's number and tried reaching her cell phone. No answer. She continued with her administrative work, reviewing the papers Dr. Wiltshire had signed the day before. Each time she finished a batch of files or discrete task, she tried Sylvia's number again. After several calls, it became clear that Sylvia was not going to answer. She was probably avoiding Kenzie, either because of her own guilt or because she, like Terri-Lyn, didn't want to chance being overheard by Cash. Or by Terri-Lyn, for that matter.

Kenzie switched tactics and tried the main house number. It was answered after two rings.

"Wade residence," a woman's voice said sharply.

"This is Dr. Kirsch," Kenzie said. "Is Sylvia around? I'd like to speak with her for a few minutes."

There was silence for a moment. Then the woman spoke again. "This is Hilda," she said softly. "You want to talk to Sylvia?"

"Yes. She's not picking up her cell."

"She isn't," Hilda agreed. "I've been trying to reach her."

"*You* are trying to reach Sylvia? She isn't at the house, then?"

"No. I don't know where she is. She didn't tell anyone she was going out."

Kenzie thought she caught a trace of concern in Hilda's quiet voice. "Are you worried? When did she go out?"

"I don't know. Sometime last night, maybe? Or during the day yesterday? No one is sure. She didn't tell anyone. She just seems to have disappeared."

"Has that ever happened before?"

"Oh, no," Hilda was emphatic. "Sylvia has always been very responsible. She is the first one who will get after a new staff member for not keeping us informed on his schedule. We can't function efficiently if people don't communicate."

"Right," Kenzie agreed. "And Sylvia has always done that?"

"Yes, of course."

"What about when she took Michael to the hospital? Did she tell you what she was doing then?"

Hilda didn't answer at first. Then a faint, "What?"

"If she thought it was important to keep everyone informed about where she was and what she was doing, then you must have known what she had planned when she took Michael to the hospital."

"No. I don't know what you're talking about," Hilda said unconvincingly.

"Was Sylvia the one who hurt him?"

"Doctor… I don't know where you are getting any of this." Her voice turned crisp. "I'm afraid Sylvia isn't here at the moment. You'll have to call back another time."

"Is someone listening in?" Kenzie guessed.

"No. I have work to do. I don't have time to go on a wild goose chase."

"Are you really worried about Sylvia, or was that just made up?"

Hilda paused, and was nearly whispering when she answered. "Yes, of course I am. But there's nothing you can do about it."

"I can. I'll have someone over there to track her down right away. You're concerned about her welfare, right?"

"Well… yes. Of course. She's never done anything like this before."

"And she could be in trouble. She might have had a heart attack out there on the grounds in some isolated area no one walks through very often. You've checked her room to ensure she's not… passed out on her bed?"

"She's not in her room. I did check." Hilda cleared her throat nervously. "I don't go into other staff members' rooms. I've never intruded on Sylvia's life before. But… I was worried when she didn't answer her phone."

"Okay. Hang in there. I'll get someone out there right away."

Kenzie called Baker and found her and Tuttle together. A tap of Baker's speaker button and Kenzie was talking to them both. "We need a welfare check out at the Wade residence. Sylvia Arnold, the nanny, is missing."

"According to who?" Tuttle demanded sharply.

"Hilda, the housekeeper. I was trying to reach Sylvia on cell and, when that didn't work, I tried the house phone, and Hilda said that Sylvia is missing. She disappeared sometime yesterday or this morning. Hilda has been trying to get her too. But she isn't anywhere to be found. And she's never done that before. She's always told everyone else how they have to let them know if they're going out and for how long."

"She's not just a short-term employee," Baker said before Tuttle could speak. "She's been there for how long, Dr. Kirsch?"

"Since Cash was a baby. That puts it at what, forty years?"

"That does sound serious," Tuttle admitted.

"She could have had a heart attack and be somewhere on the grounds."

"Or she might have rabbited if she knows something about this case that she is not willing to tell."

"I think that's less likely," Kenzie said cautiously. "But I suppose it is possible. I just don't see her leaving after so long. She must be due some kind of pension, even if she decided to quit because there are no more children to look after."

"She must have done something else between Cash being a child and Michael," Baker pointed out. "She didn't have to quit just because Michael is dead. There was other work for her to do."

Kenzie nodded her agreement. "She's right."

"We don't need to go ourselves," Tuttle reasoned. "We can send a patrol officer over for a welfare check."

"They won't let a patrol officer in the door and he wouldn't know how to insist," Kenzie warned. "When Cash or someone tells him that he can't come in and that Sylvia is fine, he'll back down. Besides, this could be your chance to get back into the house and look around."

"Hmm." Tuttle considered this. "We won't be able to do a thorough search like we could if we got the warrant. But we could at least get a peek at the nanny's room and any others close by or places Sylvia might normally have spent her time. If she was involved in Michael's death, there could be evidence in her room."

"That's what I'm thinking. You can at least see what is in plain sight. And if she isn't around and you are concerned there has been foul play, then…"

"Then we can get a warrant for a more thorough search of her rooms to collect trace evidence. Which, you never know, could lead us to some answers about Michael."

"Exactly," Kenzie agreed.

"Okay, we'll get on this. Thanks for the call."

"Any chance I could tag along?"

"Wait a moment."

There was a click, and Kenzie thought she had been put on hold so they could discuss it privately. After a few minutes, she heard Baker's voice again. "We'll meet you over there. If they object to you being there, we can't really justify it under a welfare check. But if they let all of us in without question, then you're there with permission."

"Okay," Kenzie agreed. It was as good as she was going to get, since she had no right to be there for a welfare check as a member of the medical examiner's office.

"So you might end up sitting in your car outside," Tuttle said, in case Kenzie hadn't understood the parameters. "If they say no, we're not going to try to get you in."

"I understand."

"Okay. See you there. We'll be out of here within ten minutes."

Kenzie glanced over her desk and figured she could also tidy up and be on her way in that amount of time. "See you there."

41

Hilda must have been watching for the police to arrive, because she opened the door without their having to knock. Her eyes flicked over Tuttle and Baker, and she apparently recognized them without their offering their names or badges again.

"Come in," she invited. She looked at Kenzie and, at first, blocked her from following the two detectives. "Why are *you* here?"

"I wanted to talk to Sylvia as part of my investigation. If she's here…"

"She isn't. I told you that."

Kenzie waited. She really didn't want to go back to her car while the detectives searched the property for some sign of the nanny.

Eventually, Hilda stepped back and motioned Kenzie in.

Kenzie nodded. "Thank you."

Hilda nodded. Her face was impassive, a calm, emotionless exterior cultivated over many years. But she gave Kenzie's arm a squeeze as she went by. "I really am worried about her."

"Yeah. Me too."

Hilda led the three of them to Sylvia's quarters. Rather than being on the second floor where most of the staff quarters were, her room was on the third floor with the family's rooms. The nanny slept close to her ward, naturally. They wouldn't want him disturbing his mother and father if he got up at night.

Her suite was therefore next door to Michael's now unoccupied room. Tuttle knocked on the door sharply and called Sylvia's name and, when she didn't answer, opened the door and entered.

Kenzie looked around. The room was warm and inviting. All of the personal touches that she would have expected from a woman who had been living in the household for decades. It was not the sterile room of a hotel. The suite was comprised of a sitting room and a bedroom, and boasted a full bathroom with a luxurious jetted tub. The sitting room contained a few comfortable pieces of furniture and built-in shelving that held classic books, as well as pictures of the children Sylvia had cared for, and a number of homemade trinkets fashioned by inexpert little hands. Bowls and picture frames, and a little set of pudgy barnyard animals made of lumpy clay.

After a brief look around, they headed into the bedroom. As Hilda had already looked, they knew they were not going to find Sylvia curled up in the bed, in either severe emotional distress or having something seriously wrong with her medically. Kenzie immediately checked the floor on the far side of the bed, which was not in sight of the door, to make sure she hadn't fallen off and been missed. There was no sign of her.

The bed looked comfortable, covered with a homemade quilt and several throw pillows with cross-stitched proverbs. It was neatly made, so chances were that Sylvia had not left or been taken in the middle of the night. Somehow, that didn't make Kenzie feel much better. There were more photos, with one of Michael prominently displayed on her bedside table.

She had an antique writing desk with pigeonholes, amply supplied with pretty notepaper and pens. Did she have a family of her own that she wrote to? She hadn't mentioned anyone, but that didn't mean she hadn't raised children of her own between Cash and Michael. There were pictures of more children Kenzie couldn't identify.

Baker opened the closet door. It was arranged neatly, though a couple of things had fallen off their hangers and not been picked back up. Baker pointed silently to a narrow space on the shelf that was unoccupied. Tuttle strolled over and had a look. He was the only one of them who could see the top of the shelf without a step stool.

"No dust," he said. "Something has been removed recently."

A suitcase? It was the right size and shape, and Kenzie didn't see any other luggage. A few large shoulder bags, but nothing for overnights. Nothing that might have held a couple of changes of clothing.

Kenzie stayed back, looking around, her eyes open for anything that might belong to Michael or indicate that he had been in Sylvia's room. But why would he be? There would be no reason for her to bring him into her rooms. They had everything he needed in the nursery, including the rocking chair where Sylvia sat watching him when he was sick.

The detectives went quickly through the room, looking for anything that was obviously missing, anything that was out of place, or might hint at foul play. The room was clean. If Michael or Sylvia had been hurt there, the perpetrator had left nothing behind to give him away. Maybe he had shed hairs or skin flakes. But without an obvious crime scene, there was no point in looking for microscopic evidence that could have been brought in on Sylvia's clothes or person from anywhere or anyone in the house. Cash's or Terri-Lyn's DNA in the room would mean nothing.

Once they had finished a cursory search of the rooms, the detectives spoke to Hilda, who hovered in the hallway waiting for them to finish.

"You want to come in, ma'am? Tell us if you notice anything missing?" Tuttle suggested.

Hilda walked in, both reluctant and curious. Peeking in before stepping over the threshold. "I don't go into Sylvia's rooms," she said. "So I wouldn't know if anything was missing or out of place."

"If you could just take a quick look around. You never know. Something might strike you."

She nodded and walked haltingly around the suite. Her cheeks were red, embarrassed to be there, obviously considering Sylvia's rooms forbidden territory.

"It all looks normal. Maybe a suitcase. I wouldn't know what was missing from her clothes. She wouldn't have left anything on the floor like that," she indicated the clothes that had fallen off the hangers in the closet. "Did you do that?"

"No. They were like that when we arrived."

"She wouldn't have left them like that."

"Bag them," Tuttle told Baker. "I doubt we'll get any trace from them, but you never know. There may be something significant about them."

Baker complied, putting each item of clothing into a separate paper bag and carefully labeling and signing each one.

"You think she just left?" Hilda asked, looking around and shaking her head. "She wouldn't have just left. Sylvia would not have left without a word."

"What if she was upset? What if something scared her or made her feel like she couldn't stay here?" Tuttle suggested.

"I just... no, I can't see it. She would never have done that. And..." Hilda looked awkward. "I know Michael wasn't here anymore, but she loved Mr. Wade too. Not romantically. Nothing like that. She raised him, though. She was his nanny his whole life, and she wouldn't leave him. I just can't see her doing that."

"What if she was afraid of him?" Baker asked.

"Why would she be afraid of him?"

None of them gave any explanation. Hilda looked around at the three of them. "Sylvia never had any reason to be afraid of Mr. Wade."

"He was never angry at her? I understand things have been pretty tense around here lately. Mr. Wade was under a lot of pressure." Baker's voice was quiet, non-accusatory. "It was only natural that he might have gotten angry if he was under pressure. People snap. Say things they shouldn't. Mr. Wade was a passionate person."

"Angry at Sylvia? I don't think I ever heard him say a cross word about her in all the time I've been here, and that's a long time. She said once what a hellion he'd been when he was younger, but that was when he was a teenager or young man. I doubt he'd ever raised his voice to her since then."

"Did she say how she had handled that? When he'd been a problem as a teen?"

Hilda shook her head. "I'm sure I don't know. I've seen her with teens. She has a way. She's firm, but unbending. They eventually listen."

"How *has* Mr. Wade been lately?" Tuttle asked, stepping closer to Hilda and looking down at her, being a little more intimidating than Kenzie thought was necessary. "If you listen to the news, he'd been going through a lot of stuff the last few months. I assume he had been… difficult to be around when things were not going well."

"I wouldn't talk about my employers, detective."

"Shouting? Violent?" Tuttle raised his voice as if demonstrating. "Was he aggressive? Toward you? Toward his wife? Michael?"

She stepped back from him. "He was not violent," she insisted.

"Did he fight with his wife?"

"Every man fights with his wife."

"Had it been getting worse? How did she react when she found out about his latest affair?"

"I don't know what you're talking about."

Tuttle spoke slowly and clearly as if she might not have understood him the first time. "When Mrs. Wade found out he'd been catting around again. She was upset, wasn't she? Did she threaten to leave him?"

"No. She wouldn't do that."

"Because she would lose her position if she did? Lose all of that money? And what about Michael? Would she lose him too, if they divorced?"

"They wouldn't divorce."

"Why? Because there was a prenup?"

"Of course there was a prenup. Everyone has a prenup. It would be stupid not to. But if he was the one who was having an affair, then he would be penalized, not her."

"So maybe she did threaten to leave him. To take all of that money. They've probably been stripping the paint off the walls with their arguments lately."

Hilda shook her head, but it wasn't very convincing. They *had* been arguing, Kenzie deduced. Maybe Terri-Lyn hadn't threatened to leave him, but they were arguing. And where had Michael been when they were fighting? And how did Sylvia fit into it all? What had happened to her? Had she left on her own?

"Does Sylvia have a car, Hilda?" Baker asked.

Hilda bit her lip. "No, she didn't drive anymore. There was no need for her to have one."

"How did she get around when she wanted to leave the property?"

"The chauffeur or someone else would take her. Or we would call for car service from town if no one else could take her."

"And did she call the car service yesterday or today?"

Hilda hesitated, then shook her head. So she had been concerned enough that she had already checked.

"She packed a bag but didn't call for a car service?" Tuttle challenged. "Where did she go? How did she get there?"

"I don't know."

"Did anyone drive her?"

"No… everybody says they did not."

"Are all of the cars accounted for? She didn't 'borrow' anyone else's?"

Hilda shook her head. "Of course not. She wouldn't do that. I told you, she didn't drive anymore. She wouldn't take someone else's car."

"Then how did she leave?"

"I don't know." Hilda's eyes were wide as she continued to shake her head at the questions. "I don't know where she could have gone."

Tuttle looked at Baker. "We'd better start a search of the grounds. Can you give us permission to search?" He addressed the question to Hilda.

"I'm just the housekeeper. I can't give you permission."

"Then get Mr. Wade or whoever can give us permission and find out. Impress upon him the seriousness of the situation. If he doesn't give us permission, we will be forced to get a warrant, and I will not go easy on him after being prevented from getting a warrant the past few days. If harm has come to Sylvia Arnold, and he impedes this investigation, there will be consequences. He won't be able to talk his way out of it this time."

Hilda nodded jerkily and left to find Mr. Wade. Kenzie braced herself for the explosion when he found out that the cops were back and trying to get permission to search the property yet again. And this time, it would be a broader search. The whole house. All of the outbuildings. All of the surrounding land where a woman or a body could be hidden.

42

Surprisingly, there was no explosion. And it wasn't because Cash Wade was away and therefore couldn't rage at them. Kenzie had been wondering whether they would be able to talk Terri-Lyn into a search if Cash were away. Terri-Lyn wouldn't care about Sylvia as much as Cash would. And there was also the possibility that she would refuse to do anything he hadn't directly sanctioned, forcing the police to get a warrant issued.

Instead, Mr. Wade arrived with quiet, measured tread on the thick plush carpeting. Rather than being furious that they had returned and were again demanding the right to do a further search, he looked worried. There was an N-shaped frown line between his brows.

"Hilda said that Sylvia is missing?" Cash asked, looking into her rooms from the hallway as if they might be mistaken and she was just sitting there waiting for him to show up. "How could she be missing?"

A look had flashed between Baker and Tuttle. "That's an excellent question, Mr. Wade," Baker said. Maybe they sensed he would be more amenable to dealing with a woman, more likely to be soft and sympathetic. "No one seems to know of any plans she had to leave.

She didn't call a car service. No one drove her unless maybe *you* did it without anyone realizing it?"

"No. No, I haven't taken her anywhere. She didn't go out very often. No one took her?"

"No. Can you think of anywhere she may have gone?"

"Of course not. She wasn't given to traveling." He seemed stumped. He looked into her rooms again. "She didn't leave a note, maybe?"

"There was no note."

"Her suitcase is missing," Tuttle contributed. "Maybe she decided that in light of everything that has happened, she needed a vacation."

"A vacation?" He sounded incredulous. "No, of course not. *This* was her quiet space, where she went when she needed to get away from it all and relax. She could never be relaxed on a vacation away from her family. She only traveled when she needed to accompany us on a family vacation. That's the only time she ever used her suitcase. Where would she go?" he asked the room.

No one had an answer for him.

"This is crazy," Cash said, raising his voice. "She wouldn't leave me like that!"

Kenzie found it interesting that he didn't enter Sylvia's sitting room. Was it because he thought the police wouldn't let him? It was his own house, and it hadn't been declared a crime scene. Was it because he had been trained to respect his old nanny's private space and didn't dare chance her disapproval?

"Rather than wasting time speculating on where she might have gone," Tuttle said, "Don't you think we had better begin a search? If she's had a heart attack or a stroke, or fallen and broken her hip… she could be lying on the ground somewhere, just praying that someone will find her. Don't you think we'd better look sooner rather than later? We can float all the theories we want later. For now… I think we'd better act."

"Yes," Cash agreed, looking grimly determined. "Yes, by all means. Mobilize the forces. Begin the search." He looked around for someone else to help, maybe thinking that Hilda was still standing by waiting for instructions, but she had not returned after informing him of the situation. Not finding the help he was looking for, Cash pulled out his phone and hit one of his favorite contacts. "Bill. Sylvia is MIA. She might be hurt or... anything. We need to start a search. Get the men together, and start organizing them. The police will be down in a few minutes to give them instructions." He looked at Tuttle and Baker, one eyebrow raised in inquiry.

Tuttle nodded and pulled out his phone to call for backup. They would need a lot of people to search a property that big. It wasn't just the house they would have to worry about. Kenzie thought about wells, septic tanks, and creeks. What places might exist around the property that would make the perfect hiding place for the body of an old woman, especially one as small as Sylvia?

And that was assuming that someone hadn't taken her off the property in the trunk of his car. There were bound to have been a number of people that had come and gone in the last twenty-four hours. They didn't know for sure what time Sylvia had disappeared.

"We'll want dogs," she told Tuttle, as he started to issue orders for the support he would need. "This is a big place."

He nodded his agreement. They had their work cut out for them. He and Baker were not going to just walk around the basement or the backyard and find her body hidden under a tarp. It was going to take a massive manhunt to find out what had happened to Sylvia Arnold.

Kenzie still secretly harbored the hope that they would find Sylvia alive. Maybe she had managed to talk her way into a lift into town. Maybe she had called for a ride-share service nobody thought she knew how to use. Maybe she'd had a medical emergency and was waiting desperately for someone to rescue her.

But Kenzie had a bad feeling that they would not find her in time.

It was probably already too late.

With Cash behind the search this time, there was no push-back from the police department or any of the political figures who had been making their influence known over the past few days. Quite the opposite. There was a constant stream of municipal and state police, as well as the FBI, local search and rescue, and every other organization that Kenzie could think of. She didn't envy Tuttle, trying to stay in control and coordinate everyone in the search.

She worried about evidence being trampled outside, about the woman's scent being contaminated by all of the searchers, but when the search dogs arrived a couple of hours later, they went straight to work.

They had already checked the septic tank and there were no wells, so two of Kenzie's predicted body dump sites had been eliminated.

But one of the outbuildings, an old bunkhouse that hadn't been used by the staff for years, had a root cellar with a loading passage behind the house. One of those mysterious doors set into the ground that Kenzie remembered seeing as a child in some old farmhouses. A bulkhead door.

"Medical Examiner's Office," Tuttle announced, as he escorted Kenzie through the small knot of law enforcement officers and staff. "Everyone step aside, please."

Kenzie could hear Cash bellowing like a bull, mourning the loss of his beloved nanny and threatening retribution on whoever had taken her from him. She hoped he had not seen her there, but had merely been given minimal details of what they had found.

That she was dead. That someone had hidden her body.

That they would find whoever it was and demand justice.

The keys to the lock on the door had probably been lost years before or the lock rusted shut. The killer had apparently made no attempt to unlock it, but had simply used a crowbar to pop it open.

Sylvia's small body lay at the bottom of the stairs, dumped unceremoniously through the doorway rather than carried down and set on the floor. Kenzie deduced she had been dumped by someone who didn't care about her. Someone who loved her would have taken her down the steps, stretched her out on the floor, arranged her head and her hands. She wouldn't just be splayed there, half on the floor and half on the stairs, with limbs flung in every direction.

Kenzie looked around the frame of the door before taking a step inside. She had the small scene-of-crime kit she kept in her car. Not as robust as what she would have brought if she had come from the office, but it was sufficient for what she needed to do before authorizing the removal of the body. Booties for her feet so that she wouldn't track in trace evidence embedded in the treads of her shoes. Purple gloves on her hands so she could touch the body. A stethoscope to confirm death if necessary.

Kenzie skirted the body at the bottom of the stairs and did her job stoically, walling off thoughts of the living, breathing woman she had talked to earlier in the week. The woman who had taken her precious charge to the emergency room. Who had sat and rocked beside the boy's bed when he had been hurt and sick, comforting him all night long.

She confirmed death. No heartbeat or respiration. Body cold and stiff, in full rigor. Kenzie bagged Sylvia's hands in case she had managed to scratch her attacker or get any evidence under her nails or between her fingers. She examined the woman for a fatal wound, and found no gunshot or knife wound. Whoever had killed her had been more subtle than that.

Had Sylvia seen it coming? Had she known her attacker? Known that she was going to die?

Kenzie went through the motions of taking a few pictures and looking for any trace evidence on or around the body. She gently lifted Sylvia's shoulder and head from either side to look at her upper back, neck, and head. No obvious injuries.

Was it possible that Sylvia had died naturally? Perhaps had a heart attack or stroke? And someone had been afraid of the police investigating a second death in the home and had hidden her body to cover it up? A second death to investigate would, Kenzie was sure, open up the rest of the house and grounds for a search for evidence in Sylvia's death and anything connecting the two. Kenzie's determination that Michael's death was a homicide rather than an accident would eliminate the possibility that the two deaths were coincidental.

Kenzie walked around the root cellar, looking around for anything else that had been disturbed or added to the scene. There was no weapon, no hastily scrawled note or other evidence that would point them in the direction of the killer.

Not yet. Kenzie would see about that when she looked at the

body back at the morgue. She climbed the steps back out of the cellar and dialed Dr. Wiltshire's cell, hoping he would not be too groggy on painkillers to deal with her.

He had already heard the news from other quarters and answered on the first ring.

"Kenzie. I was told you were already at the scene."

"Yes. I've had a look around. I'm ready to authorize the removal of the body, but I wanted a second opinion." She kept her voice low. "With all of the political stuff surrounding this case, I want to make sure that everything I do is double and triple checked. I don't want any accusations that I've missed anything."

"Of course," he agreed.

"I'll send you some pictures, and you can tell me if you want me to walk you around the crime scene. Or the dump site, to be more accurate."

Dr. Wiltshire made an affirmative noise. Kenzie tapped her screen to gather up the photos she had taken and send them to Dr. Wiltshire. She heard the alert on his end as they were received and waited while he looked through them.

"Not much to see," he grunted.

"No. There isn't."

She gave him a few more seconds to look at them. "Is there anything else you want to see?"

"No. But let's do it anyway, just to cover all bases. Call me back on video chat, and we'll walk the crime scene together once."

"Okay."

Kenzie hung up, then called him back again immediately on video chat. She framed the root cellar door on her screen and, at Dr. Wiltshire's instruction, zoomed close to the damage made by the pry bar. Then she walked down the steps. "I don't think I'll lose the signal, but it may glitch a bit," she warned.

Dr. Wiltshire walked her through the steps she had already completed, making her confirm them or do them again. She turned on her flashlight to walk around the body and the perimeter of the cellar, then retrieved the Alternative Light Source from her death kit and did it again. Various molds fluoresced on the walls, but Kenzie could see no blood spatters or other bodily fluids.

"That's everything," Dr. Wiltshire confirmed. "I can't think of anything that you have missed. Go ahead and release the body for transportation and have the crime techs go over the scene with a fine-toothed comb. George is already on his way over."

Kenzie thanked Dr. Wiltshire for his help and returned to the surface. She nodded at Tuttle, who was maintaining control over the scene. "ME's office releases the body for removal and transport. Our truck should be here soon. The techs can start working."

Tuttle nodded. He looked around the small yard surrounding the bunkhouse. It was unmaintained and overgrown. Kenzie would not have known that there was another outbuilding here, but supposed that anyone who had been working in the house for any length of time would have known about it. She didn't see any litter or footprints left behind by the killer. They had been careful.

"I guess I'll see you at the autopsy," Tuttle said. "You'll hold off until I can get there?"

Kenzie looked at her watch. "It's possible I could fit it in this afternoon, but it would be a squeeze, and all the stars would have to align correctly. Let's not rush it. I'll start in the morning."

"Okay. Works for me. Don't know how long we'll be here. And we'll want to go over everything you have on her," he nodded toward the body, "from your investigation into Michael Wade's murder. Any statements she made, testimony of other witnesses, whatever. We want to make sure everything is shared."

Kenzie nodded.

She noticed that, for the first time, Tuttle had referred to Michael Wade's death as a murder.

43

Kenzie arrived home late, which she knew was not a good thing. It was Friday night. Date night. She had intended to be home in good time. She tried to even get off a little bit early Friday afternoons to make it seem more special for her and Zachary, more like a break, even though she usually worked at least a few hours on Saturday and didn't take the whole weekend off.

Dr. B had suggested that they get out of their comfort zones and visit different venues from where they would normally go to. They both tended to stay home to relax, to cuddle up in front of the TV, which was a fine choice of activities but did not provide as much opportunity for chatting, learning about each other, and opening up. As they visited museums, fairs, and other cultural and tourist sites, they would naturally have more things to discuss, they would broaden their world and have more questions for each other about what they liked or disliked and get to better understand their very different backgrounds.

They had talked about going to an art show today, followed by milkshakes or another treat to make sure they both enjoyed the evening, even if one or both of them hated the show. All this came crowding back to Kenzie as she removed her shoes and outerwear after returning home. She let out a long sigh. It would be hard to raise the energy to do that tonight. She was already wiped out. They would need to eat supper, then spend at least an hour at the art show, and she would probably fall asleep drinking her milkshake. Like one of those funny videos of a toddler face-planting in his mashed potatoes or commuters nodding off on the bus or train, heads tipped back, glasses askew, snores vibrating.

She heard Zachary close his laptop in the living room and the couch springs squeak as he stood up. He walked across the room and smiled at Kenzie as she hung up her jacket.

"Long day for you," he observed.

Kenzie rolled her eyes. "Man, was it ever," she agreed.

"You look beat."

"I am. But," she kept her tone light as if she weren't dreading it, "tonight is date night, and we have plans."

Zachary grimaced. He looked at her and then at the clock. "What if I used a veto tonight?" he asked. "I'm not sure I'm in the mood for an art show and you look ready to collapse. It's not actually supposed to be torture."

Kenzie chuckled. "No, that's not the intention," she agreed. "I *am* tired."

"I think it's too much tonight. If we feel like it, we could try again tomorrow night. Tonight, why don't we just stay home? I know we're supposed to get out to explore the world on date night, but we've been doing really well at that, and I don't think it would hurt our relationship to take a break from it just once."

"We'll get back on track again next week," Kenzie said.

Zachary looked relieved. "Okay. Why don't you have your shower and I'll order us something adventurous for dinner. We can play Truth or Dare to learn more about each other."

They had *never* played Truth or Dare. Kenzie was surprised that Zachary even knew the game. It was a friend or party thing, and he'd not had close friends growing up in foster care. She laughed. "I don't know about Truth or Dare, but I'll take the rest."

"Fair enough."

"And it's not your veto. I agree. It would just be too much tonight."

He nodded cheerfully. "Okay. Off you go. Wash away the day."

Kenzie gave him a salute and headed for the bedroom and en suite bath.

Zachary's "adventurous" dinner turned out to be pizza, one of their old standbys. Kenzie had to admit that she took comfort in the familiar cheese and garlic-laden fare. She felt like she had been stripped bare and wrung out that week. The difficulty of an autopsy on an abused child, finding out she knew the victim's mother, the political pressure, and then the murder of Sylvia had all added up to feel like an overwhelming burden.

But she did her best to put it all aside during her time with Zachary. She asked him about his work and tried to focus on him for a while, giving her more time to unwind before she talked to him about her day. She was feeling much better after her shower, more like a human being, but she was still pretty raw.

The good food and conversation helped.

"Do you think we could go visit Joss this Sunday?" Zachary asked. "Since we were interrupted last week? Or do you need to be at the office catching up on everything? I understand that you might need to put in more hours than usual. Or to take a break and not have to think about going out of town. Dr. Wiltshire being gone during all of this is stressful for you."

He'd been listening.

Kenzie shook her head. "I don't know how things are going to work out this weekend, so don't promise anyone anything. If it works out, we can buzz down there for the day, but not the whole weekend. If not, we'll just push it forward another week."

"Sure." Zachary took a big bite of his garlic cheese bread and asked a question Kenzie didn't catch.

"You want to try that again without a loaf of bread in your mouth?" Kenzie asked, laughing.

He chewed and swallowed, cheeks reddening. "Sorry. That was rude. That habit of grabbing the food I want before anyone else can get it reasserts itself…" He licked his lips and wiped a few crumbs away. "How is Dr. Wiltshire doing?"

"Well, hard to say. I'm not seeing very much of him. But he at least has had his hand surgery. It has an external fixation cage that looks very space-age. But he's still in a lot of pain, trying to balance the painkillers with their side effects so he can get a little bit of productive time in. I'm hoping that in another week, it will at least be healed enough that he can back off on the painkillers and be there to sign documents, approve things, and consult on cases. I can do the autopsies without him, but I'm very slow and have to keep looking things up to make sure I don't miss anything and that it is all well-documented. It's a lot faster with him directing me."

"You'll be releasing your report on Michael Wade soon?"

"Yes. That should cause another explosion in the media. More accusations, gossip, and conspiracy theories."

"There are some interesting rumors about *how* Dr. Wiltshire broke his hand."

Kenzie had another bite of pizza and contemplated this. "Are there. It's interesting because he hasn't told me exactly how he hurt himself. Of course he isn't required to tell anyone. It's his own business. But still… it is strange that he wouldn't. We work together. I'm a doctor. He knows he can trust me. I'm not going to make fun of him or something."

"Maybe the way he broke it was embarrassing."

"What, you mean like 'tripped over my dog' embarrassing, or 'fell off the bed during sex' embarrassing?"

Zachary laughed loudly at that. "Have you ever actually done either of those?"

"I've never broken my hand," Kenzie told him. Which, of course, did not answer the question and kept things interesting.

Zachary continued to chuckle. "Okay, well, I was hearing more along the lines of broken by a bookie he owed money to or slammed it in the car door because he was distracted by a girl walking by."

"He implied that it might have been a golfing accident. I'm not sure how you smash your hand while golfing, but I guess if you swing into a tree or get in someone's way, it would be possible…"

"You can break bones doing anything," Zachary said authoritatively.

"I suppose so. I honestly don't even know if he plays golf. He jokes around about it sometimes, but he hasn't mentioned participating in a tournament, going out with buddies, or coming back on a Monday and telling me about a good score he got on Sunday. Just jokes about how his wife needs him to have a hobby that will keep him from spending too much time at home when he retires."

"Well, golf is one of those hobbies that will eat up hours of time."

Kenzie agreed. "I don't even know for sure if he is married, or if that's just a line he gives me, like a comedian doing stand-up."

She thought about Sylvia's room; all of the pictures around it of Cash, Michael, and other children she had apparently taken care of, whether they were her own, Cash's siblings or cousins, or another family altogether. She might have left the Wade family's service after Cash was too old for a nanny and rejoined them later when Michael was born.

But Terri-Lyn had said that Sylvia had recommended she get pregnant, so she had already been in place before Michael was conceived.

"Dr. Wiltshire doesn't have any pictures of his wife or children on his desk or in his office."

Zachary pursed his lips, thinking about it. "Certainly not a requirement, but it does make me wonder. Does he mention his wife by name? Or any children?"

"No, he always says 'my wife' or 'Mrs. Wiltshire'."

"I would wonder about that too."

He looked like he wanted to say something, but didn't open his mouth and ask. Which, for Zachary, showed great restraint, as he normally blurted whatever came to mind.

"What?"

"I heard that there was some more activity at the Wade residence today. I wondered whether you were involved in that. Or whether you heard anything about it."

"How did you know about that? I don't think a statement has been released."

"No, but I was doing some research on him. You know, checking to see what is true from all the rumors swirling around. And then the story broke that there were all kinds of police at the estate. More than when Michael died. And mentions of other vehicles, including a white van."

Kenzie nodded slowly. George had used the unmarked van for transport, rather than the one painted with the logo for the Medical Examiner's office, trying to be discreet in the transportation of the body. But Zachary suspected the significance of that vehicle. Maybe others had too.

"Yeah. I was back there today."

"And not to investigate Michael's case."

"Well, it is probably related. But no, we weren't back there because of Michael this time."

"Figured."

Kenzie leaned back in her chair and stretched. She should exercise some restraint if she were going to avoid putting on more weight. She was determined to take off what she had put on lately, but that wasn't as easy to do as it seemed like it should be. Especially on stressful days when one of them decided they needed to order comfort food.

"This other death was not Cash Wade," Zachary said, "Or we definitely would have heard about it."

"No. It wasn't Cash."

She gave him a warning look, letting him know she wasn't about to play twenty questions about who it was and the accompanying details. Not when there was so much speculation in the media. Once she had done the autopsy and had something to say, she would release it publicly, and she and Zachary could discuss it.

"He is in a lot of trouble," Zachary commented.

"He is? Because of the rumors?"

"No. Financial is way up there. You wouldn't think it would be a problem for him to support himself with all the wealth he inherited. Or will inherit one day."

"*Will* inherit? I thought that his parents and grandparents were all dead."

"But a lot of what he has was left in trust. So he can only access a certain amount or use it for a certain purpose. That makes it a little bit harder."

"How much financial trouble is he in?"

"There is speculation that he will file for bankruptcy by the end of the year."

"And you think that is true? Not just his detractors trying to make people think he has a problem?"

"His credit rating is pretty bad. He's been defaulting on a lot of loans and payments."

Kenzie shook her head. "I never understood how the wealthy could end up in such trouble. If you have that kind of money, you should be able to pay the bills. If you can't, you need to find a way to cut the bills down."

"Can't disagree with you there. I always thought that if you had enough money to live on, you were set. But from what I have seen... no one is ever satisfied with what they have. They always want to spend more than they have. They're always trying to make more. Win more. Make these deals that are too complicated to understand, to get around paying taxes."

Kenzie nodded.

"Why didn't you end up like that?" Zachary asked curiously. "Your family is very wealthy. You could have lived a life of leisure. Lived like your mom, just going to events and being seen, raising money for causes other than herself. You could have done anything, really, and you decided to be a medical examiner. To work for a living and pay for everything yourself," he gestured to the contents of her modest home, "rather than paying with family money. You could have something much nicer than this and not have to work."

"That didn't really appeal to me. I did it for a while after school... just drifted and went where I felt like going, with the people I felt like going with. But none of them were serious relationships. It wasn't a very fulfilling life."

"And you'd rather be living like this? Working long hours around stinking corpses? Exhausting yourself with a new case because you want to... uncover the truth."

Kenzie smiled widely. "Yes. Exactly."

"You're amazing." He pushed his plate away as well, signaling that he was finished with his meal. "Bridget was just the opposite… working class stock, but she wanted to be rich. She wanted to be elite. Someone like your mom. So she cultivated those friendships…"

"And Gordon."

"And Gordon. He's the one who fulfilled those dreams for her. She was well on her way, just by knowing the right people. She knew what she wanted. And she was willing to… do whatever it took to get it."

Including dumping Zachary when she realized he would not be a part of that picture. He wouldn't fit into that lifestyle, no matter how hard she tried to train him. She had thought that she could take an impressionable, broken man and shape him into what she wanted him to be.

She had not understood that Zachary's depression, PTSD, learning disabilities, and all of his other issues could not just be smoothed over and that he could not be forced to be a different person from who he was. There would always be friction, and he would never fit into the society she had imagined for him.

44

It was Saturday morning, and no one was sleeping in with their families or getting a few holes in on the golf course. Kenzie performed the autopsy, with George on hand to help her with anything physical. Baker and Tuttle watched from the observation room.

The body was fresh, so there wasn't too much of an odor, and the big exhaust fans whisked that away quickly, with fresh air being pumped into the room continuously. A lot nicer than a lot of morgues where the air circulation was neglected. They had tables that were easy to raise and lower with a press of the foot, voice-controlled computer systems. The observation room allowed law enforcement to observe without being underfoot. Their mics were muted unless they needed to ask a question, so Kenzie didn't have to listen to an endless discussion of the previous night's game or a new love interest. She could stay focused on the job at hand and tune everything else out.

She started, as usual, with a gross examination of the body, top to toe, front and back, noting the patient's height, weight, age, build, identifying marks, and anything else appropriate, followed by a catalog of external injuries. Sylvia's body was unremarkable. She was in good shape for a woman of her age. No surgery scars. Nothing to indicate that she'd had heart surgery. Although angioplasty would not leave any scarring on the chest. Kenzie carefully checked the usual incision sites for an angioplasty catheter and found none.

There were a few bruises on the body, but nothing of particular concern. Older people often bruised easily, and bruises on knees, shins, and forearms were very common. Kenzie didn't see any that would have suggested restraint or a fight.

She examined the eyes and ears carefully.

"Some minor petechial hemorrhages in the eyes," Kenzie observed, focusing the camera to take a few pictures for the file and for the detectives to see. "While this can be a marker for asphyxiation, it is not always present in asphyxiation cases and can also be caused by things like coughing, crying, or vomiting. We all observed Mrs. Arnold crying recently."

Nothing that caught her interest in the ears. They looked healthy. No recently ruptured eardrums. No significant scarring.

Kenzie studied the throat with the magnifying glass and under the alternative light source. She couldn't see any bruising. She had hoped there would be, providing her with a quick answer. She took x-rays of the head, throat, and torso, looking for any sign of violence. Despite the lack of bruising, she had still thought she might find a broken hyoid. At first, nothing was notable on the x-rays, then Kenzie spotted a hairline fracture.

"Here on the sternum," she pointed out the fracture line to George, who moved the mouse point around and clicked several times to mark it. "Fractured sternum can occur when someone is given CPR. We know that none of the police at the scene gave her CPR. She was already long dead by the time she was found. Did the killer try to revive her with CPR? Was it an accident rather than homicide and someone hid the body afterward simply because they were afraid they would be blamed or it would bring the family more bad press?"

There was no answer. She wasn't actually expecting one, she was just posing questions that came to her as she proceeded with the autopsy. She examined the ribs closely, figuring that if the sternum was broken, it wouldn't be unexpected for one or two ribs to be as well. She found one more hairline fracture on a rib, which George marked on the x-ray for her.

"Nothing of concern on the skull or neck in the x-rays, so I am going to go to the torso next, see what kind of damage there may be around those fractures. Looking for bruising, which we can date, or any damage to the soft tissues or organs."

She performed the Y-incision and opened up the chest and abdominal cavity. "There is some bruising, but it is minimal. Perimortem. Likely occurred very close to the time of death."

"But not the cause of death," Baker checked from the observation room.

"I haven't yet established cause of death, so I can't comment on whether it is related."

She continued with a dissection of the heart and then removal of the lungs. She noted the weight of the lungs on her autopsy report with a sigh.

"Lungs are quite heavy."

No one asked what that meant. Kenzie proceeded with a closer examination of the lungs, carefully dissecting them and noting anomalies. As she took sections for the microscopic examination, she looked toward the observation room.

"As with Michael Wade, the lungs are congested with fluid, slightly frothy. It is a clear sign of asphyxiation."

"So, does that mean homicide?" Tuttle asked.

"Asphyxiation can be caused by many things. It doesn't mean that the manner of death is homicide. But considering the fractured bones and the similarities between Michael's autopsy and Sylvia's, it is very suspicious. I'll see what else shows up in the autopsy and will review my work and confirm my findings with Dr. Wiltshire, but I believe that both will be homicide, death due to asphyxiation."

"Same cause of death for both," Tuttle said. "Pretty likely the same person, then."

"It seems unlikely that Sylvia's death was a copy of Michael's, since my findings have not yet been released. No one but the killer would know how he was killed."

"Or a witness," Baker added.

Kenzie nodded. "Yes, or a witness to Michael's murder."

"If the killer was Sylvia, someone could have exacted retribution on her, killing her in the same way."

"I suppose they could," Kenzie agreed.

"Is there anything you can tell us about the killer based on Mrs. Arnold's autopsy?" Tuttle asked. "Size of hands, strength needed, exactly how she was asphyxiated? Are we talking about a plastic bag over her head? Or something else?"

"From the broken ribs—and in Michael's case, previously broken and healed ribs—I believe that it was mechanical asphyxiation. They were prevented from being able to take a breath. In Michael's case, that would be quite easy. Any of us here would have the strength to asphyxiate a child that small. Hold him tightly against you, arms wrapped around him in a hug, and squeeze until he is unable to breathe."

Both of the detectives considered this, saying nothing at first. Kenzie could picture it herself. A bear hug. Squeezing the child until he stopped crying. Until he stopped breathing. Until, at last, it was too late to revive him.

"And doing the same to an older woman?" Baker asked. "I guess it would take considerably more strength to squeeze a tough old broad like Sylvia to death. She would have fought back. Hard. I don't think the bear hug would work as well for her. You'd need to be able to control the limbs, or risk getting scratched up while she tries to get herself out."

"With Sylvia, it was probably a little different. Either positional asphyxia, such as laying her prone while she was in handcuffs—" The way that Zachary had said that Annie had been killed in the children's center he had been held in. "—or, more likely, in my opinion, by pressure on her chest while she was lying supine."

"Lying on her back?" Baker clarified.

"Yes. Lying on her back with a weight on her chest. Someone sitting or kneeling on her."

That would account for the broken sternum and rib. Minimal bruising at the time of death, since death had been pretty quick, shutting off the body's circulatory system before the bruising could develop. No sign of a ligature or hands around the throat. No bruising around the mouth.

"So, how heavy would you have to be to do that?" Tuttle questioned.

"Not big. Just heavy enough to prevent her from breathing or throwing you off. She is a small, elderly woman; pretty much any adult could have done it."

"Great. Nice of you to narrow it down for us," he said sourly.

Kenzie smiled and shook her head. It wasn't her job to do all of the work for them. She could only do so much to find the killer. They had to take it the rest of the way.

Kenzie sorted through the evidence that had come in with Sylvia's body. The clothing she had been wearing. Some mashed receipts and change. They had not yet found her wallet. Kenzie looked at each of the receipts, but none were recent. Just slips of paper that Sylvia had left in her pockets. Incidental purchases when she had gone into town. A bottle of Tylenol from the pharmacy. A small bottle of milk. A package of candies.

Where had the killer disposed of her purse, with her wallet, phone, and other items that might help point in the direction of the killer? Where had he disposed of the suitcase? It was all together, Kenzie supposed, dumped in a river or ravine, buried under two feet of rich Vermont soil.

Cash's granddaddy had once farmed on that property. That was obvious from the extra outbuildings and abandoned equipment Kenzie had seen in the unkept areas past the rolling velvet lawns and blemish-free fruit trees.

But Cash had been raised as a child of wealth. He hadn't had to work the land like his grandfather and great-grandfather. Instead, he was inside, staring at computers, communicating with his business partners over the phone and email. Maybe not the type of work best suited to a man of his physical prowess and temperament.

He had taken his frustrations out on his wife and son. As the pressure had built, so had the abuse. Escalating until Sylvia had needed to step in and see that Michael, at least, got the care he needed. Had she treated Terri-Lyn as well? Bound up her wounds, given her Tylenol, and sponged her brow?

Kenzie suspected not. Terri-Lyn wasn't exactly well-disposed toward Cash's old nanny. She had not spoken warmly of how the woman had helped and cared for her. She had complained instead about how Sylvia had taken Michael when Terri-Lyn had been unable to care for him due to her postpartum and Michael's colic. A perfect storm. A situation dangerous enough that Sylvia had stepped in to take charge of the infant to make sure that his needs were met and his mother had time to recover. Rocking the colicky baby long into the night.

Had Cash known how much danger his child had been in at that point, or had he been like so many men, blind to how his wife was struggling, succumbing to her depression, drowning in her own black emotions?

Maybe he had. Maybe he had been the one to tell Sylvia that she needed to take charge of Michael. The very thing that Sylvia had been hoping for when she had told Terri-Lyn to get pregnant to heal the marriage.

That, as it turned out, had been a mistake.

45

The police detectives had observed the autopsy, and Kenzie, in turn, sat in on the police interviews with Terri-Lyn and Cash, separate of course. Kenzie observed from a monitoring room, watching the action on the cameras. Never face-to-face with the interviewees. It might be unusual for a medical examiner to sit in on a police interview, but she was the one who could tell the police whether what the witnesses said was believable from a medical standpoint. And she had once been friends with Terri-Lyn Wade. She probably couldn't tell the police anything about Terri-Lyn now that they couldn't deduce themselves, but it was always possible that something Terri-Lyn said could trigger a memory that would somehow be relevant or helpful.

This was no casual interview asking the witnesses if they had seen or heard anything that the police might be interested in. It was not a careful, gentle consultation with grieving parents who also happened to be politically connected to everyone at the top of crime enforcement in Vermont. Terri-Lyn was brought into the small interview room and looked around in dismay at the small table and chairs fashioned from metal tubing with a plastic seat and back screwed on, the disgusting green walls, and the bright lighting that washed out her complexion. It probably smelled as bad as it looked, and the plastic cup of water placed on the table before her had not come from a bottle and didn't sparkle. If she were expecting to be pampered in a lavish boardroom, with her whims being met by a cop playing the role of dedicated servant, she was sadly disappointed.

Terri-Lyn looked at Tuttle in disbelief, as if waiting for him to figure out that he had brought her to the wrong room. He gestured to one of the chairs. "Have a seat."

Terri-Lyn's nose wrinkled as she looked at it. Maybe she was wondering whether it had been disinfected lately. But lacking any authority here, she eventually sat down gingerly. It wasn't like she was going to catch anything from sitting in the chair used by other criminals. There were several layers of cloth between any bacteria that remained there and her pampered skin.

"I don't know why I'm here," Terri-Lyn offered, without waiting for the questions to begin. "I don't know what happened to Sylvia."

"That's fine, ma'am," Tuttle agreed. He picked up a cup of coffee that had been left on the table, took a sip, swished it around his mouth, and swallowed. "We just want to go over where you were for the twenty-four hours preceding the discovery of Mrs. Arnold's body and the circumstances surrounding your son's death one more time."

"I've already said everything I plan to on that."

"Yes, ma'am. Can you tell me your activities from Thursday afternoon through Friday morning?"

"I already told you that on Friday. I was at home. I didn't go out. I am in mourning for my son, you know. I don't need to be seen in public with all of the... well-wishers. People who want to console me. I really don't want that right now. I just want to be at home, protected, where I can... mourn the loss of my child."

"What part of the house were you in?"

"All day?"

"I don't imagine you go into every room of the house daily. Especially those areas that are set aside for the staff. You were not near Mrs. Arnold's room, for example?"

"Certainly not. Why would I be?"

"So, if someone said they saw you there?"

"They would be lying," Terri-Lyn said icily. "I wouldn't have any reason to be near Sylvia's room. If I needed her—and I didn't—I would just call her and she would come to me."

"Of course," Tuttle agreed. He looked at Baker, then back at Terri-Lyn again. "So, which rooms did you say you were in?"

"I don't know. My bedroom suite. The dining room. The gym. The pool. The morning room." She shook her head. "I can't be expected to remember exactly what I did every minute of the day."

"Of course not, ma'am. But everything that you can remember is extremely helpful. We can start to build a picture of what was happening in the house at various times. Do you remember the last time you saw Mrs. Arnold?"

"The last time? No, of course not. I don't have anything to do with her. She was Cash—Michael's nanny, not mine. That was her job and, since Michael wasn't there anymore, I had no reason to have anything to do with her."

"But you didn't fire her? Let her go since her services were no longer needed?"

"No. She could still perform other functions around the house. Cash said it would be cruel to let her go, an old woman, when she wouldn't be able to get a job anywhere else. We could pay her a pension, or continue to employ her to do work around the house. I would rather have someone actually doing work. Not just sitting around, getting paid for being alive."

"That was very thoughtful of your husband."

"He has known her for a long time. He cared about her deeply."

"Did that bother you?"

"Bother me? Why would it?"

"Because she was taking your place in his universe. She was looking after his son. He knew and loved her long before you ever became a part of his world. Some women would resent that."

"She didn't take my place." Terri-Lyn's nose wrinkled. "What a thought. That old woman? She was good at what she did, but Cash didn't see her as some... love interest."

"But she was a mother figure to him."

Terri-Lyn looked for a way to argue, then shook her head and said nothing.

Tuttle let the silence draw out for an uncomfortable length of time.

"So you don't know the last time you saw Mrs. Arnold alive?" Baker asked.

"No. I have no idea. I doubt if I saw her at all on Thursday."

"What was she doing?"

"How would I know? Sitting in her room. Reading a book. Writing letters. Whatever old women do when they have nothing else to do."

"Did she like to read?"

"I don't know."

"Like to write? Keep a journal?" Baker prodded.

"How would I know? I don't socialize with her. I have no idea what she does in her spare time."

"You know she writes letters, so you must have seen her do that. Maybe seen her sitting at her writing desk composing letters to her friends."

"I don't know. Maybe I saw her once."

46

Tuttle leaned forward. "Did you and Mrs. Arnold get along?"
"We got along just fine. She was the employee and usually Cash dealt with her. I spoke to her when I needed to." She shrugged. "That wasn't very often."

"You didn't confide in her?"

Terri-Lyn snorted. "Of course not."

"You didn't tell her about the difficulties in your marriage? She didn't suggest things would improve if you bore Cash a son?"

Terri-Lyn's jaw clenched. "She might have said something to that effect once. If she did, it was unsolicited."

"Was it. And *did* having a son improve your marital relationship?"

"No." Terri-Lyn's tone was bitter. "It was a ridiculous suggestion. Children put a strain on marriage. They don't help it."

Tuttle and Baker both nodded sympathetically. "Having kids is hard work," Baker empathized. "Men have no idea what it's like to go through pregnancy and then to try to raise a screaming, flailing baby. They think it's easy, that everything just falls into place. But there was no place for a baby in your marriage, was there?"

"Michael was a difficult child right from the time he was born. There were complications. He had colic. Then all of the teething and growing pains and whatever else. He was always crying or fussing over something and wouldn't listen to a word I said."

"It's a difficult age," Tuttle said. "They want to be able to do everything they see people around them doing, but they are not capable. It must be very frustrating for them."

"For them? Try for me! Constantly demanding attention. Wouldn't do what I said. Give Daddy a hug. Stay in your bed. He wouldn't do anything I said and had the attention span of a gnat. There was something wrong with him. That was probably what killed him, if it really wasn't the fall from the balcony. He probably had something wrong with him, but the doctors never found it. Maybe something was wrong in his brain."

"But you must have had good times together, too," Baker suggested. "Playing games. Sharing a popsicle together. And babies look like little angels when they are sleeping. Sweet cherubs."

"Cherubs?" Terri-Lyn scoffed. "When they finally wind down at the end of the day, like a mechanical toy, it's such a feeling of relief. I wished he would be quiet and sleep all of the time."

"And now he will," Tuttle said.

"You're taking it the wrong way. You know that isn't what I meant."

"He was an inconvenience to you. Nothing more. You were glad when he died."

"I was not. Ask your cops. I cried. I have been *deep* in mourning."

Nothing seemed further from the truth. Terri-Lyn didn't appear to have given her son a moment of thought in the last week. She had better things to do.

"Tell us again what you were doing when Michael died." Baker said, "How you realized something had happened."

"I was eating breakfast. I'd had a headache and slept in. Then Sylvia started screaming. I couldn't believe she would do that when I had a headache. She knew how much the noise bothered it. I thought she was screaming at the gardener or something. It went on for a few minutes before I realized it was something to do with Michael. And then… when I went outside, no one would let me close. I was nearly hysterical."

"That must have been very difficult for you," the police detective murmured.

"It was. You can't imagine what it is like to lose a child."

For a moment, Kenzie thought Baker was going to make up a story about having lost a child herself, but then her expression changed slightly. "Cash was there ahead of you? So he saw what had happened?"

"He didn't see it happen. But he was over there. Where Michael was. He saw him on the ground. For me, I never saw him after the fall. I need closure. I need to see him again to make myself understand that he's really dead."

"Didn't you say in your earlier statement that you had been doing Pilates?" Tuttle asked.

"Yes." She shrugged. "I had been. Before I sat down to eat breakfast."

"You do Pilates with a migraine? I thought you had been in bed, asleep, because all of the noise and light bothered it."

Terri-Lyn shook her head. "I know I just have to push through. I can't neglect my training program. Even now… the body-mind connection is essential, you know. If you want to feel good, you need to *feel* good."

Kenzie had no idea what Terri-Lyn was going on about.

But Tuttle had picked up on an inconsistency in her story. And it was not the only one.

"Why don't you tell us the real story about how Michael got hurt," Baker said, putting her hand over Terri-Lyn's on the table as if to comfort her. "You must want to get it off your chest. The body-mind connection *is* strong. The way that you must feel now, knowing that what happened to Michael was partially your fault… you must just feel sick about it."

"I didn't do anything to hurt him. What are you talking about?"

"The bruises and other injuries that he had. I know how frustrating it is as a caregiver. Especially with a demanding baby like Michael. Sometimes you just want him to shut up. To give you a little peace and quiet. And if you've got a migraine... well, you're not really responsible then, are you? It's extenuating circumstances."

"I didn't hurt him," Terri-Lyn maintained. "And *you* know that. These games that you're playing. You just want to lay this at my door instead of Cash's because of his position. It's much easier to get rid of the wife and then play up how sad it is. He lost his child because of what his wife did. He lost his wife, the love of his life, poor Cash. Poor, poor Cash."

"Are you saying that Cash hurt him?"

"I'm not saying anything. But if you look at the two of us, you know which one it was. Look at his size. His history. You think he was patient with Michael?" She blew out her breath explosively. "He didn't want a son. He couldn't stand having kids around. He thought it was a good idea. A good look for him. But *he* is the drunk. *He* is the loser, not me. Your precious congressman is a failure. He can't control his drinking. Can't keep it in his pants. Can't manage money. How bright do you have to be not to spend the *millions* that your grandfather left you? Millions, and he fritters it all away. We are on the brink of bankruptcy because he doesn't understand how to do a single thing. He is just a puppet. An empty suit."

"He hit Michael?"

"He hit me enough times! You ask anyone in the household and they'll tell you it's true. He gave me a black eye. He was always pushing and smacking me around, especially when he was drunk."

"And Michael?"

She rolled her eyes and shook her head, unable to understand why they weren't more concerned about her plight than they were about Michael's. "Yes, he hit Michael. If you talked to your coroner, you know that. Cash hit him. Wouldn't leave him alone. He liked to have someone to take things out on. She should have told you that. She should have told you that *I am the victim here.* I can't believe she doesn't care one bit about her best friend at school. She should have helped me."

"You're talking about Dr. Kirsch?"

"Yes! MacKenzie. She shows up at the house, blundering around, asking questions, getting Cash all wound up. And she doesn't have any idea what kind of a mess she made of things. Everybody is saying that she's protecting Cash now and is afraid to issue her report because it will implicate him. Well, she *should* implicate him! He was the one beating on me. He was the one who had no self-control. Just like my father. *He* is the one you should be looking at, not me. And I should be the congressman. Congresswoman. You think he knew what he was doing? He just followed the instructions. They told him everything to do. What to sign. Where to be. When to smile. A trained dog could have done the job. But he's got to screw it up *thinking* and trying too hard to make all these changes and decisions. He should have just shut up and smiled."

The two detectives were nodding along, looking sympathetic. Terri-Lyn was revealing a lot more about herself than she would have if they had gone in with a hard-nosed cop attitude. And Kenzie was sure that she was right about Cash. He was the one who had been hurting Michael. He was the one who could have most easily dumped Michael's body over the railing.

"What made Sylvia go looking for Michael that day?" Baker asked. "She said that she heard a sound. She must have known that he was out of bed. What do you think she heard?"

"What she heard? How would I know?" Terri-Lyn demanded.

"Do you blame her for not supervising Michael?"

Terri-Lyn considered this for a moment, then nodded. "Of course, how could I not? I know that is cruel. She loved Ca—Michael and would have done anything to protect him. But he was my son, not hers. She was supposed to be watching him. If Cash hurt him... Sylvia should have been watching him. She shouldn't have let him anywhere near him, not at that hour of the morning."

"Why not?"

"Cash was working. He had important things to do. He wouldn't have wanted Michael around, getting in the way underfoot. She should have kept him in the nursery or given him lunch in the kitchen. Michael shouldn't have been around Cash."

It was interesting to see Terri-Lyn's story start to unravel. She had played the guilt-stricken mother when she had made her initial statement. Her fault for not supervising Michael. Her fault for not knowing that he was out of bed. Now, it was Sylvia's fault, or Cash's.

Had Sylvia cleaned up after Cash? Would she have done that if she knew he had killed the boy? She had obviously loved Cash just as much as Michael. Had the whole thing been staged? Cash drops the body from the balcony. Sylvia is in place on the main floor and starts to scream?

But Kenzie had a hard time believing that could be true. Would Sylvia really have covered for Cash?

She had with her visits to the emergency room. She had made up stories of how Michael had been hurt. Given him a new identity. Given him medicine and sat up with him without saying a word about the man who had beaten him.

What was one more time?

For her grown-up little boy?

47

They took a break between Terri-Lyn's and Cash's interviews. Kenzie met in the break room with Tuttle and Baker as they refreshed their coffee cups.

"What do you think?" Baker asked Kenzie.

"Terri-Lyn's pretty happy to throw Cash to the dogs. I guess she's had enough of him."

Tuttle nodded, his face twisting into a sneer. "I've had women like that in the interrogation room before. She won't back down; I'll tell you that."

"She didn't seem really impressed with *you*," Baker told Kenzie, taking a sip of her too-hot coffee and wincing. "I think you were supposed to save her from all this."

"I'm not sure how I could have done that, even if I had been inclined to." Kenzie shook her head.

"Well, it's a good thing that you're not inclined to, because this case will be all over the news for a long time, and everybody's actions will be examined under a microscope." Baker forced another sip of the coffee and winced a second time.

"In Terri-Lyn's defense, she didn't grow up in the best family," Kenzie allowed. "I didn't see the red flags then but, looking back... I can see them now. I think her father was probably pretty abusive."

Tuttle nodded. "That's pretty much expected with a woman like this. Stuck in an abusive relationship with her spouse, possibly a co-abuser, an abusive dad is almost guaranteed. Sometimes mom. Sometimes it comes from somewhere else, but home life is the most common. If you really want to mess a kid up, just beat the hell out of them every so often. There doesn't have to be any logic to it. Best if there isn't and they can never see it coming."

"Did Sylvia keep a journal?" Kenzie asked curiously. "Or was that just a bluff?"

"It's possible she did," Baker said cautiously. "She didn't really have other people into her rooms; she cleaned it herself. It was her private sanctum. So it's hard to tell what is missing and how she spent her spare time if it isn't reflected in what is already in the room. We know that she has kept journals in the past, and we know that she wrote letters from the writing desk and pretty notepapers she kept on hand. The housekeeper and cook said she often had letters to post when one of them was going into town."

"Anyone in particular? Did she have family?"

"She had three kids. We're trying to get in touch with them. From her phone logs, she didn't keep in close touch with them. Maybe she wrote them letters, but she didn't call them, text, send emails." She shrugged. "That's not surprising. She was not really a tech person. A lot of people in her generation don't ever get into it, though some like to use Facebook to keep track of grandchildren."

Kenzie remembered the photos of other children in Sylvia's rooms. Probably her own children, then, raised during the years between Cash and Michael. "Did she still work for the Wades while she raised her own family?"

"Sounds like it. Not as a nanny, but the family employed her in other ways, just like Terri-Lyn said. Cash did not want to let her go."

"I wonder if her kids would have any insight on Cash, then. They might have heard things from Sylvia over the years. How she had raised him, what he was like when he was a boy. They would know what he was like as a young man when they were growing up in the house; they might have some interesting stories about him."

"Might do," Tuttle agreed. "We'll be sure to ask them when we break the news." He shook his head. "I can't understand them cutting all ties with her when she was getting so old. They had to know she didn't have a lot of years left."

Kenzie sighed. She closed her eyes briefly, thinking about her own parents. "You always think you have time, even if you don't. I've been trying to get closer to my parents, and it's tough. They live in a different world than I do. I have all of the day-to-day stuff that seems so important and immediate. My work. My relationship with my partner and his health issues. Visiting his family out of town. I do some work for my dad's charitable foundation, which is run by my mom, so I could just say that is my connection with them, but it isn't the same. That's business, and I deal with foundation staff, not usually dealing with my parents on a personal level."

Kenzie shrugged and rubbed her eyes. She went on.

"And I come from a pretty good family and have a pretty good relationship with them. I don't know what Sylvia's relationship was like with her kids. She seems like the motherly type, really close to the kids she was a nanny for. But... it's possible that it was different with her own kids. That they were secondary to her relationship with Cash, or were always being compared with what he had been like as a kid."

"Ugh, can you imagine that?" Baker asked, nodding. " 'This rich young brat that I raised was so much more promising than you. I love him so much.' That could definitely be off-putting for her natural kids."

"You're interviewing him next? How is he managing? He was pretty concerned on Friday when Sylvia turned up missing."

Kenzie had not seen him after being called to the root cellar. She had been very engaged in dealing with the body and had not seen him or talked to him after that. She had heard him wailing outside the crime scene when Sylvia's body was discovered.

"Not sure how he is. Today is the first day that he would consider coming in. I think he's taken it pretty hard. She was a mother figure to him. Gotta be tough."

48

They spoke for a few more minutes, and then Kenzie returned to the monitoring room to watch the next interview on the screen.

Cash showed none of his wife's concern with the setting of the interview. He seemed utterly blind to his surroundings. He sat at the table without being asked and leaned forward, elbows on the table, to talk to the detectives. He seemed intense, determined to get to the bottom of things. After Terri-Lyn's tirade about how incompetent he was in his family life and job, Kenzie had been expecting Cash to be somewhat tentative, in need of direction, and perhaps bumbling through questions, not sure why he was being interrogated as he was. But he gave an air of being absolutely sure why he was there and ready to engage with the detectives.

Yet there were a few clues that he wasn't quite himself. When she had seen him before, he had been clean-shaven, but there was a blur of blue-black whiskers on his cheeks today. His eyes were red-rimmed. When Baker put a cup of water in front of him, as she had with Terri-Lyn, he immediately drained it and pushed it back to her in a mute request for more. Baker left the room for a moment to get a refill and placed it before him again. He nodded and took one mouthful, then looked at them expectantly.

"You know why you're here," Tuttle said in a businesslike way, as if he were following a written board agenda. "We would like to review your movements in the twenty-four hours before Mrs. Arnold was found, and also to review the circumstances of your son's death."

"I was home. I've been home since Michael's... accident. I couldn't be expected to make personal appearances after that. I've taken a few meetings by video chat but stayed home, close to my wife."

"How is she taking it?" Tuttle asked with apparent concern.

"Well, you've seen her. I imagine you are as good a judge of how people react to a death as anyone."

"I saw her today, but I didn't see how she has been managing it for the last week. Things can change a lot in that time. How has she been?"

"It was very upsetting," Cash said. "It isn't like Michael died in his sleep or from the measles or some virus. The accident was very disturbing, even if she didn't have to see his body afterward. And then all of the stuff that has been going around about the medical examiner's report." Cash's lips thinned as he pressed them together. "A report that hasn't even been released yet."

"The medical examiner's office is working on it and promises to have it in shortly. But you already have a pretty good idea what it will say."

"That woman coroner said he didn't die in the fall. She has no idea what she's talking about."

"All of her work will be reviewed by the chief medical examiner. But I'm afraid that from what we're hearing... Michael was killed before he fell from the balcony. Before he was *thrown off* of the balcony."

"If he was thrown off, his body would have landed further out," Cash pointed out.

"If someone threw him further from the house," Baker agreed. "But someone who knew about trajectories might have known better and just let him drop straight down from the rail."

Cash snorted at this. "The criminal element is not exactly well known for being intelligent. All that stuff on TV about criminal geniuses is just prime-time entertainment fodder."

Baker gave a soft laugh. "I'll admit that most of our cases are exactly what they look like on the face and few of the criminals that we deal with have made more than a cursory attempt to hide what they did. It doesn't usually take hours of investigating to identify a suspect or to recognize what someone has attempted to cover up."

Cash sat back, folding his arms across his chest. His knees jiggled impatiently. He looked ready to jump out of his chair but was forcing himself to stay contained.

"In this case, for instance," Tuttle said. "It didn't take us long to figure out that the boy was dropped off the balcony to obscure his real cause of death. And it didn't work out that way, because it was quite simple for the assistant to the medical examiner to figure out the cause of death."

Cash cleared his throat and shifted. He looked around the room, eyes going to the walls, the light, the furniture, and the posts on the wall, as if he were taking in each thing for the first time, realizing where he was. Waking up to the predicament that he was in.

"I'm under a lot of stress right now," he said without any prompting. "Things are heating up in the media, and that puts a lot of pressure on me. You know you can't believe even half of what they are saying online."

"Of course," Baker agreed. "But there are a few points that we can verify for ourselves. For example, it isn't very difficult to look at your credit report."

"I have money. I don't know why everyone says I have spent it all. That's not true."

"But you haven't been making rent or utility payments on all of your properties. One of your subsidiaries did not make payroll and needed to borrow money to do so. You have defaulted on some fairly hefty business loans."

"I had a deal that did not go through. It has affected cash flow temporarily. It will be straightened out."

"That's not what your credit report says."

"A credit report isn't all-knowing. It is just a bunch of numbers and predictive analysis. You might as well ask your two-year-old to predict the future."

They were all silent for a moment, Cash's use of "your two-year-old" in such a casual way ringing in their ears.

"A credit report is just bull," Cash amended. "It is a bunch of numbers that don't have any bearing on each other or your case. What does it matter to you or anyone else whether I defaulted on a loan? Or changed a company name. Or stayed in a hotel one night when I was in town because I didn't want to wake my wife up going into the house late at night."

"Don't you have spare rooms at the mansion that you could have used?" Tuttle challenged.

"There are all kinds of rooms, but they don't come with the same amenities. I had no intention of waking the house staff up to attend to my needs when it was just as easy to go to a hotel where everything is ready for me."

Including a pretty young girl he enjoyed spending time with, if the rumors on the internet were true. Zachary believed that one was. As well as the rumors about his being forced to declare bankruptcy soon. He acted like everything was fine, but he was used to showing people a calm, confident demeanor.

"We have talked to a Miss Michelle Bentley," Baker offered. "Perhaps you would like to consider that before telling us that you only went to the hotel because they have fluffy towels and complimentary toothpaste if you forget your own."

Cash ground his teeth, glaring at her. Baker didn't push. She just sat there waiting for him to correct himself or to move on to something else.

"My personal life is none of your affair," Cash insisted. "Neither are my financial affairs."

"They both have a bearing on our investigation."

"How?"

"You weren't getting along with your wife. Going to someone else instead. You have a prenup, and you know that the fact that you were cheating on her means that she will benefit from the prenup, and you lose out. You are already having money problems, and that would ruin you."

"And what does that have to do with anything?"

"Men who are losing everything sometimes find ways to take their families out of the picture. It bothers them so much to be a disappointment to their families that they would rather kill them than to have them see their failings."

"That's ridiculous."

"An annihilator would rather see his whole family dead than admit that he has failed them. Or failed to reach whatever financial goal he thought he should have achieved. They have a wildly distorted idea of what they can accomplish in life, and when they cannot reach that goal, they feel the need to..." Baker shook her head, looking for the appropriate metaphor. "To burn everything down," she said finally.

"I haven't burned everything down."

"You're losing it."

"I am not losing it!" he raised his voice, shouting the words back at her.

Baker just smirked. "Really."

"You're trying to provoke me," he accused.

"You are not acting like the calm, collected congressman you were trying to portray when you first walked into this room."

"My son just died. And the woman who raised me. How do you think that makes me feel?"

"I think you killed both of them."

The astonishment on Cash's face was comical. Surely he had seen that coming? He had seen that was where they were going, what they were hoping to prove.

"I did not kill either one of them!"

"Prove it."

"Michael's body was found outside, nowhere near where I was. By Sylvia. How does that make me guilty of Michael's death?"

"You were in the house and dropped his body over the rail. You may think that you go unobserved in that house, that everyone just works in the background and doesn't see your comings and goings, but that isn't true. People see you. They pay attention to where you are at all times. So they can tell us a lot more about where you were and what you were doing than you think."

"I didn't do anything to hurt him."

"Oh, didn't you?" Tuttle exploded so unexpectedly that Cash jerked back from him, raising his hand to his face protectively. "You hit that boy," Tuttle accused. "Don't even try telling me that you didn't hurt him. Do you know how many people can testify to that fact?"

"How I choose to discipline my son has nothing to do with you. And nothing to do with his death. I did not kill him."

"Discipline. Is that what you call it when you beat the hell out of a toddler for interrupting you? For getting underfoot?" Baker challenged.

"That's a misconstruing of the circumstances—"

"That is *exactly* what happened. You know it, and I know it, so you might as well not even try."

Cash folded his arms again, glaring at her. But he didn't deny it. Maybe there were too many witnesses and he was trying to think his way out of the trap he found himself in.

"Do you know how often your nanny had to take that boy to the emergency room to ensure he didn't die from the injuries you inflicted on him? But this time, she couldn't get there in time to save him. She was too late. So the two of you concocted a plan to make it look like he was killed in an accident instead of being beaten to death. You would drop the boy over the railing. She would scream and attract everyone's attention. You would all play the part of hurt, grieving parents, and no one would be the wiser. That's how you thought it would all play out. You weren't planning on the medical examiner being able to tell that he had been dead before he was dropped."

"I may have lost my temper once or twice—"

"And sent him to the emergency room with broken bones, a lacerated liver, or internal bleeding," Tuttle finished grimly.

"No. I never caused that kind of damage. Never."

"We have the hospital records, Mr. Wade. He *was* hurt that badly. Just how hard do you think you can hit a kid without causing major damage?"

He shook his head insistently. "I am not that kind of person. I just... I just was under a lot of stress. He always wanted attention. He was always crying and demanding attention. He didn't know when to stay out of my way."

"Like... all of the time?" Baker suggested.

"You don't know what you're talking about. I loved my son. I loved to do things with him, to spend time with him. But sometimes he wanted to do something with me and I had work to do. Or I was... having a discussion with his mother. He just didn't know when to stop and leave me alone."

"He was barely more than a baby. You can't expect him to be able to predict human behavior. You can't expect a child that old to know when to leave you alone or to follow instructions. Both you and your wife seem to have this... blind spot where your son is concerned. It's like you think he was an adult rather than a baby. Like he chose to annoy you and was being disobedient when he couldn't do what you expected him to. He was a toddler. Can't you understand that?"

Cash put his hands over his face, trying to compose himself. "Look... I admit that I had hit him once or twice. I just got so... frustrated and angry. I've always had a temper. That's not my fault. But you can't judge me by that. I didn't kill him. I would never do that." He removed his hands and stared earnestly at the two of them, trying to convince them by his sincerity that he was innocent.

Baker looked at Tuttle. They didn't say anything for a minute, but were clearly communicating with each other. Baker stood up.

"Mr. Wade, remind me of your real name?"

"I go by Cash on everything."

"Is it Christian?"

"Crispin."

"Crispin Wade, you are under arrest for the murder of your son. I assume you will want to consult with your attorney—"

Cash covered his face again. "No, no, no! I told you, I didn't want him to die. I just... couldn't stop it."

"Mr. Wade, you need to call your lawyer. Anything that you say to us now is on the record and is going to be used against you—"

"I should have stopped. I shouldn't have let it go so far. But it wasn't my fault." Kenzie thought from the snuffling and sobbing Cash was making behind his hands that he was crying now, finally letting himself go. "How could I let that happen my son? I never thought it would go that far."

"Are you prepared to make a statement? A full and honest confession could mean a lighter sentence. People understand how difficult parenting can be, especially when you have a high-needs child and a lot of stress in your life," Baker was echoing back what she had heard Cash say, trying to prompt him to go on and tell them more details.

"I can't. I just... you wouldn't understand. You think that I'm responsible and... I guess I am, but..."

"It's time to get it off your chest," Tuttle said firmly. "But let's get a waiver signed first. Then you can explain the whole thing to us. You'll feel so much better when you do."

Baker laid her hand comfortingly on Cash's shoulder. "Come on, Mr. Wade. Try to pull yourself together. We need this signed, and then you can explain what happened. I'm sure that once we understand what took place..."

She trailed off, not promising him anything in particular. A hint of sympathy and the possibility that they could be understanding and forgive a misstep if he just explained what had happened. It was very subtle.

It took a few minutes of encouragement to get Cash back under control. He went through half a box of tissues and several spells of self-recriminations that didn't lead anywhere. They managed to get him to stop crying and positioned the Miranda waiver in front of him, encouraging him to sign it and then tell them all about what had happened.

It looked like the show was over. It was only a matter of time before they got a complete confession from Cash Wade and prosecuted him for his son's death. With his power and influence, Kenzie knew he might only get manslaughter. They would say that he had been in extreme emotional distress, that he hadn't known what he had been doing, and hadn't been able to stop himself from killing his son once he had started. But there was one problem with that.

Cash had not beaten his son to death.

49

Kenzie suspected that the house staff had a much better idea of what was going on than anyone was willing to admit. They were trained to be discreet. They had been keeping the family's secrets for too long. Kenzie didn't know if there were any others who, like Sylvia, had been there since Cash was a child. He had been cosseted and protected when he should have been forced to take responsibility for his own behavior. As a grown man, he was still trying to blame his own behavior on someone else.

A learned pattern that had been in place for many years and everyone in the household had been taught to toe the line. Cash was a golden child. The wealthy, brilliant, up-and-coming heir to the throne. Not someone who had to follow the same rules as everyone else.

What Kenzie knew was that Michael had not been beaten to death. The old bruises certainly showed a pattern of abuse. His injuries had landed him in the hospital in the past. But there was a difference between hitting and asphyxiation. Nothing Cash had said hinted at asphyxiation.

Kenzie used a quiet interview room to put a video call in to Hilda, the housekeeper. The woman had a number of problems getting on to the live video chat, pecking randomly at the screen and peering at it closely so that Kenzie got an excellent view of her nostrils. But eventually, they were face to face, Hilda sitting down with her phone propped up on the table. In the kitchen, from what Kenzie could see. She would have preferred somewhere more private, but it was essential to keep Hilda feeling comfortable and not confronted, so she let it go.

"Hilda, we need to know more about what happened the day Michael died," Kenzie told her. "There are too many different stories, too many inconsistencies. And I think you and the rest of the staff know much more about it than you have told us up until now. I know that you are used to keeping family matters quiet, but... Michael and Sylvia were family."

Hilda was already dabbing her eyes and nose with a tissue, which she balled up in her hand. "I have known Sylvia for thirty years. Had known her. Now she's gone. But I know her. She would have told us to keep quiet and not cause anyone in the family trouble. She *was* family. More than any of us. She always saw Cash as a son. Her first-born son. Even if she never carried him, she was the one who raised that boy, who took care of all of his cuts and scrapes, nourished him."

"I know. It must have been really hard for her to see what he had become. To see him being so abusive toward his own son."

Hilda shook her head. "I never saw anything," she proclaimed. "I never saw him hit the boy."

"But he did. He's admitted that to the police. And I can tell you... Michael was black and blue with bruises. Maybe you already knew that. Maybe you helped Sylvia when she bathed him or saw him running around in his diaper. He was covered with bruises."

"Maybe he had one of those diseases that makes you get bruises from the littlest things..."

"He didn't," Kenzie said flatly. "Those bruises were real. Evidence of severe abuse."

Hilda dabbed at her eyes. "I always hoped... we tried to keep Michael in the nursery, away from them, so that he wouldn't get hurt. But you can't control a toddler." She said it fondly. Someone who knew a lot more about childhood development than Cash Wade. They couldn't force him to stay and play in the nursery when he wanted to be with his mom or dad. There were probably prohibitions against locking him in or forcing him to do anything physically. Certain boundaries that a servant was not allowed to cross.

"You knew that he was being hurt."

Hilda didn't admit it or deny it.

"You knew that Sylvia took him to the hospital? Not just once, but multiple times. Because she knew he would die if she didn't."

Hilda looked away from the phone screen. The cook passed behind her. Other conversations were going on around her. Too quiet for Kenzie to hear, but there were still a lot of people aware of the conversation. Cash would not be happy if word of this got back to him.

"You knew about the hospital visits," Kenzie said, wording it strongly.

There was a very slight nod from Hilda.

"You knew that his father hit him."

"But—"

"Sylvia tried to intervene, to make sure that he got medical treatment, to save his life."

Hilda swallowed and nodded, a bit more firmly this time. "Yes. Of course. We were all concerned, but Sylvia most of all. She was the closest to him, physically and emotionally. She was his caregiver."

"Who paid for those hospital visits?"

"What?"

"Hospital visits are not cheap, especially where lifesaving surgery is required. And Sylvia never used insurance because that would tip the hospital off regarding Michael's identity. Sylvia didn't have that kind of money. So who paid for it?"

"I suppose... Mr. Wade."

"You suppose? Or you know?"

There were several seconds of silence while Hilda considered this.

"The truth will come out," Kenzie said. "Whether you say what happened or not. There are financial records. Bank transfers, deposits, payments. She wasn't paying for major surgery from the petty cash in her wallet. That money was used for things like more baby Tylenol to keep him quiet. For milk and other treats to settle him down when he had to sit and wait in the emergency room. Who paid the hospital bills?"

"Mr. Wade."

"So he can't deny that he knew about them."

"No," Hilda admitted.

"He knew how badly Michael was hurt."

"I… I guess."

"What did Sylvia hear that day?"

"What do you mean?" Hilda's brows drew down in puzzlement, confused by Kenzie's change in direction.

"Sylvia's statement said she had been working in another part of the house. She had not been with Michael. But she heard something that made her go check on him. So what did she hear?"

"I don't know."

"Was she working in the kitchen? Maybe I should ask the cook what Sylvia heard."

"She heard…" Hilda swallowed hard again and licked her lips. She looked around the kitchen, but no one supplied her with a water bottle or another drink, and she didn't seem inclined to ask anyone else into the conversation.

Kenzie was expecting to hear that she heard a scream or cry from Michael. She knew the sound of her baby's voice and dropped whatever she was doing to go to him. But she was too late to stop Cash from doing what he had. And then she couldn't make herself do anything to implicate her "oldest son" in the child's death.

Finally Hilda spoke.

"She heard an argument."

50

Kenzie felt cold. "What argument?"

"It was…" Hilda was having a difficult time speaking, putting the words together to tell Kenzie what had happened. She looked around her again. Kenzie could no longer detect any background conversations on the video chat. The other staff members were silent, waiting for Hilda to tell her story. None of them seemed to be trying to stop her, which Kenzie thought a good sign. Maybe more of them wanted to talk about it, for the story to go public so they didn't have to shoulder the silent burden alone.

"Mr. Wade and his wife," Hilda finally managed to get out.

"Did you hear the argument too?"

"I… yes. He was… very loud."

"What did he say?"

There was a long pause while Hilda thought about this, gathering her thoughts or trying to figure out all of the implications of telling someone in law enforcement what had actually happened. The story would contradict her earlier statement. At least Kenzie assumed it would. It had been left out of her account, even if she hadn't covered it with lies. And it would contradict the statements of other staff members, Sylvia, Cash, and Terri-Lyn. They had all carefully left the argument out of their accounts.

While Hilda was gathering her thoughts, Kenzie tried to picture what had happened. How had an argument resulted in Michael's death? She first envisioned the boy trying to get his father's attention while they were fighting and getting hit and thrown out of the way for being in the wrong place at the wrong time. But as she had already reminded everyone involved, Michael had not died from a blow.

"Mr. Cash, he said…"

"What did you do?" Cash screamed. "What have you done?"

His wife's replies were more difficult to make out, her quieter, higher voice not carrying through the walls and floors as easily. Cash's bellow was like that of an enraged bull. No one in the house could have failed to hear it.

"He's your son! He's only a child!"

Terri-Lyn railed at him, screams of anger and self-defense. "It's your fault!"

A crash sounded as someone's body hit the furniture or a heavy piece of furniture was thrown over.

"You said it wouldn't happen again!"

"You're never here!" Terri-Lyn screamed, "You're always off with that woman! You don't even care about your business, your home, how I will live when it's all over! You think I will be content to be your ex-wife while you marry that piece of fluff?"

"He was my son! My only son!"

"You're taking everything away from me. You thought I would just stand by while you ripped my life to shreds? And while you're gone, he's here. Whining at me. Pawing at me. Always underfoot."

"No, no, no…"

"Don't act all righteous to me!" Her voice shrilled. "You're no better than me. You come home drunk or mad because of some deal that slipped through your fingers, and you whale on him! You think I carried that thing inside me for almost ten months to see him used as a punching bag? I gave you my body! I went through pain you'll never imagine. To bear a wailing, screaming whelp who only ever shuts up for *her!*"

"You're the devil! You have no human feelings!"

More crashes, the two of them having a knock-down blowout fight.

"Because you're always sorry afterward? You think it's different if you apologize and fuss and grovel and give him a new toy? You're better than me because you feel sorry? You still hurt him!"

"I never sent him to the hospital."

"And I did? What did I ever do? Besides loving him too much? I held him. I could hold him and quiet him as well as *she* could."

"No…" Cash's voice broke off in despair. "You promised me. You got down on your knees and promised me it would never happen again. You're not a mother. You're a monster!"

"This is the end," Terri-Lyn promised. "This is the end of *your* life."

They could hear her walking down the hallway. Half-running, loud footsteps. A door opening and the familiar sound of the sliding doors being opened. There was a last moment scuffling, Cash following her, wrestling with her, trying to beat her into submission as he had before. And then a wail from him, unlike anything any of them had ever heard before.

And a noise outside. The solid thunk of something hitting the pavement.

Hilda suddenly became aware of Sylvia running through the room, sobbing in anguish. Hilda was paralyzed, unsure what to do or who to call.

Then Sylvia started screaming. The heartbreaking shrieks of a mother whose child was ripped out of her hands for the final time.

Hilda was numb as she heard Cash descend the stairs to the main floor and make his way to the poolside area. She caught a glimpse of his face as he walked by the open door. Gray skin, wide eyes, his mouth twisted into an open grimace. As he reached his son's body, others in the household were released from their game of statues and went out to assist or comfort him.

It was ten minutes before Terri-Lyn came down, dressed in a red kimono dressing gown. Her face nothing like Cash's. Quietly triumphant, superior, the horrible specter of the angel of death. She went to the back door, but not out onto the pavement where her husband knelt over the rag doll body of his son, his keening cry a faint echo of Sylvia's, the one person who had truly loved the boy and never done him harm.

And then the act began.

Kenzie's eyes moved from Hilda's face on the tablet screen to the detectives on the other side of the table, out of Hilda's view.

They were all familiar with violence. They saw it, or the results of it, on an almost daily basis. But they were not immune to it. The story of what had really happened at the mansion that day rang in their ears and was as much a part of them now as it would be of Hilda for the rest of her life.

They all shared in it now.

"It was Terri-Lyn who killed Michael?" Kenzie asked, trying to keep her voice as steady and non-judgmental as possible. "His own mother?" She remembered hearing Ben Burton's story from Zachary, similarly horrific. Mothers were held up as the example of perfect love and devotion, the highest, purest form of love. And then there were women like Ben Burton's mother. Like Terri-Lyn. Who took back the life they had given.

"She wasn't his mother," Hilda said in a disgusted tone. "It takes more to be a mother than simply to bear a child. She was never what she should have been. They gave her excuses. She was depressed. She was overwhelmed because he was so colicky, so needy, and he was her first child."

"She never bonded with him."

"Could she? The woman is as cold as an iceberg. Who would expect her to bond with anyone, much less a screaming, squalling newborn?"

"What happened?"

"You would have to ask her that. She was alone. She wasn't

supposed to be left alone with him. We all knew it could happen again. One day, she would succeed in silencing him permanently."

"She squeezed him to stop him from crying?" Kenzie asked, and she had to wipe the corners of her eyes, which were suddenly leaking hot tears, ruining her professional persona.

Hilda nodded stoically. Her tears dried as Kenzie took on the burden herself. "She never could stand him crying. She would shake or squeeze him until... he stopped."

51

Kenzie was watching the camera screen once again. Tuttle and Baker began by Mirandizing Terri-Lyn, pushing a waiver into place in front of her and instructing her to sign it if she understood everything she had been told.

Terri-Lyn looked from Baker to Tuttle, and back at Baker again, trying to decide which of the cops was more sympathetic to her story.

"What is all this? Why are you telling me this now?"

Baker spoke in a calm, even voice. Not pleasant, exactly, but removed, unemotional. "We want to make sure that you understand your rights before we ask you anything else about what happened the morning Michael died."

"I already told you—"

"A crock of lies," Tuttle snapped. "Of course you did. And now, it is time to own up and talk about what really happened. The time for cover-up has come to an end. You need to switch tracks now. We know what happened to Michael. How you killed him and dropped him off of the balcony, and pretended that it was an accident. All while telling your husband what a low life he was."

"Well... he is that," Terri-Lyn pointed out.

"No doubt," Baker agreed. "But so are you. Now tell us about what happened to Michael. The real story this time. There's no point in making us drag it out of you. Let's talk about what you did and why."

Terri-Lyn looked at Baker coldly.

"Why? I don't know who is talking to you, but if they are telling stories about me, I guess you know why already. He was ruining me."

It wasn't clear, to begin with, which "he" she was talking about.

"I didn't marry a poor man," Terri-Lyn said, a sneer distorting her mouth and nose. "I married a rich man, a rich, powerful man who was predicted to be the future governor of Vermont. This is the man I put my trust in. All of my hopes. Do you know what kind of home life I had? Did perfect little MacKenzie bother telling you anything about it? I wasn't going to live the rest of my life that way. I wasn't going to be a no one, smacked around by a no one, living and dying in obscurity. I wanted people to know who I am. Who I married. I was finished with being a nobody."

"And you hoped Cash would keep you on top of Vermont society. Everyone would know him and, in turn, know who you were. And in the beginning, it seemed like everything was going according to your plan."

Terri-Lyn favored Baker with a glare. A look that said, "Who do you think is telling this story?"

"Big wedding, big splash," Baker went on. "All of your friends and high society folks there. Congratulating you, giving you gifts. You get back to the mansion, and it's the honeymoon period. Everything is still going great. Maybe you notice a few chinks in Cash's armor, but you're willing to overlook those because everything is going great, and everybody else thinks he is fabulous."

Terri-Lyn licked her lips, maybe thinking about those early days. The whirlwind of society gossip that Kenzie had missed because she had been overseas. The splashy headlines. The first flush of married life, riding a roller coaster.

"How long did it last?" Baker asked. "How long was it before he hit you the first time? A week? A month? Maybe even a year? And then one day, when you thought everything was going great, he smacks you. Drunk, probably. You can excuse it once because he was drunk."

"How did I ever think I was going to get away from it?" Terri-Lyn demanded. "Did I think the rest of the world was any different?" She considered the question seriously. "Of course on TV, all families are perfect, even the defective ones. They still all love each other and take care of each other. MacKenzie's family, some of my other school friends... I didn't think they were like that. So it seemed like I should be able to land a man who wouldn't hit me, wouldn't stay out drinking, wouldn't turn into a ba— like him."

"But it turned out that you just picked out a higher-class jerk."

"Yeah. And not only that, but one who couldn't hold on to what he had. All of that money from his grandfather, the political appointments, all of that *promise*. He couldn't hold on to any of it on his own. It was all slipping through his fingers like water. And he was letting it go, spending his time with escorts and call girls when he had a job to do. Drinking and doping and beating on me. I wanted a man who wouldn't beat on me!"

But she'd stayed with him anyway. She hadn't been able to abandon ship. Even if she had figured it out in those first few months, she had stayed with him for years, and things didn't get better.

"I just wanted him to settle down, to stay at home, to be that stable, steady person for me... I didn't even care about the money or position anymore. I just wanted him to come home and take care of me." Terri-Lyn rubbed her forehead. "I thought I could at least have that."

The detectives nodded, making encouraging noises.

"Sylvia told me that if I had a baby, he would come back. He'd settle down and be a daddy and we could all be a family. That was how it had been with Cash's father. He had settled down when Cash was born. He'd stopped going out so much and had stayed home to play with him and take care of him. So it would be the same for Cash. When he saw his son, he would come back to me."

"But it didn't solve everything," Tuttle said flatly.

"It didn't make anything better. I was sick, I was in pain, and couldn't do anything, even after the baby was born. It was like someone had taken my body and replaced it with a different one, and nothing worked anymore. My body went flabby and weak and I couldn't get out of bed. I couldn't take care of a screaming baby all day long. How could anyone?"

"Babies with colic are a challenge to anyone," Baker sympathized. "I can't imagine how difficult that must have been with your post-partum depression."

"I was relieved when Sylvia took him. I needed my sleep, just for one night. I couldn't keep doing it. Couldn't keep feeding him and changing the stinking diapers and just... didn't have the energy to listen to one more scream. I don't know how I could have kept going if she hadn't taken him. I probably would have rolled over on him in my sleep. I was so exhausted I just wouldn't wake up. And then he would be gone."

She said it philosophically. She had, if Kenzie were right, put a lot of thought into it. She obviously knew that this sometimes happened when mothers kept their babies in bed and were too tired to wake up if something happened. She knew she could use it as an excuse. That it was just a tragic accident. Something that had been outside her control, being an exhausted mom having to deal with a shrieking, colicky baby who screamed all the time. And that would be a perma-nent solution. She would never have to worry about him again.

Had this idea festered with Terri-Lyn over the ensuing weeks and months? And then one day, she had just followed through, taking her son away from Cash.

"So Sylvia saved Michael. And rescued you from having to look after him all the time. It sounds like you were really having a hard time with him."

"I appreciated it at first. In the beginning, I couldn't think of anything I wanted more. Just for the screaming creature to be gone and to lie in my bed and sleep for as long as I needed to."

"You needed recovery time. It doesn't sound like you got it until then."

"No. I didn't." Terri-Lyn looked at Baker, her head cocked to the side, looking like a curious bird. "But then... after a while... I real-ized that she had him all the time. That she had stolen him from me. She was raising him like he was her son. He wanted her. She would rock him all night long." Her eyes got big in wonderment at this accomplishment. "This old woman, and she just rocked, and rocked, and rocked… and he slept for her. I don't know when she slept. How she got the rest that she needed. There I was, a woman in my prime, and I couldn't understand how she could do it."

"You started to resent her?"

"Yes. She was a witch. A thief. She had stolen my son from me and was trying to steal Cash too."

"How was she doing that?"

"Because Cash could go see Michael when he was with her. Meet him or pat him on the head or hold him for a few minutes, and everything was right. And Cash loved her already because she was his nanny too. She'd already stolen his heart years before. When she spoke up, when she wanted something from him, he always listened. Whatever she wanted, she could have."

"Was there anything romantic between the two of them?" Tuttle asked.

Terri-Lyn's face twisted. "Gross. No. There wasn't anything between them, not like that. But it didn't matter. He had other women to satisfy those needs. So what did he need me for anymore? I was just the wife, the arm candy, and rarely even that anymore. He was leaving me more and more, instead of staying with me like Sylvia said he would."

"So you resented him, and you resented her. And you had to do something about it."

"I had to take Michael back. At least some of the time. I had to act like I was happy to be the mommy, that I liked to be with him, that I got something fulfilling out of it."

"But you still didn't form a bond with him." Tuttle leaned forward in his seat.

Terri-Lyn shook her head, scowling. "I don't know what this bond is that they talk about. I never felt it. I don't think Michael ever felt it. He was my baby, and I tried to keep anyone from finding out that I wasn't all gooey over him like the other moms. And sometimes, Cash would come see him while he was with me, so I got what I wanted. But not often enough. And sometimes he didn't even want to see Michael. He just wanted him out of the way, and the kid was so annoying. When he was an infant, at least I could put him in a seat or a crib, and leave him there to sort himself out. Shut the door and ignore his screaming. But when he got older, more mobile, that doesn't work anymore."

"No," Baker agreed. "So you turned to other solutions…"

"It was Cash who hit him. I never hit him. He was just trying to toughen him up. Trying to get him to stop crying all the time. To listen to what his daddy told him to do. But he didn't. He was too little still. And Sylvia would get in the way, offer to take him away." Terri-Lyn rolled her eyes. "I couldn't stand that woman. What right did she think she had to my baby? Just because she rocked him a few times when he was colicky? She was the hired help, not Michael's mother."

"What did you do to stop Michael from crying?"

"I would just hold him." Terri-Lyn put her hands in front of her, curled as if she were holding Michael in front of her, hands around his torso with his legs dangling. "And I would give him a little shake." She demonstrated with a firm jerk. "And I would tell him no. No, Michael. Be quiet. No crying. No."

"And that worked?"

"Sometimes it did."

"And when that didn't work the first time, would you do it again?"

"Yes," Terri-Lyn said through gritted teeth. She demonstrated giving the baby a couple of firm shakes. Nothing that looked very violent. Her eyes were intent, drilling into the face of the imaginary baby. Firm. Telling him with her facial expression that he needed to stop. "Stop crying. Stop crying! Stop crying!"

She went still. She looked at the two police detectives. "It didn't hurt him. I wasn't doing this," she shook the imaginary child violently back and forth, so they could all imagine the baby's head flopping forward and back, brain bouncing around in his skull, causing the damage known among medical examiners as Shaken Baby Syndrome. "I wouldn't do that."

"What would you do if he still didn't listen?"

She folded her arms, looking stubborn. "Call Sylvia. Tell her to take care of him."

"Oh, I see. Even though you didn't like her?"

"Yes. She was the only one who could quiet him."

"Why don't you tell us what happened the day Michael died?" Baker said, reaching out like she was going to touch Terri-Lyn to comfort her, and then pulling her hand back so that she didn't actually touch her. "There seems to be a lot of confusion, a lot of different stories about what happened."

52

"It wasn't any different than any other day," Terri-Lyn insisted. Though surely she understood that it had ended up being very, very different from all of the days before it. But if she was only playing a part, acting like a loving, concerned mother, then maybe it was no different living her life without Michael than it had been living her life with him somewhere else in the house, out of the way so she didn't have to think about him or her failure to keep Cash in line.

"I have to get up and do my Pilates. That might seem like it isn't important, but it is. I had to build up my core strength. I had to rebuild my whole body after Michael was born. It was so awful, feeling like some alien body had been swapped in place of mine. I had always thought I would be a strong woman, that nothing could change that. If I wanted to be in a good space, physically and mentally, then I needed to do my exercise routine."

"Of course," Baker agreed.

"And then... it was a Sunday morning, you know, like it is today. That meant that Cash didn't have to work. We could have a lazy morning, just like the families on TV or in comic books. You know how they lay around, reading or smoking a pipe. I wanted that picture in my head. I got Michael from Sylvia and gave her some jobs to do in the kitchen and such. Told her that I needed her to take care of them. And I took Michael to where Cash was, sitting at his desk going over some papers. I tried to talk to him—but he wouldn't talk to me! Told me to go back to my rooms with the boy, and he'd come see him later."

She looked around vaguely at the interrogation room. But not seeing the room, Kenzie didn't think. Remembering what had happened that day. Picturing it in her mind. Trying to construct the scenario she had wanted, and what she had ended up with.

"I stayed in his rooms. Not his office, but in his sitting room. Michael wanted to play. Wanted to go back to the nursery. I told him no, made him sit, to be quiet like he was at church. I remember my daddy smacking me if I ever got out of line at church. Kids can be trained to behave the way you want them to. If you try hard enough, make them stop and pay attention."

"So he was just sitting quietly on his own?" Baker asked.

"On my lap. He wouldn't sit on his own. He would be moving around all over the place and fooling around. I could hold him on my lap and make him be still when I told him to."

"How did you do that?"

"Just held him still."

"And squeezed," Tuttle suggested.

Terri-Lyn didn't answer.

"If he didn't sit still, you squeezed him, didn't you? Or if he was making noise? If he wasn't the perfect, quiet child, you wrapped your arms around him and squeezed him tighter and tighter until he stopped."

"He always stopped," Terri-Lyn informed him proudly, as if this demonstrated her stellar parenting skills. "I would hold him tight, and he knew it was time to stop squirming and sit still with Mommy."

While she literally squeezed the breath out of him, constricting so tightly that she broke ribs on multiple occasions.

"And then what happened?"

Terri-Lyn looked at Baker blankly, her eyes dark holes. "What do you mean?"

"When Cash finished his work and came out to see his son, what did he say?"

"There were... words exchanged. He realized that he had pushed it too far this time. That he had taken too long on his stupid work and gave up on his chance to see his son. Fathers who neglect their children... shouldn't be allowed to see them."

"He saw that you had hurt Michael again. After you promised you wouldn't."

"No. Cash was the one who hurt him. He took him away from me. He was the one who threw Michael over the balcony. What kind of father does that? You see what kind of person he is? He should be locked up."

Hear, hear. Kenzie agreed. Both of them should be locked up.

"Maybe the kind of father who wants to protect his wife," Tuttle pointed out. "The kind who wants to keep her from being suspected of having done something terrible to the child. When he took Michael from you and found that you hadn't just hurt him, but killed him, he did it to cover for you. To make his death look like a tragic accident."

"He should have thought about me before," Terri-Lyn's mouth formed a pout. "He should have done something about it when he still could."

It was, all in all, an exhausting day. Kenzie found it difficult to deal with the emotion of the deaths rather than just the clinical details. The police had to deal with a lot more of that stuff than she did. She was grateful that most days she could retreat into the data and just be concerned with solving the puzzle of what had caused a person's death rather than who had done it and how and why.

Zachary had texted her a couple of times during the day to let her know that he was out on a job, doing some surveillance of an insurance claimant suspected of fraud. Giving her a little update every now and then.

Suspect on the move

False alarm. Checked the mailbox

No movement for six hours

There were definitely worse things than watching police interviews. She didn't know how he could sit for so long—and longer—without ever even laying eyes on a suspect. He would be tired when he got home too.

They both headed home at about the same time. Zachary had planned it that way, of course, so they could spend dinner and the evening together. He was very good at scheduling around their together time if he possibly could.

He beat her home and she found him downloading his camera shots onto his laptop when she arrived. He hugged her, smelling of stale sweat after sitting in a car for so much of the day. His sandpaper cheek rubbed against hers. But rather than being irritated by these evidences of his long workday, she was comforted by the *realness* of their life together. His familiar appearance, smell, and feel all provided a texture to her life that she would miss if he were gone.

She thought of how her father had been so absent from her life as a child, gone while the senate was in session, traveling to meet with clients, to press the flesh and to convince people to support his causes. She'd always been happy when he came home and spent time with them. But she had wanted him to be there more often. To be more of a part of their day-to-day life.

Zachary buried his face in the soft skin of her throat, collarbone, and shoulder, taking a deep breath to inhale her scent and scraping the sensitive area with his whiskers.

"Hey!" Kenzie pushed him away. "Cut that out! You're going to give me a friction burn!"

He laughed, kissing her and making goosebumps run down her neck and arms. Then he withdrew and kissed her on the forehead.

"How was your day?"

"Mmm." Kenzie squeezed him tightly. "Let's just say... I'm glad I don't work with psychopaths every day."

Zachary chuckled. "I think we can all be thankful for that."

"Other than the people who *do* work with psychopaths every day."

"Yes, other than them," Zachary agreed.

They moved to the kitchen together without discussing it, even though neither had yet had the time to shower off the sweat and grit of the day. Zachary poured himself a glass of water and looked questioningly at Kenzie. She opened the freezer and pulled out a pint of chocolate chunk fudge ice cream to see how much was left. She really only needed a bite or two. Just something to take the edge off the day.

They sat down at the table. Kenzie told Zachary about the interviews with Cash and Terri-Lyn, trying to impart to him the morass of emotions she had felt in watching them. Her helplessness over what had already been done, her anger at two parents who had put their own needs and feelings ahead of the little boy they were supposed to love, cherish, and protect. But he had been an inconvenience for them. A pawn that had eventually outlived its usefulness.

"And then there was the nanny," Kenzie sighed.

"What did you find out about her? Do you know for sure... which one of them killed her? How it happened?"

"I figured going into it that it was the same person as had killed Michael. Both were asphyxiation by mechanical compression, so the chances that they were done by two different people was... pretty remote."

"Did you know the mother killed him rather than the father?"

"I was really hoping that it was the father, to tell the truth. I didn't want it to be her."

Zachary nodded his understanding. "We never want to hear that a woman, a mother, could do something like that. It's... somehow it's more horrific when it is a mother than a father or stepparent. We expect all mothers to have that innate love..." Zachary swallowed hard and took a drink. Thinking, Kenzie supposed, about his own mother, abusive and negligent, who had labeled him incorrigible and abandoned them all when Zachary was ten. Another prime example of a mother who did not meet society's standards for selfless, unfailing love.

"And it's hard on us when they don't," Kenzie agreed, filling the void in the conversation. She didn't tell him it was all that much worse because she knew the mother. Had once known her closely, thought of her like a sister, a soulmate. But Terri-Lyn was not the girl she had been in the early grades. The change had already started in high school when she had realized how different her family was from Kenzie's and the families of other kids at school who still had both parents at home. When she had decided to punish Kenzie for having the perfect family by humiliating her in front of the school.

She hadn't conquered that jealous streak and that need to get retribution by taking something precious away from the person she was angry with.

"Did she confess to killing the nanny as well? Or give enough information that they'll be able to hang it on her?"

Kenzie let a chunk of frozen chocolate melt in her mouth.

"I wondered how she had gotten the nanny out there to the place in the woods where the body was dumped. The nanny was small, but even a small body is difficult to move very far without a gurney or a wheelbarrow, and there wasn't any sign that someone had pushed or pulled anything with wheels through there. It would have been pretty hard to. The ground is bumpy and overgrown."

Zachary nodded. "If there is anyone who knows about the difficulties of moving a dead body, it would be you."

"It's always best to use the tools you have. We don't lug them around in our arms or over our shoulders."

Zachary snorted at the image.

"So, how did she get her out there?"

"She didn't have to. The nanny took regular walks around the property to stay in shape. No Pilates for her."

"And the mother met her out there."

"Yeah. Waited for her or confronted her there, and then had it out about Ca—about the father and about what the mother had done. Everyone knew or had a pretty good idea of what had happened. They knew that Terri-Lyn was responsible, even if they didn't know all the details. They were loyal employees and didn't talk about it in their statements to the police. Everybody stuck to the line that they didn't know anything was wrong until they heard the nanny screaming."

"But the mother didn't think that the nanny was going to stay quiet? Figured that she was going to go to the police?"

"She couldn't say why she had gone to talk to the nanny, but I think she must have planned to kill her from the start. What else would she go out there for? It wasn't part of her normal routine. It wasn't to plead with the nanny to stay quiet. That wasn't her style. She said it was an accident."

"An accident?" Zachary repeated. "How exactly was it an accident? The nanny tripped? Had a heart attack?"

"I think that's what she hoped to convince the detectives of. But she ended up giving them a pretty full confession. She stopped the nanny on her morning constitutional…"

53

"What are you doing here?" Sylvia demanded, her eyes darting around the woods as she evaluated escape routes. "Isn't it enough that you killed Michael and ruined your husband? Why are you still here? Why didn't you leave? You should get as far away from this place as possible. Leave us alone."

"Why should I go?" Terri-Lyn challenged, her dark eyes defiant. "This is my home. Cash is the one who is responsible for Michael's death and, if they arrest him for it, do you think I'm going to do anything to save him? Do you think I would align myself with him after all he has done? I'm done pretending to be his loving, devoted wife. I'll tell the media just who he is. Not the loving family man he has portrayed himself as. He is a failure. A drunk. He has no redeeming qualities."

"You've never appreciated him," the smaller woman sneered. "You have no idea what he could have become if you'd been the person you pretended to be. If he'd had the love and support of a wife instead of a cold, hard-hearted woman who only cares for herself. You could have supported him. Lifted him up. Understood that no man is perfect and turned a blind eye to his mistakes. But instead, you have to tear him down, weaken him, drive him away. Before you came here... things were going well for him. He was a rising star. Now..."

"Now he is nothing," Terri-Lyn said with satisfaction. "He's ruined."

"I could say that *you* are too."

Terri-Lyn took a step closer to the older woman, getting into her personal space, making sure she towered over her, physically intimidating.

"You don't scare me," Sylvia said coldly, though she looked around like she was waiting for someone to show up and rescue her. "If I tell what I know, you'll go to prison for the rest of your life. So why don't you leave? So that Cash doesn't have to deal with *that* humiliation as well."

"What do you think will happen if I talk?" Terri-Lyn challenged. "If I tell them what Cash did. What he did over and over again, beating me, beating Michael. The medical examiner already knows. She's seen the bruises. All the police need is confirmation as to who did it. And I have enough pictures of my bruised body to show that he wasn't picky about who he hit."

"They wouldn't put him in prison. Not a man of his stature and reputation."

"I would make sure they did! And even if they didn't, do you think he'd ever be allowed in politics again? He'd be ruined for life. In fact, maybe that's better. Ruin his reputation. Make him walk around for the rest of his life like a ghost, with everyone knowing what kind of person he really is."

Sylvia swore and shoved Terri-Lyn, forcing her to take a couple of steps back to keep her balance. Sylvia was a tough old bird, surprisingly strong, considering she didn't follow any of the programs Terri-Lyn thought necessary for building strength. But Terri-Lyn was strong too. And she had been training. Had been trying to get back that hard, lithe body she'd had before getting pregnant. She shoved Sylvia back, driving her back farther and farther with each push. Sylvia flailed at Terri-Lyn, trying to stop her and force her back.

Terri-Lyn gave one more hard shove, this time making Sylvia trip and fall over backward. Terri-Lyn threw herself on top of the woman

and pinned her wrists in place so that she couldn't move. Sylvia struggled, but Terri-Lyn held her still. She felt again what it was like to
hold Michael in her arms, forcing him to be still, to submit to her
will and her strength, to listen to her like a child was supposed to.
When she used to go to church, they talked about children being
submissive and obeying their parents, but as far as Terri-Lyn had seen,
that was not the way children behaved. Not in modern days, anyway.

Sylvia squirmed, trying to escape Terri-Lyn's iron grip. But Terri-
Lyn wasn't letting her go. This was the woman who had stolen Cash
from her. Sylvia had stolen his heart, had made it so that Cash had
nothing else to give to Terri-Lyn. And she was the one who had stolen
Michael too, alienating his affection so that he didn't even want to be
around his own mother and was always asking if he could go see
Nanny when Terri-Lyn wanted him to be with her.

Sylvia was stronger than the baby, that was for sure. There were a
couple of times when Terri-Lyn thought that Sylvia was going to
throw her off. But she squirmed and writhed and twisted her hips and
Terri-Lyn hung on, like a fisher who had caught a marlin or a shark.
If she could just hold on long enough, she knew that Sylvia would
give in. She worked her way up to kneel on Sylvia's chest, all of her
weight on that one point. She watched Sylvia's face turn white and
then blue, gasping and begging, her mouth opening and closing like
the dying fish that she was, until, at last, she was still.

Even then, she waited, wary of a trick. Gradually, Terri-Lyn
relaxed her muscles, released her grip on Sylvia's wrists, and eventually
got to her feet and stared down at the old witch. She was a witch, just
like the one on The Wizard of Oz that got crushed beneath the house.
Because she had been evil. She had tried to take away all of the happi-
ness that Terri-Lyn had earned. And now, she was banished. Terri-Lyn
didn't have to worry about the old witch and what she might say
anymore.

Zachary shook his head, looking almost as shell-shocked as Kenzie
felt. Terri-Lyn hated Sylvia with such venom. This woman who had
raised her husband and who had rescued Terri-Lyn when her son's

care had been too much for her and helped to keep him safe. The woman who had, as far as Kenzie had seen, been the most caring and compassionate person in the Wade mansion.

Yet Terri-Lyn had seen her as a threat. As someone who had usurped her role and was trying to take away the things that she valued most. Not her husband and son, but her prestige and social position, her money, her place in the mansion. Those were things that Terri-Lyn would not give up on.

"People do evil things," Zachary offered in a subdued tone.

"Yeah. You never really know what is going on in someone else's mind. I wouldn't have thought she was anything like that. Abused, yes, but someone who would intentionally kill two other people? Her own child? I never would have thought it of her."

"You think she is a psychopath, like you said earlier?"

Kenzie shrugged. "There's no actual clinical definition of a psychopath. But yes... I think that with how she was brought up, she decided that her comfort and success were all that mattered. It didn't matter what anyone else in the family needed or did; she needed to look out for herself and never let anyone in again."

Kenzie stared off into space, thinking about it. She had another bite of ice cream.

"So, is she the only one who is being charged?" Zachary asked. "If the father didn't actually contribute to the boy's death..."

"He was certainly responsible, on some levels, for what happened. And for covering it up. He was arrested, but I think the murder charges will go away, and he'll get a pile of child abuse charges, as well as obstruction and accessory. And spousal abuse too, for that matter. He might not have killed Michael, but he could have. And he certainly contributed to the circumstances of Michael's death. From what the staff said, and the evidence of the previous rib fractures Michael suffered, it's obvious that she had done this before. Holding him so tightly that she broke his ribs and he passed out. They had been lucky to be able to revive him before. This time... she was more determined, or he took too long to get to her."

"You would think that if he knew she had done it before, he would have seen to it that she was never alone with the boy. That any time she was upset, somebody should stay with her or take him away. If they had reported the earlier incidents, she would have been in jail and this would not have happened."

"For that to happen, they would have to admit that the family was not perfect. And what are the chances they would lock him up for his part in the abuse as well? That had to be why he stayed quiet."

"That, or he really didn't care."

Zachary reached across the table to touch Kenzie's hand. A quick flutter of a touch to show that he cared about her and what she was feeling after having dealt with the psychopaths.

"What do you want to do tonight? It's Sunday, which is usually your rest day, but you'll have to get up and return to work in the morning. So these last few hours…"

"I don't know. Shower, eat, and relax." Kenzie looked at the clock on the wall. "Did you want to chat with Lorne and Pat, since we weren't able to get back down there this weekend?"

"Yeah. But they'll understand if you're busy with something else. If you need to nap or just want to veg out watching TV… it's been a tough day for you."

"Yeah. Well, after this," she took another bite of chocolate ice cream, "I'm going to shower. If you want to call after that, I'll see how I feel. I might eat while we chat, or just take some time to myself and not think about all of this. I'll just see."

Zachary nodded. "Sounds like a plan."

54

enzie picked at leftovers from the fridge while Zachary started the video chat with Lorne Peterson and Pat Parker. She wanted more ice cream. Or pizza. Or something equally bad for her. But she was trying to eat a salad and some vegetables left over from other meals. She was feeling virtuous about not having ordered in. But she wasn't actually happy with what she was eating.

Zachary was telling the two men the general shape of their week and how things had gone since they'd had to leave the Sunday brunch so abruptly. The big case that Kenzie had been working on, though Loren and Pat did not want too many details about Kenzie's cases. Zachary had a PBJ sandwich on the plate beside his computer, which certainly looked better than salad.

"Tell them about *your* case," Kenzie told Zachary. "It sounded pretty exciting."

Zachary looked at her, brows drawn down in a frown. "What?"

"Your surveillance," Kenzie prodded. "That sounded really interesting."

He took another second to realize that she was teasing and grinned. "Oh yeah, sitting around in my car for hours on end, hoping to catch some glimpse of someone lifting a child or doing gardening or one of the things that she said she couldn't do due to the accident. That's very exciting."

"And did you?" Pat asked.

"Did I what?"

"Catch her doing something she wasn't supposed to be able to do?"

"No."

They all laughed at his dour tone.

"Sometimes, our jobs suck," Zachary told Kenzie.

"Yeah, sometimes they really do. Lorne, I was wondering... when you and your wife were fostering, how many kids did you have?"

She looked around the corner of Zachary's screen to see his face for a moment.

"Oh, usually two or three at a time."

"But how many did you have in total? Do you know?"

"Oh, no. I lost track. It's possible that Lilith would know. She was the record keeper and administrator, not me. I just tried to keep things going smoothly. Provide whatever assistance I could give when I wasn't at work."

Kenzie nodded.

"Why do you ask?" Lorne asked. "You're not looking into foster care, are you?"

"No." Kenzie had to admit that the thought did cross her mind occasionally, knowing that many people found it fulfilling, and it was an important service to the community. But she also knew how difficult it would be. Zachary had been highly traumatized when he had gone into foster care and had been so high needs that he had never had a family who could take care of him for long. She knew it would mean giving up much of their time with each other. And if she ended up with a child like Terri-Lyn, with no conscience to speak of, she knew she couldn't handle that. "No, no. I was just thinking about this case. If either the victim or his killer had gone into foster care... maybe there would have been a chance for them. When I think of the number of kids that you helped... I'm very proud of you."

Lorne Peterson's face turned very pink. "Well, thank you, Kenzie. It wasn't really my doing. It was really Lilith who was in charge of the whole thing. But I did what I could."

"And I know that you did a good job, or Zachary wouldn't still be in touch with you. I know you were a good foster dad even if he was only in your home for a couple of weeks because of the way he has kept in touch with you for all of these years."

Zachary nodded his agreement. Lorne wiped sweat from his face, looking embarrassed and proud at the same time. Pat gave him a quick hug around the shoulders. "He's one special guy," he agreed.

"If you ever wanted to talk about foster care, feel free to ask," Lorne said. "I've been out of the loop for a long time, so things have changed, but the basics are still the same, and I know people who are still 'in the business,' so to speak."

"Okay, thanks," Kenzie agreed. "It's not something I'm planning on."

He nodded and didn't push it. Zachary gave Kenzie a sideways look. He would just have to trust her that it wasn't something she was asking about because she wanted to start fostering children. She wasn't even sure she wanted to have children of her own. Her parents would be delighted if she decided to provide them with some grand-babies, but providing grandchildren or even having someone to carry on the family name were not good reasons for having children. If she chose to have children, it would be because she wanted them. Being pushed into it, or encouraged to have children for the wrong reason, as Terri-Lyn had been, couldn't happen. There was nothing wrong with them just enjoying Zachary's nieces and nephews and the children of friends.

Dr. Wiltshire had been in over the weekend and had reviewed Kenzie's postmortem results and the attendant exhibits, so the official medical examiner's reports were issued hard on the heels of the news that both Cash Wade and his wife Terri-Lyn had been arrested in connection with the abuse of Michael Wade, his death, and Sylvia Arnold's death.

That was a lot for the media to handle, and it seemed like everywhere Kenzie went, she saw headlines and news reports on the deaths. She saw her autopsy reports summarized in five-word sound bites that were usually inaccurate and definitely overhyped. The cause of death itself, asphyxiation, was not as sexy as a drug overdose or shooting, so they had to find other ways to grab people's interest, usually by getting things completely backward, at least in the headline.

With the autopsies complete, the bodies could be released. Cash Wade was already out on bail, so Kenzie left a message for him about Michael's body being available for pickup by his funeral home. She wasn't sure who to contact about Sylvia Arnold's body. Despite the fact that Sylvia had been so devoted to Cash, Kenzie suspected that he would not be managing her transportation and funeral arrangements. She looked through Sylvia's phone, which had been reviewed by the police detectives, and was not needed for the prosecutions of Terri-Lyn or Cash.

Baker had told her there were three children and that Sylvia didn't keep in very close touch with them by phone. But their numbers were in the contact list, so Kenzie grabbed the number for Caden, the child she seemed to be in touch with the most often, and called him up. She explained about needing someone to claim Sylvia's remains. It always felt awkward to her to call up total strangers and to try to get them to pick up their deceased loved ones' remains. In many cases, the family members had been estranged for a long time and didn't know how to handle her call.

Caden spoke to her briefly and seemed like a nice, polite young man. He had heard the news of his mother's death and seen the headlines about Cash Wade and his wife and all the publicity swirling around them.

"Can I come there to talk to you?" he asked Kenzie. "I just... this is hard to do over the phone."

"Sure, of course," Kenzie assured him. "And your siblings, if they want to come in. But you don't have to if you don't want to. You can communicate with your funeral home and I'll deal with them. As long as the proper paperwork is signed, I don't actually need you to come in person. A lot of people don't."

"I'd just like to come in and do it face to face."

Kenzie agreed. She gave Caden her contact information and the hours she would be there and hoped she wouldn't be in autopsy when he came by. She had a couple that she needed to attend to. She needed to take care not to get behind while Dr. Wiltshire was out of commission. If she got behind, catching up again would not be easy.

By the time Caden came in, she had forgotten all about him and was immersed in her work. She looked up, smiling, when she heard footsteps coming toward her. For a moment, she was startled, thinking he was Cash Wade, but there was only a passing resemblance. He introduced himself and shook her hand. Sylvia had raised him well.

"If we could sit down together somewhere," Caden suggested, "you could show me everything I need to do to get this done."

Kenzie pulled out a form for him. "It's actually very simple. If you'll fill this out—"

He looked at the form, shaking his head. Kenzie stopped, frowning. There was no way to do an end run around the paperwork. If he wanted his mother's remains released, he would have to complete everything.

"Could we sit down?" Caden repeated.

Kenzie nodded and escorted him into the boardroom, where they sat down at the table and she again showed him the form. "It's not a lot of work, just this one form, and then I can get the ball rolling. Do you know the funeral home you want to use?"

"Yeah. I think so. But I need a hand with this, if you don't mind."

"Uh, sure. I'm happy to help." Kenzie slid the paper in front of him, right side up, and pointed out the sections. "This is your mother's information up here, her name and birth date—"

"I'm dyslexic," he told her. "It would be a lot easier if you could tell me what you need and write it down for me. Otherwise, it will take me a really long time to fill this out, and it will probably be all wrong and you'd need to do it over again afterward."

"Oh! Of course." Kenzie relaxed once she understood the problem. "My partner is dyslexic too. I know he loathes forms. Everything so densely written, and then he has trouble writing as well, so he always takes twice as long as he thinks he should to fill it out so that it is legible."

"I'd be happy with twice as long," Caden laughed. "Maybe ten times as long. It's not that I can't, but it will be much easier to get it right the first time if we just go through it together."

"Sure."

She read the questions to him, explained them when necessary, and then wrote down the information he dictated back to her. He had most of the dates and information in his head, which Kenzie thought was pretty impressive. Most family members she dealt with did not know their parent's information by heart. But with the difficulty Caden had looking information up and writing it down, he compensated by memorizing what he needed to know. He was charming and polite, and Kenzie enjoyed the short interchange as she filled in his answers.

"There. That's got it. You just need to sign at the bottom." She made an X by the signature box and turned it around for him. Caden held the pen awkwardly in a left-handed grip and twisted his body to write in a position that was almost upside down to scribble his illegible signature diagonally across the box.

"Great," Kenzie approved. The form didn't need to be machine read. The signature didn't have to fit neatly inside the box. "That should do it, then. I'll let the funeral home know that we have all the paperwork and they can pick up her remains at any time."

"Thanks for helping me out with that." He gave her a warm smile. "I always dread filling out forms. And do you have... any personal effects?"

"We can just send those along with the remains, if you want."

"No, I wanted to get them today, if possible."

"Yeah. We can do that. Give me a minute and I'll bring them to you."

There wasn't much for him to collect. Kenzie grabbed the bag labeled with Sylvia's name and returned to the boardroom to hand it to him. He looked through it, frowning.

"No wallet or purse?"

"No. The police haven't found them. It's a pretty large property, it would be easy to drop them or hide them in the woods somewhere and they would be very difficult to find. Or toss them in the septic tank or some abandoned building. I'm sorry."

He shrugged. "It's okay. Not your fault." He pulled out Sylvia's phone and apparently knew her passcode. He tapped through the apps, pulling up the photos app to thumb through the most recent pictures. He shook his head. "Should have known it would all be Cash and Michael." He grimaced. "Her other family."

"She seemed to be very devoted to them," Kenzie agreed. "It's rare to see such strong employer-employee bonds. But I understand she knew Mr. Wade from the time he was a little boy."

"Yes. Knew him way before any of us were ever thought of," Caden agreed. "We grew up on the property, knowing Cash and the household staff. It just seemed natural to us that she would live with him and that he would be such a big part of her life. That was all we had ever known. But when we got old enough to go out into the world on our own... it was a bit of a shock to realize that the rest of the world didn't have that kind of long-term, close relationship between employers and employees."

Kenzie chuckled. "I guess that would be a bit of a shock when that's how you grew up."

"He wasn't just her employer. He was her everything. She was so excited when Michael was born. Another Wade baby."

"From everything I have heard, she was a really good caregiver to him too. He had colic and... there were a number of issues. But she took good care of him. She was very patient and loving."

He nodded, swiping through some more pictures on the phone. "Yeah, she was a good mom, too. We always felt like the household was our extended family. Everyone knew who we were, would help us, give us a cookie, whatever."

"That's nice. How did your dad feel about it? It must have been strange for him to live there. Or was he part of the staff as well?"

Caden lowered the phone. "We never knew who our dad was. Or who *they* were. It was just Mom."

"Oh." Kenzie studied him for a moment, wondering if there was more, then pushed the questions away. It was none of her business.

Her job was done. Her time with Sylvia Arnold had come to an end.

55

The message was from an unknown caller. A blocked number, burner phone, or even an ancient payphone still in service. Kenzie tapped it, figuring it would probably be a cop.

"She wasn't a saint, you know." Terri-Lyn's voice was sharp and bitter. "Everyone in the media is acting like Sylvia was this wonderful person who was the perfect mother and nanny. But you didn't live with her. You didn't see what was really going on."

There was a long period of silence, and Kenzie thought the message was going to cut off there. She'd heard that Terri-Lyn, too, was out on bail. It was amazing how much easier it was for a rich person to get out on bail than a poor one. Even a confessed murderer like Terri-Lyn.

"You should have listened to me, MacKenzie," Terri-Lynn carried on. "You should have listened to your mother and helped me instead of railroading me like you did. One day, you're going to be sorry you did that."

Kenzie's finger hovered over the red End Call button, but she could see from the time code that the message wasn't yet over.

"I did the only thing I could. I was driven to it. Instead of people being sorry for what I had to go through, they're calling me a monster. A murderer. Worse." She sniffled and gulped, crying for herself. "You would have done the same thing. You don't know what they were like, Sylvia and Cash. Don't spend any time feeling sorry for them. One day it will all come out, and you'll be sorry you didn't stand by me. You just wait and see."

There was another period of silence, and this time the message cut off.

Kenzie sat staring at the phone. A knot of anxiety twisted in her stomach.

She knew that she had done everything properly, had dug as deeply as she could, and searched out all of the evidence that both bodies had to offer. As she had told Zachary, she hadn't wanted it to be Terri-Lyn.

It was out of her hands and up to the police and prosecutor to put the case together.

Wherever Terri-Lyn went and whatever term she had to serve, it wasn't Kenzie's fault.

And no amount of time would bring Michael back.

Did you enjoy this book? Reviews and recommendations are vital to making a book successful.

Please leave a review at your favorite book store or review site and share it with your friends.

Don't miss the following bonus material:
Sign up for mailing list to get a free ebook
Read a sneak preview chapter
Other books by P.D. Workman
Learn more about the author

DON'T MISS A THING! GET THE LATEST NEWS AND A FREE EBOOK

Your First Taste

PREVIEW OF SHATTERED TO DEATH

PREVIEW CHAPTER 1

Kenzie was just dropping off to sleep when her phone rang, making both her and Zachary jump.

Zachary instantly sat up and reached for his phone, even though it wasn't his ringtone. He pulled back after touching it, realizing by then that it wasn't his phone that was ringing. It took longer for Kenzie to rouse herself to some semblance of logical thought and to reach for her phone. Her phone was usually on silent mode so that it would not disturb Zachary at night. In theory, Kenzie would awaken to the phone's vibration on the side table and be able to silence it and leave the bedroom to take the call without waking Zachary. In reality, he was usually the one who awoke to the vibration and had to shake Kenzie awake to see whether it was an important call.

But tonight, she was on call and had turned the ringer on and set her volume to high so she couldn't miss a call-out. Dr. Wiltshire had attended two calls in person the night before, so it was his turn to sleep while Kenzie dealt with any calls.

It wasn't like a call-out was an emergency. It could wait a couple of hours if she didn't answer the phone immediately. It wasn't like her patients were going anywhere or would be more dead when she got there.

She liked to get to a scene as early as possible to take temperature readings and talk to the person who had discovered the body and any other witnesses about the circumstances. While most calls that the ME's office got were routine, she wanted to be on top of it if it was a potential homicide, when details like an accurate time of death could become very important. A whole case could hinge on who was or wasn't around during the relevant window.

Kenzie blinked hard and picked up her phone. "Medical Examiner's Office," she answered, after confirming that the call had been routed through the ME's office line.

"We need the medical examiner to attend a scene." The voice on the other end was male. Calm and official. But there was something in the tone of his voice that alerted Kenzie that he was nervous or excited. A slight change in pitch? His breaths coming faster than she would have expected. She couldn't put her finger on precisely what made him sound young and inexperienced, despite the definite adult timbre of his voice.

"Can I get the details?" Kenzie asked. "Address and what happened?"

It wasn't a law enforcement officer; she was pretty sure of that. They had their own particular official tone. Much more forceful and confident. Expectation, but also a hint of the routine, of a resignation that the ME might not get there for several hours and they would be left standing around the body waiting for someone to show up.

"Persons Residential Care," the voice on the other end of the phone informed her, following up with the address. He didn't answer the "What happened?"

"Got it," Kenzie agreed. "Can you tell me the circumstances of the death? I'd like to know whether I can get by with the death kit I have with me or whether I need to pick up additional equipment from the office."

"Well... I don't know. He just died."

"He just died?" Kenzie repeated. "In a medical facility?"

"Yes. I don't know what happened. Someone should come."

"I'll be there. No sign of violence? What was the patient in care for?"

"Psychiatric."

His answers were not particularly helpful, and from the muffled sounds in the background, Kenzie assumed that he was covering the mouthpiece and speaking to someone else, or someone else was talking to him and he didn't want Kenzie to hear everything being said.

"I'll be there shortly," she promised.

He hung up without any thanks or goodbye.

"Everything okay?" Zachary demanded as soon as Kenzie lowered her phone. He ran a hand over his dark buzzcut and blinked.

"Sure. Just got a call-out." She shrugged. "We both knew it could happen."

"People ought to pick a more convenient time to die," Zachary suggested playfully.

"They should," Kenzie agreed with a smile. She sighed and got out of bed, putting her phone back on the side table while she stripped off her pajamas and quickly pulled on clothes more appropriate for a scene of death attendance.

"Murder?" Zachary asked.

"No. Medical facility." She didn't tell him anything more than that. Not like she could; so far, she was completely in the dark about what had happened.

Kenzie glanced out the window. *In the dark* was right. The sun had been down for hours. People *did* choose inconvenient times to die.

"I could drive you," Zachary suggested. He had done that once or twice before, especially if he thought she was too tired to drive or needed him there for another reason.

But there was no need for him to be around in this case. No indication that it was anything other than a patient dying in his sleep. It was not an uncommon occurrence in a psychiatric facility.

"No, you stay home and get your sleep," Kenzie told Zachary, even though she knew there was no way he would sleep while she was gone. He would get up and work on his laptop or watch TV. Or just pace. "I don't know how long I will be, but I'm fine. No need for both of us to be out."

"I'd be happy to come along…"

"Not necessary. Thanks for the offer, though."

Zachary sighed. Kenzie knew that he would have preferred to go with her, but she didn't know how long she would be and didn't want him sitting around in the car waiting for her to finish her routine tasks at the scene.

Though it wasn't like he minded spending time sitting in the car. In fact, he chose to sit in it for hours on end when he was on a surveillance job. That was the life of a PI, sometimes. More often than not, he was assigned to keep an eye on someone to learn their schedule, where they worked, whether they were having an affair, or whether they were able to do more than they had told their insurance company after an accident. People actually lied to their insurance companies. Who would have guessed?

"Sorry," she told him. "I doubt I'll be too long. I should be back tonight."

"You'd better be. I don't like you stepping out on me for these stiffs."

Kenzie grinned. She finished getting dressed and ducked into the bathroom to check her hair and try to tame the wild, dark curls into something more professional. She put on a coating of her trademark red lipstick, though she knew no one but her would appreciate it, considering the circumstances. She picked up her phone and handbag as she walked back through the bedroom and got on her way.

PREVIEW CHAPTER 2

Kenzie knew generally where Persons was, but hadn't been there before. Or she might have attended there once as a medical student, but couldn't remember much about it. Maybe when she was writing a paper and needed to interview someone? It was several years in the past, and the sleepless nights of medical school had blurred the memories.

She gave her baby, a beautiful, cherry-red convertible, time to warm up before backing out of the garage and getting on the road. She was soon outside the town limits, getting away from the glaring streetlights and sparse traffic. It took a few minutes for her eyes to adjust to the dark of the country road, and then she could see stars sprinkled across the black canvas of the night, thousands of twinkling pinpricks, and a sliver of a bright moon.

She had that awake-alert feeling that she got when she was taking care of an emergency when she would normally have been sleeping. She remembered the early morning starts to vacations when she had been young, sometimes having to go to the airport in the wee hours to catch an international flight. Sleeping with her head resting on her mother's shoulder while they sat in the chairs of the waiting area for boarding to begin. But not sleeping. Staring at the dark windows and watching the preparations covertly, looking as though she was asleep, but with an alertness running through her body, her brain primed to take everything in.

The care facility was not far away. Just away from the hustle and bustle of the town. Somewhere quiet for people to recover. To take a break from their stressful, pressured lives and regenerate, get healthy before returning to the homes and families waiting for them.

Kenzie pulled into the parking lot and couldn't identify any particular parking space that she should take. It was quiet, just a few cars from the night staff were there. And a long black hearse backed into one of the staff stalls near the doors. Kenzie pulled up to the big double doors and shut off the engine.

A security guard walked out to meet her as she grabbed her death kit and walked toward the doors. He held up his hand to stop her and send her back. "I'm sorry. You can't park there. And it turns out your services are not needed. You were called in error. Just a mistake."

Kenzie frowned at him. "I'm sorry?"

"You're from the ME's office, right? I'm sorry. You aren't actually supposed to be here."

"I was called about a death."

"Yes, that was wrong. You shouldn't have been. Someone who didn't know proper procedures…"

Kenzie shook her head, brushing aside his hand as he reached out to block her and send her back.

"I'm sorry, but once I am called to a scene, I have to attend."

"But you weren't supposed to be."

"Actually, I was. The ME's office is required to attend any deaths occurring at a psychiatric facility."

"There's no need." He blocked her more aggressively.

Kenzie looked him in the eye. "Look. I've told you that I'm required by law to attend. There's nothing I can do about it. There's nothing you can do to change my mind. I can call the cops to get them to remove you so I can get to the scene. Is that what I need to do?"

He hesitated, wavering.

"Events have been set into motion," Kenzie reiterated. "I need to follow a certain procedure. Will you let me in, or do I have to call for backup?"

He lowered his hand slowly. "Well, I don't see why you have to be so stubborn about it…"

"It's the procedure I have to follow. If it's just an unattended death, someone who died in his sleep, then my time here will be very short. I'll be in and out with no fuss and bother. But you can't stop me from attending, or there will be consequences. You don't want to get arrested for impeding an investigation, do you?"

"You're not even the police," the guard grumbled, but he stepped back and grudgingly let Kenzie pass.

Kenzie preceded him into the building, but she did not have any idea where to find the body once she got there. She looked around. There was no one waiting inside to escort her to her patient. The security guard trailed her in.

"Can you point me in the right direction?" Kenzie asked. "Or should I just wander around looking for a body?"

"Down the hall and to the right," he grumbled. Then he apparently decided he should do more than just give her directions. "I'll show you."

Once they were down the first hallway, Kenzie could hear voices. Casual, routine voices, doctors or nurses talking to each other as they completed their duties. The security guard led her around another corner, and then she could see where people were gathered in the hall, pulled in by the specter of death.

There were a couple of young men in dress pants and white shirts wheeling a gurney into a patient's room. Kenzie hadn't seen an ambulance nearby. And ambulance attendants did not wear white shirts.

But she *had* seen a hearse.

"Excuse me!" Kenzie hurried forward as the two men bent over in the cramped space, preparing to lift it onto the gurney. "Don't touch that body. Get back."

They stopped and looked at her, frowning. A doctor standing outside the room, gray hair and a dark mustache, prominent creases between his eyes, turned to her.

"Who are you?"

"Dr. Kenzie Kirsch. Assistant to the Medical Examiner."

"What are you doing here?"

Kenzie motioned to the body on the floor. "Looking after him."

"You're not needed here. This is a doctor-attended death. No need for the medical examiner to be involved."

"Well, I was called, and I am required to be called for all deaths in a psychiatric facility. And you," Kenzie motioned again to the funeral home workers. "You can go. Leave me your card. I'll call you when we finish with the body."

The two men looked at each other, not sure what to do.

"You're not taking this body," Kenzie said firmly.

"Look, Dr. Kirsch," the doctor spoke to her again. "This is all just a misunderstanding. I'm sorry. You should not have been called. Just let the funeral home take care of the body, and you go home and get your sleep."

"I need to fulfill my obligations. There is a strict procedure to be followed. I'm sure you've seen it all before. It shouldn't take me too long."

There was no blood on the floor, no apparent injuries. The man had clearly not been shot or stabbed. Kenzie looked down at him, her mind already running through checklists. What she would need to see, what pictures she would take. What she would tell Carlos or whoever came from the office to transport the body, what she would tell death investigators if she needed someone else there to help collect evidence.

"This is ridiculous," the doctor complained.

"Well, it doesn't hurt you. It's just one extra step before the deceased is sent on to the funeral home. We make sure that there are no concerns, and then the family gets the body," Kenzie assured him. Of course, the doctor was old enough to know all of this anyway. He was obviously not inexperienced. He knew the way it all worked.

The doctor threw up his hands in frustration, defeated. "Fine. Do what you have to do. But it is over my objection. You don't need to be here. It is just a waste of time."

"Well, better a waste of time than having to exhume a body later on down the line!" Kenzie told him cheerfully.

The funeral home attendants backed off to let Kenzie do her examination. One of them hemmed and hawed for a minute, then handed her a business card, and he and his associate took their gurney and departed. The doctor shook his head.

"Everything would have been taken care of in five minutes. Now I'm going to still have a dead body here in two hours. Before long, we'll have patients getting up and finding out one of their number dead on the floor."

Kenzie rolled her eyes as she performed the first checks on the body to ensure the patient was properly deceased. She would have the body out of there well before patients started getting up in the morning. Unless both of the ME office trucks broke down, and if that was the case, she knew of a hearse that could probably be pressed into service...

She rested her fingertips lightly on the man's arm. "How long has he been here, Dr....?"

He hesitated, then supplied his name. "Dr. Alvarez. He can't have been there for very long. He was asleep. Must have just gotten up... maybe he wasn't feeling well and went to get help, or something for indigestion, and just keeled over."

Kenzie shook her head. "He's in full rigor."

"That can't be right."

"How long did you wait before calling someone?"

"It takes a while for people to get here," he said cautiously. "Maybe... an hour?"

It had been less than an hour since Kenzie had been called, but she knew that it hadn't been Dr. Alvarez who had called her. He had an accent and an older voice. More of an attitude, almost a bullying manner. The man who had called her on the phone had been softer spoken, younger, probably not very experienced in dealing with unexpected deaths. And that someone had called her after Dr. Alvarez had called the funeral home.

"It's been more than an hour," Kenzie disagreed. "Full rigor. That takes a significant amount of time."

But something wasn't right, because the body was still quite warm to the touch. And it shouldn't be if he had been lying on the floor for long enough for full rigor set in. Kenzie took a couple of temperature readings, writing them down and noting the time and the stage of rigor mortis. When time of death indicators did not match the witness stories or each other, there was good reason to be careful. Measure everything twice. Note everything down with dates, times, and pictures. Interview all witnesses to get their stories before they started to change.

"He hasn't been lying there for hours," Alvarez objected.

Kenzie just shook her head. She knew he was wrong or lying to her. Or there was something very strange going on with newest patient.

Shattered to Death, Book #9 of the *Kenzie Kirsch Medical Thriller* series by P.D. Workman can be purchased at pdworkman.com

ABOUT THE AUTHOR

P.D. Workman is a USA Today Bestselling author, winner of several awards from Library Services for Youth in Custody and the InD'tale Magazine's Crowned Heart award, and has published over 100 mystery/suspense/thriller and young adult books, including stand alones and these series: Auntie Clem's Bakery cozy mysteries, Reg Rawlins Psychic Investigator paranormal mysteries, Zachary Goldman Mysteries (PI), Kenzie Kirsch Medical Thrillers, Parks Pat Mysteries (police procedural), and YA series: Tamara's Teardrops, Between the Cracks, and Breaking the Pattern.

Workman loves writing about the underdog, who the reader may love or hate. She has been praised for her realistic details, deep characterization, and sensitive handling of the serious social issues that appear in all of her stories, from light cozy mysteries through to darker, grittier young adult and mystery/suspense books.

> P. D. Workman, does not shy from probing the deep psychological scars of childhood trauma, mental illness, and addiction. Also characteristic of this author, these extremely sensitive issues are explored with extensive empathy, described with incredible clarity, and portrayed with profound insight.
>
> — —KIM, GOODREADS REVIEWER

Some of Workman's titles have been translated into Spanish, French, Portuguese, German, and Italian.

Workman began writing at an early age and is a prolific reader as well as writer. She is also passionate about teaching and learning, expresses her creativity through art and cooking, and loves exploring the Calgary parks and green spaces where the Parks Pat Mysteries are set. She was a legal assistant for many years and has done extensive charitable work.

Workman was born and raised in Alberta, Canada, and is married with one adult son.

Please visit P.D. Workman at pdworkman.com to see what else she is working on, to join her mailing list, and to link to her social networks.

If you enjoyed this book, please take the time to recommend it to other purchasers with a review or star rating and share it with your friends!

tiktok.com/@pdworkmanauthor

facebook.com/pdworkmanauthor

x.com/pdworkmanauthor

instagram.com/pdworkmanauthor

amazon.com/author/pdworkman

bookbub.com/authors/p-d-workman

goodreads.com/pdworkman

linkedin.com/in/pdworkman

pinterest.com/pdworkmanauthor

youtube.com/pdworkman

Find P.D. Workman's books at

PDWORKMAN.COM

Scan the QR code below